For C
Ramcy

STORM
at the
KEIZER
MANOR

Ramcy Tietu   4/22/18

Storm at the Keizer Manor
First Edition
Copyright © 2017 Ramcy Diek
www.ramcydiek.com

This story is a work of fiction. References to real people, events, establishments, organizations, or locales are intended only to provide a sense of authenticity and are used fictiously. All other characters, and all incidents and dialogue are drawn from the author's imagination and are not to be construed as real.

Cover design by Lieve Maas, Bright Light Graphics

ISBN-13: 978-0-9983098-0-4

Acknowledgements

Thank you Jackie, for cheering me on
after I shared my first chapter with you.
Shelley Tegen, my editor.
You believed in my story, even before I did.
Your encouragement kept me going through
the entire process. I was lucky to find you.
Holly Kammier and Jessica Therrien from
Acorn Publishing LLC.
Your own experience as writers,
your knowledge with every aspect of publishing,
and your constant support were invaluable to me.
My gratitude also goes out to
Margaret, Julie, Kathy, Katrien, Barney, Lacey, Sam, Janene,
and several others, who all turned into amazing editors.
Thank you Jan Zwaaneveld, for the inspirational poem.
Dennis, your expertise as a photographer shows in my
cover photo. I'm proud to use it.
And Lieve Maas, thanks for the cover design
(and for your patience).

But of course my biggest thanks goes out to my husband
and sons. Rolf, Mondo and Cody.
You're my world. I love you.

TRIBUTE TO THE BULB REGION

The dunes curling on the horizon.
The countryside like a young blonde babe
Her locks bobbing on the wind from the sea.
So slow, so painfully slow that
only God perceives.
Look how she has put

war colors on her face
purple and pink, yellow and red, and how it
teases the rainbow. Her perfume floats gentle
as a sleeping spirit over the sand.
Her skin is indestructible young.

Cold clouds look watchful
from afar, sulking off and flinging
hail, with thunderbolts.
Their prey escapes;
it's too frighteningly alive,
too beautiful to die.

Jan Zwaaneveld

Chapter 1

WITH ONE HAND Annet grabbed her cellphone and hit speed dial. With her other hand, she reached into a brown paper bag.

"Did it ever occur to you I would've appreciated it if you'd been home?" she snapped, tossing her groceries on the worn marbled Formica countertop. Butter, chips, French bread, cream cheese, and, last but not least, a bottle of Cabernet Sauvignon, and two large pieces of chocolate and hazelnut cream pie.

"Why are you making such a big fuss?" Forrest protested at the other end. "It's still early, right?"

She glanced at the round kitchen clock above the window. "Twenty minutes past six is not early!"

"Wow, that late already? Well, I guess I better be on my way soon."

Her blue eyes sparkled like dangerous firecrackers. "Soon? Right away sounds much better. Besides, where are you?"

"I'll explain when I'm home," he replied, as always keeping his calm.

Annet brushed a few loose strands of long blonde hair from her forehead and took a deep breath, "Don't forget you were supposed to pick up Chinese for dinner," she said sweetly, letting the words sink in before she yelled, "Jerk!" and hit the red disconnect button. With a puckered brow, she slumped down on one of the rickety red leather stools at the kitchen counter.

Damn him! How could he have forgotten it was her twenty-fifth birthday? Especially after they had talked about it the night before? They had planned for her to stop at the grocery store on her way back from work, and for him to pick up her favorite meal, curry chicken with white rice from Sue Ling's Chinese Cuisine. He had promised unwaveringly everything would be ready for a relaxing and intimate evening by the time she got home. The ringing of her cellphone brought her back from her troubled thoughts. She glanced at the caller ID. At least someone hadn't forgotten her birthday.

"Hi, Mom," she answered brightly, bracing herself for the cacophony of self-centered chatter she knew would keep her on the phone for at least half an hour.

"Happy birthday, sweetheart. Are you having a good day?" Before she could reply, her mother continued, "You won't believe what happened yesterday. You remember Paula, who lives across the street from me? The old gal with the faded red wig and the two black poodles? Well, she got in her car during rush hour. That red monster with the big-ass dirt tires. I have no idea why a seventy-something-year-old granny is driving a car like that. But anyway, she backed out of her driveway, without even looking, and plowed right into traffic. I happened to be outside in the yard and saw the whole thing happen. Some kind of boring-looking sedan crashed right into her, completely crunching up the front, and …" Annet closed her eyes, hoping she could muster up the patience to sit through another one of her mother's monologs. "Chuck turned out to be such a nice guy. Can you believe that?"

"Uh, yeah," she replied, realizing she had missed a good part of the story.

"Well anyway, he asked me out for dinner, so that's what I'm doing right now. Getting dressed. I think I will wear the white mini skirt with the sunflowers I picked up at the Goodwill store a few weeks back. With my pale green blouse. If I still like him after we have dinner, I might open an extra button."

Annet could just picture her mother flirting with her next victim. She'd seduce him with her red plastered mouth and tight clothes, exposing too much cleavage and giggling as if she was still a teenager.

"Ugh! Too much information, Mom," she protested, wondering if her mother would ever be able to hang on to a man. Her entire life, Annet had seen them come and go, not one of them lasting for more than a few years, including her own father. An unwanted flicker of pain squeezed her heart, but she brushed it away. Why stress over the past? You can't change anyway. "You're telling me you're going on a date with a guy you've known for five seconds?"

"I know you pretend to be a prude," her mother said, her voice clipped. "But I know you better than you know yourself. When it comes down to it, you are just like me!"

"Sure, Mom." Not interested in another one of those talks, about how they were alike and such, she couldn't have agreed less.

"I often wonder how it's possible Forrest didn't run out on you yet," her mother continued. "I know you're gone a lot for

3

work and that you're tired when you come home, but I mean, the poor guy. He needs a warm-blooded woman in his bed, and you never seem to lighten up."

"I think I hear Forrest coming home. Thank you for calling, Mom. I have to go." Gritting her teeth, she hoped her mother didn't realize she was lying.

"Yeah, why don't you hang up on your fucking mother?" was the blunt reply.

Annet shook her head. If she and her mother had something in common, it was definitely their foul tongue, but that wasn't something you could inherit. It was a matter of upbringing and as far as that was concerned, she had received none.

"Bye, sweetheart. I love you." Her mother smacked her lips, making kissing sounds before continuing. "Have one for me tonight, will you?"

"Bye, Mom. Love you too." Annet hit the disconnect button and groaned. "Darn, I had such a wonderful day at work, but now I wish it was over." Her neck dripped with perspiration and she felt a trickle of sweat between her breasts. She peeled off her thick woolen sweater and draped it over the stool next to her, fanning her flushed face with both hands. *Jeez, what was her mother thinking, judging her like that? What did she know about her life with Forrest, about their relationship, and what they did between the sheets? Absolutely nothing. Zilch.*

About nine years ago, she had moved to the small coastal town of Dunedam, with her mother and her boyfriend at the time, Brad or Dave? It was impossible to keep track. She had enrolled in the middle of her sophomore year. During first period, Forrest entered her life. He had been tall and skinny, his blond hair too long, his face covered with acne. Trying to sneak in after class had already started, he stumbled over his own feet, landing in the chair next to her. His awkward smile and whispered apology had caused her heart to skip a beat. Without warning, she had fallen in love for the first time in her life.

A key turned in the door, the sound bringing her out of her memories.

"Honey, where are you?" Forrest rang out. Dressed in a pair of black slacks, a light grey dress shirt, and cowboy boots, his Sunday best, he walked in. "Smell," he said, swaying a plastic bag, with a red rooster printed on it, in front of her nose. The familiar aroma of curry, onions, vegetables, and rice teased her nostrils. He put the bag on the counter, took a few steps in her direction and scooped her up in a warm hug.

"Congratulations, lovelove," he whispered in her ear, nibbling gently on her earlobe. "I had an unexpected job interview this afternoon, so am I forgiven for being late?"

She leaned into him, for a moment allowing herself to relax and enjoy the familiarity of his presence and strong arms, breathing in the musky smell of the deodorant she always bought for him. Then she pushed him away with both hands. "Sorry, Forrest. Although I think that's wonderful, this time you have to do better than that. It's my birthday!"

Going down on one knee in front of her, he raised an eyebrow, his blue eyes wide open, as if he was in shock. "What can I do to make up for it? Just name it." He got hold of her hand, took it between his, and sprinkled it with warm kisses. Slowly working his way up to her wrist and the inside of her arm, he pulled her closer toward him, inch by inch.

"Get up, idiot," she replied, trying to pull her hand free, but he held on tight. The next moment, she lost her balance and fell on top of him. They both rolled onto the kitchen floor, the cheap black and white checkered vinyl cold beneath them. He wrapped his arms around her slender body, catching her lips in a warm, loving kiss.

"What are you doing?" she protested, a familiar bubble of warmth rising inside her.

"Making up for forgetting it's your birthday," he whispered between kisses, "I won't let you go until you forgive me."

His blond charm and dimpled smile were heart-melting and she was struck by the love beaming from his eyes. Damn, this happy-go-lucky, laid back, and affectionate beau of hers still dazzled her with his boyish charm. Relaxing her stance, she softened against him. With Forrest, it was always impossible to stay mad.

"How about I show you how much I love you," he offered, running his hands beneath her shirt, sensually caressing the tense muscles at the slope of her neck. "Will that grant me forgiveness?"

She wanted to protest, to pull back. This wasn't her, making love on the kitchen floor, in the middle of winter, with dinner getting cold, but somehow her mother's words nagged in the back of her head. Maybe she should lighten up, be more carefree and easygoing.

To her own surprise, a sudden heated urgency claimed her, a soft moan escaping her throat. "On second thought, I guess I wouldn't mind having a bit of the something you have to offer."

He worked his warm hands between their bodies. It wasn't until then that she noticed he had unfastened her bra. Her body reacted beneath his touch and she reached for the top button of his jeans, her fingers fumbling impatiently with his zipper.

"That's my girl," he breathed in her neck. His strong hands easily peeled away her jeans and underwear, pushing the fabric between her bare buttocks and the rigid floor, but she didn't even notice. Her blood heated and churned under her skin. She wanted him, needed him.

"Protection," he said against her lips, trying to create enough distance between them so he could reach into his back pocket.

"What?"

"A condom."

Blood roared in her ears. "Don't talk," she urged him, not wanting to lose the unfamiliar and intense passion surging through her body. It had never been like this with him.

Her fingers dug into the flesh of his back and she thrust her pelvis against his in an urgent grind. "Just touch me," she breathed ragged against his neck.

"You're sure?" he sighed between hot kisses.

Seconds later they moved together, the whole world flip-flopping around her.

After their intense passion subsided Annet paled visibly. "Oh, shit. I forgot to take the pill twice this month? What did I do?" She grabbed her scattered clothes and jumped up. "Maybe I should take a shower? See if I can undo the damage? Right?" The next moment she rushed to the bathroom, leaving him on the cold floor. He had only listened with a half ear to her rambling. She had a habit of talking herself through problems, this time self-doubt dripping from her words. Still wrapped in the afterglow of their lovemaking, he slowly got up to follow her. By the time he got to the shower, water was running, Annet scrubbing vigorously with a washcloth between her thighs.

"That won't help baby, you know that just as well as me," he said, looking at her wet, naked body with admiration. Her long legs, unblemished alabaster skin, and full breasts. He sure was a lucky guy to have her.

"I know," she replied, "but I have to do what I can. Damn, I should have taken the time to..."

He could tell she was upset and joined her under the spray. Pulling her close to his naked body, he mumbled, "It's all right, honey. It was just one time without protection so what are the chances?" In an attempt to make her forget her concern, he tried to catch her lips.

He caught the doubt flickering in her expressive blue eyes before she turned her face away.

"That's all it takes. One time!" She freed herself from his embrace and stepped from the shower.

"Don't go yet," he protested as she reached for a towel. "I want you to wash my back."

"Dinner is getting cold," she replied, drying herself off with brisk movements, "I'm hungry."

Acknowledging the romance had gone up in smoke, he let the water splash over his hair and face. "You know I wouldn't mind if you got pregnant, right? I'm ready for it." He reached for the shampoo, waiting for her reaction.

Annet rolled her eyes and walked out of the bathroom, leaving him to his own thoughts.

"I really don't understand why you think it's time to have a baby," Annet told Forrest after he joined her in the kitchen. The microwave beeped and she took out their dinner. "I only just turned twenty-five. There's still plenty of time for that later. Besides, we can barely make ends meet on my wages alone."

He followed her into the living room with the bottle of Cabernet Sauvignon and two wine glasses. They sat down on their comfy brown couch, both dressed in sweatpants and a T-shirt.

"Every penny goes to rent, food, utilities, car insurance, and all that, leaving no room to pay for a baby's needs," she continued, dishing up two plates while Forrest poured the wine. "We would need to move to a bigger apartment. You know there's no way we can afford that as long as you're unemployed."

"You're right, I know." Forrest tone was defeated. "This economy sucks. There are no jobs in my field out there, and the interview I had this afternoon isn't going anywhere either. The guy was a jerk."

They ate in silence, both deep in thought.

"Maybe I should apply at the local hardware store for a clerk position," Forrest suggested once his plate was empty. "I noticed this afternoon they had a help wanted sign in the window. Or at the auto parts store in town. They seem to have trouble keeping their employees." He held up the bottle. "Do you want more wine?"

"No, why don't you get the two pieces of pie from the fridge. It's chocolate and hazelnut cream and I totally feel like indulging."

He poured himself another glass. "I'm serious, Ann. Ever since we graduated from high school and moved in together, you have been the one who worked, supporting us, managing to make it all work on so little money. Now I'm finally done with college, it's time I start to make a few bucks. Since nobody is hiring engineers nowadays, I should at least do something."

She folded her legs beneath her and took the last sip of her wine. What he'd said was true. He had never brought in a penny. But that wasn't his fault. He wanted to become a civil engineer and with his 3.9-grade point average, he'd qualified for several scholarships. It would have been crazy not to pursue an education. Besides, all she had wanted was to work, to get away from her flighty mother. Talking him into sharing an apartment immediately after their high school graduation, she had found the one bedroom unit in the White Castle Apartment complex online. It was the only affordable place in town, but there was nothing castle-like about them. The apartments were small and cheaply built, with most of the tenants on government assistance, single mothers, recovering addicts, struggling artists, and the like. The only reason they'd never looked for something else was that they couldn't afford anything better.

"You were able to obtain those amazing scholarships that paid for your tuition and books," she said after he came back into the living room, balancing two pieces of pie. "That amounts to a lot. You should be proud of yourself."

He handed her one of the plates and sat back down on the couch next to her. "What good does all that do me when I can't land a decent job?" He took a bite and smacked his lips. "This pie is almost as delicious as you are."

"Bullshit," she grinned.

Chapter 2

ANNET PEDALLED TO WORK against the strong westerly wind that had been howling all night, her bicycle set into the lowest gear. It was blowing so hard, she had to squint against the fine sand that blew into her face. She could taste the salt from the ocean spray on her lips. Almost there. She stood onto her peddles to conquer the last dune before she reached the top and descended down the long, paved driveway leading to the parking lot of the Keizer Manor. The three story, impressive manor was constructed around 1850, but the passage of time had barely made an impact. It still stood firm and proud at the edge of the dunes, just outside Dunedam. The manor had originally been built as a summer retreat for the wealthy Keizer family who lived in the neighboring city of Heemstead, but was currently used as a museum and housed the collection of oil paintings by one of their family members, Alexander Keizer, a famous nineteenth century painter.

The normally easy three miles from her apartment to work had seemed to take Annet forever today. She reached the covered bicycle area and stepped off quickly. After locking her bike, she rushed up the five concrete steps onto the terrace and pushed open the heavy oak door that took her into the main hallway.

Beverly was sitting behind the reception desk, all primped up as usual. Her boss had hired the twenty-two year old girl a year ago, convinced she was perfect for the job as a fulltime receptionist. Her resume indicated she had received some kind of Assistant Certificate for her so-called great communication skills, and basic knowledge of accounting, data entry, payroll and spreadsheets. What she failed to mention was it had taken her a full year to finish the two terms and still barely passed.

Beverly looked up from behind her computer at the sound of Annet's approaching footsteps on the marble tiled floor and raised a perfectly shaped eyebrow. "You must be on your bike," she said, disapproval dripping from her voice. Beverly limited her jewelry to tasteful pearl earrings, her conservative blouse and dark blue suit jacket with matching skirt accenting her pale skin, not to mention her properly coiffed hair and impeccable makeup.

Okay, she had to give her that, the girl knew about style, Annet thought, raking her fingers through her hair to smooth it out.

"Forrest needed the car," she explained. "He's job hunting, and he better find something today or I'll kick him out of the house."

Beverly gave her a startled look, her right hand covering her mouth. "You can't be serious."

Annet rolled her eyes. "Ugh. That was a joke, Beverly." She took off her gloves and stuffed them in the pockets of her coat. "I almost didn't make it over that last dune. That damn wind is brutal."

"It's just an excuse for being late," Beverly snapped. "By the way, that's not a very smart move when you're expected to attend a meeting."

Annet shrugged casually, "Did they start already?" She rounded the black, beige and gold marbled reception desk and headed toward her office.

The receptionist's stare followed her. "You forgot about the meeting, didn't you?" she said, her eyes scanning over Annet's faded blue jeans, worn cowboy boots and oversized sweater. "Because not even you would go dressed like that."

As long as Annet made her minimum of forty hours per week, she could start work at whatever time she wanted. Usually she preferred to be there early, but she hadn't slept very well last night. Images of babies and dollar bills kept fleeting through her mind, the nine o'clock meeting totally slipping her mind.

Beverly must have noticed something in her reaction, because her tone changed from snippy into one of pity. "At least comb your hair and put on some lipstick." She swiveled her chair around and started hacking away on the keyboard of her computer.

Checking the time on her smartphone, Annet left the reception area and hurried into her office. She grabbed a notebook and pen, and dashed into the meeting room down the hall. Wood grain laminate tables were set up in a U-shape, the smell of fresh coffee and sugary donuts in the air. Fortunately, the meeting hadn't started yet, most attendants still standing around, chatting with one another, one of them pouring coffee.

Annet slid into the empty chair next to her boss of seven years, Dan Mockenburg, the director for collections and exhibitions. His eyes were glued to the screen of the laptop in front of him on the table. She nudged him on the shoulder of his suit jacket.

"Glad you could join us," he said, giving her a friendly nod.

"I wouldn't miss it for the world."

Dan closed his laptop, straightened his tie and raked his fingers through his thick mane of grey hair. "Thank you all for coming this morning," his voice resounded. "As we all have seen, there is a very important guest in our midst this morning. Because of that I would like to make quick introductions."

Annet looked up from her minutes, noticing the flamboyantly dressed elderly lady who had been hidden from her behind a coworker's broad shoulders.

The unfamiliar lady nodded in greeting, her gold-and-turquoise earrings dangling down, matching rings decorating her fingers.

"For all of you who haven't yet met her, let me introduce to you Mrs. Caroline Rothschild, a direct descendent from Alex Keizer, and one of the museum's benefactors."

Annet had never seen a grandiose lady like her, with purple hair swept into an elaborate bun, intricate jewelry around her neck and wrists, and strange layers of colorful clothing reminding her of Africa.

"Mrs. Rothschild is joining us today," Dan continued, "not only to offer her help with the two-hundredth anniversary celebrations on May 18, but also to tell us everything about an exhibit she wants to set up especially for this occasion."

The well-dressed men and women around the table mumbled welcoming words. Dan quickly introduced them all with a brief description of their function, ending with Annet. "That brings me to my invaluable administrative assistant,

Annet Sherman, who also has a big hand in our marketing and public relations. Caroline, could you fill us in?"

"It's very nice to meet you all," Caroline Rothschild started off. "As you can imagine, as a direct descendent from Alex Keizer, this museum has always been very close to my heart." She gave a sad smile. "Unfortunately, since my brother's passing last year, there are only a handful of us left. Me, my children, grandchildren, and a few distant cousins."

"Sorry about your loss, Mrs. Rothschild," one of the older women at the table said.

"My brother was sick for a long time. It wasn't unexpected."

"Do you live in Dunedam, close to the Keizer Manor, Mrs. Rothschild?" Annet asked.

"No, after living abroad for most of my life, I moved in with my brother at the original Keizer Estate in Heemstead. It's where I was raised, and where I belong." She paused for a moment, straightening her shoulders and clearing her throat. "Okay, that's enough about my personal life. I am here today to share with you and the public my mother's extensive collection of eighteenth and nineteenth century dolls."

With careful hands she opened the box in front of her on the table, lifting out a porcelain doll, wearing a long layered yellow gold satin dress with brown trim.

"I brought this doll because it is one of the finest examples." She placed a wooden stand on the middle of the table which supported the doll, so it could stand up straight on its own. "All of her clothing is hand sewn, including her tiny leather shoes, hat, and lace parasol."

Over the next two hours, they talked about the planning of the anniversary until Dan leaned forward indicating the meeting was over. "Annet, why don't you join Mrs. Rothschild in *"Storm*

Hall"? That's where she prefers to set up her collection, and I'm sure she'll have a lot of logistical questions. When you're done, would you escort her to my office? I'd like to take her out for lunch."

"Of course," Annet replied, collecting her papers. "Whenever you're ready."

Dan helped Mrs. Rothschild up from her chair and gave them both a friendly nod before leaving.

"It's a pleasure to finally meet you," Mrs. Rothschild smiled up to Annet. "Dan speaks very highly of you and all the talent you bring to the museum." Annet at five foot eight towered over the petite older woman. "Tell me," she continued. "is it true you were hired as a clerk in the museum's gift shop after you graduated from high school, working yourself up in a few short years?"

"Guilty," Annet replied, holding the door open and escorting her from the meeting room. "It was the first job I ever had. I've loved working here from day one."

"Then you must be very interested in art," Mrs. Rothschild said.

Annet felt a flush appearing on her cheeks. "To be honest, when I applied for the job, I only knew the Keizer Manor was a museum with paintings and not much else."

Mrs. Rothschild raised her eyebrows. "If you weren't familiar with the Keizer Manor, you must not be from around here."

"You're right," Annet acknowledged, directing her guest into the main entrance hall. "I grew up in Heemstead, on what they call the wrong side of the tracks, and didn't know anything about art." She laughed at the memory. "I even took a watercolor class for beginners, thinking it would help me understand the fascination. After a few weeks, I realized the world was not waiting for my creations."

"Oh, the blissfulness of youth." Mrs. Rothschild smiled. When they reached Storm Hall, she momentarily paused before entering. "This museum holds such a special place in my heart. Don't you love the architecture, the intricate woodwork, the double staircase, the grandeur?"

"I've always felt there was so much love put into each single detail," Annet agreed. "The architect must have been a talented guy."

The solid oak doors opened and several visitors walked out, holding one of the heavy doors open so they could enter.

Storm Hall was grand and dim, the ceiling high. Stained glass windows colored the walls. It felt like they had entered a church, demanding peace and respect. The only sounds were their own footsteps on the rust-colored tiled floor and the soft whispers of the other guests as they approached the center of the hall and stopped.

Side by side they gazed at Alex Keizer's masterpiece, which dominated the far wall. *Lost in the Storm* portrayed a slender young woman wearing a long white dress that resembled a simply made cotton nightgown. The little girl she had by her hand wore similar clothing. Both walked through a desolate landscape during a lightning storm. Dark, threatening clouds and dangerous flashes of light loomed overhead. Their plain clothes were completely soaked, clinging to their bodies. Large drops of water dribbled down their skin, their long hair hanging flat and dark from the heavy rain. They seemed to wander around, lost and desperate, a haunting expression etched on their pale-white faces.

"I've seen this painting many times, but every time I come in here it takes my breath away," Mrs. Rothschild said, breaking the silence. "To tell you the truth, I'm honored to be Alexander Keizer's great-great-granddaughter. What an unbelievably talented and brilliant artist he was."

Annet looked away from the haunting scene, goose-bumps on her arms. Although it was an amazing painting, something about it gave her the shivers. She swallowed several times, her throat constricted, before nodding in agreement.

"Yes he was." Then she forced herself back to reality, turning all businesslike. "Now what was it you had in mind exactly?"

Chapter 3

"YOU ARE PREGNANT," the doctor confirmed.

The last few weeks, Annet had felt weary and slightly nauseous in the morning, her temper flaring up over nothing. That her cantankerous mood had everything to do with her terror over a possible pregnancy, she had realized all along.

Although she had braced herself for the news, when it came she was not prepared; doubt, regret, excitement, and fear assailed her all at the same time. "What am I going to do?" Sighing, she hid her face behind her hands in an effort to compose her thoughts.

The doctor raised his eyebrows. "Most women are happy when I give them the news, but I can see this comes as a shock to you. Don't worry, Annet. You have about seven months to figure everything out."

Annet got up from the chair in the examination room and put on her coat. Six months, three weeks and two days to be exact. Why hadn't she been more careful? She had never behaved that primal in her entire life. Now, here she was with the consequence of her impulsive and irresponsible action.

The doctor scribbled something on a piece of paper and handed it to her. "Take these prenatal vitamins, an extra dose of folic acid, and make an appointment with my secretary before you leave. I want to see you again in three to four weeks."

But what if I don't want this baby? she protested in silence, leaving the doctor's office. Forrest still hadn't found a job. Mainly because he was overqualified, but when he had begged the appliance store in town to give him at least a chance, they had still turned him down because he had no sales experience. At least he was helping out around the house, and when she got home he was busy making dinner. Despite how she felt, the meal smelled pretty darn good.

"Chicken sausages with potatoes and asparagus," he announced, giving her a quick kiss before turning his attention back to the stove. "How was your day?"

"Great," she replied dejectedly, dropping the car keys on the kitchen counter. She slumped down on one of the kitchen stools, watching him turn the sausages over with care. Well, at least one person in the house would be elated with the latest news.

He looked at her over his shoulder. "Something wrong? You're so quiet."

"Yes, something is wrong," she sighed. Her whole being felt deflated and her head dropped. "I'm pregnant. How is that for something being wrong?"

"What was that?" He dropped his meat fork and stared at her with his big blue eyes, too taken by surprise to know quite what to say. Then he abandoned his sausages and scooped her up in his strong arms. "I knew it!" His voice filled with joy. "Oh, I love you so much, Annet! You have no idea."

"Stop it, you're crushing me!"

He released her from his tight embrace and helped her sit back down on her stool with exaggerated care. "We can't have that. Are you comfortable now?"

Pushing his hands away, she smiled with self-deprecation. "You don't have to lay it on so thick. I'm not going to break."

Forrest raised both his arms above his head and whooped with joy. "I can't believe it. I'm going to be a daddy." He danced around the tiny kitchen until their eyes met in midair. Immediately he stopped and furrowed his brow. "What? Why are you looking at me like that?"

She was trembling, struggling to control her apprehension, fear and anxiety.

"Come on, Annet. Aren't you as happy as I am?" He took both her hands. "Because, really honey, this is the best thing that could ever happen to us. We are going to be parents. Don't you get that? It's unbelievable."

She gave him an irritated glance. "You know how I feel about it. We're not ready for this."

He dropped down on one knee in front of her, taking both of her hands in his. "Don't worry. We will be fine. Oh, Annet, you make me so happy." He lifted her right hand up to his mouth and kissed each finger, his eyes holding hers. "Do you want to marry me?"

"Are you out of your mind?" she gasped. "Marry? Whatever gave you that idea?"

Forrest wasn't discouraged by her harsh reply and got up, his eyes full of excitement. "Come on, let's tie the knot, make it official. What do you say?"

She threw up her hands in exasperation "You know I don't believe in marriage, Forrest. Look at my mother. She's divorcing number four while already on the prowl for number five!"

"But it will be different for us," he protested. "You're nothing like her! You know that!"

Her heart ached when she saw hope and unqualified love radiating from his eyes. Tenderly, she took his face between her hands, pressing her mouth against his forehead. She had seen it too often around her. A wedding changed a relationship, making lovers into enemies, divine people into devils.

"It's not going to happen," she replied resolutely, the smell of burning food biting at her nostrils. "Besides, how do you think you can take care of a baby if you can't even take care of your sausages?"

"I heard good wishes are in order," Mrs. Rothschild said when she walked into Annet's office several weeks later. "How are you feeling, my dear?"

Annet stood up and pulled out a chair for the elderly lady, inviting her to sit down. "Much better, especially since I know my woes have everything to do with my unexpected pregnancy."

Mrs. Rothschild looked unconvinced. "Dan said your blood pressure had been too low, and that the doctor recommended you stay at home for at least an entire week, but here you are. Do you consider that wise?"

"You don't think I could sit at home, twiddling my thumbs, while there is so much to do before the anniversary, right?" She brushed her concerns away. "The catering, the ordering of the tables and chairs, the press releases. I have so much last minute stuff to take care of." An excited laugh escaped her lips. "But we're getting it done! The personal invitations have been sent out, the radio commercial is on the air. Decorations are being delivered as we speak, and the new brochure is ready to go to the printers. I have a proof right here."

Mrs. Rothschild opened the tri-fold flyer. "The Keizer Manor Museum, famous worldwide for the important works of art created by nineteenth century painter Alexander Reginald Keizer, is celebrating its two-hundredth anniversary and invites you and your family to share this milestone with us," she read out loud. "Since the expansion of the historic mansion was completed last year, we have been able to increase our art classes and enhance the Museum's programs and collections tremendously. Throughout the coming year, the museum plans to enrich the lives of our visitors even more by engaging, informing, and inspiring them through exciting new exhibits. The latest permanent collection of antique dolls, donated by Mrs. Caroline Rothschild-Keizer, is dazzling those young and old."

"Well, what do you think so far?" Annet asked, anxiously waiting for her reaction.

Mrs. Rothschild lowered her hands in her lap. "I have to be honest with you," she began.

"Darn, you hate it," Annet concluded, falling back in her chair, disappointment on her face. "Please, tell me what needs improvement. It's not too late to make a few last minute changes."

"You crazy girl," Mrs. Rothschild laughed out loud, the fine wrinkles at the corners of her eyes deepening. "When I met you at that first meeting a few months ago, I honestly thought Dan Mockenburg had lost his mind, hiring a lanky teenager as an assistant and marketing manager. But I soon came to realize you were a hardworking, strong, and decisive young woman."

"Yes, a real bitch. I know," Annet interrupted.

Mrs. Rothschild had trouble catching her breath, she was laughing so hard. "It's rare to meet someone with your kind of dedication and bluntness," she hiccupped. "Although I don't always appreciate your choice of words, I find you an amazing young woman. Really, I have to tell you, working with you has given me inspiration and a tremendous amount of joy."

"You give me way too much credit, Mrs. Rothschild. I'm just doing my job," Annet told her, uncomfortable with the praise. "Now about that brochure?"

Mrs. Rothschild handed it back to her. "I would have preferred to see more color in it, but you know me," she said with a wink. This morning, she wore a wide deep-purple and gold pants-set with a matching headwrap draped around her purple hair. On her feet she had a pair of mustard colored canvas slip-on Toms. "All the years we lived in Africa heavily influenced my style, as you can tell."

"I figured that," Annet replied. "What took you there?"

"My husband was a physician, specialized in the diagnosis, treatment, and care of individuals with illnesses transmitted through insect bites. He was sent all over the world to educate other doctors. I followed him wherever he went, even during the time we raised our three children."

"That must have been difficult," Annet said.

"I would have followed him to heaven if I had been able to," Mrs. Rothschild smiled sadly, getting up.

After she was gone, Annet's hands fell silent, wondering if she would be willing to give up her job and her life in Dunedam to follow Forrest if he found employment elsewhere. Probably not. She didn't even want to think about moving out of the area, let alone to a country where infectious diseases were rampant.

Chapter 4

ANNET RAN AROUND THE APARTMENT, nervous as hell. Today was the big day, which she had worked many hours of overtime for, to make sure nothing could go wrong. The thought that she might have forgotten the smallest detail almost made her knees buckle.

"Forrest, I can't find my shoes," she muttered, rushing into the bedroom. The blankets moved, a head with tousled blond curls peeping out from under them. He stretched his arms above his head and yawned. "Why aren't you in the shower yet?"

He stretched one more time and pushed the blankets away, showing himself in his full naked glory.

She ignored him and opened the closet for the second time, throwing out all the shoes from the bottom shelf. The next moment, a pair of arms circled around her waist, pulling her against a warm, firm body. Forrest cuddled her close to him, but she pushed him away. "Please, can't you be serious for once?

We have to be there in less than an hour. I still have to eat breakfast, find my shoes, and put on make-up. Dan insisted on it."

Forrest threw both his arms up in the air. "All right. I give up." He turned around and headed toward the bathroom.

"You promised you would help today," she yelled at the closed door. "Please, hurry!" She dove underneath the bed on her stomach, not the most pleasant position at four months pregnant, locating her hated black high heeled shoes. In front of the mirror, she topped off her short black dress with a crème colored tailored suit jacket and the fake pearl necklace she had bought at a thrift store. She was ready to face the world.

Five minutes later, Forrest joined her in the kitchen. He had showered and was clean shaven, dressed in his favorite jeans and dark blue, black and white plaid shirt. "I know this is an important day for you, and I *will* be there for you," he promised her. "Starting with one bit of advice. Try to watch that potty mouth of yours today."

"I'll try," she grinned, giving him a quick peck on the cheek.

Fifteen minutes later they pulled into the parking lot at the Keizer Manor at the same time Sofia Henderson, the manor's accountant, and her husband Geoff did. Forrest parked their car next to them and stepped out.

"I guess we couldn't be luckier with the weather," Geoff said. "Not a single cloud in the sky."

The four of them crossed the parking lot. The doors of the manor stood invitingly wide open, an abundance of colorful balloons floating gently in the early morning spring breeze.

A bulky man wearing blue coveralls entered behind them and headed toward Beverly, who was busy polishing the reception desk. "I'm here to deliver the tables and chairs. Where do you want them?" he asked.

"The auditorium," Annet replied, immediately taking charge. "You can use the delivery entrance around back."

When she turned towards Forrest, she noticed Beverly ogling him. It was no secret she had the hots for him. Annet quickly pushed him toward her office.

"So, what's the exact schedule for today?" he asked.

"The doors will officially open at 10AM. All visitors will be welcomed by volunteers, who hand out brochures and maps, answer questions, and explain the details about the treasure hunt that will guide them through all the exhibits."

She smoothed out her dress. "You can't tell yet I'm knocked up, right?"

Forrest scoffed. "Since when do you care what people think of you?"

"I don't," she grinned. "Come, let's go to the auditorium. We will have an official reception there that starts at 3PM, followed by a dinner buffet from 5PM to 7PM for select members, beneficiaries, and VIPs. I would appreciate it if you can help me oversee the setup."

As a steady stream of visitors made its way through the manor, Annet got pulled in a hundred different directions. She was completely in her element: multi-tasking, problem solving, answering questions, and giving directions. It was what she loved, until she found Forrest on top of a ladder, messing around with a light fixture. Beverly looked up to him, handing him a screwdriver, the top buttons of her blouse undone. That girl was really beginning to piss her off. Quickly, she steered away from the scene. This wasn't the time for a confrontation. With her hands clenched in a fist, she entered *Storm Hall*. Caroline was busy talking to visitors about the history behind her dolls and their wardrobes, her exhibit drawing a lot of attention.

"I need a short break before the reception starts," Annet confessed. "Do you know what time it is?"

Caroline glanced at her golden bejeweled watch. "Almost three o'clock. That gives you about ten minutes."

"Is it normal to be so freaking emotional when you're pregnant?" Annet asked. "Believe it or not, just before I joined you here, I felt a strong urge to punch someone in the nose."

"Oh, it is, my dear," Caroline assured her. "Just like other common symptoms like feeling tired or run down, tender breasts, feeling dizzy or faint, and abdominal twinges or cramps. Remember what the doctor told you, take your prenatals and mind yourself."

"Darn," Annet groaned. "How am I going to be able to live with myself the next five months?"

Caroline smiled kindly. "Pregnancy is such an exciting time. Just try to look at it as a nine-month adventure, filled with hope and fear. Besides, I'm sure Forrest will be by your side at all times."

"He will. He's a sweetheart," Annet assured her. "No matter what I throw at him, he never gets angry. And that says a lot!"

"You don't give yourself enough credit," Caroline replied. "Did I ever tell you that you remind me of my granddaughter, Kara?"

Annet smiled courteously. Caroline was so proud of her granddaughter that she had told her that at least three times already.

"Okay, I know," Caroline admitted. "But what I didn't tell you is that she mastered in Art Conservation, her degree awarded last week. I've been talking to Dan about asking her advice on the condition of Alex Keizer's paintings while she's coming to visit me this summer. In my humble opinion, they need a professional cleaning."

Annet stretched the sore muscles in her back. "You're probably right," she said, giving Caroline a warm hug. She had become very fond of the older woman. "Thanks for the talk."

There were at least one hundred and fifty people gathered in the auditorium, walking around with glasses in their hands. A speaker squealed as Dan Mockenburg tapped against the microphone to get their attention. "Welcome everyone," he said.

Annet listened with a half ear to the speech she had prepared for him, her eyes scanning the crowd in search of Forrest.

Dan's speech came to an end and he made room behind the microphone for the young, vibrant new mayor of Dunedam.

"Everyone is familiar with the name Alexander Reginald Keizer," the mayor started, silencing the crowd by raising a single hand. "But what do we know about his personal life? His family? Yes, we know he was married, his wife ahead of her time, a force to be reckoned with. His children continued his legacy. But what do we know about the man, other than he became one of the greatest artists of the nineteenth century?"

People were quiet, glued to his words.

"Last but not least," the mayor concluded his talk about the brilliant painter, "after this reception, everyone is invited to enjoy the buffet that is set up behind the folding paneled wall, for casual networking and to listen to the fantastic music from The Straight Arrows. Thank you!"

He jumped off the stage, landing next to Annet. "Here is another force to be reckoned with," he said jovially, shaking her hand. "Great work, Annet!"

They exchanged a few pleasantries until the mayor mingled back into the crowd. Annet took off her suit jacket and started looking for Forrest. Since the day was coming to an end, there wasn't much left to be done. She reached her office, finding the door wide open, Forrest lounging in her chair. He was laughing with a woman who sat pontifical on top of her desk. The woman's entire posture was one of seduction; her skirt pulled up high, almost showing her underwear. It was Beverly.

"What the hell is going on here?" Annet cried out in anger. She couldn't believe the girl's gall.

Beverly slid off the desk, throwing Forrest a hand kiss before she headed to the door. "We'll have to do this again sometime soon."

Annet's fingers closed vicelike around her wrist. "Stay away from him, you bitch." Anger made her voice dangerously cool, her eyes flinging daggers.

"Gee whiz, Annet. What's wrong with you?" Beverly said, trying to break free from her painful grip. "We were just talking, nothing more."

Barely managing to control the impulse to scratch out the younger girl's eyes, she let go of her arm in disgust. Then she turned around to confront Forrest. "I will be there for you, huh? My ass!" Before he could reply, she spun toward the door and slammed it shut behind her.

Stumbling precariously on her high heels, she crossed the hall and rushed out the front door, leaving visitors and volunteers gawking behind her.

It didn't take long before Forrest ran after her. "Come on, Annet. Stop!" he yelled, his long legs soon catching up with her when she entered the dunes. "This is crazy!"

He grabbed her arm, forcing her to an abrupt halt. "What's wrong with you?"

She lashed around and pommeled his chest with both fists. "You son of a bitch!"

"Stop it!" he protested, getting hold of her wrists. "What in the world has gotten into you?"

He forced her down in the sand, her face beet red, her breathing labored.

"Every time I needed you, you were busy entertaining Miss fucking Beverly," she spat out with an accusatory glare.

"Come on. I was just being friendly. She doesn't mean anything to me!" he defended himself. "Besides, I worked my ass off the entire day. I dragged furniture around, fixed light fixtures, unplugged toilets, took out trash. I even cleaned up vomit!"

She turned away from him, all of a sudden feeling ridiculous. With her back turned against him, she picked up a handful of fine warm sand, letting it seep between her fingers time and again, until her rapid breathing and heartbeat slowed down, her unexplainable rampant emotions turning into downright embarrassment and regret.

He watched her face soften and her anger dissipate with each deep comforting breath of refreshing sea air, replacing it with a sense of serenity and peacefulness. The dunes and the ocean never failed to calm her down, no matter how upset she was. He scooted over until he sat next to her, draping his arm around her shoulders. "You want to talk about it?"

"Not really," she replied, resting the back of her head against his chest. "Although I do want to confess I'm starting to get fond of this little bubble growing inside me."

He pulled her even closer. "I knew you would. I love you. I always will."

"I love you too," she replied, her words floating away on the warm breeze.

They sat in harmonious silence, the only sound coming from the dull roar of the ocean in the distance, until she felt collected enough to go back to the manor and face the world.

"Let's go for walk instead of heading back," Forrest suggested. "You've worked too hard lately. It's obvious all that stress is taking its toll."

She hesitated, her responsibilities weighing heavily on her shoulders, but then she gave a nod of assent. "Yes, you're right. I need a break. Besides, they can probably make it through the rest of the day without me."

Forrest picked up her shoes and extended his hand to pull her up. "You want to walk to the beach?"

Holding hands, they climbed up against the first steep dune, their feet sinking deep into the warm loose sand, when a dark cloud passed across the sun. It sent a shadow over them and a light breeze suddenly chilled the air. They stopped to look at the late afternoon sky turning from a deep blue into a bizarre brownish green color. Patches of scattered dark clouds billowed around them, driven upwards by some mysterious force.

"It seems like those clouds are coming out of nowhere," Forrest commented in surprise. "I've never seen anything like it."

They looked up at the darkening sky, mesmerized by the rapid fluctuations of color and the unnatural formations, until the sun was no more than a pale ball of light behind the heavy curtains of mist that fanned above them.

"It's actually kind of scary looking," Annet quivered.

The temperature dropped and the fog gradually thickened into an intimidating heaviness, ranging from a disturbing brown color to an unnerving deep dark green.

Forrest pulled her against him. "It looks like we can forget about our walk along the beach," he commented, trying to make light of the situation, but the concern in his voice gave away his true feelings.

Annet wrapped her arms around his waist, huddling against him for protection. "I've never seen anything like this either. It's creepy," she said, her voice strangely muffled by the heaviness of the air surrounding them. It was almost pitch dark now, except for the eerie shafts of pale green and pink light streaming up the sky casting an eerie glow.

A loud steady rumbling made them look at each other in wonder. Was that thunder? Or was it something else entirely?

The rumbling grew louder, vibrating the air around them until they could feel it in the sand beneath their feet. Their legs trembled and they had to let go of each other's hands to protect their eardrums against the deafening roar.

Having lived at the coast her entire life, she had experienced many storms, but what was happening now was something entirely different. "If this isn't what the end of the world feels like, you can shoot me!" she yelled, trying to make herself heard, but she knew it was useless. She couldn't even hear her own voice. The next moment, she felt a drop of rain on her bare arm. Then another one. Darn, what else was Mother Nature going to throw at them?

She just finished her thought when the winds kicked up, dust and sand whirling around her. Barely able to stay on her feet, she searched for Forrest, but couldn't even see her hands in front of her face, sand trashing into her mouth, ears and eyes. This was some serious tempest. She lowered herself to the ground and pulled up her legs. With her hands over the back of her head, she pushed her face between her knees, trying to protect herself and her unborn child against the extreme elements, her fingers already numb from the bite of the wind and the pelting raindrops. This better be over soon. They were only five minutes into this wicked crazy storm and she was already cold to the bone. Stifling a sob of fear she warily looked up, but what she saw made her cringe. Disturbing wild lightning flashes shot in every direction against the green and brownish sky, sand and debris thrashing dangerously around in the whirlwind. "Forrest! Forrest?" she yelled.

Trembling with fear she squeezed her eyes shut, curling herself up in a tight ball, her muscles tense. She was drenched all the way down to her underwear, shaking uncontrollably. This was it. She was going to die. In a complete state of panic, she listened to the hurricane-force wind and the terrifying rumble until everything around her exploded like an atomic bomb, so earsplitting and violent, that her entire nervous system shorted out. The next moment, there was nothing.

Chapter 5

FORREST'S HEAD HURT like a son of a gun, his nerve endings crackling. *What in the world had happened?* He moved his fingers and toes. All accounted for. At least that was something. He opened his eyes and leaned up on his elbows. It was morning. That bizarre light, the booming noise? The explosion blowing him off his feet, knocking him to the ground? Had it left him unconsciousness all night? That couldn't be! Shivering, he got up, sand crunching between his teeth, irritating his nose and ears.

A soft breeze came in from the ocean, moving the tall grass. White morning clouds moved gently in a western direction, seagulls flew overhead. The only evidence of last night's tempest was the raindrops, glimmering on the Marram grass, his soaked clothes, and his irritated red skin. It felt like he had been sandblasted. He ran his hand over his face and through his hair, a coating of sand puffing into his eyes.

"Annet?" he shouted, blinking rapidly to get it out so he could look around. "Annet, where are you?!" No response. He pulled his cellphone from his pocket, finding it unresponsive. Cursing the device to hell and back, he widened his loop, yelling her name with his hands cupped around his mouth. The only answer was the squeal of a seagull. With each step, panic began to replace his initial unease and concern. Where was she? Was she hurt? Was the baby okay?

He reached the top of a dune, his heart pounding, blood ringing in his ears. Nobody around, anywhere. Deciding she must have returned to the Keizer Manor, he began making his way through the dunes. Twenty minutes later he walked onto the parking lot of the Manor. Only four cars sprinkled the large lot; their own red clunker, an unfamiliar white pickup truck, and a full size sedan. The fourth car was Dan Mockenburg's all-wheel drive station wagon. He picked up his pace, taking the terrace steps two at the time, until he reached the entrance and pulled on the door handle. Locked.

"Dammit," he muttered, banging his fists against the solid wood. "Hello, anybody there?" His throat constricted with renewed fear. If she had made it back, why was the door locked?

When nothing happened, he walked to one of the windows on the side, knocking hard against the historic stained lead glass until he noticed movement in the hall.

He made it back to the door just as it opened, an elderly man dressed in a blue security uniform regarding him suspiciously. "We're closed. Please come back later," he said, trying to re-shut the door, but Forrest pushed it wide open and flew past the stunned guard into the hall, yelling, "Dan? Annet? Are you here?"

The guard hurried after him, protesting, "You can't just walk in here! The museum doesn't open for hours."

Forrest ignored him, rushing into Dan's office with the guard in tow.

Dan sat behind his desk, frowning at the clock and his unexpected visitor. "What are you doing here so early? Is everything all right?"

Forrest planted his hands on the massive antique desk, trying to catch his breath. "Annet?" he croaked, swallowing hard. "Have you seen her?"

"She's not here," Dan replied, regarding him with unease. "What in the world happened to you? Your clothes are torn, you're all scratched up and bleeding!"

"That's not important," Forrest brushed his concern away. "Annet's gone. I can't find her anywhere."

The guard still lingered on the threshold, uncertain what to do.

"Jim, would you please bring Forrest a cup of coffee," Dan addressed him, looking at the floor. "Also, tell the janitor we need a broom to sweep up the sand." Next he turned back to Forrest. "What are you talking about? Annet is gone?"

Forrest fell down in a chair, raking his hands through his wild mane, his breathing ragged. "We got caught in that thunderstorm last night," he began. "I got hit by lightning and was unconscious all night. When I woke up, Annet wasn't there."

Dan raised his eyebrows in question. "It rained a little last night, but a thunderstorm? What are you talking about?"

"Jeez, are you kidding me?" Forrest protested fiercely. "I've never experienced anything like it. The sky was green, there were bolts of lights dancing around, the constant rumblings of gunshots and cannon fire sounding like war."

Dan gaped at him in disbelief. "I hope you realize how bizarre this sounds, because all we had were a few sprinkles. That was it."

"Well, I don't care what you believe," Forrest retorted indignantly, getting up from his chair. "All I care about is finding Annet."

"Just call her," Dan replied.

Forrest held his dead cellphone up in the air before tossing it carelessly on the desk. "Piece of garbage must have fried in that thunderstorm."

In answer Dan pushed an old-fashioned desk phone in his direction. "Press nine for an outside line."

Forrest picked up the hook and punched in her number. A few seconds later, the faint sound of a ringtone came from the office next door.

Dan got up from his chair. "Do you hear that?" He followed Forrest through the door into the connecting office, finding the space empty. The ringing came from the top drawer of her desk. He pulled it open, finding the vibrating smartphone.

"The pockets of Annet's suit jacket weren't big enough for her phone. That's why she left it in there," Forrest explained.

Dan glanced around the desk. "Her purse is still here as well," he commented, pulling out the familiar colorful tote from underneath, her flip-flops sticking out.

Forrest jangled with the car keys in his pocket. "I guess I'll drive to our apartment. Maybe someone gave her a ride and brought her home." He slipped her phone in his pocket and walked out of the office, her purse hanging over his shoulder.

Dan followed him to the front door. "Maybe you shouldn't drive," he said. "Something obviously happened to you last night. You seem confused and distraught."

"Sorry, pal," Forrest replied. "I got to do this."

Disobeying the speed limit of thirty miles an hour, Forrest sped through Dunedam. Of course she would be home, he encouraged himself, cutting a corner and hitting the curb. Someone must have given her a ride from the dunes. She had been so exhausted last night, she was probably still sleeping, snuggled warm and cozy underneath her favorite quilt. With screeching brakes, he stopped in front of their apartment, unlocked the door and flew inside. "Annet!"

No reply. His pulse quickened, his skin cold in a sudden panic. With a few frantic steps he covered the tiny kitchen, living room and bedroom. Nobody. He threw open the bathroom door. Empty.

"Come on, Annet, where are you?" he growled, hitting his fist against the doorjamb in utter frustration.

He stared at himself in the mirror, shocked at what he saw. There was dried-up blood on his face, his clothes were torn and his hair was a mess. He couldn't face the world looking like that? Stripping, he turned on the shower, throwing his wet, sandy clothes in a heap on the bathroom floor. Without waiting for the water to warm up, he washed his hair and rinsed off the sand.

"Hello?" a woman's voice called out. "Anybody there?"

In a hurry, he toweled himself dry, slipped into his boxers, and rushed out of the bathroom, finding Caroline Rothschild in the middle of the living room.

"I knocked several times, but when no one answered I tried the door," she apologized, her fingers fidgeting with her long beaded necklace.

"It's all right," Forrest replied, trying to sound casual. "What can I do for you, Mrs. Rothschild?"

"Dan Mockenburg told me Annet is missing? Is that true?" she said, trying to look anywhere but at his bare hairless chest, red boxers, and long muscular legs.

"Yes it is," Forrest said. "Do you have any idea where she might be?"

Caroline straightened the colorful turban on her head, her eyes directed to the ceiling. "No, I don't, but I'm sure there's a simple explanation for her absence. She was so tense the entire day."

"Yes, she was," he agreed. "But I know that has nothing to do with her disappearance." He rubbed the morning stubble on his chin wondering if he should share with the old woman what had happened. "To relax we walked to the ocean just when that wicked storm rolled in out of nowhere. I tried desperately to hold on to her, but we somehow got separated."

"I don't know anything about a storm," Mrs. Rothschild replied, pointing toward a cut on the underside of his arm. "You're bleeding. What did you do?"

Forrest grimaced, turning his arm, so he could look at it. "The winds were so violent, thrashing us around, and I got hung up in a barbwire fence, briars, and bushes." He grabbed a dishcloth from the counter and pressed it to the wound before he hurried into the bedroom to slip on his jeans and a T-shirt.

"You might have been caught up in a tornado," Caroline commented after he came back into the kitchen. She sat on a barstool at the counter, her colorful bejeweled appearance a peculiar sight in their sparingly furnished and modest home.

Forrest's eyes shot wide open in renewed fear. "A tornado? Do you think it might have picked her up? Oh, no! If that's the case, she could be seriously hurt. I have to alert the police."

"I think you should," Mrs. Rothschild agreed, a frail wrinkled hand against her throat in obvious concern "Unless you can think of another place where she might have gone."

He slapped himself against his forehead. "Of course! My parent's house." Relief was evident on his face. "They only live about a mile and a half from the Manor. Why didn't I think of that before?"

Grabbing his car keys, he escorted Mrs. Rothschild from the apartment. "I will keep you posted," he promised, stepping into his car and speeding off.

Forrest made it to his parents' in record time and parked behind his father's SUV in the familiar driveway. Like most coastal homes around it, the main living area was above the ground by one level, the parking area below. He climbed the outside stairs onto the deck. The curtains were drawn, but that wasn't unusual at 9AM on Sunday morning. His teenage brother and sister had probably come home late last night and his parents liked to sleep in on the weekends. He found the backdoor unlocked, and entered the kitchen. Empty. Still clinging to hope, he walked straight down the hallway and knocked on the door of his parents' bedroom, waking them up.

"Have you seen or heard from Annet?" he asked with his head peaking in.

His mother rubbed her eyes. "Forrest? Annet? What are you talking about?"

Forrest paled visibly. "Damn, I'd so hoped she would be here."

"Language please!" his father's voice came from underneath the blanket.

With her short blonde hair disheveled, her face puffy from sleep, his mother stepped out of bed and grabbed her flannel

41

robe. Knotting the belt at her waist, she followed him into the kitchen. "We haven't seen Annet since the reception yesterday, honey. Are you all right?"

She opened the curtains and drew up the blinds, sunlight streaming in. "Wonderful. Another beautiful spring day."

Forrest sank down at the kitchen table, hiding his face behind his hands to ward off the pounding in his head.

"Did you and Annet have a fight?" his mother asked, filling the coffeepot with water. She scooped the coffee in the filter, switched the machine on, and opened the bottom cupboard.

"No, of course not," he replied, not even trying to hide his irritation. "She was upset. Tired. But it was nothing important. Just an overreaction due to the stressful day."

His mother set five breakfast plates on the table, stifling a yawn behind her hand. "She seemed a little tense when we talked to her at the reception, but that was to be expected. After all, it was a very important day." She continued setting the table. Although he felt horrible, he automatically got up to help.

"Annet must have been pleased with the outcome," his mother continued. "There were so many people."

"Oh, it was a great day," he admitted, "but she needed a break. We decided to walk to the beach. It was perfect. Blue sky, warm, peaceful. And we talked. But then the weather turned. Did you notice that incredible weird color in the sky? It was unearthly, bizarre."

Bare-chested and barefoot, wearing only pajama bottoms, his father walked in, trailed by Spunk, the family's old black Labrador. "I did see that," he commented, pouring the hot dark liquid from the coffeepot into three mugs. "But it seemed to dissipate quickly. We never even got a drop of rain." He was as tall as his son, his head completely bald since he shaved off all his hair when it had started to thin in his early thirties.

"We got caught in the middle of it," Forrest said. "I've never experienced anything like it."

His father stretched his back and his mother tried to push her curls in place, both working to wake up fully.

"The wind howled, sand thrashed all around us, the rain coming down in sheets," he continued. "We struggled to stay on our feet." He made a choking sound, reliving last night's terror. "The last thing I remember, before everything got black, was seeing her yell something, but her voice never reached me. When I woke up this morning, I was drenched, covered with sand, and she was gone."

His mother placed her hand on his arm in deep concern. "That sounds terrible, sweetheart! What could have happened to her?" Then, she turned toward her husband. "Gerhard, did you hear that? Forrest was unconscious, maybe hit by lightning. Don't you think he should have himself checked out at the emergency room?"

"I'm fine. I'm not going to the doctor," Forrest protested. "I need to find Annet!"

His sister Jackie entered the kitchen, dressed in bright orange fleece sleep pants and a matching short-sleeve top. At seventeen years of age, she was more concerned with texting one of her dozens of friends than giving her brother a proper hello.

"Mom, Dad, why are you up so early?" she asked, pushing her long blonde hair behind her ear before she addressed her brother, "What are you doing here?" She plopped down at the table, pulling her bare feet underneath her.

"Annet didn't come home last night," his mother informed her.

Jackie shrugged not bothering to look up. "So what?" Her thumbs typed with rapid speed on the keyboard of her phone.

Forrest rubbed his fists across his eyes. "Mom, we have to do something. I'm really worried."

His sister scoffed. "It's not like anything serious could have happened to her, for Christ sake. This is boring Dunedam where nothing ever happens."

"Well, she's a grown woman," his father said, trying to cheer him up. "Who knows? Maybe she spent the night at a friend's house?"

Forrest didn't reply, knowing they were wrong. Dead wrong!

Chapter 6

Annet found herself lying flat on her back, with her arms and legs spread out, like she was making snow angels. Blood was pounding in her temples, her limbs crackling as if they were charged with electricity. Her muscles twitched involuntary. What the hell happened to her? She opened her eyes and bright rays of sunshine stabbed straight into her brain. Moaning, she raised her arm and covered her eyes. Had she been in an accident? Why was she outside? With no memory of what had happened, she moved her head from left to right, her neck muscles protesting under the small movement. Maybe she should lay there for a moment.

She drifted in and out of awareness, curling herself in a ball when the sun set on the horizon and the temperature gradually dropped. Covered in goosebumps, she woke for the second time. Pushing herself up on her elbows to look around, every muscle in her body objected. Darn, she was somewhere out in the dunes. Why? She tried to wet her parched lips, but her tongue felt like leather.

Muttering, she struggled up, a wave of dizziness overwhelming her as the first inkling of the previous night's events popped up in her fogged brain. There had been a tempest, unlike she had ever experienced before. Had she been caught in a tornado and spat out? Had she been hit by lighting? Or had the world come to an end, she the lone survivor? The sun had set on the horizon, the temperature dropping significantly. She shivered, her black dress not nearly enough protection against the chill of the early evening air.

And where was Forrest? She forced herself to stand up and look around, but all she saw were dunes, and more dunes. Carefully, she took a few steps, her muscles protesting with pain and spasms. He wouldn't have left her here by herself now, would he? He had to be here somewhere, right? Struggling to stay on her feet, she took another step.

"Forrest!" she yelled, her voice raspy. "Forrest! I'm pregnant and I'm hurting! You need to help me!"

Light headed, she stumbled around, looking for something to support her trembling body. There was nothing to hold onto, just dune grasses and sharp bushes. She craned her neck from left to the right, wondering if she should keep on looking for him in the little bit of daylight that was left, or if she should try to make her way out of the dunes to find help? She hesitated a few minutes but then made her decision. She couldn't afford to lose the last bit of her energy on a search for him. She had to think about the baby and find her way out of the dunes before it got dark.

On bare feet, she stumbled through the deep sand, the dark heaviness that lingered in her brain increasing. A lump of despair formed in her throat and tears stung her eyes. She was disoriented and numb. With every step, her knees buckled underneath her, the last morsel of her strength evaporating fast.

The final remnants of sun dipped below the horizon and darkness surrounded her. Like a blind person, she struggled on for what could have been seconds, minutes or hours, until she tripped over her own feet and fell forward into the sand. Her body hit the ground, knocking the wind out of her.

"Awww," she cried out, curling herself into a ball. "My baby!"

Stars twinkled softly in the night sky, and an almost full moon rose, lighting up her surroundings. She lay motionless between the tall grass, confused and paralyzed by fear.

During the night, she woke up several times. Not until the morning dawned crisp and bright did she try getting back up. Covered in sand, she took a few steps, her head exploding, her skin burning red and tender beneath her touch. Choking back sobs, she forced herself to walk, pushing herself forward as the morning progressed. The sun gained strength, gradually warming her body, until the wind picked back up. Looking up at the darkening sky, the fear that had firmly settled into her brain turned into complete terror when she noticed dark ominous clouds moving in around her. By now she remembered clearly the unearthly event leading up to this moment. *No please,* she panicked feverishly, not again! The first spatters of rain hit her head and she raised her face up to the sky, trying to catch a few drops of precious liquid. She was cold and hot at the same time, barely able to stay on her feet. Trembling violently, she sagged down onto the ground and licked the liquid off her skin. Her fingers were numb, her limbs stiff, her motor functions gone.

"Oh my God," she sighed, the weight of her desperation too heavy to bear. This was it. She had nothing left.

Cuddled under a heavy blanket, she stretched her legs. Nothing felt better than waking up, refreshed and renewed, after a good night's sleep. The feeling of comfort only lasted for a moment before the real world began to filter through. Her head hurt. So did her hands, her shoulders, her throat. Moving her legs, the heavy cover scratched her sun and wind burned skin. *What was laying on top her?* It was so thick. She felt suffocated. She tried to push the blanket off her and shifted in search of a more comfortable position, but something poked her behind. When she shifted again, she got stabbed in her back and arm. A cold anxiety washed over her. Bedbugs? Was she being bitten?

She opened her eyes and looked around. The room was small. It smelled damp and it was cool. The walls were bare, except for a simple wooden cross made out of two pieces of wood tied together with a piece of twine. A narrow window high above her bed, the glass grimy and thick, allowed only the brightest of light to come through. A wooden door stood slightly ajar. She let out a sigh of relief. At least she wasn't locked up.

Her attention shifted to the bumpy mattress beneath her. Straw poked through the coarse cotton material, jabbing into her flesh. The dark grey woolen blanket scratched her skin. When she pushed it with her feet to the bottom of the bed, she realized she wore an ankle-length loose cotton gown. Its condition gave away the fact it had been worn many times before. The white fabric had a grayish tint, the collar and cuffs frayed, and one of the four tiny round buttons was missing. Lacking the strength to raise herself, she drifted off to sleep content in the knowledge she was alive.

When she woke it was dark in the room, except for the light of a candle flickering on a small table next to her bed. She raised herself up on her elbows, her eyes darting around the dingy cell. The heavy blanket had been pulled back over her body, and a table and candle had appeared out of nowhere. She sat up, her brain not as foggy, her body less sore.

Someone had been in the room, leaving a metal cup filled with water, a chunk of bread on a plate. Bread and water. Maybe she was in prison? She shifted on the coarse uncomfortable mattress until she sat with her back against the cold wall. How long had it been since she had eaten last? Two days, three?

She gulped the water down, wishing they had left an entire gallon. Its coolness soothed her painful throat. She attacked the bread. It was dry and hard, but she didn't care. She was famished.

Chewing the last morsel of the bread, she realized not a single sound had penetrated into her room. No banging noises from fellow inmates, no guards roaming the hallway. Was she somewhere else altogether? There were no bars on the window, the door open, indicating an ability for her to leave if she chose to.

Had Forrest brought her here? Was he somewhere outside the room? Jeez, what was she doing here, sitting on her ass? She needed to find him, tell him she was okay. Instead of moving, she stayed in bed, something holding her back.

If he was around, why wasn't he sitting next to her bed? To check up on her condition? To see if she and their unborn baby were safe and sound? Why wasn't he here, holding her hand?

Well okay, she had to admit, it was dark, probably way past midnight. Maybe he had been here while she had been unconscious. But if he had been here, why hadn't he taken her to a hospital, making sure she was hooked up to an IV, with monitors beeping, fresh clean sheets, an emergency bell to push, and nurses running around to come to her aid?

Agitated, she shifted around on the bed. Where was she? What kind of place was this? It was then she heard light footsteps and the murmur of a whispered conversation. Finally, she would get some answers. She waited for the door to open, but the voices faded away. Damn it. She lowered her legs, the hard concrete floor cold beneath her bare feet. With the cotton nightgown tightly wrapped around her body, she shuffled the few steps to the door, supporting herself on the cast-iron handle until she was sure her legs were steady enough to continue. Behind the door was a long corridor sparsely lit by what appeared to be oil lamps attached to the wall. The first one flickered only a few feet away from her door. She studied the gilded cast iron wall bracket, the glass reflector and the circular wick surrounded by a yellowish glass chimney. The antique lamp seemed well made and in excellent condition. Why would someone go through the effort of hanging such an antique lamp instead of fluorescents? Why was there no carpet or vinyl on the floor of the barren corridor?

Annet walked down the corridor to a window and pressed her face against it to look outside. Besides twinkling stars and a sliver of moonlight tucked behind the clouds, she couldn't make out a thing. Where was she?

Supporting herself against the hard stone wall, she scuffled forward.

"Hello?" she yelled, her voice echoing down the hall. "Anybody there?"

There was no answer, the only sound the sputtering of the lamps.

At the end of the corridor Annet was overtaken by the enormity of the hall that lay before her. High concrete arches supported a cathedral ceiling. Hanging at various places were candle lit chandeliers. Two long rows of wooden tables and

50

benches stood in the center, a huge fireplace with real burning logs was built into the wall. Quivering from exhaustion, she sat down on one of the bare wooden benches surrounding the hearth, stretching out her legs and arms toward the fire.

Light footsteps made her look up. Two women dressed in long black habits, their hair tucked underneath a white coif and a black veil, walked in, carrying large pieces of wood in their arms.

"Hi, there," she said. The words exhaled out of her mouth in relief. Of course, she was in a convent. That explained her surroundings and accommodations.

The two nuns stopped in their tracks.

"Sorry I startled you," Annet apologized. "I had to get out of that horrible desolate little chamber they put me in. Jesus. The bread and water were nice, I really needed that, but the potholed mattress and horrific blanket were just about to kill me."

The nuns' mouths dropped.

Annet pulled up her long white dress, showing them her bare legs and feet. "I need some Aloe after-sun lotion, or another kind of moisturizer. I'm sunburned severely."

At the sight of her bare legs, they almost jumped out of their habits.

"Yeah, I know," Annet grinned. "It looks pretty bad." She pulled up one of her sleeves. "Look, it's even blistering in several places. I can only imagine what my face looks like."

With a loud thud, the nuns dropped their load of firewood right in front of them on the concrete floor, crossing themselves before they fled.

"Hey," she cried after them. "Where are you going?" Exasperated by their quick departure and lack of information she turned back to the crackling fire. Maybe they had just left in a hurry to get her the medical care she needed. Or better yet, maybe they had left to get Forrest. She wanted to see him so badly, it almost hurt.

A few moments later, she heard the murmur of voices. *Hallelujah, something was happening.*

The two young nuns returned, accompanied by five others. Slowly they moved towards her, their brows furrowed, silently looking at her and then at each other. The nun leading the group stopped next to her, a large silver pectoral cross hanging from her neck. She was obviously the lady in charge.

"Our two novices informed me you were up," the nun said, her voice soft and warm. "It gave me great pleasure to hear that."

From the deep wrinkles in her face, Annet estimated she had to be at least in her late sixties. "You're darn right," she agreed. "Thank you very much for setting me up in your nunnery. That's very kind of you, and I don't want to be offensive, but how did I end up here instead of the hospital?"

The nun took a few steps closer, observing her with concern. "The dairy farmer who brings us fresh milk twice a week noticed you sprawled out in the dunes. He brought you here. Don't you remember?"

Vague memories of her lying on a hard surface between tall gray metal canisters, a disturbing continuous bouncing motion, and a humming bearded man surfaced in her brain.

"Although we don't have an infirmary in the monastery, we do take care of people falling ill. It was completely understandable he brought you here instead of all the way to the hospital in Heemstead." She lifted Annet's chin, inspecting her face. "You're awfully pale beneath that sunburned skin. How are you feeling, my dear?"

"Thirsty," Annet replied. "But other than that, I think I'm okay."

The group of nuns whispered among themselves. The older sister snapped her fingers and they immediately fell silent, bowing their heads in respect.

"We are poor ladies from the Second Order of St. Francis, Sisters of St. Clare," the older nun informed her. "I am Mother Superior, the prioress of this monastery. The two novices you first met are Sister Rudolpha and Sister Clarissa."

Annet got on her feet to introduce herself, a wave of dizziness bringing her perilously close to falling.

Mother Superior rushed to her side and supported her before she fell. "Sisters," she ordered. "She's still too weak. Let us support her back to the dormitory. When she's settled, bring her food and water."

The two novices rushed to her aid and guided her with gentle hands out of the refectory toward her room, followed by Mother Superior.

"I was there when the farmer brought you in," one of them told her after they made it into her room and carefully lowered her down onto the bed. "You were mumbling about a Kaiser that lived in a manor in the forest. Do you recall?" They lifted her legs and pulled the blanket over her trembling body.

Hearing his name was almost too much for her unsettled state of mind and she flew back up. "Forrest. You have to call him. I'm sure he's worried sick about my whereabouts."

With gentle hands, they tried to press her back down on the mattress, looking at Mother Superior for help. They stepped back when she approached the bed and placed her hand on Annet's forehead. "Calm, my dear. This is not the time to overexert yourself. You have a light fever and need to rest."

Annet grasped her arm before she could walk away, fighting against her tears. "My name is Annet Sherman. We live in the White Castle Apartments on Sixth Street in Dunedam, right behind the new library. My boyfriend's name is Forrest Overton. You have to find him!"

"I understand," Mother Superior soothed, stroking her hair. "Trust me. We will send somebody to Dunedam right away."

"For crying out loud. Just call my cellphone or the Keizer Manor," Annet cried frantically, holding onto the sisters' arm so tightly, her knuckles turned white. "I can give you the numbers."

Mother Superior wrestled her arm from her tight grip and positioned her hand on the blanket, patting it a few times before she stepped away from the bed. "Don't worry, Annet. We will call on him right away. Now, repose while Sister Rudolpha prepares your food. After you've eaten, you have to close your eyes and sleep. I promise, when you wake, your Forrest will be by your side."

Chapter 7

FORREST LEFT HIS PARENT'S HOUSE and drove back to
their apartment. "Please, Annet, be there," he begged out loud,
desperately hoping she had miraculously reappeared during the
time he had forced himself to finish a bowl of oatmeal. But their
apartment was just as cold and empty as before. Trying to stay
optimistic, he stepped back in his car and headed toward the
Keizer Manor. Sunday was usually Annet's day off, but due to
this weekend's ongoing celebrations all employees had been
ordered to be present no later than ten o'clock. Admission was
still free and it was bound to be busy again. So if she wasn't
hurt, or worse, he knew she would be there, for sure.

As he entered the museum, the hallway was already
crowded with visitors, Beverly waving at him from behind the
reception desk. "Hi Forrest," she smiled, taking him in with an
approving smile, "I heard Annet is missing? Is that true?"

"You haven't seen her today?" he replied, his hope deflating. "Damn!" He punched his fist in the palm of his left hand. Without waiting for an answer he opened the door to Dan's office, finding him on the phone behind his desk.

"One moment," Dan mouthed, pushing one of the empty office chairs toward him. Its wheels rolled over the vinyl floor and came to a stop in front of him. Forrest swiveled the seat around, sat down, and rested his elbows on his knees, hanging his head. *Where was she? What the hell had happened to her?* His frustration increased by the second. Damn, he couldn't just sit here and listen to some bullshit conversation. He had to do something, like call the police, organize a search party.

"I understand," Dan said, the one-sided dialogue lingering on.

Growing increasingly anxious, Forrest stretched his legs out, swinging the chair back and forth, until finally Dan placed the phone back on its cradle. "From the look on your face, I can tell she wasn't home," he said, rubbed his chin in deep thought. "Could she have gone to a friend's house?"

"Of course not," Forrest shot up. "Besides, you know she would have shown up by now, or at least would have called in if she couldn't make it for some reason!"

"I know," Dan agreed, pushing his chair back. "This is completely out of character. Come, let's start with talking to every person who saw her yesterday after the reception. Someone must have an inkling of where she might have gone."

Around one o'clock, Forrest had talked to a good deal of people, all expressing their support and uttering caring words, but nobody seemed seriously concerned about her absence.

She's fine, they assured him. Annet could take care of herself. He didn't have to worry. She was able to fend off any

56

danger. Besides, nothing ever happened in their rural community. Dunedam was peaceful and quiet. Everyone knew everyone. The only crimes ever committed were nonviolent, like drunk and disorderly, reckless driving, vandalism, or the occasional break-in. What was he thinking? That Annet had been kidnapped or met foul play, while the most violent crimes ever committed in the town's history were the abduction of a child by a noncustodial parent and vehicular manslaughter? What a crazy idea! No one from Dunedam had ever vanished in thin air, not even a cat or a dog! Furthermore, besides the occasional routine traffic patrol, they never even saw a police cruiser in town. So nothing serious could have happened to her. Right?

Of course they were right, Forrest tried to make himself believe. He knew from his own experience nothing ever happened in Dunedam. He always read the weekly newspaper that focused on the obituaries, the volunteer of the month, and advertisements from local businesses and restaurants. Two dollars off a large pepperoni pizza, and two-for-one burgers on Tuesday night at the grill bar. This week, the hot topics on the front page had been the re-zoning of a residential street into commercial use, the need for a new roof on the building that housed the grade school, and of course the two-hundredth anniversary of the Keizer Manor.

Okay, Annet's disappearance probably had nothing to do with misconduct, but he also knew with one hundred percent certainty, something was keeping her from coming home. It was up to him to find out what it was.

Tension knotted the muscles in his neck when he placed a phone call to the sheriff's office dispatch center, explaining the situation.

"I understand your frustration Mr. Overton," the dispatcher said. "However, with a missing adult, we usually recommend waiting twenty-four hours, unless there are special circumstances, or evidence a crime has been committed."

"She's pregnant. Isn't that reason enough?" he protested.

"I will relay the message to the officer on duty," the cool voice from the dispatcher replied.

Forrest shut the cellphone with a decisive click, ready to throw it against the wall. *Those lazy bastards, why didn't they jump into action?*

"Is there anything I can do?" Mrs. Rothschild asked. She had abandoned her precious dolls and followed him into the entrance hall where a handful of people had gathered in the hallway, eager to scour the dunes in an unorganized search party. Among them were Ed and Chantal Winters, Sofia Henderson, her husband Geoff, Lucy Hilda, Renée DuBois and his parents. All the people who knew her best and cared for her the most.

"Thanks for offering, Caroline," Forrest told her. He appreciated her willingness to join in the search, and although she was in good shape for her age, toiling up and down the dunes would be too much for her. "Why don't you stand guard at the door? Maybe she'll be able to make her way out of the dunes and it would be wonderful if you were here in case she does."

For a brief second, he contemplated calling Annet's mother to inform her about the situation, but decided against it. She was so self-absorbed and wouldn't listen to his concerns anyway. Besides, he didn't have the patience to sit through one of her monologues. He'd much rather postpone the dreaded phone call forever if he could.

Forrest led the group through the dunes, taking them to the exact spot where he had seen Annet last, splitting up in various directions when they got there.

Where are you, my gorgeous, pregnant hothead? he thought, walking around in circles, searching for any sign of their footprints or any other evidence they had been there, but last night's storm had wiped everything away in the ever-changing sandy landscape.

By the time it was four PM a stiff breeze picked up, blowing away even his most recent footsteps within minutes. Forrest's spirits dropped. He was dog-tired and longed to take home a frozen pizza, crack a beer, and watch TV. His head still hurt, his nerves were frazzled, and he just wanted for his life to be back to normal, with Annet safely home, reading a book, playing on the computer or talking on the phone, while he watched soccer.

Oh girl, where are you? What happened to you? The sting of tears he hadn't yet shed burned his eyes. He wasn't religious, but by this time he was ready to pray to anyone or anything.

At five o'clock, the museum closed its doors. On Dan's orders, all the employees and volunteers gathered in the meeting room. The purpose of the informal gathering had been to festively close the weekend and thank everyone for their extra work and support. Annet had bought snacks and bottles of soda, wine and beer on Friday and would have been busy setting up. Instead people just helped themselves, opening bags of pretzels and pouring their own drinks.

There were at least thirty people talking loudly amongst each other, about the successful weekend, the unpredictable spring weather, and Annet's possible whereabouts. Speculations about her sudden disappearance had grown rampant as the day progressed and Forrest could barely take it. He was at his wits' end.

With his head in his hands, he sat at a table, listening passively to the continuous hum of voices around him. All he wanted was talk to the police and make them understand the seriousness of the situation. Without their help, he wouldn't be able to find her. Mrs. Rothschild sat next to him, patting his hand in a futile effort to calm him.

At the sound of a shrill and accusing female voice, he raised his head. It was Beverly.

"We all know what happened!" he heard her yell loud and clear. "They were fighting before she disappeared into the dunes!"

Silence fell while everyone looked in the girl's direction, until Sofia Henderson took a step forward. "What exactly are you implying, Beverly?" she demanded to know.

"I'm not the only one who witnessed Annet flying out of her office in a rage!" Beverly continued, looking around for support. "I know for a fact she and Forrest had words. I witnessed it myself."

"I saw it too," someone backed her up. "Annet was obviously angry and Forrest chased after her into the dunes. I never saw them come back."

Sofia walked toward Beverly and pointed her finger at her chest in warning. "Not another word, Beverly!" she said, her voice dangerously low. "All of this is gossip."

"What were they fighting about Beverly?" someone else asked, walking over from across the room.

Beverly pushed Sofia's accusatory finger away. "Annet was jealous," she shouted for anyone to hear. "They were fighting because Forrest preferred my company over hers." The spiteful young girl tossed her long brown hair back in an arrogant manner, her smile triumphant.

"I believe you were the one who was flirting," Sofia countered. "I've seen you in action more than once."

"True, I like Forrest," Beverly admitted with a smug grin. "And no one can blame him for looking in another more willing and friendlier direction. Especially since Annet became an even bigger bitch after she got pregnant."

Forrest flew out of his chair and got face to face with Beverly. "Bullshit!" he yelled at her. "You shut your filthy mouth!"

Everybody started to talk at the same time.

"Are you out of your mind?" Sofia yelled.

"Come on. Give her a chance to talk," a woman shouted.

There was complete chaos in the small meeting room, the mood shifting from kindness and support to uncertainty, doubt, suspicion, and even allegation. Dan Mockenburg pushed his way through the crowd until he reached Beverly. Without hesitation, he grabbed her by the arm and pulled her out of the room. It wasn't until they reached the hallway he let her go.

"Get out," he told her, pointing toward the exit doors. "I don't want to see you here anymore. You're fired!"

The tension in the meeting room was palpable after Dan forcefully escorted Beverly out. Forrest looked around, detecting the accusatory glances thrown at him.

He felt a strong urge to defend himself. To tell them Beverly was lying, explain they'd only talked for a few minutes, and that he didn't give a rat's ass about her. He struggled to keep his rage under tight rein. He loved Annet more than anything in the world, and would never hurt her. But all these people were Annet's colleagues and friends. Although he had met several of them over the years, even had them over at their apartment on occasion, he was the outsider. They didn't know him, and after Beverly's convincing tirade, some of them were bound to believe he had flirted behind Annet's back, causing a fight. His jaw tightened as he ran a hand through his hair.

Before he could do or say anything he might come to regret, Dan returned and took him by the arm, this time escorting *him* out of the room. He allowed himself to be led away to Dan's office. He was exhausted, his ears still slightly ringing, his nerves singing with anxiety.

"Let *me* call the police for you," Dan said, forcing him into a chair. "You're in no condition to keep your calm."

Dan sat down behind his desk and dialed the non-emergency phone number of the police station in Heemstead. "Yes, I would like to report a missing person," he said. "A twenty-five year old woman. Her name is Annet Sherman. S-H-E-R-M-A-N." He listened. "No, I'm not a relative. I'm her employer, but she didn't show up for work this morning and that's completely out of the young lady's character, so we are very concerned."

Another silence.

"The last person who saw her? Oh, her boyfriend, Forrest Overton."

Forrest cringed when he heard the word *boyfriend*. It sounded casual, offhand, and unimportant.

Dan opened the lid of a small card holder on his desk and leafed through the index cards until he found one and pulled it out. "Her address is White Castle Apartment Complex, apartment number 14 on Sixth Street in Dunedam. Her boyfriend has her cellphone. The number is 527-834-0491. Thank you. We'll wait for his call." He put the phone down and looked at Forrest. "She said something about an Amber Alert and a car pileup on Interstate 33, but promised a police officer or detective will call you as soon as possible."

Right at that moment, Annet's cellphone rang in Forrest's pocket, and he pulled it out. "Hello?" His shoulders sagged when he recognized his father's voice. "No, nothing, but we just called the police."

"You want to come to the house and have dinner with us?" his father asked on the other end.

Although he was tempted, he declined. "No, I won't be good company tonight and would rather wait at home for the police to call me back. I'll keep you posted."

When he got home, he plugged Annet's phone into the charger and cracked a beer. Gulping, he sagged down on the lonely couch and turned on the TV to fill the silence. The game he had wanted to see just ended and Excalibur, his favorite soccer team had lost. *At least he wasn't the only one who had lost something today.*

The phone stayed silent as he sat through the recap of the game and an hour of news, his mind with Annet and the horrible storm. *What could he do instead of hanging out on the couch? Damn. Why weren't the police calling him, those cocksuckers? Were they not interested because it was Sunday evening and soccer night? Was it because Annet was an adult and not a child? Or would they have reacted differently if they had been married?* When Dan told the officer who had taken the call, even to his own ears, the word boyfriend had sounded hollow. That definitely had to change.

63

Chapter 8

After tossing and turning for hours, Annet awoke, weary and agitated. She opened her eyes and found herself alone. The sun shone in through the small window above her bed, a bright square of light visible on the wall. It had to be late morning or early afternoon.

During her restless slumber, the uneasiness lingering in her brain had gradually shifted into a definite inkling that something wasn't right. She stared around her bare chamber, taking in its oddities. *Why weren't the walls freshly painted? Why weren't there lights on the ceiling? Why was the bed so uncomfortable? And what was up with the breakfast they had served her?* Although the milk had been fresh, the bread had been stale, and when she had complained about it, Sister Rudolpha had kindheartedly explained she had to soak it in the milk. *What was up with that? Why didn't they give her fresh orange juice, bacon and eggs, or hot cinnamon oatmeal? And where was Forrest?* Mother Superior had promised he would be here.

Her door squeaked and sister Rudolpha entered, carrying a bundle of clothes. She nodded courteously in Annet's direction, placing the small stack at the foot of the bed. "We gathered a chemise, drawers, a corded bonnet, woolen shawl and dress for you," she said, laying the pieces out one by one. "Unfortunately you have very large feet for a woman and we couldn't find any shoes that might fit you, so I brought you these." She looked at her apologetically, holding up a pair of brown leather sandals and black wool stockings.

"Ah, thick woolen socks and Birkenstock sandals. Are you trying to turn me into a hippie?" Annet remarked.

Sister Rudolpha gave her a quick puzzled glance before she returned her attention to the clothing. "This is what you wore when they brought you in," she said, lifting a small bundle of black fabric in the air. Annet recognized her bra, panties and black dress. "I've never seen such interesting, soft and stretchy material," the young nun continued. "You must come from a rich family if you can afford something this exquisite."

Rich? I wish, Annet thought. For the majority of her life she had lived in a single wide trailer, among the white trash of Heemstead. The only things her life had been full of were cuss words, yelling, and emptiness. It wasn't until her mother had married her third husband and they moved to Dunedam that her life had improved. But rich? Far from it.

"Any word about Forrest? Is he on his way?" she asked.

Sister Rudolpha shook her head sympathetically. "Mother Superior sent out the gardener hours ago, but he hasn't returned yet."

"Hours ago?" Annet cried out with angry impatience. "Jeez, if this monastery is located on the outskirts of Dunedam, it should only take fifteen minutes to drive back and forth."

The young nun flushed after her outburst and took a few nervous steps in the direction of the door. "Maybe if he could fly, Miss," she replied. "But on horseback it takes a lot longer."

"On horseback? Are you out of your mind?" She was ready to pull out her hair. "What century do you actually live in? This is ridiculous!"

Sister Rudolpha cowered against the wall, her hands covering her ears. "The nineteenth."

Annet pushed the covers away, stepped out of bed and held up her index finger in front of the trembling nun. "If this is a practical joke, I will kill you," she yelled and stomped into the hallway toward the refectory, her eyes blazing. Her patience had run out. She was going to get some answers from good old Mother Superior.

She flew through the refectory and down another hallway, leaving shocked nuns in her wake. Reaching the library, she found two nuns sitting behind a square wooden table, almost hidden between the book-covered shelves. In front of them sat a large volume with lots of scribbles.

"Where is Mother Superior's office?" she demanded.

They pointed to a door and Annet burst through it, her bare feet sinking into soft burgundy carpet. The empty room was colorful and decorated with long curtains along the tall windows, dark wooden furniture and a chest with ten drawers, adorned with small statues. *Probably images of the Virgin Mary, Saint Francis and Saint Clare,* Annet thought. Against the wall, behind a heavy looking desk, hung an olive wooden crucifix with an INRI acronym. Her hand trailed over the back of a carved wooden chair with red velvet padding as she took in the serene atmosphere. There was no doubt in her mind this office belonged to Mother Superior.

Since nobody was around, she searched the desk and other surfaces for the phone, but there wasn't one to be found. With a sinking feeling she turned toward the crucifix. "Absolutely nothing makes sense here," she said to the figure of Jesus Christ. "Isn't there anything you can do for me?"

She waited for whatever to happen, but the stillness around her only seemed to deepen, until she detected faint voices coming from behind a closed door on the other side of the room. Great, someone was coming. It was time to get some well overdue answers.

The door opened and Mother Superior walked in, accompanied by two men.

"But I don't understand no one is missing her," Mother Superior said, before she caught sight of her unexpected visitor. A frown of disapproval furrowed her forehead. "Annet, what are you doing here in your night shift?" She grabbed the black woolen shawl that was draped over the back of her chair and hurried over to her, pushing it into her hands. "Quickly, cover yourself."

"I'm not taking orders from you," Annet replied, tossing the shawl on the floor. "Where is Forrest? And what's up with this nineteenth century baloney? I want answers, and I want them now!"

Mother Superior gasped sharply. "No one in my monastery ever dared to defy me in such a horrible manner. This is unacceptable."

Annet's eyes burned with indignation. "I don't know what's going on here, with this no electricity and no phone nonsense, and people running around on horseback, but if this is a practical joke, I assure you, I'm not laughing!"

"The tone of your voice is very disturbing, young lady. We don't tolerate that around here," Mother Superior said with a pinched look, trying to retain her regal composure by straightening her pectoral cross. "Especially not after we took you in, fed and clothed you, and pulled our gardener away from his duties by sending him to Dunedam."

One of the men, who had accompanied Mother Superior into her office, stepped forward, his boots leaving muddy footsteps on the spotless carpet. "After hearing you rant and rave like that, I'm coming to understand why nobody seems to know you in Dunedam," he said with disdain. His thumbs looped behind the leather suspenders holding up his breeches, his face red and pockmarked. "They probably don't want to."

Annet turned toward the ill-dressed man, wondering if he was the gardener they had sent to look for Forrest. "Instead of looking, you probably took a nap beneath the apple tree. This is bullshit!" she snapped at him.

"What was that?" The gardener raised his voice, "I spoke to many good folks out there in Dunedam. No one had ever heard your name or your husband's. Sixth Street? Behind the library? What manners do you have to send a man in search for places that don't exist? You should be ashamed of yourself."

"You're lying," Annet cried out. There was stark pain under her accusation.

Mother Superior took a step forward. "I'm sure there must be a simple explanation," she said. "Please, let's discuss this as sensible adults."

The gardener turned around on his heel, aversion plastered on his face. "I'm not talking with a mad woman," he said before marching out the door.

After a long moment of taut silence, Mother Superior sat down behind her desk and cleared her throat. "Annet, let me assure you our gardener did everything he could to find your husband. When he found himself unsuccessful, he even took the trouble to find Mister Keizer for you, since you kept on asking about him. Aren't you happy to see him, at least?"

Annet's mouth dropped. "Mister Keizer?" She turned around to face the second man in the office. He leaned casually against the chest with the holy statues, one of them precariously close to falling down.

"At your service," he said. His strong white teeth flashed in a smile before he bowed at the waist, his velvet blue cloak touching the ground.

Even in her frantic state of mind, she couldn't help but notice he was strikingly handsome with long wavy dark brown hair and impossibly green eyes. Nice Jack Sparrow boots too, she thought.

Her face organized itself into a smile of false amenability. "Well of course, now I understand," she smirked. "We're on a hidden camera show or Funniest Home Videos, and you're trying to make me believe I traveled back in time without the use of a time machine or a DeLorean. Very funny!" With a haughty shrug she turned around and walked out of the office.

Chapter 9

A BRIGHT YELLOW RAY OF SUNLIGHT crept through the window, waking him from a deep sleep. Forrest lay curled up and reached to the other side of the bed in an automatic gesture, his eyes still closed. Finding it was cold and empty, he awoke fully, realizing where he was and what had happened. A suffocating emptiness engulfed him. Groaning loud and deep, he opened his eyes. The clock on Annet's nightstand told him it was almost seven-thirty in the morning. He couldn't believe he'd slept for five hours straight.

Not wanting to face the day without Annet, he pushed himself up until he sat at the edge of the bed with his head in his hands. His limbs were heavy, his shoulders sagged. After sitting miserably like that for several minutes, he picked up the cellphone from the bedside table. Not a single call or text had come in.

Disheartened, he used the bathroom and brushed his teeth. Glancing in the mirror above the sink, he barely recognized the sad image it reflected. His face was strained, his eyes hollow, and his hair a mess. What a transformation from the happy-go-lucky guy he used to see. He contemplated taking a shower in the hope it might make him feel better, but he lacked the energy. Instead he started the coffeemaker and sat down at the kitchen counter with the phone in his hand. It was time to call the police again. To tell them how serious the situation was. She was pregnant, for Christ's sake. Half in anticipation and half in dread, he hesitated. Suppose they told him she'd been found, severely injured, or worse, that she would never come home again. He wasn't sure he could handle that.

A loud knock on the door shook his nerves.

"Mr. Overton? Are you there? This is the police."

With his heart pounding in his chest, he hurried through the living room and opened the front door.

Two men waited outside, the older one dressed in blue jeans and a plaid shirt, the other one in uniform. Their police cruiser stood in the parking lot.

"I'm Detective Jaeger," the older man said. "This is Deputy Collins. We're here about a missing person?"

Blood drained from Forrest's face. "Yes, please come in," he said, taking a step back so the two men could enter. He was barefoot, his clothes slept in. He knew he looked terrible. Not a good start with the police.

"We'd hoped to get here sooner," the detective said, his eyes taking in the apartment. Then he mumbled something under his breath about a busy weekend, a missing three-year-old and a partner on vacation, but Forrest paid little attention. Since he didn't work, he always kept the house clean, did the laundry, bought the groceries and prepared dinner, and he didn't want the two men to think he never picked up after himself. With the detective's staring at his back, he gathered last night's beer cans and the empty bag of chips.

"Is it your partner who's missing?" Detective Jaeger asked, his bushy mustache bobbing as he spoke. He pulled a notepad from his back pocket and flipped it open. "Annet Sherman, female, age twenty-five."

Forrest squeezed the beer cans in his hands so tight, they crumbled under the pressure. "Have you found her? Do you have any news?"

Jaeger shook his head. "We're here for more details."

Forrest let out a heavy sigh. At least there was still hope she might walk through the door, unaware of what her disappearance had done to him, teasing him, and calling him a wuss for worrying so much. "Do you care for coffee?" he managed to ask.

They declined, but sat down at the kitchen counter while he poured himself a cup, trying to act normal and behave in an adult manner.

"Tell us exactly what happened," Jaeger said, his pen ready to take notes.

Forrest talked for several minutes, not leaving anything out. Not even the silly misunderstanding they had had, and Beverly's fabricated lies and accusations.

"You'll have to come to the station for an official statement, and have yourself examined by a physician," the detective told him.

"I feel fine and don't want to see a doctor," Forrest rejected the detective's professional concern, ignoring his headache and the persistent ring in his ears. "I just want to find Annet,"

The men got to their feet. "I insist!" Detective Jaeger said on his way to the door. "I'll have a deputy set up an appointment at the hospital in Heemstead. He'll let you know what time you're required to be there."

Forrest walked them out. Before they stepped into the police cruiser, Jaeger turned to face him,

"I'll arrange a search of the dunes. Since you told me you got hung up on the barbed wire fence at the Government Research Center, the surrounding area will be our primary focus. We'll branch out from there."

Chapter 10

Annet woke up after a long, restful sleep and crawled out of bed. Mother Nature was calling. Yesterday, they had told her to use the chamber pot, stored underneath her bunk. Right now she had bigger business to take care of, and she wasn't about to use it for that. Dismissing from her mind what they had told her about living in the nineteenth century, she left her cell, opening doors along the corridor with curiosity. Cramped chambers, bare walls, beds neatly made, black habits, and long white robes hanging from hooks on the wall in each tiny room.

Her tongue slipped over her front and bottom teeth. She hadn't brushed them in days and they felt like they had moss growing on them. Disgusting. She couldn't face the world like that?

Rows of nuns sat at the long tables in the refectory, spooning their breakfast in complete silence. Ugh, silence, again. How did these women do that?

"Can anyone please tell me where the bathroom is?" she asked.

"Just use your bedpan," one of the nuns whispered. "I'll empty it in the cesspit after you're done."

Annet shook her head. She might be pregnant, but she definitely wasn't an invalid. "No way! Besides, I need to take a shower, brush my teeth, and comb my hair. I'm sure I look like a zombie from the living dead by now."

"Living dead?" the nun shrieked, forgetting to keep her voice down.

One of the older nuns got up from the table, took her by the arm and forced her back toward the hallway.

"Hey, you're hurting me," Annet protested, rubbing her pained arm after the nun finally let go. "Jeez, all I want to do is go to the bathroom, clean up, and get the hell out of here. Is that too much to ask?"

"We have never encountered a more disturbing guest than you," the nun countered. "You are insolent and ungrateful, and don't deserve to stay under our roof. Please, go to your room and do your business in the provided pot. In the meantime, I will fetch what you need, so you can get ready for your departure."

What a bitch, Annet thought, acknowledging she had met her match in the old nun.

Soon, Sister Rudolpha entered her room with a bowl of hot water, a towel, and a few toiletries. "Will you be all right, Annet?" she asked. "You seem distraught."

Annet gave her a confident grin. "Sure, don't worry about me. I always land on my feet."

Left alone, she wet the towel to wash her body, washed her hair with soap, and looked at her "new" clothes. A long brown dress with white lace, a chemise, and drawers. It couldn't get any worse. She stuffed the bonnet and toiletries, along with her nightgown and black dress into a burlap bag. After she slid her feet into the sandals, she walked to the refectory.

"Mr. Jonkers is waiting outside," Rudolpha said, handing her a loaf of bread and two apples. "Here, take this on your journey."

Annet followed her past the chapel to the main entrance. "Who's Mr. Jonkers?"

"He's the dairy farmer who brought you here," Rudolpha explained, opening the convent door. "He inquired after your well-being and offered to give you a ride back to the Dune Road."

A horse-drawn wagon loaded with metal milk churns sat on the cobblestoned drive in the courtyard. A bearded man stood beside the chestnut workhorse, adjusting the reins. At the sound of their footsteps, he turned around.

"Russell Jonkers, at your service," he said, raising his straw hat.

Doubts assaulted her. Could that wagon really be her method of transportation back to Dunedam? This time-travel nonsense was really starting to piss her off.

Russell helped her on the narrow wooden bench of the wagon, and sat down next to her. "Ready?"

She inhaled a shuddering breath. *What was she getting herself into?*

The dairy farmer clacked with his tongue, and the cart rolled over the cobblestone away from the monastery.

"Here we go baby, hold on," Annet whispered, bracing herself on the rickety seat, her hand protectively covering her belly.

The horse kept a slow steady pace as they drove down a dirt road. Miles and miles of empty moorland surrounded them, none of it looking even vaguely familiar. "I can't believe how far away we are from civilization," she commented.

Russell chewed on a piece of straw, the reins loosely in his hands, "Around the next bend, you can see the church tower of Dunedam," he said.

It was a beautiful morning, bright with sunshine. It felt great to be outside of the depressing walls of the convent and on her way back home, to Forrest.

"I'm pleased to see you've recovered well from your ordeal in the dunes," Russell commented. "How are you feeling?"

"Other than thinking I've lost my mind, I believe I'm okay." She grimaced and then cried out in fear when one of the wheels sank into the soft shoulder of the road. Several empty milk churns in the back tipped over. As if nothing had happened, the horse pulled the four-foot wheel from the ditch and continued down the narrow road.

"Damn, we almost had to call Triple A," she cried out, wiping the perspiration off her forehead. "That was close."

Russell raised an eyebrow. "That a friend of yours?"

Annet cracked a smile. "With a clunker for a car like we have, we got to know them pretty well."

They drove around the bend. A few hundred feet further, Russell pulled the reins, bringing the wagon to a stop. "That's where I found you," he said, pointing to a shallow dell surrounded by Marram grass and sand reed.

She gawked at him. "Right there? Are you kidding me? We're in the middle of nowhere!"

"I have no reason to lie," Russell frowned. "I came down the Dune Road, noticing you all sprawled out. I picked you up and took you to the convent."

Afraid she was losing it, she breathed deep in and out in an effort to control her panic. "So you're telling me this sandy track is the main road that connects Dunedam with Lisk? I don't believe you! You're a liar!"

Russell skewered her with a glance, throwing the burlap bag with her meager belongings in the sand. "I'm not a liar, Miss, and this is where we're parting ways."

Chapter 11

AFTER THE POLICE LEFT, Forrest called his parents, Dan Mockenburg, and several of Annet's closest friends. Next, he placed the dreaded phone call to Annet's mother, Barbara. She had divorced her fourth husband, and was now living with Chuck, the man she'd had a date with on Annet's birthday. Forrest hadn't met him yet, but from what he'd heard so far, he wasn't missing anything.

"Oh, my poor baby!" Barbara cried out at the shocking news. Forrest could hear her sobbing at the other end of the line, and then his stomach dropped even further when she said exactly what he'd feared. "We're coming down as soon as possible." Damn, that was the last thing he needed.

Over the course of the morning, Annet's cellphone didn't stop ringing. People wanted to find out the latest news, convey their concern, and offer their help. The police had called to inform him he had to undergo a complete physical evaluation at two PM at the hospital in Heemstead, and that a search party was scouring the dunes.

And then there was Barbara. She had called half a dozen times or more, asking him for an update. Despite his protests, she stated they were loading up the car and heading his way.

"You can't stay at our apartment, Barbara! It's too small, you know that!" he tried frantically, hoping to get through to her. He had to keep her away!

Forrest showered, shaved, and changed his clothes before he headed to the hospital. While he waited for his appointment, he phoned Detective Jaeger for an update.

"The Coast Guard has a chopper in the air, flying over the dunes and along the coastline," the detective told him. "Search-and-rescue is patrolling on foot. Don't worry, Mr. Overton, we will do everything we can to find her."

"Thank you," Forrest sighed, grateful tears blurring his vision. This was a lot more than he had expected in such a short period. He covered his face with his hands and stifled a dry sob. Thank God they were taking the situation seriously.

A few minutes later, a nurse called his name and escorted him down the hall to a private room. Half an hour later, he was back in his car, a cotton ball held by a piece of medical tape in the crook of his arm. Feeling a tad woozy, he stopped at a fast-food restaurant and sat down in a booth behind a burger, fries and coffee, wanting his phone to ring with good news, but when he pulled it from his pocket, the damn thing had died. "Damn, no wonder it had stayed quiet," he muttered, grabbing his food to go. The minute he got home, he plugged it into the charger. Before it had the chance to come back alive, his door banged open and a strange man wearing black suit pants beneath a bulging stomach walked in, carrying two huge suitcases.

Forrest's mouth dropped. "Who the hell are you?"

"The name is Chuck," the man replied, his voice booming through the room. "Where do you want these?" His light blue shirt was open at the throat, exposing a grey wedge of chest hair, and his sleeves were rolled up to his elbows, revealing several unsightly faded tattoos.

Was this old coot Barbara's latest suitor? Forrest thought. *That couldn't be. He had to be at least twenty years older than her.* "You've got to be joking me," he moaned and walked past him. A small white pick-up truck with an extended cab was backed up to his front door. Annet's mother was pulling futilely on another suitcase.

"Can you give me a hand, Forrest," she cried out when she spotted him.

"No way!" he protested. "What are you doing here, Barbara? I told you not to come!"

She pouted her red lips. "But dear, how could I stay away when my only daughter is missing?"

"I don't have room for you! You know that!"

Crocodile tears sprung into her heavily mascaraed eyes and his gut tightened, knowing he was fighting a losing battle.

"Nonsense," she replied, giving up on the suitcase. "Since Annet isn't here, Chuck and I can stay in the bedroom and you can take the couch." She spread her arms and walked toward him, her trim body swaying seductively under her tight fitting coral-red sleeveless jumpsuit. Much could be said about her, but she kept herself in great shape and didn't look a day older than forty. She wrapped her arms around his middle and rested her head against his chest in a warm hug, the heavy smell of her perfume adding to his misery.

His neighbor's door opened and he cringed. The situation was already difficult enough. He couldn't handle another worried female, but the door opened further and his longtime neighbor, Mrs. Graham, stepped outside. She was very old, her hair white, her face finely wrinkled, and she leaned on a cane.

"I noticed a police cruiser in the parking lot this morning and heard Annet is missing? Is that true?" she asked, her voice so soft he could barely hear her.

"Yes, it is," he replied, prying himself loose from Barbara's tight grip.

"Oh no, my dear Forrest, you must be devastated," the old woman croaked, reaching out to him with a quivering hand, her skin translucent and covered with liver spots.

Forrest took her arm. "Come, Mrs. Graham," he told her, guiding her back into her apartment. "You don't have to worry. The police have a helicopter in the air, search and rescue is on the ground. They'll find her."

After he had settled her down into her recliner, he rushed back into his own apartment and heard voices coming from the bedroom. He walked in and almost exploded. Chuck was lying on his bed with his shoes still on and Barbara stood in front of their closet with both doors wide open. She handed him a stack of his neatly folded T-shirts. "You have to make room for my clothes, Forrest."

The look he shot at her could have killed her. "Fine," he said, gritting his teeth. "But if you just so much as touch Annet's clothes, I'll kick your skinny ass back to where you came from."

Chapter 12

Dumbfounded by the curt dismissal, Annet watched the milk wagon roll down the road until it was out of sight. Then she turned around to look in the other direction, the dirt road stretching on until it curved around the dunes, disappearing into nowhere.

Instead of going in the direction of Dunedam, she entered the dunes to investigate. There was no fence to keep her out of the fragile environment, no sign to keep her from trespassing, the uncanny quietness around her only disturbed by the distant tweeting of a few birds and the screech of a seagull. She had had enough of silence! With sagging shoulders, she turned around and walked back to the Dune Road, heading toward Dunedam. After five hundred feet she gave up. There was nothing in sight. It was hot. She had no water. Not knowing what else to do, she turned around yet again and followed the wagon's tracks. By the time she approached a farmhouse, she perspired heavily underneath her dress, her hair sticking to her forehead, her cheeks burning from the sun. The familiar milk wagon stood parked on a courtyard down a short drive, horse and owner nowhere to be seen.

She let herself in through the gate, retied the rope around the wooden post and headed toward the house. The farm house was one story, with a straw covered roof, and red and white shutters next to the windows. Chickens clucked around, accompanied by several waddling ducks. A small brown dog with floppy ears wandered around in front of a barn, a stick in his mouth. When he noticed her, he wagged his tail and came running in her direction.

Hoping he was friendly, she waited until he stopped in front of her.

"Hello dog. Where is your owner?"

"Woof," said the dog, the stick dropping from his mouth in front of her.

The farm door opened and a young woman appeared, a red handkerchief tied around a burst of curly brown hair.

Annet gawked at her very pregnant middle, the waistband of her full dark blue skirt pulled up just beneath her heavy breasts. "I'm pregnant, too," she said, for the first time feeling proud of her small bump. "About four months."

"Are you coming for eggs?" the robust young woman asked.

"No, she's not," Russell Jonkers interrupted. He had come from the barn, a wide brush full of horsehair in his hand. "This is the odd female I discovered in the dunes."

Annet regarded him. "I truly apologize for my outburst, Mr. Jonkers. I'm normally not that rude. It's just that I have the feeling I'm somehow completely misplaced in the circle of time and all I want is to find my way home."

The friendly dog kept on begging for her attention, playfully rolling over and jumping up against her skirt, leaving dusty footprints. She knelt down to pet him.

"Since my dog seems to like you, I guess you can't be all that bad of a person," Russell commented. "His name is Duke. He's a six-year-old Cocker Spaniel." Then, he turned toward the young woman. "Trudy, take her inside for a meal."

Through a mudroom, where they took off their shoes, they entered a modest kitchen. It was pleasantly cool inside.

Trudy gestured toward one of the straight-backed wooden chairs surrounding the table, and Annet sat down, looking around the tidy and comfortable kitchen. What she didn't see was a refrigerator, microwave or coffee machine.

"Care for beef, potatoes, and vegetables with gravy?" Trudy asked, busying herself behind the wood-burning cook stove. She used the hand pump next to the sink to fill a glass of water. Next, she picked up a wooden ladle, filled a bowl, and placed it in front of Annet on the table.

While Annet ate, Trudy sank down in a chair next to her, her right hand bracing her back. "Hope you don't mind me asking. How on earth did you come to be alongside the road?"

Taking time to think about what she would say, she slowly finished her mouthful. "I got lost in the dunes, looking for the Keizer Manor. Do you know where it is?"

"You're looking for Mr. Keizer?" Trudy asked.

Annet's index finger followed the red and white checkered pattern of the tablecloth. "I have an important message for him," she lied.

"Mr. Keizer left for Heemstead. He probably won't be back til later this week. Do you want to leave the message here since he always stops by on his way for fresh eggs and milk?"

Annet thanked her good fortune. This young woman proved to be a great source of information. She finished her bowl and got up. "That's kind of you, but I'd rather deliver it in person. Can you point me in the right direction?"

Trudy walked her out. "Take a left at the end of the drive. After about half a mile, you'll see a wooden post marking the trail leading to his abode."

Before she could leave, Trudy got hold of her arm. "Are you feeling well enough to walk? You seem distraught."

For a moment Annet was taken aback. "I'm fine," she replied, straightening her back before she hurried down the drive. Without a doubt, the wisest thing for her to do was leave before she started bawling, spilling her guts. She felt so lonely, so abandoned.

Duke followed her until she reached the Dune Road, wagging his tail and barking loudly until she disappeared out of sight.

Chapter 13

FORREST SPENT A MISERABLE NIGHT on the couch and left early in the morning, buying an espresso and a blueberry muffin at the Dark Roast Drive-Thru along the main road out of town. He didn't want to see his unwelcome houseguests more than he had to.

With the cup of steaming coffee in his hand, he cruised along Dune Road, thinking about last night. Although Chuck had said little, thank God, Annet's mother made up for it. She continuously bawled over her missing baby, rattling on about the wonderful childhood she had given her and how much she missed her. By the time they retreated to the bedroom, he was ready to pull his hair out. But visualizing Barbara and her big ox in their bed had driven him crazy, as if his apprehension over Annet's whereabouts wasn't enough to drive him mad.

This morning an organized search party of friends, locals, and other volunteers from neighboring towns would leave the

Keizer Manor's parking lot around ten. The police had concentrated the search on the direct area surrounding the Government Research Area, where Forrest had seen her last. They had found one of her black high heeled shoes, but nothing else, and had expanded the search to a five mile radius.

The editor of the Dunedam Pioneer offered to write a story about her disappearance in their weekly edition. Strangers were handing out missing person posters, and posted them everywhere around town, in the library, at the post office, the banks, and stores, on fences, light posts and traffic signs. Annet's photo on the posters was perfect. Her long blonde hair fell in soft waves around her shoulders, her deep blue eyes glistening with excitement, her lips curved in a bright smile. Looking at it made his heart and throat constrict with grief.

Dan Mockenburg had set up a base-camp in the auditorium of the Manor. He had also contacted HLDB-FM, the radio station that aired out of Heemstead, and they had offered to broadcast free daily updates on the search, and any latest findings from the police.

After cruising aimlessly around for an hour, Forrest checked in at the police station to give his official statement. He was met by the young deputy who had come to his apartment the other day and was ushered into an interrogation room. The cameras mounted in each corner, and the obscured and barred windows caused his stomach to clench.

"Take a seat," the Deputy said, sitting down at the table himself, a digital recorder and a notebook in front of him.

Forrest sank down on one of the hardback chairs under his cold, scrutinizing glare. *Why was he staring at him like that, instead of showing empathy and concern?*

"For the records, can you state your name?" Deputy Collins started the interview. The same questions he had answered before were thrown at him. He felt like a suspect, his clenched stomach starting to hurt as his apprehension grew.

"So you're an unemployed civil engineer and your wife, uh … girlfriend, supported you all the way through college," he repeated as he jotted down the information. "You've been in a relationship for eight years. You have no credit card debt, no outstanding loans, no car payments, and no life insurance. And you have one car? How do you get around?"

"Annet likes to take her bicycle to work, unless the weather is bad. I bike around a lot myself too," he answered, trying to contain the anger in his voice because of the way he was being treated.

The hour-long interrogation ticked by in a way that made it feel like precious time was being taken away from finding Annet. After the deputy took his fingerprints and a swab from the inside of his cheek for his DNA, he left the room without a word, leaving Forrest shaken up and unsure if he was free to leave. Screw it, he thought, rushing out of the precinct office to his car. He drove to the Keizer Manor to join the search party scheduled to depart at ten.

It was Tuesday and the group of volunteers, consisting of retirees, students, and housewives scattered around the dunes. Forrest decided to search on his own. He wasn't in the mood for company, his nerves jagged.

Although he had been honest, not leaving anything out that might be of interest, he had the distinct feeling the cops didn't trust him anymore; that they believed he was lying or hiding something.

He considered himself an uncomplicated, jovial, and easy-to-get-along-with man, who bore no secrets, except that he sometimes drank a little more than he should, but what the heck, who could blame him? It wasn't always easy to receive another rejection after a promising phone interview, or having to ask your partner for a few bucks if you needed shaving cream, or a new pair of socks.

Hadn't he been cooperative enough, by giving them unlimited access to their apartment, and letting the forensic team comb through their car? Or was the fact that husbands or boyfriends always ended up being the culprit enough for them to make up their mind?

After hours of wandering through the dunes, his search hadn't turned up anything. He was wet and cold from the drizzle, and feeling depressed.

Caroline Rothschild sat behind the reception desk when he returned to the Keizer Manor, her eyes widening at the sight of him. "You look terrible," she cried out. "Have you been sleeping at all?"

He looked haggard, still wearing the shirt he had slept in last night. It was wet, wrinkled and hung down from his sagging shoulders. "What are you doing here?" he asked, to steer the attention away from him.

"I have no clue," Caroline said with a grimace. "But since Annet is missing and Beverly has been fired, the museum is understaffed. Of course the counter can't be left unmanned, so I volunteered."

"I see," he mumbled. His hair was dark from the rain, water dripped from his clothes onto the floor, and his socks squished in his sneakers.

"Go home, and get some rest!" Caroline ordered him. "You can barely stand on your feet, and you can't help Annet when you're like this."

Although going back to his apartment was the last thing he wanted to do, he had no other choice. He needed a few hours of sleep, a shower, and clean clothes.

Chapter 14

A nnet made her way through the dunes, feeling like a tracker, but instead of following footprints, she followed mounds of horse manure. It was blistering hot, the sun shining unrelentingly down on her. Fine white sand filled her sandals and burned her feet. Her dress was plastered to her back and perspiration trickled down her temples. It had to be close to one-hundred degrees, maybe even more, making her wonder how it could be so blistering hot in May. She struggled on, concerns for her baby's well-being and the lack of drinking water troubling her more with each step. *Please, let this nightmare end. Please, universe, swallow me up and take me home.*

After rounding yet another hill, the landscape leveled and she stepped into an oasis of green tranquility. A small fen, fed by groundwater, with grasses growing in abundance around it, glistened in the midafternoon sun. Willow and pine trees provided shade. A cabin with a porch and a small shed stood sheltered by large dunes, a cast iron water pump above an oval washtub nearby. She hurried toward it, raised the handle and pushed it down. In return it produced a shrill protesting sound. The second time she moved the handle, clear water rushed out. Thank you, good Lord.

She quenched her thirst before washing her hands and face, relishing the cool fresh liquid. Next, she looked around. It seemed no one was around. Pretending she didn't have a care in the world, she strolled to the cabin and knocked on the door. "Hello? Anyone home?"

When it stayed silent, she tried the handle and the door opened. Her pulse beat nervously as she stepped over the threshold into the oppressive heat inside the room.

"Hello!" she tried again, taking in her surroundings. An old couch with protruding metal springs sat beneath a window. In the center stood a rickety table with four chairs, and there was a small kitchen with a sink. Everything was covered with a thick layer of dust, the grime-coated windows full of cob webs, the bare wooden floor layered with sand. No wonder they didn't see a reason to lock the door. There was nothing of value inside.

She tossed her bag onto the couch, throwing up a cloud of dust. "These people are lousy housekeepers," she muttered and sneezed.

Realizing no one was home, she opened an inside door and entered a bedroom, blankets and pillows strewn about. An oak dresser stood to the side, wrinkled, and paint splattered clothes spilling from the open drawers.

She shut the door, squeezing her nose to prevent another sneeze, and peeked into a second room. Shelves, loaded with jars of paint in all colors and sizes, and others jammed full with a variety of paint stained brushes, covered two entire walls. On the floor, against the opposite wall, she noticed at least thirty paintings lying on top of each other, all of them carelessly discarded. In the center stood an easel with an unfinished painting of what could either be a landscape with trees, or the skyline of a city with skyscrapers.

Okay, she had found the studio of a painter, that much was clear, but was it really Alex Keizer's?

She picked up the painting on top of the stack and turned it around in her hands.

"What the hell! This is Alex Keizer's *Spring Flowers*. What is it doing out here?"

She placed it against the wall and picked up another one. *Earth meets Sky, Defiance, The Poseidon, Zeus and Hera.* Her hands trembled when she carefully went through the paintings. The yellows, greens and oranges so bright, the paint so fresh, she could smell it!

With her eyes fixated on the paintings, she slumped down to the ground, trying to wrap her mind around everything that had happened since the anniversary party. Although proof was laughing in her face, it was too difficult to fathom she had actually landed in the nineteenth century. It just couldn't be true. It had to be a hallucination.

Now, if she could only fall into a deep sleep and wake up in her own bed, next to Forrest, his hand protectively covering her stomach, where their baby grew, everything would be fine again. She curled herself up in a ball and squeezed her eyes shut.

Chapter 15

WHEN HE OPENED THE DOOR to their apartment, Forrest almost took off running. Besides the nauseating aroma of perfume and bacon grease, the smell of stale male sweat hung in the air. It had to be at least eighty degrees inside. Barbara and Chuck sat on the couch, watching TV. The moment he crossed the threshold, she jumped all over him.

"Where the hell have you been?" she lashed out. "You can't just leave us here and make us fend for ourselves. We're your guests!"

Swallowing hard, he stared at the mess in the kitchen. Egg caked plates, and dirty pans stacked up in the sink, grease splatters all over the stovetop. He was ready to strangle her.

"Thanks for your concern over Annet's wellbeing," he said, his voice dripping with sarcasm.

In the blink of an eye, her demeanor changed from the scornful raging witch to the loving and caring mother she was supposed to be. "Oh my, oh my. Is there any news?"

He scoffed and turned his back to her.

Showered and dressed in a pair of black jeans, a flannel shirt, and a V-necked burgundy sweater he sat at the kitchen counter. Although his persistent headache and the constant ringing in his ears had diminished, he could not have felt worse. He was at the brink of exhaustion, physically and mentally, his mind in constant turmoil. Where was she? What had happened to her? Was she swallowed up by the dunes? Had the storm picked her up and taken her to sea?

The repetitive beep from the microwave brought him back to reality. Dragging himself up, he pulled out the Hot Pocket, carefully opening the wrapper. There was a brick in the place where his stomach used to be and with distaste he set his teeth in the buttery crust.

"What are you having?" Barbara yelled from the couch. She was simultaneously watching reruns from Judge Judy, How I Met Your Mother, and Top Model, zapping rapidly between channels, while Chuck sat next to her, his head leaning backwards, his mouth wide open. He was snoring loudly.

The relentless chatter of voices, the suffocating heat, the smell of food, and Chuck's constant grunting sounds were more than he could bear. "I need some air," he said, walking out of the apartment and into the rain that was still falling. There were huge puddles in the parking lot and he hesitated, but going back inside was not an option. He dug out his keys from his pocket and dashed through the rain toward his car, jumping in. He placed his hands around the steering wheel. They were cold but sweaty, his vision blurry as he stared straight ahead. The rain drummed on the roof. Although it was chilly and damp inside, the car felt like a protective metal box around him. For the first time in days, he relaxed his shoulders. Mesmerized, he stared at the few cars driving by and splashing up water, until his eyes became heavy and everything around him faded away.

The ring of Annet's cellphone woke him with a start. He fumbled in his pocket to answer.

"Hello? Is this Forrest?" The female voice on the other end was hesitant.

"Yes."

"This is Renée DuBois. You remember me? I'm the gift shop manager at the Keizer Manor."

"Of course I remember you," he said, not pleased to be woken up.

"I was just listening to HLDB-FM on the radio. They had breaking news. Did you know they found a female body this morning?"

Paralyzing shock hit him like an explosive. "A body?" he croaked.

"Sorry, I thought you knew," Renée whispered and disconnected the line.

The horror of what he'd just heard slammed like a fist into his gut and he doubled over onto the steering wheel. Oh, no. She was dead. The desperation surging through him was almost more than he could muster. He sat for minutes, until his panic and nausea subsided enough for him to raise his head. The rain had stopped, the sun was out, and the sky deep blue, but he didn't notice, his brain mulling over what he had just heard. Then he got mad as hell. If they had found her, why hadn't they called him first? To make sure he didn't have to hear it through the grapevine? This was uncalled for! Those assholes! His fingers trembled when he opened his cellphone, hitting Detective Jaeger's number.

"Is it her?" he yelled after the detective answered.

"What are you talking about?" Jaeger replied. "Who is this?"

"The body you found!" he croaked. "Is it Annet?"

A brief silence ensued.

"Mr. Overton, maybe its best you come to the police station, so we can talk," the Detective said.

Forrest's heart lurched into his throat, and he swallowed hard. "This uncertainty is killing me, Jaeger. Talk to me. Please. I have to know."

"Just get to the station, will you," was the answer, and the line went dead.

"Shit!" Forrest threw the phone on the passenger seat, started the engine, his foot hitting the gas pedal. The car shot from the parking lot as he struggled with his seat belt, maneuvering through traffic at a daring speed, adrenaline shooting through his veins. In less than fifteen minutes he parked right in front of the Heemstead's police station main doors.

"I'm Forrest Overton for Detective Jaeger," he told the desk sergeant, rushing through the automated glass doors. The place smelled like Pine-Sol and dirty socks.

The sergeant picked up a phone, talked for a minute and nodded. "Right through the door, Mr. Overton. They're waiting for you down the hall in the meeting room, third door on the right."

The door buzzed open and Forrest entered an empty corridor, trying to hold onto his anger instead of turning into a blubbering mess. The wet soles of his sneakers screeched on the shiny polished floor as he made his way down the hall, the annoying sound adding to his anxiety.

He found the third door on the right already open and knocked on the wooden trim, his gut tightening in dread of what he might hear.

Detective Jaeger stood in front of a large window, blowing into a paper cup filled with hot steaming coffee. He narrowed his eyes at the sight of Forrest. "Come on in," he said.

Two police officers sat at a long rectangular table. They stopped in the middle of their conversation, staring at him blankly.

At the end of the room, a woman with curled black hair and puffy cheeks stood next to a white dry erase board on wheels. Her starched lab coat stretched tightly over her solid bosom. She stared out the window, avoiding his gaze. The tension in the room was palpable.

"All this time …," he whimpered, the suffocating dread so heavy in his limbs, he could barely move. He sunk down in the nearest chair, his fingers shaking as he massaged his forehead. "All this time I've been clinging to the hope of finding her alive, but she's dead, isn't she?" He glanced around the room with a tortured expression on his face. "Please, tell me …" His groans turned into unrestrained sobs.

Papers rustled, one of the police officers coughed behind his hand, and a chair scraped on the floor as Detective Jaeger walked up to him. "It's not her," he said.

Forrest raised his head, looking at him with dazed puzzlement.

"A full autopsy still needs to be performed, but we know with one hundred percent certainty it isn't her." His tone was apologetic.

Forrest stared from one person to the other, trying to comprehend what he had just heard.

"Mr. Overton," the heavyset dark-skinned women in the lab coat said. "My name is Julia Van Pelt. I'm from the coroner's office." The paperwork in her hands crinkled in her tight grip. "Late this morning, a body was brought into the morgue ...." She looked for support in Detective Jaeger's direction.

The unsociable and arrogant investigator raised his hand. "Let's give Mr. Overton a minute to compose himself."

Forrest batted unshed tears from his eyes and heaved a deep shuddering sigh. "Sorry," he uttered. "These last few days have been a terrifying rollercoaster ride."

"No apologies necessary," the coroner said, giving him an understanding smile. "We know how hard this situation must be for you, and I apologize for the unnecessary extra strain this put on you this afternoon."

Detective Jaeger paced the floor, clearing his throat. "This morning, a survey crew conducted an inspection on bridge work in a forested area, just off Highway 31 outside the town of Lisk, when they noticed what looked like a pile of clothing. They radioed it in to their employer after they found out their discovery was a lot more gruesome than that. The local police were informed and people quickly jumped to the conclusion it had to be the body of your partner, Annet Sherman." He stopped for a moment, his watchful eyes monitoring his reaction. "But it wasn't her. An elderly Lisk woman, suffering with Alzheimer's disease, had gone missing several weeks prior. It turned out it was her body they had discovered."

The Detective poured another cup of coffee and placed it in front of Forrest. "Here, you look like you might need this."

"Good luck to you, Mr. Overton," Coroner Van Pelt said.

Jaeger walked her to the door and they talked briefly before she left, followed by the two police officers.

Jaeger closed the door behind them. "We didn't call you, because we were waiting to hear from the coroner's office," he explained. "You understand?"

Forrest nodded. "I appreciate everything you've done for us so far," he said, trying to pull himself together. "Thank you."

He got up to leave, but the Detective laid a strong hand on his shoulder, forcing him back down. "Yes, about that," he said, dropping his understanding undertone. "I think it's time we talked."

Forrest puckered his brow in immediate concern. "I hope you're not implying you're giving up the search?" he asked. "It's only been three days, and I know she's still alive. I can feel it in my bones!"

The detective walked around the table and sat down in the chair on the opposite side of him. "As you know, suspicions were raised about the argument you had before your girlfriend's disappearance. The fact you saw her last doesn't help the situation either. We have to look at every angle and I want to go over all the details one more time. Just to make sure we didn't overlook anything." He rested his arm along the back of the empty chair beside him, staring at him with a penetrating glare.

"You're suggesting I have something to do with it," Forrest remarked, knowing that was exactly what the detective was implying. "That all of a sudden, I am a suspect. Right?"

"Let's say, for now, you're a person of interest," the detective replied with a careful undertone. "On Saturday, May 18, the day of her disappearance, you were at the Keizer Manor to help with the two-hundredth anniversary celebration." He opened the folder that lay in front of him. "Around five, just before the dinner-buffet, you were in Annet's office together with Miss Beverly Tjaverski. Did I pronounce that right?"

"I don't know what her last name is!" Forrest protested. "I barely know the girl!"

The attentive atmosphere in the office changed into one of harsh interrogation. Beneath the heat of the demanding questions, he quivered in alarm, afraid that if they didn't believe him, they might detain him and throw him in jail. "I was knocked unconscious and didn't hurt her. How many more times do I have to tell you that?" His shoulders were turned in, his head bowed, as if all he wanted to do was vanish, just like her.

"Those scrapes and scratches on my arms? I got hung up on that barbed wire fence, in blackberry thorns and briars. Ask the doctor who examined me. He knows!"

"We won't have the medical report from Dr. Simmons until tomorrow," Jaeger said. "Anyone else you spoke to the next morning, besides Dan Mockenburg and the janitor at the Keizer Manor?"

"Like I told you before. I talked to Caroline Rothschild and my parents!"

Jaeger leafed through his notebook. "Caroline Rothschild came to see you at your apartment, right?"

By now, Forrest was fed up. "Please, can't we continue this another time?"

Jaeger flung his pen across the table. "All right, but don't leave town or we'll have you picked up." The threat in his voice was loud and clear.

Forrest ran out of the room and down the hallway as fast as he could. When he reached the exit doors, he barged through and sprinted to his car as if the devil was chasing him.

Chapter 16

One moment, Annet had been in a deep sleep, the next she woke up. Frantically she looked around, finding herself on a hard floor, the smell of paint and turpentine around her. *Darn, she was still stuck in the same freaking nightmare. How long was this going to last?*

She crawled up and stretched her stiff muscles, preparing herself for another freaky day. It was morning, the sun already up, and she was hungry. But first things first. She stepped outside. A translucent fog caressed the dune tops, the sea air fresh and salty. Hoping the smallest outbuilding of the two was an outhouse, she opened the door. *Hurray. One problem solved.*

She washed her hands and face at the pump and went back inside. Munching on one of the apples Sister Rudolpha had given her, she roamed around the cabin, not wanting to sit down at the dirty kitchen table. How someone could live like this, she didn't understand. Look at that filthy wood-burning cook stove.

It could sure use a good scrubbing. Not used to having nothing to do, she searched for a cleaning rag, thinking it would be better to make herself useful than snooping around even longer. She filled a metal bucket with water and began scrubbing the windows. After they were clean she moved on to the table and wood floor, forcing her mind to focus on the chores at hand instead of worrying about her predicament.

Humming the melody of an Adam Lambert song, followed by her favorites from Bruno Mars and Taylor Swift, she worked unrelentingly for hours. She was so engrossed at the task at hand, she didn't hear the sound of a horse nickering, or the rattle of an approaching wagon. The silhouette of a man blocking the light streaming into the cabin made her look up.

"Hey, why are you sneaking up on me?" she shrieked, recognizing Alex Keizer. "You scared the living daylights out of me."

He stared at her from the threshold, his eyes glaring. She fretfully wet her lips. This wasn't the way she had envisioned this encounter, with her hair a mess, wearing a wrinkled bag of a dress, her face hot and flustered. Damn. She had hoped he would find the cabin clean and sparkly, with fresh flowers on the table, after she had spruced herself up and changed into her sexy black dress.

"What are you doing here?" he thundered. "Thinking you would find something of value to steal?" He took a threatening step in her direction, his grim look causing a sudden stab of alarm.

"Oh, no. I would never steal," she hurried to say, working hard to keep her voice from shaking. She didn't frighten easy, but at the moment, she was scared. He was so tall, with the broad shoulders of a body builder, his fierce expression making her heart thud in alarm. Why hadn't they ever informed her Alex Keizer had a temper?

He clutched his fists, struggling to keep his rage under rein. "Nobody, I mean nobody, has ever set foot in this house. This is my sanctuary."

She stretched her arms out in front of her, backing away. "I'm so sorry. I didn't mean to invade your privacy. Please, don't hurt me."

"Then why are you here?" he roared, his eyes challenging her.

He was barely two feet away from her when her back hit the crude wooden wall. The essence of the outdoors clung to his clothes, his emerald green eyes sparkled with fire. She couldn't help but notice he was undeniably attractive; his features aristocratic, his skin darkened by the sun, an afternoon stubble on his strong jawbones.

"Instead of keeping those valuable paintings hidden, carelessly thrown on top of each other, I'm here to tell you the time has come to share your talent with the world," she improvised, lifting her chin with all the bravado she could muster.

With a sharp rebuff, he threw his arms up in the air. "Until a few days ago, I didn't even know you existed. Now you brazenly invade my private domain, rebuke my life, and tell me what to do with my paintings? They should have locked you up! You mad woman!"

"No, no, no!" she cried out. "You don't understand. You'll be famous! Admired all over the world. Your paintings will be worth millions."

He stretched his arm, pointing with his index finger to the door. "Out! Right now!"

She regarded him for several long moments, defeated and dispirited. "You're right," she admitted. "I probably wouldn't have believed me either if I was in your shoes."

Close to tears, she trudged toward the door. She had always been an optimist, always able to see the bright side of life, even when everything turned against her, but right now she was a heap of despair. She was exhausted, hungry, and at the end of her endurance.

Spending her last energy, she made her way into the dunes, her feet dragging through the sand, her shoulders slumped. After this long day, she wasn't sure she would be able to make it to Dunedam. Bitter tears rolled down her face into her mouth, blurring her vision.

When she heard rapid footsteps behind her, she kept on walking, her anguish too deep to care. It wasn't until a strong hand got hold of her arm, forcing her to stop, that she looked up in a panic.

Alex stood in front of her. The top opening of his white linen shirt showed perspiration simmering on his skin, his wavy dark hair loosely tied in a ponytail. "In this heat, I can't take the chance you'll get lost in the dunes once again," he said, his expression distant. "Come."

She gave him a watery smile. "Is that an apology for your rude behavior?"

"Don't push your luck," he answered, turning around.

Without uttering a word, they reached the cabin where he ordered her to sit. Her mouth watered as he unwrapped a loaf of dark brown bread. After he cut a thick slice off and slid it onto the plate in front of her, he took a step back. Folding his arms across his chest, he watched her eat, his expression brooding.

Intimidated by his presence and unrelenting stare, she tried to ease the tension. "Thank you for hauling my ass back to the cabin. I'm sure I would have died out there."

He didn't reply.

"You are Alex Keizer right?" she broke the nerve-wrecking silence.

He scoffed. "Yes, I am, but what that means to you, I still have to discover."

"Besides the Jonkers' farm, are there any other homes, farms or buildings around here? Like a Manor, maybe?" she tried, although she already knew the answer.

Alex uttered a stream of swear words and walked out. When he didn't come back, she got up to find him.

The door of the shed stood open, a tall black horse with two white socks nibbling on young green grass next to it. He had a halter made of rope around his head, but wasn't tied down with a rein. A water bucket had tipped over, spilling its contents. Giving the magnificent horse a wide berth, she peeked inside the shed. It was about ten feet high with an open rafter construction, just large enough to house a stall and a minuscule tack room. A hay rack was mounted to the wall, straw covering the dirt floor. It was dusty, speckled with spider webs. Just like the cabin, it needed major cleaning.

"Anything I can do?" she asked, as Alex spread handfuls of straw.

He took off his shirt, and hung it on a protruding nail next to the door, exposing broad shoulders and dark hair curling on his chest. Then he grabbed a brush and walked over to his horse. With short, firm strokes he brushed its neck, and body, the dull black coat becoming shiny under his steady strokes.

She watched from a safe distance.

"Are you afraid of horses?" he asked.

107

"Hell, yes," she admitted. "He's so impressive. Until yesterday I'd never even been this close to one."

He frowned. "Then stay away from here and try to make yourself useful. You can unload supplies or prepare dinner. I brought fresh green beans and potatoes."

The wagon parked in front of the cabin was loaded with firewood and a hefty supply of provisions. He had already unloaded a burlap bag full of potatoes, a metal milk churn and a bulky sack of flour. She pulled on the white hand woven bag. It was far heavier than she had thought and it didn't want to budge. Then she turned toward the metal churn, almost tipping it over. Darn, her host was already pissed off enough. She didn't want to add fuel to the fire by spilling its contents. Maybe she should stick to the lighter items. She hung a wicker basket full of brown eggs on her arm, lifted a wheel of yellow cheese, and entered the cabin. No refrigerator. How could they keep it cold?

She put the perishable foods on the kitchen table and brought in candles, dried meats, and canning jars filled with various fruits and vegetables.

Alex soon followed with the bag of flour on his shoulder. He dumped it on the floor and knelt down. Next, he rolled up the shabby olive rug, pulled on a recessed metal ring in the floor and drew open a wooden hatch. Cool, damp air escaped from the square opening.

"You have a basement to store the cold stuff," she commented. "Smart."

He disappeared down the creaking wooden ladder into the darkness, the heavy bag on his shoulder.

"How often do you buy supplies?" she asked after he resurfaced, a spider web caught in his hair. She resisted the temptation to remove it, knowing he wouldn't appreciate the gesture.

"Twice, sometimes three times a year," he replied.

There was little known about his private life. Considering his reluctance to answer even the most innocent of questions, she understood why.

"Did you hear a weather forecast, by any chance?" she asked when he came back inside with the bag of potatoes. She knew they hadn't invented television yet, but maybe they already had radio.

"I can foresee thunder on the horizon if you don't keep your peace for once," he barked.

For a moment she was taken aback, but just before he turned away, she detected a sparkle of humor in his eyes and a small gurgle of hope bubbled up in her throat. Hmm, maybe he wasn't such a grouch after all. With a little luck she might penetrate his shield of indifference.

With the use of flint, he lit the cook stove, ignoring her smart remarks about how much easier it would be if he used matches.

Going through the cupboards, she found two pans and filled them with water. Half an hour later, she dished up their plates, calling down into the cellar where Alex was organizing the supplies. He resurfaced, whisking the dust from his clothes before washing his hands.

"I've never been much of a cook," she confessed as he sat down at the table with her. "But these beans came out great."

"Tell me, what could possibly go wrong with a simple meal like this?"

"Oh, if you knew me, you wouldn't ask that question," she grinned between mouthfuls.

For a fleeting moment, the guarded expression on his face disappeared. "You are a woman full of surprises," he said. Then his expression grew serious again. "I think the time has come to explain why you are here and what you want from me."

Chapter 17

A lex noticed Annet shifting in her chair.
"I prefer not to talk about it right now," she said, her eyes avoiding him. "Can't you just let it go?"

Gone was the upbeat, chatty demeanor she had presented since showing up at his home. She rose from the table, gathered the dishes and placed them in the sink.

Deep in thought, he followed her every move. When the gardener from the convent had left a message at Russell Jonkers' farm that a young woman was asking for him, he hadn't been interested. But when Russell explained he had found the same woman unconscious alongside the road, minimally dressed, he became curious. It didn't happen every day that someone got lost looking for him, especially not a young woman. Against his better judgment, he'd gone to the monastery, to talk to Mother Superior, thinking maybe the woman had been on her way to deliver a message, but he barely got the chance to find out more about her. They had just entered the office when she had appeared out of nowhere, dressed in a long white nightgown, her hair a long blonde mess, her clear blue eyes like glittering chips of ice. The chaotic scene had thoroughly amused him. That woman wasn't an innocent lost soul, she was a calculated vixen.

He had felt sorry for the anxious Mother Superior, who had even apologized to him on behalf of the wild and unruly woman in her office, but he had brushed off her concern. It wasn't often someone astonished him these days, and the brazen woman in her nightclothes had truly surprised him.

On his way back to the city, he hadn't been able to put the bizarre encounter out of his mind. Even the next day he had been thinking about it. He had never seen anyone so young and attractive be so outspoken and behave so rudely, especially in a convent. He still had to grin when he recalled how she had blatantly walked out of the room, leaving Mother Superior in complete dismay. That took a lot of nerve and he admired her for it. But he was less amused when he stopped at the Jonkers' farm to buy his provisions and found out the daughter-in-law had told the eccentric female how to find his house.

He had left the farm in a hurry, noticing her footsteps on the trail and around the cabin, soon realizing she was inside. His anger had flared up, but he wasn't prepared for what he found inside.

In his memory, she had been lofty, tall and stout, like an Amazon, the celebrated female warrior in Greek mythology. Instead he found a vulnerable, slender and fearful young woman, red faced and tired from scrubbing and cleaning. Her turbulent blue eyes the only proof of her feisty spirit. Knowing how shamefully filthy his home had been, he'd recognized she'd been at work for hours.

"You owe me an explanation," he said, tapping his foot against the wooden planking of the floor.

Almost a full minute of thoughtful silence elapsed before she turned around to face him.

"I could feed you a nice bullshit story. Beg for your compassion and understanding," she said, "but I won't, because I hate liars."

He kept a stern face to hide his astonishment, appreciating her spunk and honesty more than he should.

"But I'm also not going to tell you the truth, because you wouldn't believe a word I say."

"What?" he breathed in disbelief, forgetting that a minute ago she had touched a soft spot inside him. "You want to play games?" He was out of his seat like a rocket, covering the distance between them in one long stride. With her back against the kitchen sink, she leaned away from him, her hands clenched into small fists.

He gave a short, bitter laugh. "Patience has never been my best virtue," he said, "But I would never beat a woman."

He turned away from her, wishing there was a way he could wrench the truth from her. That damn woman. He should just throw her out, instead of letting her get to him, but chivalry won out.

"For tonight, I think its best you take the bedroom and I sleep on the couch," he growled before he slammed the door of the cabin shut behind him.

Chapter 18

WITH HIS FOOT PRESSING HARD against the accelerator, Forrest sped along the familiar streets. As if on autopilot, he parked in front of the Clipper, his favorite watering hole. He needed a drink, maybe two. After his eyes adjusted to the darkness inside, he made his way to the bar and sat down.

"Hi Forrest," the bartender said, pouring his usual drink, rum with one ice cube.

He frequented the bar often, since it was in close vicinity to the two temporary staffing agencies where he had posted his resume. It was also close to the library and the grocery outlet store. The bartender knew him well.

Forrest downed the drink in one big gulp. "Give me another one."

The barkeep refilled the glass and watched Forrest stare with brooding sadness at the bottles of booze lined up behind the bar. "Hey pal," he said with empathy, propping pieces of lemon in four bottles of Corona. "I heard what you're going through. This one is on me." He placed the bottles on a tray and delivered them to one of the tables where four young men laughed loudly over a card game. After he came back he rinsed several beer glasses clean, before leaning over the bar. "What do you think happened to her?"

Forrest looked up with bleary eyes. "I wish I knew," he said, unable to keep his voice from cracking. Hoping to find some solace, he emptied his second glass and slid it back to the bartender. "I'll have another refill."

The barkeep frowned, poured his third drink, and left him to dwell.

A country song droned from speakers hanging in the corners of the dark pub, the few patrons laughing over beer and bad jokes. Ignoring everything around him, Forest stared at the silent TV behind the bar set on the Weather Channel. Rain throughout the night for the entire region. The sky cried with him. Good!

Sipping his fourth drink, he replayed the cross-examining he had been subjected to. *That son of a bitch Jaeger, making him a person of interest.* He scoffed. He might as well have accused him of her disappearance, because that had been on the insensitive asshole's mind. If he only had access to Annet's extensive unrefined vocabulary, he would have known what to say instead of running out of the station with his tail between his legs.

The bar door opened, admitting a cold gust of wind and a patron. He looked up and recognized Keith, one of the five o'clock regulars. As always, he was wearing khaki coveralls and a camo T-shirt, his heavy boots leaving muddy footprints on the rug and the floor, the varnished boards worn from years of traffic, and many attempts of cleaning spilled beer and liquor.

Forrest reached for his drink and downed it. Keith was a gabber, and he wasn't in the mood for small talk or gossip. He pulled out a twenty dollar bill and threw it on the bar. "See you later, Pete," he shouted and headed toward the exit, but in passing, Keith grabbed his arm.

"Hey, Forrest, buddy! You don't want to join me for a drink?" he said. "I'll buy."

"No thanks. I've already had more than I can handle," Forrest declined, not appreciating the undisguised curiosity coming from the guy's eyes, staring at him from beneath the bill of his camo baseball cap. He staggered to the door, bumping into a barstool.

Keith grabbed his arm to steady him. "You look like shit, man. Are you okay?"

"I'm fine," Forrest replied, steadying himself against the doorjamb.

"Jeez man," Keith laughed out loud. "If getting rid of your old lady did this to you, why didn't you just keep her around?"

Forrest stiffened, turning around with squinting eyes. "What did you say?"

"Well, you know," Keith replied, sheepishly backing away. "This is a small town, and the word goes around you were all fighting and …"

Forrest took a threatening step toward the cowering man and then another. "You asshole, you filthy rumor spreading cocksucker!" He clenched his hand into a fist, a red mist of rage clouding his perspective. "How dare you spread those unfounded spiteful accusations? I love her!" He took a swing with his right arm, hoping to connect with Keith's cheekbone, but all he hit was air. The force of his own blow caused him to lose his balance. His shoulder hit the floor and his face smacked into the leg of one of the barstools, tipping it over. The skin on his forehead split open. "Damn." Blood oozed into his eyebrow and down his temple. Cursing to himself and the world, he tried to sit back up and regain his senses. What had just happened?

The barkeep rounded the bar and pulled him up with one strong arm. "You're completely unraveling, aren't you, poor man?" He handed him a stack of napkins to staunch the bleeding cut. "Now take my advice. Go home before more rumors fly."

Forrest hung his head and let himself be led out of the bar, but after he unlocked his car the barkeeper grabbed his keys. "On foot."

It was a short distance to his apartment, but he hesitated on the sidewalk. Why would he go home? There was nothing for him there but Barbara and Chuck. He certainly didn't need them adding to his already awful day. He opened the backdoor, pushed a few empty cans and food wrappers onto the floor and crawled onto the worn seat. Groaning, he lay down. He hurt everywhere, his cut bleeding onto the fabric, but he didn't give a darn. All he wanted was for Annet to be found. To have her safe, back in his arms. He closed his eyes and pulled himself into a ball, mumbling to himself in a drunken stupor. "I'll make them understand I'm innocent. That something undefined took her away from me. Maybe a rapist? Or a monster? I will find out who or what it is. Tomorrow."

Chapter 19

Annet awoke to the sound of rain pelting on the metal roof. The sun wasn't up and it was much cooler than the day before. She stretched, got up and opened the curtains. The deep puddles around the cabin indicated it might have rained all night, the disconsolate landscape reflecting her own dark mood. But then her spirit lifted. Maybe they would have thunder and lightning today so she could magically transport home.

Footsteps in the room next door, followed by a scraping noise and a heavy thud, startled her from her thoughts. She heard loud grumbling.

Worried Alex had hurt himself, she opened the door to the kitchen/living area. The room was empty.

"What a way to start the day," she heard him complain. Annet tiptoed to the doorframe of his workroom and peeked in. He was down on all fours, a small jar of dark red paint splattered all over the wood floor. He was trying to save what he could by scooping it up with his bare hands. There was paint all over his face, arms and sandals. It was such a comical scene, she burst out laughing.

His surprise over her sudden appearance was momentary. "What are you laughing about?" he scowled.

She shrugged. "Nothing. I was just wondering what you're doing on the floor?"

"I was trying out something new," he explained. "Mixing oil with water, but so far I have been unsuccessful."

Relieved to see his anger from the night before had diminished, she handed him a rag. He wiped up the last of the paint before opening a glass bottle of turpentine.

"Don't waste your time with water colors. Stick to oils on canvas," she told him, knowing all his paintings were oil based. "That's where your talent lies."

"What could you know?" he scoffed. He poured the yellowish solvent over the rag, exuding a sharp biting odor, and wiped the paint off his hands and feet.

With professional concern she looked at the valuable landscapes, portraits, and still-lives in the room. "You should protect your work instead of discarding them in a heap," she told him. "Oil paint dries by oxidation, not by evaporation. Although it might be dry to the touch, art conservators don't consider an oil painting completely dry until it is decades old."

Alex searched through his paint supplies and found another rag. "Why in the world are you so concerned about my deplorable works of art," he commented, wiping the paint splatters from his nose and cheeks. "Or is it the spirit of the Amazon in you, trying to help and defend the poor, wretched artist?"

She raised her eyebrows. What did he know about Amazon, the website she used to buy music for her phone and the occasional e-book? "Amazon? What are you talking about?"

He picked up a thick book with a brown hardcover, handing it to her. "The legendary Amazons were strong fighting women. They lived near the southern shore of the Black Sea where they formed an independent kingdom under the govern of a queen. It's from Greek mythology."

She turned the book over in her hands. It had a full leather binding and a smooth spine, gilt ruled into compartments. It looked brand-new. She leafed through it, the print bold, illustrated with mythological creatures. Gods, goddesses, and monsters. Damn, she had found out more about Alexander Keizer in twelve hours than she had in all the years she had worked at the Manor. Maybe she should write everything down, so she would remember it all when she got back home. Caroline Rothschild and Dan Mockenburg would be ecstatic with all the information.

"Is it okay if I interview you later today?" she asked.

He narrowed his eyes and walked out of the room. She rushed after him. This was too good of an opportunity. She couldn't let it pass by. "Like in I ask the questions and you give the answers. Don't you think that would be fun?"

Dangerously slow, he turned around to face her, his green eyes blazing with anger. "I can't believe you!" he shouted. "You are an intruder in my home, who doesn't have the decency to explain who she is and why she's here. Then you shamelessly dare to ask me to join you in a dialogue about *my* life. To give up *my* privacy! How dare you?" He raked a hand through his already mussed hair, breathing through his nose like an angry bull.

Damn, he was right. Why hadn't she thought her actions through? Well, okay, this obviously wasn't the right moment, but maybe, when she was sneaky, she could make him share a few things. "You don't have to blow up like that," she said defensively. "All I wanted was to find out more about your paint techniques. That isn't too much to ask, is it?"

He grabbed her by the shoulders, opened the door and pushed her outside.

"What the hell are you doing?" she protested. "Are you throwing me out?"

With a decisive click the door closed in her face.

"I can't believe it?" she yelled. "You throw me out in the rain? In my nightgown? What kind of man are you?" She tried to pull the door open, but he had locked it from the inside. With both fists she banged on the rough wood until her hands hurt. "You can't do this! You asshole!" When he still didn't reply, she sank down onto the porch and slumped forward. Now what?

It was still drizzling, but a glimmer of sun shone through the dark clouds, the weather clearing. Her hope for a juicy thunderstorm evaporated as the blue spot in the sky grew larger and the clouds changed from grey to white. Such luck.

How long had it been since she transitioned over here. Was it ten days? Two weeks? Whatever. It was too long. She had to find her way home. Forrest would be totally freaked out by now, sick from worry. So would her friends and colleagues. She had to get back, for the sake of her unborn child and everything else she held dear. She needed another one of those freaky thunderstorms.

With her eyes on the sky, she sat on the porch, vulnerable and hollow. The chill and dampness of the early morning hours penetrated every cell of her body. If she stayed out here much longer, she would end up with hypothermia, but it was obvious the arrogant painter didn't seem to care about it one bit. The jerk!

"Okay, you win," she yelled. "I'll tell you everything you want to know." When he didn't answer she got up on her feet. With both hands around her mouth she bellowed, "Did you hear me? Everything!"

After what seemed like an eternity, she heard a click and the door opened. Nonchalantly, he leaned with his shoulder against the doorjamb, a glint of triumphant gloating in his eyes.

Chapter 20

What an oaf, Annet thought, struggling to keep her cool. He held all the cards and she was damn well aware of it. "Can I please come back inside? I'm freezing my ass off."

"Under one of condition," he said, stepping aside so she could enter.

She glared at him suspiciously.

"You have to obey all my rules."

"And that's what you call *one* condition?" she replied heatedly. "I call that slavery!"

He crossed his arms in front of his chest and blocked her way, his expression changing from mild amusement into unyielding impatience.

"Okay," she sighed in defeat, knowing she had no choice but to give in. "Whatever you say." She hurried past him into the bedroom and changed into the heavy brown dress. It was the ugliest piece of clothing she had ever worn. She hated the boring color, the scratchy stiff material, the tatted borders. But with everything else that life had forced upon her lately, she had no alternative.

The delicious smell of food made her stomach growl. When she opened the bedroom door, she found him busy behind the stove. The room was pleasingly warm, the tingly feeling in her toes and fingers disappearing.

"We're having scrambled eggs, bread, and milk for breakfast," he said.

She sent him a grateful smile and sat down at the table. Maybe he wasn't such a bad guy after all.

They ate in silence. After they finished, she offered to clean up. Without objecting, Alex left the cabin. After she finished her chore and stepped outside, she noticed he was busy in the shed. With nothing else to do, she continued cleaning the cabin, hoping he would be in a better mood after he noticed how spic and span his house had become. When he came back inside, he ignored her and her hard labor and disappeared in his so called atelier.

Hours later, she added two pieces of wood to the fire in the stove and fixed them a small lunch. Alex ignored her futile attempts to start a conversation, only to return to his workroom after he'd finished his last bite, obviously avoiding her.

To break the charged silence and to alleviate her stress, she doubled her cleaning effort, chasing cobwebs on the ceiling with a broom, making as much noise as she could, until she heard a rumble in the far distance. She stood stock-still, pricking her ears. Was that thunder? The next moment, rain came down on the metal roof and when the dim room lit up with a flash, her heart surged with hope. Maybe this was her chance? She reached for the door and stepped onto the tiny porch. Heavy black thunderclouds grumbled in the west. Without a second thought she ran as fast as she could toward the incoming storm, lightning flashing beneath the heavy, black clouds.

"Forrest!" she yelled. "I'm coming!"

She tripped and stumbled through the brush and tall grass into the dunes, the deep loose sand making it difficult to put one foot in front of the other. The rain pounded down, each drop piercing her skin, soaking her to the bone within seconds. With her arm pressed against her forehead, to protect her eyes from the unrelenting rain, she flew forward, until she found herself in the center of the storm. Raising her face up to the sky, her arms spread wide, she spun around and around. "Here I am! Please, come and get me! Take me home!"

Chapter 21

With all his might, Alex tried to ignore the racket coming
from the living room, wondering if he would ever get
anything done today. His unwanted houseguest exasperated him.
He wanted her gone. Maybe he should load her onto his dray
after the rain stopped. Ship her off to Dunedam or Heemstead.
There were always people willing to take in the unfortunate. Or
maybe the shopkeeper, from whom he bought his pigments and
brushes, would take her off his hands. His wife had fallen ill,
and he had mentioned he wanted to hire an extra hand.

He registered the distant rumble of an approaching lighting
storm followed by a flash. It looked like Mother Nature was
working against him. That was unfortunate. It meant he would
either get soaking wet, which didn't appeal to him, or he would
have to keep her in his house for another night.

The next moment he heard the loud thud of his door
banging against the wall. He dropped his brush and rushed from

his workshop, finding the living room empty and his front door wide open. A cold wet wind swept inside, the floorboards at the entrance already soaking wet. He hurried onto the porch, looking around, just in time to see Annet disappear into the dunes. *That foolish woman!*

For a moment he stood there, wondering if she would reappear, but when the rain and thunder intensified he went back inside and closed the door. Problem solved. She was gone.

Without comprehending what he did, he donned his cloak and headed back outside. Cursing at himself, he crossed the grounds and entered the dunes. *He shouldn't go after her. She had invaded his privacy. He should be relieved she was gone, so he could concentrate on his work instead of being distracted by her antics. Besides, she wasn't his responsibility.*

With every step, the storm intensified, the wind howling around him, pushing him backwards, its velocity swelling as he moved closer toward the ocean. This was a hell of a tempest. He hunched his shoulders, bringing his collar up to his ears. His progress was slow, her footsteps increasingly difficult to detect in the growing darkness. Damn that crazy woman!

The rain was so heavy and the gusts so fierce, he missed her disappearing footsteps several times, forcing him to retrace his own. Although he knew the landscape around his cabin well, even he lost his sense of direction in the blunt of the storm.

In the gathering dusk, temperatures dropped fast. He shuddered beneath his saturated clothes, his concern over her wellbeing increasing. It would be dark soon. If he didn't find her before then, she could be in serious trouble. He plowed through the vegetation and up another dune, grains of sand crunching between his teeth, when he detected the faint sound of a woman's voice.

"Amazon?" he yelled, hoping his imagination wasn't playing tricks on him. "Are you there?" He stopped and listened for a reply, wondering if the brutal wind had overpowered his voice.

"Hello? Can you hear me?" he bellowed with his hands around his mouth.

Inaudible words floated toward him. He shifted direction, yelling, "I'm here, I'm coming! Stay where you are! Don't move!"

With each step, the sound of her voice grew louder until he could distinguish the silhouette of a woman, her arms stretched out toward him.

"Forrest? Forrest?" he heard her scream. "Is that you?"

She was a miserable sight. Her blonde hair, dark from the deluge, hung flat against her skull. Her dress was torn, her face deadly pale. When their eyes met, he saw her overjoyed expression disappear and change into one full of rage.

"You!" she cried out in accusation. "I don't want to see *you*! NOOOO!!!" The next moment she hid her face behind her hands, sank down on the sand and wept without restraint, her sobs hysterical, her slender shoulders shaking violently.

Her reaction left him dumbstruck. Motionless he looked down at her, his face dripping, his hair soaked, his green eyes never leaving her, until his patience ran out. That ungrateful creature. Without hesitation, he grasped her arm and forced her up.

"Don't think I want you in my house, but I won't leave you here. Come, let's go!"

She protested wildly, trying to free her arm from his vicelike grip, but she was no match for his brutal strength. Screaming, she attacked him, her nails clawing in his chest and at his eyes, her bare feet kicking him wherever she could. "Let me go, you son of a bitch. I have to go home! Let me go!"

He let himself get beaten, kicked, and scratched as he tried to control his own rage with considerable effort. Although he considered himself a patient man and had never hurt a woman before, after she drew blood in his face and neck, he saw no other option than to give her a hard slap across her cheek, to snap her out of her frenzy. "You are hysterical and under no condition will you stay here," he told her, his face wiped of all expression, his eyes the temperature of absolute zero. "You are coming with me, like it or not."

In a matter of seconds, all the fight went out of her. Wrecked by emotion, she sagged down against his chest. In an automatic response, his arms went around her quivering body, steadying her. Over her wet head, he gazed into the distance while they stood in silence, the wind tugging on their clothes, water dripping from their bodies. When she shifted against him, he gradually released his firm grip.

"Come," he said, hoping she'd cooled off enough. "Let's get you out of this torrent and back to the cabin."

With his arm around her shoulders, supporting her, he guided her through the dunes. The rain eased off and clouds blew away from the setting sun, their path lit by the reddish light of a spectacular sunset, but he didn't notice. He was cold, wet and unhappy. His day was lost, his inspiration vanished, his peaceful retreat ruined.

When they arrived back at the cabin, he pushed her in the direction of the bedroom. "Take off your wet clothes and wrap yourself in a blanket."

He closed the door behind him, hung his cloak out to dry, and cranked up the stove to heat water for tea. Minutes went by, and not a single sound came from the bedroom. Uncertain of what to do, he waited a while longer. By now, the room was sweltering hot and the tea ready, but when she still didn't reappear, he tapped on the door.

"Amazon, are you all right?"

He waited, tapped again, but no answer came. With growing concern he opened the door. She was rolled up underneath the blankets, in a deep sleep, her quiet face ashen, her clothes in a wet pile on the floor. Pensively, he gazed down at the feminine contour in his bed. Questions piled up in his head as he listened to her steady breathing.

Who was she? Where did she come from? And where did the over-whelming sorrow in her eyes come from? The desperation? The longing?

But most of all, who had she hoped to find out there in the middle of nowhere?

Deciding not to wake her, he quietly left the room.

Chapter 22

AFTER SPENDING THE NIGHT in his car, Forrest drove to Gloria's diner on the Market Square. It had a nice view of the Old Historic Pump and the surrounding impeccably manicured park. The pump had been restored because of its cultural historic value, but didn't function anymore.

Feeling grungy, his first stop was the bathroom where he tried to wash himself clean of the prior day's events. Realizing it was a futile effort, he left and slouched down in the last empty booth. Without looking at the menu he ordered a three-egg chef's omelet with cheese, hash browns, toast and coffee.

While he waited for his food, he turned his phone back on, noticing he had five missed calls. Three from Annet's mother and two from the Keizer Manor. Still nothing from the police or a-hole detective Jaeger. He stared through the window. Cars were driving by, pedestrians walked along the sidewalk. A woman sat on one of the concrete benches next to the Old

Pump, crumbling up a slice of bread, feeding the birds. All these people's lives continued as they always had while he had lost control of every aspect of his own life. *Why was this happening? Why had everything gone so wrong?*

The busy waitress served him coffee and rushed away. As he stirred cream in his cup, he noticed she regarded him curiously every time she passed his table, questions in her eyes. Dunedam was a small town. He knew who she was. She had graduated from Dunedam High a few years ahead of him. Deliberately he evaded her eyes. When he looked the other way, he caught the other waitress gawking in his direction, as was a group of grey-haired ladies and the middle-aged couple in the booth next to him, their probing eyes riveted on him. He recognized most of the people around him, including one of Annet's girlfriends, understanding he was the subject of their interest and appraisal. Morosely staring down into his coffee, he tried to ignore the ripple of attention his arrival had created.

By the time his breakfast was served he'd lost his appetite. Instead of eating, he folded his napkin, then unfolded it and folded it again, wondering if they believed he had nothing to do with Annet's disappearance, and that he was the victim of horrible circumstances. Or if they had already judged him to be a skirt-chaser, an abuser. Or worse, a killer?

He forced a few mouthfuls down his throat and finished his coffee. Not able to deal with the curious and accusing stares any longer, he tossed down his wadded napkin and a ten dollar bill and left.

Needing to see a friendly face, Forrest pulled into the Keizer Manor parking lot. He parked and stepped out, realizing it was far too early for anyone to be there, except for the security guard, and he didn't want to see him.

Standing with his hands on his hips he gazed into the dunes, listening to the morning sounds. The wind was still, the sun shining brightly behind him, projecting his silhouette on the sand. It was the kind of morning that made everybody feel bright and alive, aware of all the magnificent wonders Mother Nature offered, but he was too wrapped in his misery to appreciate it.

Maybe I should drive to my parents' house, he contemplated. They had always been there for him whenever he needed them, ready with an embrace, with words of encouragement, and unconditional love. But he couldn't tell them he was a suspect now, forbidden to leave town. He didn't want to share that with anyone. It was too humiliating.

The second car that pulled in he recognized as the janitor's, but he didn't want to talk to that man either. He was a grumpy, old coot and would only bring his spirits down further, if that was even possible.

Indecisive, he hung around for another ten minutes until he noted Dan Mockenburg's all-wheel drive station wagon pull into the parking lot. He stuck his hand up in greeting, and joined him.

"You're looking worse for wear, Forrest," Dan commented. "No wonder the police are tuning in on you."

An electric jolt ran through Forrest. "What? Who told you that?"

Dan pulled out a set of keys from his pocket and unlocked the side door of the Manor. "They were here yesterday around closing time, asking questions, talking to the night guard, the janitor, and whoever else. As expected, they pulled the security tapes." He held the door open so Forrest could enter, locking it again behind them. "Husbands, boyfriends. They're always the primary suspects in a case like this."

"I realize that," Forrest admitted. "I have to prove my innocence, but how do I do that?"

They walked into the meeting room and Dan started the coffeemaker. "It would be easy if you had an alibi, but unfortunately you don't have one."

As always, Dan was dressed immaculately in a white shirt and a dark charcoal gray suit, his silver hair carefully styled, his black shoes polished. The Keizer Manor's president and coordinator was a man of standing in the community, and Forrest appreciated his support more than he could express.

"But they also need motive, right?" he tried. "And I don't have a single reason to hurt her."

Dan observed him. "People who don't know you might consider the unplanned pregnancy a motive, but I know it was Annet who had doubts. Lack of money could be another motive, but since Annet was the breadwinner, that won't hold up either."

"You sound like a cop," Forrest commented. "But go on. I appreciate the honesty."

"Don't expect me to sugarcoat it," Dan told him. "This is a very troubling situation. The lack of motive might be the only reason you haven't been picked up yet."

Forrest diverted his eyes from Dan's penetrating gaze and stared at the ground in embarrassment. "Was Caroline still here when they came?"

Dan poured coffee in two cups and handed him one. "Yes, she was. They talked to her."

Forrest grabbed creamer packets and followed him into the adjacent office.

"You should have seen their faces after they realized Caroline was eighty years old." A smile flashed on Dan's face. "What in the world did you tell them?"

Despite the seriousness of the situation, Forrest cracked a smile as well. "I told them she was there when I walked out of the bathroom in my boxers. After hearing that, I guess they assumed I was having an affair with her."

"I knew it had to be something like that, because Caroline was furious after they left," Dan chuckled. He turned around and sat down behind his desk, empty coffee cups and stacks of papers on top. "This is what happens when you're understaffed," he muttered.

"Can I help, since I have nothing else to do but bite my nails and wait for the phone to ring?"

Dan looked up in surprise. "Can you type? Are you familiar with Word and Excel?"

Compared to the civil engineer software programs he had mastered to design infrastructures and to monitor bridges and roads, Excel was a piece of cake. "Of course," he replied. "I'm an expert in creating resumes and filling out job applications on the computer."

"Then I won't decline your offer." Dan rummaged through his desk drawer and pulled out a key. "Go home, get cleaned up, then pick up the mail at the post office. Box 90."

Forrest drove home, finding Barbara and Chuck once again sitting useless on the couch. It seemed they had been there since yesterday, never leaving their seats, except for the bigger mess in the kitchen. He ignored them and walked to the bathroom. Although he had tolerated Barbara throughout the years for Annet's sake, he didn't care for the woman. There was no doubt in his mind the feeling was mutual. She had given him her non-flattering opinion numerous times, not to mention all the times he had overheard her telling Annet behind his back that he was a fucking three-time loser, a failure.

"Hey, the police called me yesterday and came to the house," she yelled at him. "They wanted to know about your relationship with Annet, search the house, and lift fingerprints."

He felt his heart sink. "What did you tell them?"

"Well, the truth of course," she told him from the couch. "That you're high school sweethearts. That Annet was bringing in the dough, because even though you might be smart, no one wanted to hire you. Not even as a dishwasher."

Thanks, you spiteful witch, he thought, hoping Detective Jaeger had seen through her, and understood how hard it was to find a job with the current recession.

Barbara got up from the couch and joined him in the kitchen, her skinny blue jeans hugging her hips, the first buttons of her blouse undone. "You look horrific. Aren't you getting any sleep?"

Now that was the understatement of the year.

"Can I fix you something?" she continued, opening the refrigerator. "There's potato salad left from last night."

"Don't worry," Forrest replied. "All I need is a shower and fresh clothes."

Barbara slammed the refrigerator door shut and turned around, her eyes blazing. "Have you always treated this apartment as a hotel, and my daughter as your chambermaid?" She planted her fists on her hips. "Can you believe him, Chuck? Just waltzing in to shower, drop his dirty clothes, and breeze out. No wonder Annet left."

This woman was outspoken, biased and as subtle as a sledgehammer. He had to get her out of his house or he was going to go berserk. "How long do you plan to stay here?" he asked bluntly. "Because I need my house and my privacy back."

"Your house?" she scoffed, rolling her eyes. "Sorry, bud, but we'll stay here for as long as it takes."

A glint of exasperation flickered in his blue eyes. "Takes for what?"

"As long as it takes for Annet to come back, you dumbass. Even after that we might stay for a while. The apartment we lived in is on the market. The owner wants to sell. We were served an eviction notice a few weeks ago. While we were looking for another place, we put our stuff in storage and might as well stay here until we find one."

Darn, he might be stuck with her and her fat ass stinking suitor forever if Annet didn't come home. What was he going to do? He couldn't live like this! Crestfallen, he walked to the bathroom, but then turned around in his tracks. "Hey, Barbara? About what you said earlier. Do you really believe Annet walked out on me, and that I didn't hurt her?"

She emitted a harsh bark of laughter. "Now, if you were missing instead of her, I wouldn't be so sure," she cackled, pointing with her finger at his chest. "But you, hurt her?" She stood only inches away from him. He could see the thick layer of foundation makeup on her face, the wrinkles underneath it. Smudges of black mascara and eyeliner clung around her eyes, the deep-red blusher on her cheeks reminding him of a clown. Why someone would go through so much effort to look like a harlot, he couldn't fathom. Still, it was nice to get support from an unexpected angle, even if it came from an aggressive foul-mouthed hellion.

"You're such a good for nothing whoosh!" she sniggered and walked back to the couch.

After he had cleaned himself up, he drove to the post-office and returned to the Manor with the mail.

"Glad to hear you're taking over some of Annet's duties," Caroline Rothschild remarked from behind the reception desk. "Dan is a little overwhelmed with her and Beverly gone."

One of Annet's many duties was to open, sort, and distribute the incoming correspondence, including faxes, emails, memos, and art submissions. Although he felt uncomfortable doing her work, it made him feel closer to her; the small stack of mail was a lifeline between the two of them.

"Dan has been so helpful and understanding. This is the least I can do in return," he replied, sending her a warm smile. He already loved the fragile colorful lady. She was enthusiastic, positive, and a tremendous supporter, but she looked weary, apprehensive, and out of place in the receptionist's seat.

Beverly's tasks included answering the phone, directing calls, greeting visitors, and collecting their admission. She also performed simple tasks like making coffee, keeping the reception area and meeting room in order, and supporting Annet and Dan with general office duties. All those tasks were a lot to expect from an eighty-year-old who had never worked in an office before.

"How are you holding up, Caroline?" he asked. "You look a little tired."

Caroline gave him a tense smile. "All I do is answer the phone and greet visitors. Other than that I have no idea what I'm doing and this computer is abracadabra. I'm too old to learn."

"I'm sure everyone appreciates what you're doing," Forrest assured her. "But I could take over for the rest of the day if you want."

"Oh no," she declined. "I know you already have more than enough on your plate, especially now with the added pressure from the police, and Annet's mother staying in the house."

"It will keep my mind busy," he grimaced. "Go home. I'm sure your two cats will be happy to see you."

Caroline laid her hand on his arm, giving it a squeeze. "Why don't you come over for dinner at my house tonight? Annet told me curry rice is one of your favorite meals. It just so happens it's one of my specialties." She picked up her silk shawl from the back of the chair and draped it around her shoulders.

Forrest didn't have to think twice. "Are you serious? That would be great!" Anything would be better than an evening in his apartment, where he missed Annet even more. "What time?"

She smiled. "I'm glad that, if only for one second, you lost that perpetual intense wretched expression on your face. Does six sound right?"

Forrest's smile faded. "There's a lot people who believe I'm involved in Annet's disappearance. I can't tell you how much your trust and support means to me."

"You have to thank Annet for that," she replied. "She told me what a gentle, caring, supportive and endearing partner you've always been. She's a wonderful, talented young woman. I completely trust her judgement."

Chapter 23

Annet awoke, memories of the night before flitting through her mind. Too bad it hadn't worked out. The storm just hadn't been fierce enough. It had also lacked the precarious green and brownish sky, and the continuous deafening rumbling. At least she had tried, and would try again the next time a thunderstorm rolled in.

Besides the disappointment she felt, her head hurt like a son of a bitch. She had scratches on her hands and arms. But other than that, she seemed in one piece, back in the relative safety of Alex Keizer's cabin. It was warm in the bedroom, and she began to feel revitalized. Ready for another challenging mind-boggling day, but the awareness of her shameful behavior kept her from getting up. She dreaded having to face him, knowing he would demand answers about her past. About her awful, bizarre, and ungrateful behavior. *How could she explain?* Telling how she had somehow traveled back in time would convince him she belonged in a psychiatric hospital. Confessing that last night, in the rain, she had lost control because *he* had been there instead of Forrest would prove she needed to be locked up with the key thrown away.

She pounded her fists into the mattress beneath her. *Damn, why had she made such a mess of her short stay here?* She had disgraced Mother Superior, humiliated Alphons the gardener, had been rude to Russell Jonkers, and now she had attacked Alex Keizer. Tears of embarrassment and frustration mingled with those of despair. Never had she behaved so rudely, so disrespectful, and never before had she succumbed to such fits of temper. But then again, never before had her world been so unmercifully turned upside down.

The sound of someone whistling a cheerful melody outside her window caused her heart to skip a beat. It seemed someone was in a good mood. She sat at the edge of the bed, the blanket wrapped around her body, looking at the pile of wet and crumpled clothes on the floor. She couldn't wear those. Well, then there was only one solution. She had to borrow something from Alex.

In the closet hung a green wool hunting coat with sharp M shaped lapels and a long sleeved white cotton shirt. *Probably size XL*, she thought, but it could work. She also found several pairs of breeches and picked out sapphire blue ones that tied around her waist. They reached well below her knees. Very cool looking and comfortable. She pulled her hair back in a ponytail, tying it with a leather shoelace she'd found on the floor. Hoping her host wouldn't be upset she had borrowed his clothes, she walked outside, finding him harnessing his horse in front of the wagon.

"Good morning," she said, her heart skipping a beat. Was he leaving?

141

He studied her before an approving grin appeared on his face. "Maybe a little too big, but those clothes suit you, Amazon."

Relieved he wasn't angry, she smiled back at him. "Did you have breakfast yet?"

He nodded. "There's tea, and plenty of bread."

His horse gave him a gentle nudge with its nose and he turned toward the animal. "I'm not forgetting you," he said, stroking his horse's neck with an affectionate strong hand. It was obvious horse and owner had a strong and loving bond, something she was unfamiliar with. She'd never had a pet, not even a guinea pig or a cat.

She walked back inside and poured herself a cup of tea. Alex soon followed her in.

"We're going to Dunedam," he told her.

He had several nasty scratches on his face, making her feel terrible. She had had no right to vent her frustration on him. He had been good to her, and didn't deserve her wrath.

"I have business to take care of and you're coming with me," he continued, standing with his hands on his hips, his feet apart.

"Why not," she agreed. "I'm curious to find out what the town looks like."

He stiffened. "Get ready. I want to leave as soon as possible." Brusquely, he turned around and marched out.

Now what's suddenly his problem? Damn, he was hard to read.

She walked outside, pulled herself up on the wrought iron handrail of Alex's wagon, and landed on the buckboards wooden bench. The seat was more comfortable than the one on Russell Jonkers' dairy cart, with a rail to hold onto, and a pillow underneath her butt. Life was improving.

Without a word, he sat next to her and drove the wagon over the trail toward the Dune Road. Other than a few puddles, there was no proof of last night's thunderstorm. The day was warm and glorious.

They drove on, Alex's tenacious silence irritating her. Deciding it would be better to let him stew, she occupied her mind by admiring the rural scenery, shielding her eyes from the harsh sunlight. They passed the Jonkers' farm and the turnoff to the monastery, already familiar terrain.

"Didn't you say you live in Dunedam," Alex asked semi-casually.

"I do," she replied.

"Then why did you say you would like to find out what it looks like?"

So that was what had pissed him off. He thought he had caught her in a lie. Phew. Her life had become so complicated. She couldn't even make a casual remark or it got her in trouble.

"I don't know. Sometimes I'm just a dumb blabbermouth," she replied, trying to wiggle her way out of it.

He grimaced, not hiding his discontent. They continued their trip in tense silence, the tower of Dunedam's Catholic Church the only recognizable feature in the unfamiliar and empty landscape. No pavement, no cars, no houses or apartment buildings. Just endless moorlands, pastures with cows, and farmlands with crops as far as the eye could see.

Alex waved at a farmer who walked behind a horse drawn plow, tilling the dark brown soil. The red-faced man, wearing blue breeches and a work shirt without a collar, lifted his straw hat and waved back.

The day was heating up. She took off the wool coat and rolled up the long sleeves of her white cotton shirt, pleated with ruffles at the cuffs and collar. She had never worn anything so dressy. Alex wore a similar shirt, his decorated with large frills on the front and on the cuffs. It had a laced-up V-neck opening, reminding her of shirts worn in the Pirates of the Caribbean. Totally awesome.

They passed several scattered homes alongside the gravel road, laundry hanging to dry on long clotheslines, dogs barking in the yard. When they reached a tiny village, the wagon wheels rumbled and clattered over cobblestone, a wooden sign with Dunedam engraved in it stood next to the road.

The Dunedam she knew was a thriving community, with an approximate population of thirty five hundred people. The main employer, the Dunedam Ocean View Lodge, accommodated tourists visiting the beach and the Keizer Manor. So this tiny village couldn't be Dunedam. There were hardly any houses, the streets practically empty, except for a few women in long plain dresses with white aprons and bonnets, and a young boy pushing a wheelbarrow.

After they rounded a street corner it got slightly busier. Wagons were parked alongside the road and homes built closer together. She saw a shop selling feed and grain, a saddle and harness maker, a general store. It wasn't until the wagon made another turn that she recognized the two-story post office between the bank and the drugstore, all three buildings still standing in her time. She craned her neck. This was Main Street and they were approaching the Market Square.

"Look," she said, grabbing Alex's arm. "That's the old library! And over there, the building on the corner with the print shop and Stoever's Hardware. That entire building burned down to the ground a few years ago. Oh, I can't wait to find out what the Market Square looks like, with the Old Pump. Are they actually using it right now? Is that where that man with the two buckets full of water is coming from?"

"I seriously believe your imagination is your worst enemy," Alex commented, pulling the reins. The cart stopped. "Besides that, who do you hope to find? Your husband? Your children?"

She touched the now evident swelling of her tummy, thanking Mother Nature for taking such good care of her baby under the primitive and challenging circumstances she encountered. "I'm not married," she said softly.

Alex gave her a quick inquisitive look before his hand disappeared in the pocket of his breeches, pulling out a handful of coins. "Here," he said, handing them to her. "I have to attend to business. In the meantime you can order yourself some decent clothes. Walking around in men's clothes is inappropriate, and that ugly brown dress looks dreadful on you."

"I couldn't agree more," she smiled, sliding down from her seat onto the street.

He looked at the clock on the church tower. "I'll be back here around two. Be ready." The wheels of the wagon creaked, horse and owner taking off.

She waited until he was out of sight before she leisurely strolled in the direction of the Market Square and the Old Pump, the heart of Dunedam. Town folks nodded friendly as she went by, eyeing her with curiosity. She acknowledged their greetings, eying them just as curiously in return. Some of their dresses and wardrobes were remarkable in their splendor and finery, while others were plain and tedious, the difference between rich and poor evident. It must have sucked, if they could tell by your clothes if you had money or not, she thought, but then she realized in her time, it wasn't all that different.

"Hi girls," she said to the five women visiting around the pump. "What's happening?"

Three of them, dressed prim and proper in stylish garments, reminded her of the Victorian Age. With tight corsets and

145

gigantic hoop-skirts, their long hair caught up in elaborate chignons. Their feathered hats perfectly designed to accommodate their elegant hairstyles. *These were women with style and money, no doubt about it.* The other two women dressed conservatively and plain, their long grey dresses and white aprons extending all the way to the ground, their hair arranged in a tight bun at the base of their necks beneath cute miniscule white bonnets. They had to be the servants.

"I couldn't wait to check out this good old pump," she said, grabbing the giant iron handle. "It's a hot one and I'm dehydrated. Aren't you girls hot too?"

Despite the high temperatures, their clothing covered their arms and shoulders. With the layers of lavish materials, the petticoats and the restrictive corsets, they had to be smoldering underneath.

Observing her guardedly, they smiled politely.

"We weren't sure if you were a man or a woman," one of them remarked, giggling behind her hand. Her gorgeous blue velvet button-down dress was decorated with lavish ribbons and lace fringes.

"You're kidding me, right?" Annet grinned, not the slightest bit offended. She had always dressed according to her own style, favoring bright colored shirts, blue jeans, and boots. But when she got back home, to her own time period, she would consider wearing breeches and white shirts with puffed up sleeves, like the ones she was wearing now. Alex Keizer had great taste in clothing.

"I have fresh water in these two buckets," the taller maid said.

Annet knelt down, formed her hand into a bowl and dipped it in the sturdy galvanized-steel bucket, drinking thirstily, sluicing the water over her face and neck. "Man, that's refreshing. Thank you." She raised her arm and dried her dripping face with her sleeve.

"You are not from around here," the blue velvet lady inquired. The other two women had retreated a few steps, their expression aloof.

Darn, she thought, her fingertips twiddling with the end of her long blonde ponytail. *Another one of those tricky questions she didn't know how to answer.* "I was born in Heemstead," she replied, deciding to stick to the truth. "How about you?"

"I'm Juliette LaRouge," blue velvet introduced herself in a tone stating everyone was supposed to know that. "My father owns the Citizens Bank of Heemstead. He prefers to spend his summers at our country house in Dunedam over our villa in the city. So, that's why I'm here." It was obvious from her demeanor she didn't agree with her father's choice. "These are my friends Dorothy and Rebecca Parsons. They are sisters. Their father is Heemstead's most important solicitor."

"A solicitor?" she asked. Wasn't that someone who rung each and every doorbell, trying to sell magazines, his or her religion, or anything else?

"Yes, he handles my father's legal matters."

Losing interest in the conversation with the hoity-toity young woman, Annet smiled obliquely. "My name is Annet. I'm in need of new and comfortable clothes." She put the emphasis on comfortable. "Is there a store around here you can recommend?"

"Dunedam doesn't have much to offer. We do all our shopping at our personal tailors in Heemstead, don't we girls?" Juliette replied with condescension.

The two sisters were dressed just as elegantly as blue velvet. Their sophisticated gowns had full caped sleeves with lace cuffs, and pearl-studded high collars, their trained skirts embellished with applied woven braid.

Although well-designed and classy, Annet had no intention of ever wearing a corset or anything so lavish and ornate. It had to take hours to get dressed each morning, with all the frills, sash and ribbons, their hair genuine pieces of art. Who had time for that?

The Parsons sisters nodded in unison, their soft, white hands playing with their lace parasols.

"Mary," Juliette LaRouge said, addressing her servant, "where do you buy the fabric for your clothes?"

"Me, my lady?" The young housemaid blushed, uncomfortable under the sudden attention.

"Yes, don't you frequent Marvin's Mercantile?"

Mary's color deepened and she stared at her mistress, confused and afraid. The other servant, the one who had given her the water, took a step forward, draping her arm around the quivering Mary's shoulders. "The Mercantile has a nice selection, Miss LaRouge," she said.

"Thank you, Angie," Juliette said, throwing her servant an irritated stare. "Then maybe you want to be so kind as to give our visitor directions." She raised her blue parasol above her head and turned on her heel, her layers of petticoats rustling as she walked away. "Come girls, let's go." The two sisters immediately followed in her tracks.

Aren't we a little bossy? Annet observed the threesome strolling down the Market Square, chatting and giggling, probably gossiping about her. Well, she didn't give a rat's ass.

"I hope you will forgive poor Mary, Madam Annet," Angie said, picking up the two buckets. "The only clothes she has are a calico dress she made herself and the uniform given to her by the LaRouge's housekeeper."

STORM AT THE KEIZER MANOR

"Oh, no worries. I totally get that," Annet reassured them before they rushed off after their mistresses.

Annet wandered in the opposite direction, recognizing many buildings that were still standing in her own time although they housed different business. The cellphone store was now a butcher shop, the liquor store a dry goods store, the deli a cheese shop. Cheese? That sounded great. She pushed the door open. A set of bells clanked. A bulky man with bushy eyebrows emerged from a back room. He wiped his hands on his apron, which hung down to his knees over navy gingham check trousers. "What can I do for you, lad?"

The strong, rich aromas of the cheeses played in her nose, transporting her back to a picnic she and Forrest took one summer. They had splurged on fancy cheeses and crackers, and paired it off with a cheap, no name wine. "I would like to buy a pound of your mature cumin seed cheese," Annet said, digging in the pocket of her loose breeches for the coins.

The cheese maker lifted a large round wheel from a wooden shelf behind the counter and placed it on a butcher-block. With a double handle knife, he cut the cheese in half, before cutting off a smaller piece. "That should be about a pound," he mumbled, weighing it on one of the brass dishes of the large scale hanging down from the ceiling. "Nineteen cents, please," he said, wrapping the cheese in a sheet of wax paper and handing it to her.

For the first time since she had landed here, she felt like a normal human being. Doing her shopping, without being judged, analyzed or criticized. She smiled when she handed him a coin.

The cheese maker looked at her mouth, turned beet-red, and stammered, "Oh my Lady, I had no idea."

Annet frowned. "No idea about what?"

"Well, uh…" He blinked hard as though clearing his vision. "Your clothes, my Lady. I apologize."

"My clothes? What about them?" she pressed on.

"If it wasn't for the strange outfit you are wearing, I wouldn't have been so callous. Please, forgive me for not treating you with the respect you deserve."

"Damn it, man," she replied heatedly. "You were the first one in weeks who didn't eye me suspiciously, or make me feel horrible. Now tell me, what triggered this crazy reaction?"

"I've never seen such a beautiful smile among the common folk, my Lady," he explained, stumbling over his words. "You have the smile of royalty."

"I see," she replied, taking the cheese and leaving the shop. As she passed Second and Third Street, she studied the people's clothing, their shoes, and their demeanor. Making her way in the direction of Sixth Street, where her apartment with Forrest would be, homes became scattered. Besides a few children playing with pebbles and a woman washing her windows, the streets resembled an abandoned ghost town. It wasn't until the cobblestones transformed into gravel, gravel into dirt, then into tall weeds, that she came to an abrupt stop. *Something was wrong. Had she missed Fourth and Fifth Street? And where the hell was Sixth?*

She retraced her steps until she arrived at the house with the window washing woman. She stood high up on a ladder, brushing away cobwebs and dirt, a bucket filled with water hanging from a hook.

"Sorry to bother you," she said, "but I believe I'm lost."

The woman looked down. "Who's asking?"

"I'm Annet Sherman. Would you be so kind as to give me directions to Sixth Street?"

"You're a lassie?" The woman came down the ladder. She was scrawny and pale, her mouth set in a condemning straight line. "Hasn't your mother told you anything about decency and modesty?"

"Modesty? What in the world are you talking about?"

"No bonnet, men's breeches, bare feet, and revealing your legs!" The woman breathed through her nose, two angry red splotches on her puny cheeks. "We don't want women without morals in Dunedam. Get out of here, harlot!"

"What?" Annet cried out in outrage. "Do you think I'm trying to sell my puss? That I'm a whore? God, are you out of your freaking mind!"

"How dare you take the Creator's name in vain?" the woman shrieked, raising her brush in the air, threatening to hit her. "You will be damned to the eternal fires of hell." Her face was blanched with fury.

Annet took a few steps back, raising her hands in defense. That crazy bitch scared the living daylights out of her. When the woman came charging at her, she took off as fast as she could.

"Vanish from this town or you will be burned at the stake!" she heard the woman yell after her.

Frantically looking for a place to hide, Annet hurried on until she noticed two barn doors standing wide open. Breathing raggedly, she stumbled inside.

A wagon loaded with empty burlap bags caught her attention. Without hesitation, she climbed onto the back and hid underneath them. Oof, that was close.

Her labored breathing slackened, her heart rate slowing down. She had outrun that crazy bag of bones, that religious fanatic witch. But her euphoria only lasted until the seriousness of her situation sank in. She was more than four months pregnant, in a strange town, full of antique people. There were no cars or telephones, no Keizer Manor, no White Castle Apartment, and no Forrest. Just women in long dresses, horse drawn carriages, nuns, dirt roads, and miles and miles of nothing. Never had she felt so forsaken.

Immediate tears rolled down her cheeks, into the coarse material of the bags. She was more dismally alone than she'd ever been in her life.

Chapter 24

A little past two, Alex's wagon rolled onto the Market Square, his hope of being released from his unwanted houseguest by leaving her in the care of someone else vanished.

The shopkeeper, from whom he had bought new red pigment and a very expensive weasel hair brush, had taken his wife's younger sister in to help for the duration of his wife's illness. Next, he had gone to the town's doctor, hoping he could help find a suitable place for Annet to live. The doctor's wife told him she had already heard about the poor damsel from the convent's gardener. In a small town, everyone knows everyone, gossip spreading as rapidly as a grass fire in the heat of summer. Unfortunately, the doctor had risen at dawn to make his rounds, not expected to return before sunset. Alex didn't intend to sit around, and wait that long. Patience had never been one of his virtues. However, she had promised to pass on the message about the stranded lass.

His last stop had been at the school, in the hope the two teachers would have a suggestion for Annet, but they had informed him not to expect a rapid solution. Although times had improved since the deprivation and famine, poverty was still widespread. People were afraid and cautious, making it almost impossible to find a household willing to take on an extra mouth to feed. Both teachers had promised they would keep an ear out, hoping they would hear about a family needing a nanny for their newborn, or a caretaker for an elderly family member.

Alex wished that would be sooner than later. He needed his peace and quiet back, and didn't want the responsibility for a badmouthed, vociferous and forceful maiden any longer.

Glancing around the Square, his foot tapped impatiently against the wooden floorboards of the wagon. *Where was that blonde vixen?* Cussing and grumbling to himself, he tied his horse to a tree and paced around the pump. He had told her to be there at two. That damn woman.

The afternoon air around him was motionless and suffocating. He opened the top buttons of his shirt, drops of perspiration beading on his face and chest. It was the hottest time of the day, heat radiating up from the concrete sidewalk. To cool off, he stuck his mouth and head underneath the streaming water. Coming from deep below the ground, the cold water was a welcome refreshment.

Another glance at the clock told him only ten minutes had passed. He became increasingly impatient as passersby greeted him. The obvious curiosity on the familiar faces was not lost on him. He nodded politely, ignoring their looks and attempts of conversation. He didn't want to talk or explain himself. Why he was lingering around the Square was none of their business.

With his long dark hair dripping onto his shirt, he walked back and forth like a caged bear, his temper rising with each passing minute. But when the clock tower struck three times, he got the inkling something might have happened to her. Unease attempted to replace his anger and impatience, but he deliberately fought that unwanted feeling off. He shouldn't worry about her. She wasn't his responsibility. But he also couldn't just abandon her, or dump her off on somebody else's shoulders. Cursing, he continued to wait.

Chapter 25

The itch in her nose and the musty smell of the bags were intolerable, but it wasn't until she heard approaching voices, that she hastily crawled from the wagon. She was dusting her shirt and breeches down when two men entered the wooden shop building. The tallest was dressed formal, and stiff, wearing a frock coat, cravat, and vest. His top hat looked like a stovepipe. The other man was dressed more casually. His cotton fall front trousers off white, his hat made of straw.

"Good day," she said, as she strolled to the door, hoping they would either ignore her or believe she belonged there. But she had no such luck.

"Halt, there!" Mr. Top Hat yelled, blocking her way out, his voice stern and accusatory.

Annet stopped in her tracks.

"What were you doing in here?" He turned toward the friendlier looking straw-hat and motioned in her direction.

"Check his pockets!" Without hesitation, the man approached her, ready to pat her down.

"Don't you dare touch me," she hissed, her eyes darting between the two men and the door, calculating if she could make a run for it.

"Oh my," the approaching man grinned over his shoulder. "It looks like we have a fire spewing lass on our hands."

"Hey buddy," Annet said, hoping to distract him. "I was supposed to meet someone at two. Can you tell me what time it is?"

The man pulled a watch from his breast pocket, and gazed down. Immediately, she seized the opportunity to dash toward the door and barrel outside.

"Stop her, you fool!" the nobleman bellowed. "She's getting away!"

For the second time that afternoon, someone was chasing her through the streets of Dunedam, but this time she wasn't sure if she could outrun her pursuer. Her sandals weren't the right footwear, and she had no clue where she was. The loud thumping of heavy footsteps behind her became louder. "Stop that thief!" her chaser yelled. She could almost feel his breath in her neck.

With adrenaline powering her run, she flew over the cobblestones, avoiding carriages, pedestrians, and other obstacles, until the pursuit noises behind her faded, but she had no illusion he had given up the chase. Noticing the increase in people and traffic, she was convinced she neared the town center. When she rounded a corner, she recognized the cheese makers shop and the pump, a familiar wagon parked next to it. She gulped a sob of relief. "Alex! They're chasing me! Help!"

At the sound of her screams he looked up. She waved wildly with both hands in the air. The next moment she crashed into him, throwing her arms around his neck and clinging onto him. "Oh, my God. I'm so happy to see you," she cried out, tears of relief glistening in her eyes.

Almost losing his balance under her sudden weight, he protested loudly. "Have you lost your mind, you idiot!" He ran his strong hands over her back, calming her, while he looked over her shoulder at the man who had been chasing her. He was huffing and puffing, his face beet red and sweat pouring down from his forehead.

Alex frowned. "What seems to be the problem, Andrew?"

Andrew Mullins owned several drays, the strong low carts used to haul heavy burdens. Alex had employed him several times throughout the construction of his cabin, to transport lumber, his cook stove and other bulky materials. Their business dealings had been mutually satisfying. He knew him as an honest and decent fellow.

"We found her inside Mr. Hoffman's warehouse," the drayman explained, leaning with his hands on his knees, trying to catch his breath. "She was hiding something in her pocket. He thought she was stealing."

Annet clung to Alex's neck, not willing to let go, his physical strength and comforting presence like a lifeline. He drew her away, just far enough so that he could see her eyes.

"What were you doing in that warehouse?" he asked, regarding her earnestly.

The concern in his voice took her by surprise and their gazes locked, his green eyes resting on her with unexpected warmth. She let out a deep sigh of relief. Thank God he wasn't angry.

"I was hiding," she answered, pulling out a package from her pocket. "What he saw underneath my clothes was the cheese I bought."

Alex turned her around, so she could face her accuser, his hand resting reassuringly on her shoulders.

"I apologize for sneaking inside the warehouse, Mister Andrew," she said. "I got lost."

The two men observed each other over her blonde head, until the drayman lowered his head. "I'll explain the situation to Mr. Hoffman, but I'm sure he won't drop the matter until he's certain nothing is missing from the warehouse."

"Thank you, Andrew," Alex smiled civilly. "But I'm sure everything will be in order. Miss Sherman might be an unusually brazen woman, but she's not a thief." Taking her by the arm, he led her toward the wagon. "Your list of explanations has just doubled," he whispered in her ear, before he helped her onto the seat.

"Dunedam sucks," she muttered between her lips.

Chapter 26

"What kind of people live in that pathetic little town these days?" Annet commented on the way back. "They looked down on me, accused me of whoring and stealing. Everything was so different. The streets, the houses, the stores. I still can't believe it!"

Alex grinned. "Not a single woman would dare to go into town wearing breeches. I admire you for that, Amazon, but do regret not warning you." He pulled the wagon into the courtyard of the Jonkers' farm. "We need supplies," he explained. "And since you didn't buy any clothes, maybe Amelia Jonkers or her daughter-in-law can help you out."

At the sound of their approaching wagon, Duke, the Jonkers' cocker spaniel appeared. Annet jumped off the cart, and squatted down next to the barking dog. She held out her hand, allowing him to sniff her fingers. "Hi, Duke, do you remember me?" Duke's tail wagged excitedly, leaning toward her, eager to be petted. "Yes, you remember me, don't you?" Laughing, she scratched him under the chin.

"I can't believe you actually know how to make a friend," Alex commented with a sly smile.

Annet glanced at him, wondering if he had made a joke. Then she burst out laughing. He was right. From the moment she had woken up in the convent, she had blatantly offended someone or had unintentionally run into trouble. Wherever she went or whatever she had done, she had created a huge mess. Maybe it was wise to tread more carefully from now on. After all, until she'd figured out how to transport herself back to the future, she depended on the people around her.

The door of the farmhouse opened and Russell Jonkers appeared, followed by a heavyset woman. She couldn't be taller than five feet. "Looks like she found you," Russell commented, indicating with his head he was talking about Annet.

"Yes, it looks like she did," Alex replied. "We stopped by to buy more eggs and sausage." Then he turned toward Russell's wife. "Amelia, Annet needs a dress, a shift, stockings and a bonnet. Can you help her with that?"

Annet seriously doubted if she was interested in what the heavyset woman could offer, regarding her modest cotton skirt with matching laced bodice. An apron completed her outfit.

"Trudy couldn't stop talking about you, and neither could my husband," Russell's wife smiled, the ruffles from her cotton day cap tight around her pleasant face with a chin tie. She preceded Annet through the mudroom into the kitchen. Trudy sat at the table, knitting with soft gray yarn.

After the frenzied last two days, the relaxed, laid-back atmosphere in the cozy kitchen was a welcoming change. "What are you making, Trudy?" she inquired. "It looks darling."

"It will be a baby jacket. Have you started a wardrobe for your baby yet?"

Annet shook her head. "No, I'm only half way through my pregnancy."

"Maybe you should," Trudy told her. "Those months go by much faster than you can imagine."

The women drank tea and ate freshly baked cookies, chatting about the weather and the clothes she needed.

"Do women really wear a corset every single day?" Annet cried out, holding up a heavy cotton, intricately seamed, whale boned garment. "It looks so uncomfortable and painful."

"Of course," Amelia replied, a look of astonishment on her face. "Once you wear it, you automatically get used to it, until one day you feel naked without it."

Annet laughed. *I highly doubt that.* "So the sole piece of underwear you wear is this short sleeved shift?" The one on the table was pieced from rough cloth, the neckline gathered up on a drawstring.

By the time they were done, the table was covered with dubious garments. A shift, three layers of petticoats, a bodice, a skirt, a blouse, shawl, and a bonnet. This was ridiculous.

"Since we're among women, how about personal hygiene these days?" Annet asked. "Like washing your hair, bathing, menstrual pads, and brushing your teeth?"

After the cheese maker's remark about her smile, she had paid close attention to the condition of the teeth from the people around her, realizing most of them probably never used a toothbrush.

"We use chew sticks and toothpowder we make ourselves from brick dust or crushed pottery," Amelia explained. "I prefer to mix ours with sugar to make it taste better."

"You use dirt and sugar as toothpaste?" Annet cried out in utter horror. Ever since she was a child, they had told her to brush her teeth. But how could she instill the same habits in these uninformed farmers, who had never used a toothbrush in their life?

"What else would we use?" Amelia replied, irritation pinching at the corners of her mouth. Her chair scraped on the floor as she got up.

"Oh, no, I'm sorry," Annet apologized as fast as she could. It hadn't been her intention to offend her host, but hearing about the unintentional damage she did to their teeth had shocked her. "Please, Amelia," she continued. "You taught me so much this afternoon. In return, I want to explain why you should never use that toothpowder again."

"If you have to," Amelia shrugged, the look of discontent still on her face.

"Look, the material you use in your powder is abrasive, causing considerable damage to your tooth enamel. The sugar you add to the powder, combined with bacteria, will cause cavities. Do you understand?"

"What's enamel, and what are bacteria?" Trudy wanted to know.

Annet exhaled a slow sigh. "Okay, forget about all that," she said. Although she realized her explanation had been too complicated, her whole demeanor inappropriate and overbearing, she wasn't going to back down on this one. Even if it meant they would find her a bitch. "All I want to suggest is using a toothpick, rubbing your teeth with a clean cloth, and rinsing your mouth with water after each meal." It was what she'd been doing for the lack of anything better, but she intended to talk to Alex. If they could make paintbrushes, they should be able to make toothbrushes as well.

"Will my teeth become just as beautiful as yours then?" Trudy asked, showing her yellow teeth and plaque lined gums.

"Probably not," Annet admitted. "But if you start right now, it will prevent severe toothaches in the future."

"That sounds like a lot of work to me," Amelia muttered and strode out of the kitchen.

Worried, Annet looked at Trudy. "Do you think she's mad at me?"

"No," Trudy whispered behind her hand. "She had a tooth pulled several weeks ago and this is a sore subject."

The kitchen door opened. Alex and Russell walked in followed by a man who couldn't be anyone else but Scott Jonkers. He was the spitting image of his father.

"How are you, dearest?" Scott said to Trudy. He planted a kiss on the top of her head, patting her large stomach with a calloused, dirty hand.

Trudy smiled up at him, love radiating from her eyes. For a minute, the two of them seemed to forget the entire world around them.

"Those two youngsters still behave like newlyweds," Russell Jonkers remarked in a gruff voice, his face glowing with pride.

With pain in her heart, Annet stared at the young couple, remembering the day she'd told Forrest about her pregnancy. How he'd whooped with joy over the news and dropped down on one knee, asking her to marry him. Tears welled up in her eyes when she thought about how much she missed him.

Alex's hand squeezed her shoulder. "Are you all right?"

Finding all eyes focused on her, her defenses flared up. "Jeez, I'm fine." Getting up, she shrugged off his hand.

Alex soon followed her outside with the pile of clothes, climbed on the seat next to her and clacked his tongue. They drove off, both deep in thought.

"I don't understand why you're so nice to me, because I'm such a royal pain in the ass," Annet started out a few minutes later.

Alex cast an exasperated glance. "I don't think I've much choice in the matter."

"Maybe not," she admitted. "But I still want to thank you. You've been very kind."

They drove on in silence, the horse's hooves thudding rhythmically on the dirt road. It was peaceful and quiet, the landscape still undisturbed, the air free from pollutants like chemicals, metals, ozone, emissions and carbon monoxide.

"I believe the only advantages of living in the nineteenth century are the serenity, the stillness, and the clean air," she remarked, breathing audibly in and out. "You can smell the freshness and the high level of oxygen. I will definitely miss that."

"You plan to stop breathing?" Alex grinned.

"No, jerk, I mean when I'm back home." She lowered her head and continued feebly, "Whenever that's going to be."

They left the Dune Road, their wagon shaking forcefully when a wheel hit a rock. She bounced from her seat, in alarm grabbing a hold of his arm. "Holy moly! What was that?"

"I'd hoped to shake you out of your melancholy," Alex remarked, a teasing quality in his voice.

"You did that on purpose?"

When he didn't answer, she shook his arm. "Did you?" She studied the strong features of his face, his straight nose, the long wavy dark brown hair flowing over his collar, until a slight twitch at the corner of his mouth gave him away. "You asshole,

I could've fallen off," she replied with stiff dignity. "I could have hurt myself!"

His green eyes sparkled mischievously. "You were wallowing in self-pity. I had to shake you out of it, to get the color back in your face."

At first she was too stunned to speak, then when she did, her voice shook with exasperation. "Oh is that how you want it to be? Well, I got news for you. I will cry and wallow as much as I want. Do you hear me?"

Unimpressed by her threatening words, he burst out laughing. "If you weren't such a grouse, I wouldn't mind keeping you around," he howled. "I haven't had so much fun in years!"

She watched him with brooding eyes until they approached the cabin. It was splashed by the late afternoon sunlight, the surrounding views vivacious, the foliage luxuriant. Mosquitos and other insects danced above the pond.

He has chosen a perfect spot for his hideout. It almost looked like paradise. Maybe she should try to approach this entire experience as a vacation. She hadn't had a week off in years and could look at this weird adventure as a relaxing time, away from all her responsibilities, like a well-earned retreat.

Chapter 27

"These last several days have been very pleasurable and unobtrusive," Alex commented over breakfast a few days later. Annet agreed. Besides the struggle with the laundry and the cook stove, she had tried to unwind while Alex had locked himself up in his workshop for hours on end, still experimenting with the red dye, oil, and water.

"It's been too hot to do aything," she complained. Normally she would have loved the sun-drenched days and brilliant blue skies they were experiencing, but now, it had been disappointing. There hadn't been a single cloud in the sky, let alone the desperately desired thunderstorm. All she had gotten out of it was a little color in her face.

"Is the heat bothering you?" Alex continued. "You seem distraught, and you're so quiet, almost listless."

"Are you complaining?" she replied. "If so, I could organize a rave party, with loud electronic music, smoke machines, free drugs, and psychedelic mushrooms?"

"Music sounds good," Alex said, taking the last bite of his eggs. "If you want, we could go to church."

She raised her eyebrows. "To church, why?"

"Because it's Sunday."

"Oh, it is? Damn, I haven't thought about what day it is in quite a while." Plunged in thought, she ran the tip of her thumb across her lips. "Come to think of it … is it still May, or is it June already?"

He stared at her. "You don't know it's September?"

"What?" she cried out in disbelief. "That's impossible! The anniversary was in May and that's barely two or three weeks ago!" She sunk down in her chair. *Had those horrible "time travel folks" not only propelled her back two centuries, but also played another trick on her by landing her at the end of the summer?*

Alex stared at her from the other side of the table, his fingers drumming on the wooden surface.

"No, I don't want to go to church," she snapped at him. "But I'm not holding you if you want to go."

"Don't worry. I never go to the church when I'm here," Alex said. "Then maybe you want to do something else?"

Annet scoffed. "Yeah, something fun like going for a Sunday drive in your automobile? Or visiting the friendly folks in Dunedam? Hell, no! I'm staying here."

"Suit yourself," Alex replied, getting up. "As long as you don't expect me to hang around and watch you sulk."

The moment he walked out of the door, she regretted her outburst, but her pride kept her from running after him. Screw him. She had disappeared in May and landed here in August.

With him out of her hair, she should go sunbathing before the weather turned and fall made its entry.

She grabbed a large towel and the book she'd chosen from Alex's meager collection, titled "Persuasion," thinking she might learn something from it about the current customs and etiquette. It was written by Jane Austen, the author of Pride and Prejudice, a novel she had read during her senior year in high school.

Leaving the dirty dishes on the table, she walked outside. Next to the cabin was a shallow hollow in the dune, the sand warm, clean and inviting. It was the perfect spot for what she had in mind. She draped her towel down at a comfortable angle and peeled off her short sleeved shift. Wearing her bra and panties, she lay down and made herself comfortable. The sun stood hot in the blue sky, concerns over her lack of sunscreen, and exposure to UV radiation popping up in her head. Deciding not to worry about it, she opened her book. It was a perfect morning, a soft breeze moving the air just enough to keep it comfortable. She read a few pages about the financial trouble of the Elliots of Kellynch Hall before she closed her eyes. Birds chirped in the trees and frogs croaked in the distance. Around the pond, she had seen a large variety of cawing sea gulls, doves, kestrels, and sparrows, deer and rabbits. Alex had told her there were also owls and foxes around, but she had yet to see one of those.

She dozed a little, her hands covering the swelling of her tummy, until the sound of approaching footsteps and a measured cough made her look up. She raised herself up on one elbow, finding a broad shouldered man gazing down at her. Despite the hot weather, he was completely dressed in black, a wide brimmed hat decorated with a peacock feather planted on top of his head, his long dark hair tied in a ponytail. All he needed was a black pencil-style moustache and a mask, and he could be Zorro.

"Who are you?" she asked, her hands searching for her shift. When she found it, she held it in front of her breasts to protect herself from his piercing stare.

"I thought people had been telling tales about a blonde harlot living with my brother, but I guess I was mistaken," the man said with disdain. "Where is Alex? I need to talk to him."

Annet scrambled up, pulling the shift over her sunbathed body, sand scratching her skin. "He went for a walk. Is there anything I can do for you?"

He scoffed. "You're a disgrace! Don't you have any shame?"

"Shame? What for?" He was actually an inch or so shorter than her, and not nearly as impressive anymore, the smell of cologne and cigars in his clothes.

"My God," he said, his eyes fierce with resentment. "How dare you parade yourself in front of me. I'm a married man. Cover yourself, you shameless slut."

Annet got angrier by the second, her lips barely moving as she spat out. "If you think I'll shake in my boots because you bark at me like a baboon, come again!"

She stared at him for a long moment, struggling to tamp down her anger. After all, this pompous tyrant was Alex's brother and she didn't want to cause more problems than she already had. "Sorry," she said demurely. "Can I make you a cup of coffee while you wait for Alex? I'm sure he'll be home soon." She grabbed her book and towel and hurried back to the cabin.

To her astonishment, her unwanted visitor followed her up the steps and through the door. Arrogantly he roamed around the cabin with his hands folded behind his back. Ill at ease, she added a piece of wood to the still smoldering fire, ground the coffee beans, and filled the percolator with water, contemplating how she could work him back outside. With every move she made, she felt his eyes burning a hole in the back of her neck, heightening her anxiety. When the coffee brewed in the two-tier drip pot, she excused herself, and disappeared into the bedroom, to dress more appropriately and escape his intense gawk. She donned the ugly brown dress and pulled her hair into an untidy ponytail. When she reentered the living room a short minute later, he studied the sunflower painting in the windowsill.

"Instead of working, like everyone else, my brother wastes his time painting flowers," he commented with contempt before he blatantly looked her over and smirked, "I liked that flimsy white thing much better on you."

"Yes, you made that noticeably clear, Mister," she replied. The coffee sputtered on the stove. She grabbed a pot holder, stiffening when she felt him behind her. With trembling hands, she poured him a cup, the atmosphere laden with tension and unwanted vibes. Hoping he would follow her to the relative safety outside, she headed toward the door.

"Why are you suddenly so skittish and prudish?" he asked, following her out on the porch. "Afraid I'll tell my brother how you displayed your goods for me?"

She stepped down from the deck onto the sand, relieved he was on her tail. "You can tell him whatever you want," she replied, handing him his coffee. "He's right there."

He looked up as Alex appeared from the dunes, his hair flowing in wild curls around his shoulders, his shirt unbuttoned. At the sight of him, her heart did a strange erratic dance. It was wonderful to see him. What a relief!

As he came closer, she knew he was livid, his mouth set in a straight line, his eyes cold and blank. "What are you doing here?" he said, towering at least four inches over his brother. "You know this is forbidden territory!"

"I don't know why you're all fired up," their visitor replied, nonchalantly flicking an imagined dust particle from his immaculate black clothes. "Because I can see you don't mind entertaining a dubious, but attractive member of the opposite sex out here."

Alex shot him a glare that could have set a log on fire. "This is my property and I'll prosecute you for trespassing if you don't get the hell out of here, Leo."

That's right, Alex, Annet thought, *let him have it*.

"Come on, Alex, calm down," Leo replied. "Father sent me because you didn't appear at the meeting last Thursday. Damnation, he told you on numerous occasions how imperative it was."

They stared each other in the eyes, grim-faced and hostile, until Leo smirked. "Believe it or not, Father thought you might have been in an accident and was worried, but when he heard from James Hoffman you were seen in Dunedam with a blonde streetwalker, he was furious. I won't repeat what he said, for the sake of that same particular hussy here, but let me assure you it wasn't pleasant."

"Would you please refrain from calling me a whore," Annet cut in heatedly. "You don't know anything about me!"

"Oh, is that right?" Leo commented, highly amused. "I know you have commendable legs and a voluptuous bosom. Now how would I know that if you weren't such a harlot?"

"What are you talking about?" Alex exploded, pushing Annet out of the way. The situation was close to spinning out of control, the two brothers challenging each other like a pair of vicious bulldogs, until Leo scoffed. When he turned away, Alex seized his arm, the coffee mug flying down into the sand.

Annet rubbed her fist across her forehead. If she hadn't shown up at the cabin, Alex would have gone to the meeting, and his father wouldn't be mad. This was all her fault. She had to defuse the tension.

"Please," she said, placing a calming hand on Alex's arm. "Don't fight with your brother. It's not worth it."

Leo yanked himself free and rubbed his skin. "Father wants you home. Today!" he snarled, turning around on his heel.

They watched him stride toward the brown horse tied down next to the shed. He swiftly mounted it from the ground and rode off, leaving a cloud of dust in his wake.

Alex breathed out loudly through his nose. "I know he's my brother," he said, "but I would've gladly punched him in the face for the insults he threw at you." He looked at her with concern. "Are you all right?"

"Me?" she asked. "I can better ask you that question? Damn, Alex. I really appreciate I can stay here until I figure out a way to return home, but you can't neglect your responsibilities because of me!"

"Your home on Sixth Street in Dunedam, right?" he said mockingly. "Did you try to find it last week while we were there?" Without waiting for an answer, he turned around and headed back to the cabin.

With a frustrated sigh, Annet picked up the empty, sand-covered coffee cup and followed him.

"Yes, I did," she told him after she caught up with him on the porch. "But it wasn't there yet."

"Aha!" Alex said, spreading his arm in ridicule. "Who would have guessed?"

"You're a jerk!" Annet countered. "Just like your ass of a brother. Care for some coffee? There is plenty left."

"Sorry, this time I won't allow you to change the subject," Alex replied. "I expect an explanation. About *everything*. Where you came from, why you were looking for me, and why you can't go home."

She sat down at the table. "Look, for days I've been bursting to tell you the truth. I hate lying and having to be so evasive, but like I told you before, you won't believe a word of what I say."

"Try me," Alex challenged her.

"Okay, then, here we go." She sighed and then blurted out, "I come from the future and traveled two centuries back in time."

He stared at her blankly. "Right."

"Oh, I'm so glad to have that off my chest." She fell back in her chair, a smile on her face, her shoulders relaxed. "Now you can understand my dilemma, because I have no clue how to get back there."

"You traveled in time and landed on the side of the road," Alex said, leaving his spot next to the kitchen counter to pace the floor. "Russell Jonkers found you and took you to the convent. Is that it?"

Annet's smile became even brighter. "Oh, Alex, you understand." She got up and threw her arms around his neck, not noticing the darting look in his eyes. "You're such a wonderful man!" A warm glow burned inside her. She had found an ally! From now on everything would be better.

"Forrest and I walked in the dunes, all dressed up for the museum's anniversary party. All of sudden these weird brown-greenish clouds gathered over us, followed by the deepest rumbling we had ever heard," she explained, releasing him from her strangling embrace. "The air was laden with eerie shafts of pale green and pink light streaming up the sky."

She was so engrossed in her own story, she missed the disbelief on Alex's face first change into irritation, then to disappointment and finally into compassion.

"Sand moved beneath our feet and we had to protect our ears against the deafening noise. Hurricane-force wind howled, pushing us over, until everything around us exploded like cannon guns, so loud my eardrums popped. It was terrifying!"

"I see," Alex said, rubbing his chin between his fingers, his eyes concerned. "That must have been unnerving."

"Oh, it was," she agreed. "When I eventually came to, I was hurting everywhere, and freezing my ass off in my dress."

Alex shook his head. "Incredible. What an ordeal."

"Wait here," Annet said, "I want to show you something." She ran into the bedroom and took off her clothes. Next, she slipped into her short black dress and topped it with her fake pearl necklace. Without a second thought, she ran back into the room where Alex waited for her.

"Look, this is the dress I was wearing." She paraded in front of him, eagerly awaiting his reaction to the sight of her bare legs and tight fitting classy outfit, not realizing her small baby bump was clearly visible. "Professional, but stylish. Don't you agree?"

Her question hovered in the air for at least sixty seconds, then two minutes, the strained silence becoming intolerable until he made a snorting sound full of disgust.

"Or you could have said, I'm a fallen woman because I became pregnant without being married and my family kicked me out of the house!" His voice rose louder as he completed his tirade. "I can't believe how stupid I have been! Believing in you!"

He fell into a gloomy silence while the atrocious understanding of what he had found out sank in. "I'm such a fool," he grunted. "Look at you! My brother was right. You are a whore, indeed."

The horror of his startling response slammed into her gut. Oh, no, he didn't believe her at all. Not a single damn word of it. Doubling over, she swore she would be sick. He thought she was lying! Making it up to cover an unwanted pregnancy.

A chair went flying through the room and his coffee mug shattered on the floor. "Gather your belongings and get out of here! Now!" he yelled.

Tears burned in her eyes as she watched him march out of the door, leaving her in shambles.

Moaning, she leaned over, clutching her arms. He had been so disappointed in her, so deeply hurt. Sobs of despair wracked her body, debilitating her, and she didn't resist when two strong arms enfolded her. Alex had come back into the cabin and sat down next to her on the floor, his features drawn with sorrow and unease.

"Honestly, I didn't lie," she cried out, her voice choking with emotion. "You have to believe me. Please, I'm begging you." Desperate and afraid, she leaned against him until her ragged breathing slowed down.

"Amazon," he said with compassion in his voice. "Do you understand how hard it is to believe you? Traveling in time through some kind of tempest. You have to admit it sounds ludicrous."

"I know," she replied miserably. "And there is no way I can prove it, other than by telling you about the future. About what life is like. Or to tell you what I know about the past. I've always been interested in history and know quite a bit."

Alex drew away from her. "Suppose you are telling me the truth. What do you think happened to your friend Forrest?"

Hot tears welled back up in her eyes and spilled down her cheeks. "I don't know." She spoke barely above a whisper. "He could be hurt, or he may have ended in a different time period, but whatever happened, I'm sure he's worried sick. Just like my mother, my colleagues, and friends."

Alex got back on his feet and pulled her up next to him.

"Here." He handed her a towel. "Blow your nose and wash your face. You look terrible."

"Gee, thanks," she muttered. "I can't tell you how much better that makes me feel." She splashed cold water in her face and washed her hands, still feeling shaky after her emotional turmoil.

"Sit down while I fix us something to eat," Alex ordered. "Hopefully that will revive your spirit."

Clutching the towel against her chest, she stared into nothingness, the noises he made in the kitchen sounding dull and far away. She had hit rock bottom and she knew it.

It wasn't until he put a plate in front of her, that she emerged from behind the dark clouds in her brain.

"I'm sorry about everything," she began. "Usually I'm not such a drama queen, but this last month has taken me through the wringer." A faint smile trembled across her lips. "To tell you the truth, at first I thought someone was playing tricks on me, but now I know it's reality. I'm stuck in the nineteenth century, with you."

"Well, it doesn't sound all that bad," he replied, and sat down at the opposite side of the table. He had made sandwiches with ham and grilled onions. She took a bite, trying to settle her stomach, and force herself back to normality.

"Why don't you tell me something about yourself?" Alex said. "About your parents, your siblings."

"I'm more than happy to tell you everything, Alex, and I will," she replied. "But first you have to understand a lot has changed in two-hundred years. Some for the better, but a lot for the worse."

"Telling me about your family can't be all that difficult to understand?"

Annet scoffed. "You would be surprised." A frown appeared on her forehead. How could she best explain the circumstances under which she had grown up, knowing Alex would have a very hard time understanding the dramatic shift in traditional values related to sexual attitudes and all the societal changes that had occurred in the twentieth century. The feminists, gay rights, hippies, multiculturalism.

"I barely remember my father," she said, "He walked out on us when I was three. Since then, my mother married three more times and is now dating an unemployed sixty some year old truck driver. His name is Chuck. You know that in many countries the divorce rates are higher than forty percent? That's why Forrest and I never married. We don't believe in it."

"You lost me," Alex interrupted. "Walking out? Divorce? Truck?"

"Oh, Alex," she cried out in frustration, "it will take me days to explain everything."

"I'm not going anywhere," he said, making light of the situation.

"But you have to go to Heemstead, to your father!"

He massaged the bridge of his nose with his thumb and forefinger. "This is more important right now. Why don't you start at the beginning, and we will keep on talking until I know everything there is to know about you."

Chapter 28

In the days that followed, Annet introduced Alex to life in the twenty-first century and her own past. Where and when she was born. That she had been an only child. How she had taken care of herself from a very young age. This took her to her mother's plentiful, but short-lived marriages, and relationships, and to Forrest. How they met in high school, and lived together for seven years when she got pregnant. So far, she felt he understood, but when she told him about the trailer park where she grew up, she ran into the first complication. What is a trailer? What is a mobile home park?

She had detoured back to the invention of the automobile, which he had been very interested in, but the step from car to train and plane had been incomprehensible.

Talking to him about her job had also caused difficulties, because he had found it inconceivable she had been the breadwinner. The idea he would have his own museum and be famous all over the world, had made him roar with laughter.

But whenever the conversation became too difficult, she tried to make light of it. She couldn't expect him to take everything in in a few days, while it had taken centuries for mankind to get there.

At least their relationship improved. She was building trust, and days filled with dwindling summer sunshine drifted by in a new found, quiet comradery. Days in which they took long walks in the dunes, fixed their meals together, and talked and laughed. Evenings were spent on the porch, where they gazed at the unbelievable dark sky and admired the brilliance of the Milky Way, the stars and galaxies without interference of light-pollution.

In return Alex told her about his brother Leo, who had been thirteen years old when he was born after countless miscarriages. He also told her about his mother, who he had lost four years ago due to an illness of her heart. She had been the only one who understood his passion for art and his need for reclusion. Therefore, she had left him the land in the dunes that had been part of her heritage.

"Now what do you miss most about your life, besides the people?" Alex asked a few days later.

"Prenatal care and a long hot shower," was her immediate response, explaining to him about the vitamins she was supposed to take, and about four walls, a water heater, and shower head. "That would be so luxurious compared to your water bowl on a washstand."

"Maybe I can build you one. It doesn't sound too complicated," he offered, raising his eyebrows in questioning at the sound of approaching horses and creaking springs.

"You're expecting company?" she asked.

Alex pushed his chair back and walked to the window to look outside. "It's my father," he told her. "I'm sure he'll want to come inside. For his sake, do you mind changing into something more modest and feminine?"

She was wearing one of Alex's shirts and paint splashed knickers. "Don't worry. I don't want him to have a heart attack when he sees my shapely calves," she joked.

Alex grinned in reply and walked outside the moment a coachman jumped down from the driver's box of a shiny black carriage. It was four-wheeled and enclosed, with doors on the sides and room for luggage on the roof. The custom made carriage was pulled by two robust horses, but wasn't designed to drive outside the city and off the main road, causing it to look misplaced in the deep sand, between the dunes, and the tall grasses.

The door of the carriage opened, and Leo stepped out. He extended his hand, helping his father down the black metal step. Both men were dressed in similar double breasted frock coats, cravats, breeches, and low heeled black shoes with square golden buckles. Each had their thick hair tied in a ponytail, one grey and one black.

To Alex's surprise, a beautiful woman with flawless porcelain skin, a dainty little nose and perfect soft pink lips, emerged from the carriage. It was Elise, Leo's wife, who almost never left the house except to go to church on Sunday.

"Hi, Alex," she smiled, extending a gloved hand, her other hand fanning to cool her face.

"Elise," he said, "what a wonderful surprise to see you here." He bowed courteously, wondering what could be so important she had accompanied the two men to his humble abode.

181

"Your father insisted I should come," she explained, her voice soft and tinkly, her eyes warm and caring, "but I'm glad I did, because your place is lovely."

His father placed an affectionate hand on Elise's shoulder. "After hearing about your concubine, I decided to remind you what a real lady looks like," he remarked. "Come let's step out of the sun. This heat is too much for your sister-in-law."

Alex cringed at his father's arrogant words and the way he took control of the situation even though he'd never set foot inside his house.

"I told Elise to accumulate several outfits for your courtesan after I heard she was either running around in men's clothes or practically naked," his father continued. "Jason, our coachman, will bring them in."

Alex's mouth fell open in astonishment. His father wasn't the man to listen to rumors and certainly not about a "useless" and "unimportant" woman, but then he noticed Leo who was trying hard to keep a straight face. When their eyes met, his brother burst out laughing.

"Sorry brother," Leo grinned. "but I had to warn father about this wild and foolish strumpet you're involved with, before the word gets out and you ruin our good name." He tilted his head arrogantly to one side before he took his wife by the elbow, and supported her through the loose sand and onto the porch, waiting for Alex to open the door so they could enter.

The snob! Alex thought. Before he could oblige, his father pulled him aside and spoke with a hushed tone, "Her standing and intolerable behavior aside, I was relieved to hear from Leo you're finally involved with a *woman*."

Alex's jaw dropped. Although he was still a bachelor at thirty-two, keeping his affairs private didn't mean he wasn't interested in women.

"Why are you even here?" he asked. Fighting to conceal his irritation, he pulled out a chair for Elise, inviting her to sit down.

"This is a delightful home, Alex," she commented, oblivious to the tension. She gathered her skirts before she sat down, and looked around with genuine interest. "It's so cozy and clean."

"She's right," his father agreed, looking around for himself. "I am pleasantly surprised, indeed." He put the dossier he carried under his arm on the table and took a seat. "Now let's get to business."

Aha, his father was trying to kill two birds with one stone, Alex concluded. The first one trying to form an opinion about his alleged relation with Amazon, the second one the legal papers that had to be signed.

At that moment, the bedroom door opened and Annet stepped out. Instead of the brown dress she'd been talking about, she was wearing the clothes Trudy Jonkers had given her. The voluminous ochre skirt was wrinkled and a tad short, but paired with the bodice, its elegant bishop sleeves and ruffled cuffs, she looked fabulous. Her long blonde hair was pinned into an attractive chignon at the back of her head, and her sun touched skin radiated health and vitality. Her blue eyes sparkled with dynamism and wit. Alex's heart jumped at the sight of her, rushing over to her side, his eyes reflecting his surprise and appreciation.

"Father, it's my pleasure to introduce Annet, a woman unlike any other."

"Hello everyone," Annet smiled and curtseyed.

His father cleared his throat before answering, "Well, my son, I have to admit, I am pleasantly surprised, *again*."

"She sure cleans up nicely," Leo commented, his eyes blatantly roaming the length of her before he punched his brother on the shoulder. "You've worked wonders with her. How did you do that, brother?"

Alex noticed the unmistakable sexual interest in his brother's eyes and he glared at him. "She's beautiful inside and out," he replied. "No matter what you think."

He pulled out a chair for Annet. "Annet, this is Elise, Leo's wife."

"It's so nice to meet you," Elise said as Annet sat down next to her. "I was told you were in desperate need of garments, bringing several stunning gowns along, but I can see this is not the case. You look lovely."

"That's very nice of you to say," Annet replied. "but trust me, this is the only decent dress I have and I can sure use a lesson in nineteenth century dress code. Tell me about the intricate shawl you're wearing."

The two women engaged in a frivolous conversation about clothes while Alex's father pulled out his paperwork. "These are the documents about the settlement of your grandfather's estate you were supposed to sign during the meeting two weeks ago," he said. "It can't be delayed any longer. Jason can function as a legal witness." He slid the papers over the table in Alex's direction, ordering Leo to walk outside and fetch the coachman. Next he pulled out a dip pen and a tiny bottle with black India ink from the inner pocket of his frock coat.

"You have to sign and date the third page and last page," he said, pointing it out.

Alex opened the bottle of ink. The sooner this was taken care of, the sooner his unwanted company would leave.

"Great," his father said, pulling a watch from his pocket. "Just what I thought. Leo and Elise, time to leave." He stuffed the papers back into the dossier, got up, and headed to the door.

Alex followed them outside and helped them get settled back inside the carriage. But before he could close the door, his father leaned out. "You had three weeks of fun," he said. "Now it's time to get rid of that unscrupulous woman and come home, son. This is an order!" Then he pounded his cane against the ceiling, the sign for the coachman they were ready to leave, and leaned back into his comfortable red plush seat.

Taken aback, Alex shut the door of the carriage, watching the strong horses pull their heavy load around. When they were out of sight, he filled a bucket with water. His horse nickered when he entered the shed.

"Sorry I'm late," he said, stroking his neck. He poured the water into the horse's trough and added hay to the empty rack. "Sometimes life is just too complicated."

He rested his elbows on top of the stall door, contemplating what had happened over the past weeks, staring into nothingness. In a few days he had no other choice than to go back to Heemstead. He was forsaking his duties and surprised his father's patience had lasted this long.

But what about Amazon? He couldn't leave her here. Soon it would be autumn, followed by winter, and staying here would be impossible. The walls and the roof of the cabin were too rickety and insubstantial to keep it warm inside, even with the woodstove burning at full blast. His water pump would freeze over, and often for weeks on end, the roads would be impassable by snow and ice.

"Oh, there you are!"

He turned around and saw her standing in the doorway of the shed, her elegant chignon gone, her long blonde hair fanning around her shoulders. She had also loosened the laces of her bodice, showing the slight swelling of her pregnancy. Her long sleeves were pushed up to her elbows, her feet bare. His skin began to burn and his groin stirred.

"It's way too hot for all these clothes," she complained, raising her skirts so cool air could flow around her legs.

Her behavior only added to his discomfort. *Where were you my entire life,* he wondered and shuddered as reality slammed through him. What was he dreaming about? He only met her one month ago and barely knew her. Besides, she was spoken for by another man, carrying his child, and all she wanted was to return to him, even at the risk of being struck by lightning.

She walked further in his direction but he held out his arms, regarding her coldly. "I don't want to see you. Please, leave me alone."

"But why?" she protested. "Did I do something wrong?"

Already feeling what it would be like to lose her, and the emptiness she would leave behind, he walked past her, ignoring her objection. He entered the dunes with long strides. He needed time for himself, to sort things out.

Chapter 29

Alex kept on walking until he reached the ocean. The early afternoon sun reflected off the water, inviting him in. Without hesitation, he stripped and walked into the surf, the cool and salty water pooling around his feet. He waded in deeper and when a large wave rolled toward him, he dove in. Swimming with angry strokes, he wondered why he had allowed her into his life. Why he believed her ridiculous stories about her time travel and the future. People flying in the air with machines, lights that turn on after you flip a switch, people talking to each other through a square device, even if they resided in another town. He couldn't fathom it.

He swam past the surf, and floated on his back with his eyes closed, gentle waves bobbing him up and down, until splashing sounds came toward him. He opened his eyes and couldn't believe what he saw. Annet swam in his direction, her rhythmic strokes strong, slicing through the water, her body propelling forward. When she reached him, she started to tread water and smiled.

"You can swim?" he said incredulously.

"Of course, I love to swim, and even took synchronized swimming lessons when I was in junior high. Here, I'll show you."

She disappeared beneath the surface, and he was afraid she was drowning until he noticed one foot slowly rising from the water, followed by an elegant calf and knee. Another foot followed in the same slow manner, her toes pointed, her legs moving like scissors in the air before they disappeared again. Under the surface, he saw her body turn around several times, her white shift swarming ghostly around her body until her face came back up followed by her neck and her shoulders. She seemed to rise from the water. He had never seen anything so mysterious and beautiful in his life.

"It's a combination of ballet, swimming, and gymnastics," she explained, breathing heavily. "I used to be able to hold my breath much longer, though. I'm so totally out of shape."

He slid his arm around her waist. "Are you okay?"

She held on to his shoulders to catch her breath. He looked at her with concern. "Let's get back to shore. You think you can make it?"

"I'm fine. I'm pregnant, not a sissy," she told him, letting go of his shoulders. "Hey, handsome!" A teasing sparkle appeared in her eyes. "You want to race me to the beach?" She splashed a handful of seawater in his face, and disappeared into the surf, a high wave picking her up, giving her an immediate advantage.

He instantly dove under water following suit, but before he could catch up with her she rose from the water, the thin material of her shift clinging to her body like a second skin. She was breathtakingly beautiful, and he stopped swimming to enjoy the view.

"I won!" she exulted, waving at him. She proceeded onto the beach and squeezed the salt water from her hair, before lowering herself onto the warm sand next to his discarded clothes.

He waved back, but lingered in the surf. He was stark naked. Then he threw out his feelings of hesitation and modesty. She didn't have a single prudish bone in her body, and had seen a naked man before. He rose from the sea and approached her.

"Holy cow, Alex," she commented, her blue eyes sparkling with blatant admiration. "You have a gorgeous body!"

He picked up his breeches and slipped them on before he sat down next to her, feeling much safer now his manhood was invisible from her scrutinizing gaze.

"So do you," he replied.

He forced himself to relax, but the fresh sea air, mixed in with the irresistible scent of her body and the warm glow of her skin drew him toward her. His body responded and there wasn't a damn thing he could do about it.

All of a sudden the sun disappeared behind the clouds, a gust of wind chilling the air.

Annet pulled up her legs, hugging her knees to her chest, and he watched her shiver. "Are you cold?"

The spell was broken.

"A little," she replied.

He handed her his shirt. "Why don't you use this to towel yourself dry," he said, turning away. Staring at the dark clouds gathering overhead, his breathing slowed, his imminent lust diminished. "I think we better head home before we get caught up in a wicked summer storm."

The moment he stopped talking, they heard the boiling clouds grumble in the distance. Alex got up and wiped the sand off his hands. "Come, let's go. It looks like this could be a thunderstorm."

He took her hand, but she yanked herself free. "I'm not leaving. I'm staying here," she declared, her eyes stubborn.

"No, you don't. It's too dangerous," Alex argued. "We're out in the open, with nothing to protect us against a lightning strike. Come!"

He tried to get a hold of her arm, but she stepped away from him. His temper heated.

"Damn, I can't let you stay here." He would never leave her here by herself, vulnerable to the elements.

"Don't you understand?" she cried out. "This could be my chance! Look at the sky. Those clouds are brown and green, aren't they?"

The first drops of rain pelted down and lightning flashed beneath the heavy, black clouds.

"No, they're not! They're black and grey, and very dangerous, you fool!"

The wind picked up fast and the rain pounded down, each drop a small pebble, piercing down hard on his bare skin. Within seconds, they were soaked, any pretenses to make it home before the brunt of the storm hit vanishing.

He stared at her for a long time and she stared back, her face determined, desperate, and terrified. Unspoken paragraphs exchanged, and he knew her mind was made up. She would try to return home. Although he desperately wanted her to stay, he had no choice but to let her go.

He wrapped his arms around her shivering body while the wind thrashed relentlessly around them. With one arm around her waist, the other protectively around her neck, he pressed her face against his shoulder. "Was it like this?" he yelled into her ear.

"Yes," she replied, her voice barely detectable above the fury ravaging around them.

He let his fingers dive into her hair and their eyes locked.

"I will miss you!" he declared.

Lightning splintered the darkened sky and water gushed down their faces as he lowered his eyes to her trembling lips. Unable to control himself, he lifted her face, and kissed her with barely controlled savagery, unleashing all his pent-up emotions. If she would disappear from his life, and he would never see or hold her again, at least he got to taste her once.

As the raindrops continued their ravage on the earth, he kissed her thoroughly and free from restraint. Each time he withdrew, she pushed back up against him, pressing herself more fully into the warmth of his mouth. When their lips separated so they could breathe, she trembled in his arms. He pressed her face against his neck, kissing her head. His hands slid down her back and curved over her hips. Now he knew what it felt like to be in heaven.

Jagged streaks of lightning struck around them, but they neither flinched nor moved. They stood together as if carved in granite, waiting for what was to come. Each filled with thundering emotions, each with their own wish.

When the heavens parted and a glimmer of sun shone through the dark clouds, they lifted their faces up to the sky, releasing their tight grip.

"Do you think it worked?" he asked. Everything around him still looked the same, but he hadn't expected the dunes, the beach and the ocean ever to change.

"If so, you must have gone with me," she replied, the wind tugging on her skirt, trying to push her over. "Do you think you could handle that?"

He touched her colorless cheek with the back of his finger. "If you could handle my century, then I should be able to handle yours."

"Yeah, right," she replied and grinned, knowing the last four weeks had been close to a catastrophe.

The heavy rain turned into a steady drizzle. Hand in hand, they left the beach, anxious to find out where they had ended up.

Chapter 30

FORREST HAD ENTERED Caroline Rothschild's address into the G.P.S. app on Annet's smartphone. With one eye on the road and the other on the moving dot on the screen, he drove through an unfamiliar part of Heemstead. The wide streets had immaculate sidewalks lined with ornamental cast aluminum street lighting, and sprawling trees. Enormous homes were widespread, mostly hidden behind stone walls, high enclosures, and towering shrubs, oaks, firs, and other foliage. Security cameras were mounted at most entry-gates, and on top of tall wrought iron fences.

Glancing from left to right, he passed one impressive and stunning mansion after the other, still following the G.P.S.'s instructions, until it told him he had reached his destination on his right. He used the turn signal. Driving through a wrought iron gate onto a long drive, he wondered if he was at the right address. The grounds were humongous, the trees gigantic, and from what he could tell, this could be where the President or Bill Gates might live.

The paved driveway curved along an old two-storied coach house. It was slightly dilapidated, the wooden roof shingles green from all the moss, the siding in need of a fresh coat of paint. The first floor was lived in, the second floor boarded up. Unsure if this might be where she lived, he parked and stepped out, the sound of blaring music coming from the apartment throwing him off. Hard-rock was definitely not Caroline's music of choice.

He knocked. When no one answered, he tried the door, opening it far enough to peek inside. It was a warm spring evening, but all the windows were closed and heavily draped. Music blasted from two stacks of speakers on either side of the murky room, two guitars and a drum set standing in the center, along with several microphones on stands. A young guy lay on the couch, his long legs stretched out at their full length. He was bare-chested, and clad in torn faded blue jeans.

"Sorry to bother you," Forrest yelled, trying to make himself heard over the music. "I was looking for Caroline Rothschild?"

The man raised himself, turned down the volume, and walked on bare feet into the tiny kitchen area where he opened a refrigerator and pulled out a bottle of beer. "You want one?" He pried off the top with an opener. The metal cap flew off, landing amongst many others on the torn up brown linoleum floor.

"No, thanks," Forrest replied, pointing toward the instruments. "Do you play in a band?"

The man nodded. "The Dirty Dandies. This is where we practice." He extended his hand and they shook. "I'm Rix, lead vocals and guitar. All we need are some backup vocals and we're complete. Can you sing?"

"Forrest Overton, nice to meet you, Rix. And no I can't sing. I'm actually looking for Caroline. Does she live here?"

Rix took a long swig from his beer and wiped his mouth with the back of his hand. "Caro? No, she's my landlady and lives in the main house. It's hidden behind those tall junipers and firs. Just follow the driveway until the end. You can't miss it."

"Thanks, man," Forrest replied and walked out, the music getting cranked back up the moment he closed the door behind him.

He followed the driveway, soon spotting what had to be the main house. *Holy crap. What was an old lady doing in a gargantuan mansion like that?* It had two stories, two wings, and a huge terrace with pillars. She would be completely lost in it.

He parked his car and hurried up the marble steps onto the promenade. The two front doors stood wide open. "Caroline?" he bellowed, his voice echoing against the walls in the empty hallway. "Are you there?"

He hesitantly crossed the threshold, gaping at the stunning woodwork of the staircase, the molding and the wainscoting, the marble floor and cut-glass chandeliers hanging down from the towering ceiling. Everything had a slight air of neglect, but he could tell by the craftsmanship and the details the house had been spectacular in its heyday.

Footsteps ticked on the marble tiled floor down a corridor to his right. "Forrest, is that you?" She entered the hallway, followed by two identical grey cats, beckoning him to follow her. "You're perfectly on time. Dinner is almost ready."

He followed her down the hallway, the cats regarding him suspiciously.

195

"What are you doing in such a huge house by yourself?" he asked after they entered an oversized sparkling-clean kitchen. It smelled like curry and some kind of cleaner. "It's bigger than the entire White Castle Apartment Complex where we live."

"I know," Caroline admitted wholeheartedly. "I grew up here with my brother Gerry. After I married and moved away, my brother stayed here. Unfortunately, he and his wife Mathilda never had children. After their passing, the whole caboodle landed on my bony shoulders. Did you know this is the original Keizer Estate?"

Forrest shook his head. "I had no idea, but that's very interesting. How many generations of Keizers have lived here?"

"Honestly, I don't know," Caroline replied, turning her attention to the six burner stove. "Since my son took early retirement, he's been working on a family tree. Isn't that exciting?"

She stirred the contents of a small pan. "The rice is done and so is the sauce." She opened the oven and pulled out a shallow baking pan with her mitts. The chicken, smothered in onions, peppers, and carrots was sizzling hot and smelled incredible. She placed the steaming pan on the stove and poured the sauce over it.

"Time to eat," she said, setting the plates on the kitchen table. "I always eat here instead of in the formal dining room. It's warm and comfy. Don't you agree?"

Forrest looked around. "I still can't believe you live in such a huge house all by yourself, Caroline. How can you ever keep up on the maintenance?"

"Don't you worry," Caroline grinned. "I have Rix who keeps an eye on me. He's rented the coach house for about two years now. Nice kid. And the bottom floor of the left wing is rented out to two brothers. They've lived there the last fifteen years. Strange, eccentric men. They never use the kitchen. Just a toaster oven and a microwave they set up in their quarters, and they make espressos. It's one of their hobbies."

"I met Rix," Forrest told her, taking a gulp from his glass of water. "Wow, you make a mean curry, Caroline."

Chapter 31

"I don't think it worked, Amazon," Alex said. "Why?"

He stopped and knelt down. "Because I think we are retracing our own footsteps."

She acknowledged he could be right, but wasn't ready to give up hope. "They don't have a name on them and could be anybody's," she objected.

During the storm, the temperatures had dropped, Alex's shirt too thin to protect her from the wind and the continuous drizzle. Goosebumps covered her legs and arms. They hurried through the dunes until they reached the familiar cabin.

"Damn, you were right. It didn't work," she cried out in frustration.

As soon as they were inside, Alex added firewood to the stove and followed her into the bedroom where he stripped and pulled on dry clothes right in front of her, but she didn't even blink. Something had changed in their relationship and somehow it felt normal.

"Don't just stand there," he told her. "You have to get warm or you'll get sick."

She peeled off the soaked shirt, Alex looking on with interest. "You want me to help?" he offered. The twinkle in his eyes made clear what he had in mind.

"By making me a cup of coffee? That would be great!" she laughed him off, watching him close the door behind him, her smile disappearing.

When they had just met, Alex had been a closed door, and she a ranting obnoxious diva. Gradually their relationship had changed. Doubt, frustration, worry, and suspicion had turned into trust. An easygoing friendship had developed. But now they had kissed, complicating everything. No, taking their relationship to a different level was not an option. Not if she wanted to be able to look Forrest straight in the eyes when she got home.

"I could sure use that hot shower now, Mr. Keizer," she muttered, taking off the rest of her wet clothes. She snuggled into one of Alex's shirts and a pair of wool pants. With a blanket wrapped around her body, she entered the living area and sat down on the couch. Despite the warmth in the room, she still shivered.

Alex was fixing dinner. "I'm baking chicken with grilled onions and squash," he said. "Oh, and there's tea."

"Awesome," she replied. Without energy, she poured herself a cup and migrated to the table.

Alex turned around, her lack of enthusiasm not going unnoticed. "You appear hot and flustered. Does that usually happen after a little cuddle?" he teased, but the concern in his eyes was apparent.

"I'm not hot! I'm freezing," she replied crankily. Her head ached and she was shivering.

"Maybe dinner will make you feel better," he tried to cheer her up and dished up two plates. It smelled delicious, but she wasn't hungry. Instead of eating, she pushed her food around, thinking about the kiss Alex had stolen from her in the brunt of the storm. It had been a tense and dangerous moment, and was understandable under the circumstances. After all, it was intended as a goodbye kiss. What else could she have done but give in.

"About that cuddle," she said. "Is that the way you always say goodbye to your female friends?"

He took hold of her hand, giving her a half-grin. "I wasn't saying goodbye, Amazon." His thumb stroked the top of her hand, his eyes meeting hers with potent intensity. "I was trying to hold on."

His intimate touch sent electric shocks up her arm and she drew her hand away, aware she had let him hold it for far too long.

One moment, all he wants is to be left alone, the next he wants me to stay. No wonder my brain is muddled, she thought. "You're a jerk for sending out such contradictive signals! You know that?"

She loosened the blanket. It felt like the temperature in the room had skyrocketed in the last few minutes, drops of perspiration beading her face.

"I'm glad to see a little color return to your face," he remarked. "But you're not eating. Maybe you should go to bed. It's been a hectic day."

She gave him a dull smile. "Dinner is great, but you're right. It's as if I ran the New York marathon. I'm aching all over my body and feel like crap."

"Marathon? As in the legend of the Greek messenger, who's sent from the battlefield of Marathon to Athens, to announce the outcome of the battle? According to my Greek Mythology book, he ran the entire distance without stopping, and died after his announcement."

"That sounds about right," she replied with a touch of dry humor. "Except that I hope the dying part is not going to happen to me."

She headed toward the bedroom and dove straight under the covers, but sleep eluded her as she tried to come to terms with the disappointment of another lighting failure and the contradictive emotions that had beleaguered her after they had left the beach. Why in the world had he kissed her, making her feel like a wanton? Like the shameless and immoral woman they accused her to be. She could almost feel his lips back on hers. Why was that? She didn't care for him the way she cared for Forrest, her lover, her best friend. But for the first time she realized that if she returned to the twenty-first century, it would also imply she would never see Alex again. Somehow that thought constricted her throat. Damn, her situation was so screwed up!

The next morning, she felt even worse. Her throat hurt, her nose was clogged up. What had started as a light throbbing in her temples had changed into a serious headache. She dragged herself out of bed to use the outhouse, and then joined Alex for a cup of tea and a breadcrumb.

"It's just a cold," she brushed off his concern. "An ibuprofen or two and I will feel much better. Do you have any?" But of course he didn't. He hadn't even heard of aspirin yet.

"Then what do you do to treat a headache?" she asked grumpily, her cold not helping her frame of mind.

"I've heard doctors prescribe laudanum for pain, but other than that, you just have to suffer through it," he told her, his eyes soft with compassion. "Just stay in bed for the day and let me nurse you back to health. I'm very good at that."

After another twenty-four hours her condition had only worsened. Mucus had built up in her nose and sinuses, she coughed continuously and couldn't even force herself out of bed.

Alex became increasingly worried, deciding to get help after she had been in bed for three days without the slightest improvement. Wrapped in blankets, he picked her up and carried her outside.

"What are you doing?" she objected between coughing fits. "Don't you know I'm ill?"

Ignoring her protest, he loaded her on the back of the wagon, stuffing a pillow under her head. Next, he climbed onto the coach box and set the cart in motion.

"Oh, my skull," she moaned between gritted teeth, her nose red, dark circles bruising the skin beneath her eyes. "It's about to explode."

As careful as possible, he made his way onto the Dune Road, passed the Jonkers' farm, and turned into the road to the monastery.

"Where are you taking me?" she whined. "I want to go home! Please, don't do this."

Every other minute, he turned around in his seat, checking to see if she was all right. "You're very sick, Amazon," he told her. "You need to see a doctor."

Two minutes later, she tossed and turned, pushing the blankets away, perspiring heavily. "My lips are dry. I'm so thirsty," she complained. Racked with fever, she tried to push herself up. Alex quickly stopped the cart. With caring hands, he lifted her head in his lap and helped her take a few sips of water from his flask. After settling her back in, he continued the three-mile trip that seemed to take forever. Despite the drop in temperature they had experienced these last several days, his hair and shirt were soaked in perspiration when he pulled up in front of the monastery. "I'll be right back," he told her before he rushed toward the entrance of the chapel. The door was unlocked, and he hurried in, returning a few minutes later followed by two nuns.

One of them touched her burning forehead. "You were right to bring her here, Mr. Keizer. She's very ill. Why don't you carry her inside?"

As if she weighed nothing, he lifted her up and followed the two sisters. It was cool and dark within the thick stone walls of the convent. He adjusted his eyes, Annet moving restlessly in his arms.

"Where are we?" She squinted through watery eyes, protesting weakly when she recognized her surroundings. "You can't bring me here! They hate me!" She squirmed and pushed against his shoulders until he got angry.

"Damn, woman! Do you want to get better or not?"

She slumped back down against his chest, her lungs wheezing, her energy gone.

"We will send someone for the doctor immediately," a nun said, while the other one guided him through a long hallway, into an empty room.

"Just lay her down on the bed," she told him, immediately scooting him out of the door after Annet was safely tucked in.

"But I want to stay with her," he protested.

"Absolutely not," the nun refused. "You're an unmarried man, and this is a nunnery."

They cooled her down with wet sheets, forced her to drink water, and did whatever they could to make her as comfortable as possible. A nun kept watch on her bedside as she battled her fever in an almost comatose state.

The doctor gave her a bitter tasting reddish-brown medicine, called laudanum. It was an analgesic and cough suppressant, keeping her so relaxed that in an occasional waking moment, she wondered what kind of potent narcotic the alcoholic herbal preparation contained. It gave her vivid hallucinations and concerns over her baby's wellbeing troubled her.

After three days, her fever broke. She refused the spoon full of laudanum; she wasn't taking more of that hallucinogenic medicine. Her unborn child had had enough to endure.

"So doc," she asked the physician when he came to see her. "Did I have a bad case of the flu, or was it something else?"

"Looking at your symptoms, I believe you had pneumonia," he told her. "That's a very dangerous lung illness. Many people die from it. Fortunately, you were in good health. I believe neither you nor the baby will have any long-term complications because of it."

It took two more days for her spirit to revive and to have enough energy to waddle around the room, supported by Sister Rudolpha.

"It feels like I have risen from the dead," she told her as she carefully placed one foot in front of the next.

Rudolpha crossed herself and kissed the small crucifix that dangled on her rosary, her cheeks flushed.

"I didn't mean to make a comparison with Jesus Christ," Annet apologized demurely. Rudolpha had been watching over her every day, nursing her back to health with affable attention and utmost dedication. The last thing she wanted was to offend her in any way.

"At least it proves your spirit is unbroken and you are convalescing well," the young nun said, puffing up her pillow and helping her back into bed.

This last week had been traumatizing as she had fought for her life, her fever-racked body shaking with teeth-chattering chills, her oxygen deprived lungs coughing up green mucus. If it hadn't been for the compassion and care she had received, she probably would have died.

"You're an excellent nurse, Rudolpha. I want to thank you for everything you've done for me." Her illness had jumbled her emotions, making her realize how vulnerable life was. She could have been gone, unable to see Alex or Forrest ever again. That was a very scary thought.

Chapter 32

The next morning Annet felt strong enough to join the sisters for breakfast in the refectory. They greeted her like a long-lost friend, their kindness unexpected, and when Mother Superior expressed her delight over her swift recovery she became a blubbering mess.

Jeez, ever since I got pregnant, I'm such an emotional sap. It was time her hormones settled down and she became her old self again. She was getting sick of herself.

After breakfast, Sister Rudolpha assisted her back to her room. The trivial physical exertion had wiped her out. It wasn't until the afternoon that she was energized enough to get out of bed again.

A nun brought her a blue cotton calico dress with coat sleeves, a white collar and white cuffs. It was much better than the brown one, the material soft, and comfortable. It almost reached to her ankles, but had belonged to a heavyset woman.

She would have drowned in it, if it wasn't for her prego belly. She was almost in her third trimester, her baby noticeably stirring inside, making its presence known.

"Hello baby, how are you doing today?" she whispered, massaging her stomach. "What do you think of this environment? It could use more color and a fresh coat of paint, don't you agree? And carpet on the floor wouldn't hurt either."

When she was dressed, she roamed around the hallway and proceeded into the peaceful courtyard. It had rained earlier in the day, everything still wet. The early autumn air was cool and fresh, the scents from the garden tweaking her nose. Two sisters were busy weeding the vegetable garden, another one collecting the last ripe tomatoes of the season in a wicker basket. A small statue of Mother Mary stood between rows of hedges, guarding the harvest.

"Those tomatoes look delicious," she commented, watching the nuns work for a while until a coughing fit immobilized her. Her lungs wheezed a high-pitched raspy sound. She sunk down on a concrete bench at the far end of the garden until her cough subsided. It might still take days, or weeks, to fully recover, but she was grateful to be out of the confinements of her room. She was experiencing cabin fever, ready to leave the convent and go home. At this point it didn't matter if that was Alex's cabin or her White Castle Apartment.

The three hard working nuns disappeared and she sat by herself, enjoying the quiet serenity of her surroundings, thinking about her time-travel problems and Alex. They had informed her he had stopped by every day, begging to see her. Except for the doctor and the priest, the dorms were strictly forbidden for men. Consequently, they had denied him access to her room. She hadn't seen him for more than a week and missed him. He was the only connection to her former life. The only one she

could talk to without telling white lies, so when she heard
footsteps approaching and realized it was him, she jumped up
and rushed into his arms. "Alex!" She threw her arms around his
neck and began to cry, again. "I'm so happy to see you!"

He pulled her close against him, letting her weep into the
shoulder of his chocolate colored work shirt, his strong hands
comfortingly stroking her back. They stood that way for several
minutes until he pushed her away.

"I was so horribly ill and convinced I would die," she
sniffled. With one hand she clung to the lapel of his shirt,
touching the side of his face with the other, her fingertips
trailing over his afternoon stubble. "I was terrified and wished
they hadn't been so prudish about not allowing you to see me."

Her lungs wheezed noticeably and she coughed to clear her
throat.

Alarmed, Alex forced her back down on the concrete
bench. "Now don't overextend yourself Amazon," he warned,
concern on his face.

"I don't want to sit down," she protested, reaching out to
him. "I feel strong enough to go home now, with you."

He sat down next to her, ignoring her extended hand.
"Well, about that, ..." With a straight back, he stared out in
front of him, his hands on his knees, making sure their bodies
didn't touch.

"Why are you suddenly so stand-offish?" she asked,
noticing his aloofness. "They can't force me to stay here, if
that's what you're worried about."

A fly buzzed around his head and he chased it away,
avoiding her gaze.

"What's going on?" she cried out, taking hold of his arm
and shaking it. "Are you holding something from me?"

He slowly turned toward her, his gaze boring into her. "Are you aware of the fact that everybody knows you're pregnant?"

She shrugged indifferently. "Who cares?"

"This is the nineteenth century, Amazon," Alex sighed. "Where people condemn sexual immorality. I know you're very well aware of that."

"Oh, come on, Alex," she replied impatiently, letting go of his arm. "Do you think I'm worried about what they think of me? That I care about my reputation?"

"Do you ever think about anyone else but yourself?" he lashed out, stiffening noticeably. "How about *my* reputation, living with an unmarried pregnant woman. Or more importantly, do you ever think of your unborn child? What it will be like, to be raised as a bastard?" He stood up and paced back and forth in front of her, his face like a thundercloud. "The Bible says no one born of a forbidden marriage, nor any of their descendants, may enter the assembly of the Lord. There are priests who refuse to baptize out-of-wedlock children. You can't do that to your child!"

She gaped at him. "But I won't be here anymore when my child is born. So why would I worry about that?"

He stepped in front of her, his eyes blazing. "How do you know that?"

"I won't have my baby here!" she cried out, stubbornly trying to hold on to the conviction that three months was a long time and anything could happen. For example the miraculous appearance of a space ship. Or simply waking up in her own bed, finding out it had all been a dream. "I need Lamaze classes and a sterile delivery room in the hospital. What if I need a cesarean section or an epidural? No way will I give birth here!"

"You may not have a choice!" Alex said, still pacing over the gravel path, his brow furrowed.

In the long heavy silence that followed, only her labored breathing, and the sounds of nature could be heard. They were left undisturbed until two nuns walked by, looking at them curiously.

Annet coughed to clear her airways, her face deadly pale. "What are you suggesting I should do?"

He stared down at her, with his legs set apart, his arms folded across his chest. "It's simple. You'll have to marry me."

She laughed tiredly. "Marry you? Why?"

He reached out and lifted her chin, forcing her to look him straight in the eyes. "I can't bring you back to the cabin and let you live with me without us being married. Too many people know about your circumstances."

"Okay, I get that people around here are old-fashioned prudes, but it still doesn't explain why you would sacrifice yourself by marrying me."

He sat down next to her, draping his arm around her shoulders, pulling her close. "I care about you, Amazon. More than I should. You know that."

She exhaled a shuddering sigh and rested her head for a brief moment against his shoulder. "I care about you too, but I still think it's ludicrous and can't accept your offer." Resolute, she freed herself and got up. The world spun around her, almost making her lose her balance.

Alex rushed to her side, steadying her.

"Sorry," she excused herself, irritated with her own weakness. "This horrible illness gave me a beating."

He supported her through the garden toward the monastery. Before he opened the door he turned her toward him. With his hands on her shoulders, his breathing noticeably shallow, he stood, opening his mouth, then closing it again. She could tell from the way he tried to gather his words that what he was about to say was important.

"If you don't want to marry me, this is goodbye, Amazon."

"Oh Alex," she sighed exasperatedly. "I'm involved with Forrest. He's the father of my child and I can't let you take on that responsibility."

A look of discontent appeared on his face, his body stiffly looking as he dropped his hands.

"It wouldn't be fair to you," she continued, trying to make him understand. "Besides, suppose I figure out how to get back, I wouldn't be able to marry him since I'm married to you. That would be so screwed up! You get it?"

"You're not thinking this through," he said. "When you return to the future, I will be dead."

She gave him a blank stare and his stance softened. "Just think about it. I will come back tomorrow for your definite answer." He opened the door, nudged her inside, and left.

Chapter 33

Annet's skin felt hot and clammy as she huddled around for most of the night, her thoughts chaotic. Damn, why wasn't she stranded in the future, where people flew around with their personal flying mobiles, where robots did the work and computers all the thinking? A time where people would be open-minded, and tolerant.

No, instead she had to land in a time where the only form of transportation was a horse or a carriage, where women had to obey their husbands, where people were antiquated in their thinking and straitlaced. Damn, she wasn't willing to trade in her career for the kitchen. She loved her job and her independence, and getting married had never been part of her plans. Not even when she was a little girl, pretending her dolls traveled the world in a camper. With Ken and Barbie taking turns behind the wheel, towing their pink Cadillac behind it. As a teenager, the idea of being together with the same man for an entire lifetime seemed terribly boring. Then, after meeting Forrest, she had learned the value and importance of companionship and friendship, but she still had taken their relationship one day at the time. People changed. People fooled around. People disappeared out of your life.

At last, she heard several nuns passing by her bedroom. She followed them into the refectory. Until the sun crept up, she sat quietly at one of the long wooden tables, turning everything over in her mind as she had done a million times during the night, her nerves stretched and frazzled, her gut tightened in trepidation.

Marrying Alex Keizer was the easiest solution. He was a righteous, dependable man, generously willing to offer her a home, the protection of his name. Besides that, he was undeniably deliciously attractive, his sex appeal irrefutable. And that was the problem. After their passionate kiss during the thunderstorm she hadn't stopped thinking about how his lips had felt on hers. How they had stirred her insides, her passionate reaction taking her completely by surprise. There was no denying it. She was attracted to him, the idea of sharing his bed stirring up disturbing sensual desires. If she married him, she would step into a danger zone, a minefield, the consequences for her heart and soul too disturbing.

No, she couldn't marry him. She would get too involved, her feelings undermining the resolve to return to where she belonged. Besides, she didn't need him. She knew how to take care of herself. She always had.

Annet ate a few breadcrumbs and returned to her room hoping sleep wouldn't elude her any longer since she had made her decision, but the anxiety about his impending visit kept her awake. What was she going to tell him? How was she going to explain her reasoning?

After tossing and turning for several more hours on her bumpy cot, she got up and headed back to the courtyard. Maybe fresh air would clear up her headache and the cobwebs, but there was a chill in the air that hadn't been there yesterday. Autumn was definitely upon them. The same two nuns from the day before were cleaning out the garden, all the vegetables picked.

"It seems you're making the garden winter ready," she commented.

They looked at her with concern. "It's too cold for you to be outside, Miss Annet," one of them told her. "You have to go back inside."

"You're right," she admitted, shivering in her dress, "but I was restless and needed fresh air."

"We just saw Mr. Keizer pull up with his wagon. He's talking to Mother Superior."

"He is?" Deciding to get it over with, she turned around, intending to find him the moment he entered the courtyard from the hallway leading to the chapel. She had been in there before, seeking desperately needed solace, the plastered ceiling with Gothic patterns, the tessellated tiles on the floor, and colorful stained glass windows making it a true sanctuary. Candles burned in front of another statue of Mother Mary, tenderly looking down at baby Jesus in her arms. It had warmed her heart. Soon, she would be a mother too.

"They told me you were here," Alex said, taking her by the arm and pulling her toward the door. "You shouldn't be outside in these low temperatures without a coat, bonnet or shawl."

She yanked her arm free. "You can't boss me around!"

Gaunt, and with dark circles under her eyes, she placed her hands on her hips, trying to make a stand, but she failed miserably. She looked like the tiniest breeze could blow her over.

His eyes softened. "Since you don't seem to take care of yourself, maybe I should," he said, chuckling. He opened his cloak and wrapped it around her, pulling her close against his warm body.

At his smile, her stomach made a strange little flip-flop, and with tired, worn-out eyes, she placed her palms on his chest. "I haven't been able to sleep all night."

"I can tell. You look abominable and have lost weight."

"Thanks. That's just what I wanted to hear," she sighed, instigating another coughing fit.

He held on to her until her coughing subsided, his hands massaging the tense muscles in her neck and back, her body coming alive under his soothing hands. OMG, his touch was magical.

"Why are you so good to me?" she moaned. A soft yearning sound escaped from her throat as he lowered his face close to hers. When his lips brushed over hers, pyrotechnics ignited within her.

"I love you, Amazon," he sighed against her mouth.

"You do?" she stammered. Hissing soft swearwords of pointless protest she burrowed her fingers in his hair, melting in his embrace.

In answer he took another kiss, then another one, a deeper one. By the time the lengthy kiss ended, her body was weak and fluttery with longing.

"Mr. Keizer!" a stern voice interrupted them.

They looked up and saw Mother Superior, her face frozen in a look of disapproval. "In case you forgot, you're in a convent where the inhabitants took vows of poverty, obedience, and chastity."

"I'm sorry, Mother. It won't happen again," Alex grinned sheepishly, and continued. "Is everything arranged?"

"Yes," the stern nun replied. "Father Castricum is taking confessions. He'll be ready in about an hour."

"Ready for what?" Annet asked.

"To take your wedding vows, of course," Mother Superior said before leaving them.

"He what?" she replied stupefied, turning to Alex. "But I decided I *don't* want to marry you."

"Maybe you did," Alex said, guiding her through the door, into the hallway. "But I believe you have changed your mind."

"No, I haven't," she objected. "What gave you that idea?"

"You did of course," he continued, his eyes daring her to contradict him. "Because it's obvious you're as attracted to me as I am to you."

Her eyes darted around through the empty hall toward the doors of the chapel. "Don't you think we should talk about this a little more," she said panicky, struggling to impose order on her confused thoughts. "I don't know anything about weddings and don't even have a dress."

"Russell and Amelia Jonkers are on their way. They are bringing you a dress..." He stopped in mid-sentence, hitting himself against his forehead. "Oh, I forgot to tell you. Scott and Trudy can't attend the ceremony because Trudy just gave birth to a healthy nine pound baby boy."

"That's wonderful," Annet replied, "but I don't want you to change the subject." She locked gazes with him. "You're telling me that within the hour, a priest is going to marry us here in the chapel." *This was ridiculous.* "You know I'm not religious, and who knows what they'll make me promise? I can't do that!"

He took her hands. "All we will promise is to love, comfort, honor, and keep each other, in sickness and in health, and that we will forsake all others for as long as we both shall live. That won't be so hard, will it?"

They heard voices and soon were surrounded by the Jonkers and a group of nuns chattering with excitement. Annet was stupefied and stared around.

Sister Rudolpha was amongst the nuns and approached her. "Mr. Keizer asked Mother Superior for a witness on your behalf. She suggested I should do it. Does that comply with your wishes?"

"Of course, Rudolpha," Annet replied with an apprehensive smile, "I couldn't ask for a better witness."

They were interrupted by a bright-smiling Amelia Jonkers.

"Alex sent me to a tailor in Heemstead for a wedding dress," she said, a long crème colored cotton gown hanging over her arm. "I guessed your measurements and hope it fits."

"I'll help you get dressed," Sister Rudolpha offered, taking the dress from Amelia. "Shall we go?"

Feeling she was brainwashed, making a colossal mistake, she followed Rudolpha.

Half an hour later, Annet walked toward the chapel in her simple but elegant wedding gown. The embroidered bodice sat high above her waist, her floor-length skirt wide and layered. She was confident nobody could tell she was six months pregnant.

Rudolpha helped her get dressed, brushing her long blonde hair until it shined and pinning it up, leaving a few strands hanging loosely around her face. She had also picked a handful of wildflowers that grew around the building, binding them together in a small colorful bouquet. All in all, Annet felt like a real bride; panicky and excited at the same time.

Almost too nervous to take another step, she stopped on the threshold of the chapel. Bright sunlight filtered in through the colored stain glass window panes, the rows of flickering candles providing a joyous and spiritual picture. The wooden pews, arranged in rows facing the altar, were filled with whispering nuns, waiting in anticipation. In front of the white marble altar, Alex waited for her, flanked by Russell Jonkers. She barely recognized him in his formal black waistcoat, grey striped trousers, and starched shirt, his hair combed down with grease. He reminded her of an undertaker, and she had trouble keeping a straight face.

Amelia Jonkers joined her. "Are you ready?"

The nun behind the organ started to play and all nuns rose, joining in a hymn. The priest stood behind the altar, wearing a black robe with a long white stole.

Overwhelmed by the entire setting, she walked down the aisle. Was this for real? Was she actually getting married? Her eyes flitted from left to right until they landed on Alex. Unlike her, he seemed at ease with the situation. A triumphant smile curved his mouth and she wanted to smack him.

The hymn ended and Father Castricum made the sign of the cross over the entire congregation. "In the name of the Father, the Son, and of the Holy Spirit."

"Amen," everyone mumbled.

At first, Annet listened to the unfamiliar rites and verses, but bemused by the rapid and dramatic changes in her life, her mind began to wander. She had come close to dying from a lightning flash, dehydration, and pneumonia in a few short months. Now, here she was, getting married to Alex Keizer, a person who had been important in her life as a historic figure, as the master painter who created magnificent pieces of art. Her heart constricted a degree tighter as she tried to make sense of it all, vaguely hearing Alex taking his vows.

The priest turned toward her. "Annet Sherman, will you obey him, and serve him, love, honor, and keep him, in sickness and in health?"

What? Did she hear that right? *Obey? Serve?* Wait a minute! Had he asked Alex the same questions or was that submissive baloney just for her? Alert and distrustful, she spun toward Alex and yanked his arm. "What's all that about?" she hissed.

With a tender, dreamy smile around his mouth, he looked down at her, his eyes radiating love. "Don't worry. I love you, and everything will be fine," he whispered.

In a trance, her mouth formed the words, "Yes, I do."

Alex bowed his head, her lips awaiting his kiss, but before they touched, she whispered, "You can forget about that obedient baloney, buddy!"

"A promise is a promise," he replied against her mouth, the tip of his tongue tracing the soft fullness of her bottom lip, his arm strong around her waist.

A warm, heady sensation spread through her body, but when their lips parted, he gave her another triumphant smile. In an exasperated reply she clutched his wrist and pressed her fingernails hard in his skin. "We'll see about that!"

"You little witch," he grinned, rubbing the moon shaped indentations she had left.

Chapter 34

Annet fell asleep on the way to the cabin. After they arrived, he lifted her off the coach box and carried her over the threshold.

"Even though you're pregnant, you weigh less than a bag of potatoes," he remarked.

She wrapped her arms around his neck, nuzzling into him with her nose pressed to his neck. "I know. Kate Moss and Claudia Schiffer can be jealous of my figure."

"Friends of yours?" he asked.

She chuckled. "They wish."

He lay her down on the bed and pulled the covers over her. "Sleep," he told her. "You need it."

"Oh, did the bossing around already begin?"

He smiled down at her before leaving the bedroom. The moment he closed the door behind him, she was already gone.

When she woke up, it was early in the morning, the sun just coming up. She left the bedroom and found Alex sleeping on the couch underneath a throw. His hair hanging loose around his face, his handsome features relaxed.

After using the outhouse, she searched for a piece of bread and sat down at the kitchen table, watching him as it slowly got lighter in the house. *How bizarre. I'm married, and the man, snoring softly on the couch, is my husband.*

Alex turned around in his sleep, exposing his chest, and one bare leg. She took every inch of him in, admiring his broad shoulders, strong arms, and muscular legs until her skin burned, a yearning ache developing between her legs. She shifted in her chair, the wooden legs of her chair squeaking faintly, but he had heard it. He opened one eye, then another, a sleepy grin appearing on his face when their eyes met.

"How long have you been sitting there?" he asked, pushing himself up. The throw almost fell off the couch, exposing a naked well-shaped thigh. Without modesty, he tapped the seat next to him. "Come over here. You're so far away."

She got up, her clothes wrinkled, her hair a tangled mess.

"You're still wearing your wedding dress?" he commented, extending his hand. The second she took it, he pulled her onto his lap.

"Hey, what are you doing?" she protested meekly.

Emotion darkened his eyes and his arms twined around her, pulling her head down. "Before our wedding night is over, the least I want from you is a kiss," he said, rubbing his lips over hers, the tip of his tongue teasing.

She brushed a strand of hair from his forehead and smiled, "I'm okay with that."

He gave her a long and deep look before his mouth covered hers, his tongue slipping between her lips, tenderly probing, tasting, exploring. Her body began to tingle.

"I'm trying to seduce you. Am I succeeding?" he sighed in a strangled voice, giving her the chance to pull away, but instead, she moved closer into his arms.

This was exactly what she needed, a lot of tender loving care. "Yes, it is, and you better stop talking before I change my mind," she replied, forcing every memory of Forrest to the back of her mind.

He laughed with a low, contented rumble, his fingers struggling with the laces of her bodice, before impatiently pulling the piece of clothing over her head and discarding it on the floor. With their lips fused in a deep and passionate kiss, he pushed his hand inside her shift and placed it on her breast.

She gasped into his mouth, burrowing her fingers in his shoulder blades. She had never been more aware of her own body. How did he do that with just one touch? "I want you," she sighed, kissing him zealously in search of his mouth.

"You're sure?" he asked, giving her one more chance to draw away. "Because I can never let you go once I've made you mine. Do you realize that?" He eased her down on the couch, the throw falling to the ground.

In answer, she raised her hips so he could pull her shift away, her whole body aching and pounding. "Yes, I'm damned sure," she breathed, "This is exactly what I want."

"That was unbelievable," she told him as they lay intertwined on the couch, both spent and exhausted from their lovemaking. He had awakened a ferocious sensuality in her she had never known existed. She stifled a moan of pure animal pleasure when his hands closed possessively around her bottom, pushing her against his groin.

"I was almost dying of wanting you, and hope I wasn't too rough," he admitted with unbridled exhilaration.

"You were perfect," she whispered in his neck, wantonly rubbing her breasts against the dark hair covering his chest. "If you're not too tired, do you think we can do this again?"

They made love for the second time, slow, and intense. Afterwards they fell asleep in each other's arms. When she woke up, with her head on his chest, sun poured in through the windows, tiny specks of dust dancing around in the bright beams.

Alex kissed her hair and placed his mouth against her ear, "I have a wedding gift for you. Do you want to see it?"

She chuckled. "I have seen it, and loved it."

"No, this time I mean something else," he grinned, getting up and taking her hand.

"Outside?" she protested when he pulled her toward the door and opened it. "But I'm naked."

"As you should be," he replied.

She playfully tried to smack him on his bare behind when she followed him outside.

"I built something," he said, pointing towards a second structure next to the privy, with a wooden rain barrel mounted on top. He opened the door and she looked inside. It was empty, except for a weird piece of sewn leather extending down from the ceiling, a metal clamp at the bottom.

"Come on, get in," he said, pushing her inside and stepping in next to her. "I built you a shower." He raised his arms, removed the metal clamp, a gush of lukewarm water flowing on top of her head and down her body.

A warm glow of gratitude and love bubbled up inside her. "I can't believe it," she cried out, throwing her arms around his neck. They stood together enjoying the feel of each other's naked body, and the sensation of his first, and her sorely missed shower. "This is heaven."

Alex picked up a bar of green soap from a wooden shelf he had mounted in a corner, and washed her shoulders and back. They took turns with the soap, their bodies soon reawaking.

"You woke an insatiable appetite inside me, do you know that?" he confessed, entering her swiftly.

They moved in union in the confinements of the shack. Lifted on the wings of their passion, they soared for the third time.

"I couldn't ask for a better honeymoon," Annet commented days later.

They were lying on the couch, Alex's hand on top of her belly, the baby moving inside.

"I believe it's time to visit a doctor," he said. "The baby is kicking stronger every day. It's telling us it wants to be born soon."

"I have at least ten more weeks," she replied, stretching lazily. "It's weird. I was originally due around the middle of October, but according to the time here, the baby could very well be born on my own birthday in January. Isn't that crazy?"

"It will actually be October the fifteenth tomorrow," he replied, getting up from the couch. "Soon the rains will come and it will be too cold to stay in the cabin."

She shot up. "Too cold to live here? What do you mean?"

"The cabin is merely a summer retreat, Amazon," he explained, picking up his shirt from the floor. "We can't stay here when the weather turns."

She was horrified. "What are you talking about?"

"We have been fortunate with the mild weather, but it won't be long before storms roll in, and winter will be here in earnest. You know that."

"But where will we go?" she cried out.

"To my father's house, in Heemstead. I want to start preparing for our departure no later than tomorrow."

"No way," she replied, crossing her arms in front of her chest in a stubborn gesture. "I won't live in the city with your father, and arrogant ass of a brother. Besides, I'm still waiting for the perfect storm to transport me back."

Alex stared at her, a frown between his brows. "You can't keep on running into the dunes the second you hear a thunderstorm roll in. Next time it might kill you."

She scoffed. "I'll just buy an umbrella, and a waterproof slicker." Chewing a fingernail, she lowered her head, pouting.

"You don't want your baby to be born here," Alex told her. "The closest doctor is miles away, and he's gone visiting patients most of the time. We can't take the chance of delivering the baby without medical help."

"But how about your family? They don't want me there! Besides ..." She glared at him. "Do they even know about our marriage?"

The tension between them mounted.

"I talked to my father when I picked up my suit," Alex said. "He promised to prepare my quarters for my bride and the baby. They're expecting us."

"Your own quarters?" she asked, hoping he was telling the truth, because the last thing she wanted was to run into his dear brother at every turn she took.

Alex finished getting dressed. "I want you and the baby to be safe," he said, his tone making it clear arguing was useless.

"Oh, all right," she replied crossly, recognizing winters in Dunedam were harsh, with violent storms passing through, and temperatures often dropping far below freezing. Living in a cabin without insulation, power, or running water would be difficult, and although she didn't mind a little cold and a few minor inconveniences, she wasn't a survivalist by any means. Her nineteenth century adjustments were already stretching her limit. "But what about your paintings? We can't leave those here!"

He smirked. "I'm not taking those. They're worthless."

"Oh, so you still don't believe me, Mister Alex Keizer, Master Painter," she said in an exaggerated tone.

"No, I don't. But since you're so concerned about them, I'll store them in the cellar."

"Absolutely not!" she countered. "They're coming with us! All of them!"

Chapter 35

AFTER THEY FINISHED DINNER, Forrest helped with the dishes and got ready to leave. It was eight and he figured Caroline would want to retire soon.

"How are you holding up?" Caroline asked as she walked him out.

"Depressed. Heartsick. Lonely. That's about the extent of it," he sighed with a heavy heart. "And when I get home, I have to deal with Annet's mother Barbara and her latest partner, Chuck. Those two practically live on the couch, littering it with food crumbs, empty wrappers, and other trash. Then they expect me to sleep there. I can't stand it." As soon as he had vented his frustration, he regretted it. "Sorry, Caroline, I didn't want to burden you with my problems." He shoved the blond curls off his forehead with aggravated fingers.

Caroline took him by the arm. "Come, let's walk over the grounds, so you can tell me all about it."

The sun was about to set when they strolled down a narrow flagstone walkway. Arm in arm, they passed an empty fountain and walked further down through what could have been a rose garden.

"Annet was raised by her mother and lived here in Heemstead," he said after they had walked for another few minutes. "When she was sixteen, her mother married for the third time, and they moved to Dunedam. I met her in high school." He grinned at the memory. "She was wearing cargo pants, an oversized denim man's shirt, and black army boots, her long blonde hair pinned up, and hidden underneath a worn baseball cap. I was late, the only available seat in class next to hers, but I hesitated to sit down. Her blue eyes stared at me so ominously."

"You were afraid of her?" Caroline laughed.

"Oh, yes I was," he admitted. "Her clothes were all oversized. I didn't even know if she was a boy or a girl. She freaked me out."

Caroline chuckled. "I have a hard time believing that."

They left the rose garden, continuing their evening stroll through the dense trees and shrubs that tried to overgrow the mossed-over walkway.

"I dropped my backpack next to my seat and tripped when I sat down. The chair tumbled over and I landed on the floor. She laughed so hard! Of course I was pissed, and embarrassed, but when she helped me up, I noticed concern in her eyes. From that moment on, we were inseparable, and I miss her so much. What in the world could have happened to her and my baby? " His voice broke, and Caroline squeezed his arm.

"Now tell me about her mother," she encouraged him.

Forrest told her about Barbara and Chuck, how they had taken over his apartment, creating a mess, until they made it back to where his car was parked.

"Maybe you should spend the night in one of the guestrooms instead of going home," Caroline suggested.

Forrest shook his head. "That's kind of you, but I can't do that."

"Nonsense," Caroline reasoned. "You know I have plenty of space in the house. It would be a pleasure to have you here." She stifled a yawn. "Come back inside. I'll give you clean sheets and a towel. Several of the rooms upstairs have beds and adjacent bathrooms. Just pick out the one you like best."

After wishing his host a good night, Forrest climbed the stairs. When he reached the top, his gaze swept the wrought iron banister, the hardwood parquet, the wainscoting, and the long hallways to either side of him. The place reeked of serious old money.

Not knowing why, he decided on the left wing and opened the first door which proved to be the biggest walk-in closet he had ever seen. The second door opened to an enormous master bedroom with a four-poster canopied bed. It looked handmade with carved figures on the posts and enormous bulbous legs. He tried to imagine how it might have looked like back in the day, with heavy fabric hanging down on both sides, creating a private hideout.

Feeling out of place, he sat on the side of the bed, rubbing his forehead. The headache that had been brewing for hours had leaped into full, vicious life, all the stress and sleepless nights catching up on him. Listlessly, he unfolded the blanket Caroline had given him, and sank down onto the pillow. Without undressing he closed his eyes.

The next morning, his headache was almost gone and he felt revived. Longing for a shower and a toothbrush, he went in search of Caroline, finding her in the kitchen where she flipped through a magazine, a cup of coffee in her hand.

"Good morning, my dear. Did you sleep well?" she asked.

"I did," he answered, realizing he had slept dreamless throughout the entire night. "I feel restored and ready to take on another day."

"That's wonderful," she smiled. "Do you care for coffee? I made a full pot."

Self-conscious about his appearance, he poured himself a cup. "It's already eight-thirty and I promised Dan I would be at the Manor around ten this morning. I hope you don't think it's rude of me to rush out of here, but before I can show my face I have to stop by my house and clean up."

"Don't be late on my account," she assured him. "Just remember you're more than welcome to come back. This house gets awfully lonely sometimes."

"I might hold you to that," he replied, blowing her a kiss when he walked out of the kitchen.

Chapter 36

The dreaded day of their departure approached far too soon, but she knew Alex was right when the first fall storm passed through. Temperatures dropped, the cabin creaking and groaning beneath the violent gusts, wind blowing in through the cracks between the wall boards.

After the cabin was cleaned up, and everything secured or loaded up on Alex's cart, they made their way out, stopping at the Jonkers' farm for a short visit. Trudy and Scott had named their baby boy Russell Junior, after his grandfather. Annet peered down into his crib. He was so small, his baby hands clenched in tiny fists, his cheeks rosy. Her own pregnancy had become very real, her baby fluttering inside, her stomach growing, her skin stretching.

With a heavy heart, Annet said goodbye to Trudy, and they drove off in the direction of Heemstead. Every time the wagon jolted, she glanced over her shoulder at Alex's paintings in the back.

"Don't worry, I'll be careful," he said. "I know I'm transporting a very valuable load."

She knew he wasn't talking about his paintings.

They drove further down the Dune Road, one of Alex's hands on the reins, the other resting intimately on her leg. The weather had cleared, the sun was out, and a mild breeze moved the air. The emptiness of the landscape caused her heart to cringe. She was homesick. Maybe it wouldn't be so bad going to Heemstead. At least there would be noise around her, and hopefully people who would be able to help her find her way back.

They entered Dunedam, and stopped at the pump, letting the horse rest and drink water. When they continued their journey, her nerves flared, thinking about what it would be like in his father's house.

"Everyone will look upon you with respect," Alex said, reading her mind. "My name will protect you."

Annet raised her eyebrows. "What are you talking about? You're not famous yet."

"My family is wealthy, Amazon," Alex replied.

"Wealthy? Like Bill Gates or Jack Ma? Or maybe more like middle class rich?"

"I don't know those people, but the Keizer family is one of the richest in the county," Alex said. "My grandfather, on my mother's side, invested in a merchant ship, and began importing cotton, spices, tea and much more from India, and China. Soon after, he expanded his trading business into new territories like the Caribbean Islands, and Australia, investing in two more vessels and real estate. My father's family owned a textile manufacturing and trade company. They bought imported cotton and silk, and sold textiles made with wool." He paused for a brief second. "Both sides of my family moved in the same circles, doing business together, hence the marriage between my parents."

Annet placed a caring hand on his arm as he talked about his late mother.

"Right now, my father is mainly concerned with the merchant side of the business, while Leo stepped into the textile manufacturing, furthering my grandfather's endeavor."

They passed several farms and unassuming homes. Alex nodded at the people walking along the side of the road or working the land. A carriage pulled onto the road behind them, and two other horse drawn carts came from the opposite direction as they approached Heemstead.

"My grandfather started the change from manual labor, draft animals, and water wheels into steam engines and machine-based manufacturing with the use of coal. I don't know if this is the right development, but I believe it can't be stopped."

"No, it can't be stopped," Annet told him. "It's what will be called the Industrial Revolution, a very important period in the history of humanity."

"So, do you think this is progress?" he asked.

She thought for a moment. "It will bring technological, and economic progress if that's what you mean."

Supporting her stomach against unexpected jolts, she looked around, but as they drove further into the city her initial curiosity changed into shock and dismay. People, children even, dressed in rags, lay down in gutters or hung against rundown buildings in dilapidated side streets and alleys. The horrible, overwhelming stench of human waste, horse manure, rotting garbage, and dead animals made her sick to her stomach. She had never seen such human misery and wretchedness before. "Do you see those poor children with bare feet running around in filth?" she cried out in shock, her heart aching at their misery. "I've never seen such a slum! What the hell is going on around here?"

"Heemstead is a dynamic city, full of opportunity," Alex replied, his features drawn. "Dramatic growth has also resulted in the disquieting aspects of current urban life. Housing is in short supply, space becoming increasingly valuable, and public hygiene deteriorates. That's why I was wondering about the progress we talked about earlier."

A horse-drawn omnibus full of people came from the opposite direction.

"Those are the city's workers. The lucky ones," Alex commented grimly. "They're clerks, teachers, nurses, dockworkers, builders, chimney sweeps, messengers, and coachmen; but the growth of the vast slums in this part of the city has been horrendous."

"Why doesn't anyone do anything about those poor people? Why don't they clean up the streets? All that filth and litter is a health hazard, and will cause diseases."

"We've had several outbreaks of cholera in the city," he said. "Do you think that has anything to do with this?"

"Of course," she cried out. "It's an infection of the small intestine that's transmitted by either contaminated food or water."

He looked at her with hope in his eyes. "Maybe that's why you were sent here. To educate the people!"

They left the depressing underprivileged neighborhood and drove through wider streets, lined with sprawling trees. They were at the full height of their autumn glory, their colors gold, orange and fiery red. Stately homes were partially hidden behind stone walls and ornate gateways.

Their cart stopped in front of a wrought iron gate between two towering pillars. Alex pushed them open and they drove onto a pebble-stone driveway, winding through a lush garden. The landscaping was formally designed, with spiraling gravel pathways bordered by decorative green grass, manicured lawns, a fountain, ornamental vases, statues and urns.

He stopped in front of a coach house, the size of a villa. Jason, the coachman, appeared, followed by a young stable hand.

"Welcome home, Mr. Keizer," Jason said, taking the horse by its reins, rubbing and scratching its neck.

"Hello Jason, good to see you," Alex said, jumping off the box before helping Annet down. "Will you take care of our belongings?"

"Of course," Jason bowed. "We will bring them to your quarters."

"Be very careful with those paintings," Annet warned him. "They're extremely valuable."

Alex took her hand, steering her to the grand mansion. It had two stories and two wings, with a colonnade supported by six columns, reminding her of Greek architecture and the White House in Washington D.C.

From the red brick walkway, they stepped onto the white marble terrace.

"You weren't kidding when you said your family is loaded," Annet said.

"That's an interesting way of describing it," Alex commented, and pushed the heavy front door open, the huge brass handles shining brilliantly in the afternoon sun.

The entrance hall was huge, with a sparkling marble floor and a carved marble fireplace featuring leaves, roses, lion's paws, and intricate swirls. Crystal chandeliers with candles suspended from the high ceiling, the circular marble staircase with wrought iron spindles, a wooden railing running at least six feet wide. At the bottom stood two white marble columns with twelve branch candelabrums.

"Marble must have been on sale when they built this castle," she remarked, uncomfortable with the splendor. "Wow, Alex, it looks like a palace."

"I know," Alex acknowledged. "It's hard to breathe here, but it's not all that bad. My father had running water, central heating, and gas lighting installed. Since you're from the future, you will probably appreciate those luxuries."

"In my time, those aren't luxuries, but basic necessities," she replied.

With his arm around her middle, he walked her toward the bottom of the stairs where she turned around to face him. "Are we going straight to the bedroom?"

She poked him in his side and he squirmed away from her. "Of course, why not?" he laughed, trying to tickle her back. When they reached the landing he pulled her in his arms and kissed her intensely.

"What's all that commotion?" a loud voice barked from downstairs.

Alex leaned over the wrought iron banister, still grinning. "Good afternoon Father," he said.

"It's about time you came home," his father replied with a disapproving frown. "I need to talk to you. Meet me in the library in fifteen minutes."

"Yes, Sir," Alex replied, taking her hand as they walked over the hardwood parquet down the hallway. He opened the second door on the right and closed it behind them.

Annet sank down on the solid oak, four poster canopied bed with carved figures and bulbous legs. "Are you worried about your father?" she asked, her finger trailing the intricate golden letter K embroidered on the hand-woven sheets and pillows.

Alex sat down next to her, his expression turning serious.

"No, I'm not concerned for myself, but I am for you," he said. "You see, Amazon, in our era, the attitude of men toward women differs from what you're used to, and they may want to change you. Like demanding you wear your hair up." Her long blonde hair fanned down her shoulders and he tugged a stray lock behind her ear. "They will also expect you to wear elaborate gowns, sway with a lace hand fan, and keep yourself in the background."

"I'm flexible. I can do that," she replied confidently. "If that's what it takes."

"Unfortunately, it will take more than that," he continued. "Most men feel the woman's place is in the home, by the hearth with her needles. Perceptive women of independent and original thought, like you, are frowned upon."

"But I can't change my personality," she protested, sliding off the bed. "Can you envision me in a lavish gown, taking tea, and making cross-stitches? No way, José, that ain't me!"

"I don't want you to change," Alex assured her. "I love you the way you are, but in our circles, the only goal a woman has in life is marriage."

"Well, screw that!" she blew up. "Besides raising my kid, I want to work. Make myself useful." With her hands placed on her hips, her fingers pressing against her lower back to support her growing belly, she paced the waxed hardwood floor.

Alex's eyes followed her every step. "I understand you don't want to hear this, but I have to explain it to you so you can prepare yourself."

"What do you mean?" she cried out "Is it getting worse?"

He hesitated, looking for the right words. "All the qualities a gentlewomen needs are innocence, honorability, and obedience. Most women in our circle are perfectly content with this state of affairs. They take pride in taking care of their household and are exactly like Elise. Dutiful, fragile, delicate, flowers, incapable of making decisions."

"Oh, come on, Alex, that's ridiculous!" she protested. "If they expect me to live like that, I'll die of boredom!"

He patted on the mattress. "You're too agitated. Come sit down and relax."

But she wasn't sitting down. She was mad. "You're a jerk for not warning me about all this," she told him.

"I know you were well aware about our state of affairs," Alex defended himself. "You told me yourself how the values have changed, about the women's liberation movement, and the struggle for gender equality."

She sank down next to him, feeling dejected. "Yes, but that was before I realized how rich your father is, and what kind of environment I have to live in."

She had envisioned his family in a country home, her mind invoking images of a modest house with a pitched roofline, charming dormers, stone siding, gridded windows and freshly painted wooden shutters. In her mind, she had seen a warm and appealing living space, and a wraparound porch where they would sit on rocking chairs, drinking tea, and playing with the baby. Not a mansion where she was afraid to touch anything, or make a single sound!

She grabbed one of the dozen pillows, wrapped her arms around it, and hugged it. "Living like royalty is out of my league."

"We're not royalty?" he laughed. "We go to work every single day but Sunday. We worry about business decisions, go to meetings, and argue all the time. Trust me there's nothing royal about this family!"

She relaxed her stance, her eyes softening. "Don't laugh at me!" She raised the pillow, threatening to smack him.

"You're the smartest woman I've ever met, Amazon," he grinned, taking the pillow from her. "It might take a few adjustments, but I'm confident you'll do superbly." He stood up from the bed and straightened his clothes. "It's time to meet my father, but don't worry, I'll be back soon."

"Yes, go," she said. "And tell him ..."

A soft knock interrupted their conversation and Alex opened the door. Jason stood in the hallway. "Where would you like the paintings, Mr. Alexander?"

"That's up to my wife," Alex replied, turning back toward her. "What did you want me to tell my father?"

She blew him a kiss. "Never mind, just thank him for having me here. After all, it can't be easy for him to accept you're married to your 'concubine'."

When Jason brought in the last load, he was followed by a young girl. "I can hang your clothes in your adjacent boudoir, Mrs. Keizer," she offered, curtsying, her dark grey skirt and matching pinafore apron sweeping the ground.

Mrs. Keizer? That sounded weird. "Sure," she replied, not wanting to let on she didn't even know she had a dressing room.

As the girl busied herself with her meager supply of clothes, Annet picked up one of Alex's paintings and held it in her hands. All the paintings in the future Keizer Manor were framed and securely fastened on the walls, protected by alarms and security cameras, but yet here there were many of them, lying in a stack on the floor of her bedroom. With careful hands, she placed them one by one against the walls around the room. They needed to be framed. Finding an experienced picture framer would be one of her first undertakings.

For a minute, she lay down on the bed with her hands protectively over her stomach, closing her eyes, until a gentle touch and warm lips against her cheek woke her. Alex sat next to her.

They smiled into each other's eyes, hers sleepy, his filled with passion.

"I love you," he told her, and kissed her until her head spun, but then he pulled away. "I want nothing more than to devour you, but dinner will be served in an hour and we're expected to attend."

Still groggy and dizzy with passion, she stepped out of bed, noticing he had changed. His camel trousers sat tight around his narrow hips, with six small buttons on the front and a narrow clasp on the back.

"You have a very nice butt in those fall front trousers...," she commented, pinching him playfully.

Alex wrapped his arm around her neck, pressing her face against his chest in a stronghold. "You better be careful, or we might end up in bed after all," he whispered in her ear, and let her go. "Come let's get you presentable." He opened a connecting door. "Here is your powder room."

"That's right. Didn't you mention something about running water?" she said, noticing a walnut-burl six drawer vanity with a mirror, a wooden washstand with a bowl and a pitcher, a chamber pot, and a marbleized zinc bathtub.

"A private water company supplies water to the stables and the kitchen, but if you want to take a bath, the maids will have to bring up warm water."

"Do you know I've never taken a bath in my entire life?" she told him, astonished by the fact herself. She had always lived in a single wide trailer or apartment, and the bathrooms never had a tub.

"Then you should have one later this evening," Alex decided.

An hour later, she descended the stairs on Alex's arm.

"Tomorrow, I'll ask the housekeeper to hire a personal maid for you," Alex told her. "So you have someone who can help you with your clothes and hair."

"I don't need a maid," she protested. "You did a remarkable job helping me pin up my hair, and closing my corset just now."

"Maybe so," he grinned, "But you don't expect me to carry up all those buckets with hot water for your bath, do you?"

As they reached the bottom of the stairs, she stopped him in his tracks. "Do they know I'm expecting?" She knew there was no possible way to hide it. She was very pregnant, and walked like mother goose.

"Yes, they do. To avoid complications, I told them its mine."

"Okay, that's cool," she replied, grateful for his resourcefulness. She didn't want to create more difficulties for him than needed. With a measured stride, she walked next to him, trying to steel her nerves. When they reached the dining room, they were greeted by a tall, gray-haired man, elegantly dressed in a long black coat and black trousers. "Mister Keizer, Madam," he said with a slight bow. "Welcome home."

How many people did they employ? she wondered There were the coachman, the stable boy, the young girl in the pinafore, a housekeeper, a cook, and now a butler?

"Thank you, Jackson," Alex said. "It's good to be back."

Liar, she thought, clinging to his arm when they entered the dining room. Like the rest of the house, it was lavishly adorned. The beautiful white and gold wood paneled walls lined with gold framed mirrors, candle holders, and paintings. None of them Alex's, she noticed.

"Unbelievable," she whispered.

"What was that, Madam?" the butler asked.

"Oh, nothing, Mr. Jackson," she replied, extending her hand. "Nice to meet you. My name is Annet."

The elderly butler hesitated, a careful smile tugged at the corner of his mouth. "Likewise, Madam," he said, and turned to Alex. "Dinner will be served in a few minutes."

Standing erect in front of the fireplace, dressed in a formal black tailcoat, his hands folded behind his back, Alex's father commanded the room with his presence. "You're late," he said, the stern look on his face setting the tone.

Alex ignored the reprimand. "Where are Leo and Elise?"

"Just like you, it seems they forgot how to tell time."

Jackson pulled out one of the sixteen chairs surrounding the mahogany dining table. On each end of the table stood an eight-arm candelabrum. Next, he turned toward the door, greeting Leo, who entered with Elise on his arm.

Leo nodded vaguely in their direction, but Elise rushed toward them and grabbed Annet's hands. "You two are married. I wish we had been able to attend." She kissed the air on each side of her face. "Congratulations."

"Yeah, that would have been great," Annet replied. "It was a lovely ceremony."

Elise took a step back, inspecting her dress, "That's not one of my gowns," she said, trying to hide her disapproval. "But it looks ... delightful."

It was obvious, Elise didn't like her clothes, but Annet didn't care. She didn't like them either. They were uncomfortable and she could barely breathe.

"No, it isn't yours," she assured her. "Look at you. You're so tiny, and I'm at least six inches taller than you. Amelia Jonkers gave me this dress. It belonged to one of her neighbors."

"You can't walk around in hand me downs," Elise replied in a whisper, extending a compassionate hand. "You should tell Alex to buy you a wardrobe of your own."

"Oh, my gosh, no," Annet replied dismissively. She didn't need more clothes for the short time she would be here. "What I have will suit me just fine, at least until the baby is born."

Grief welled up in Elise's eyes and she swallowed arduously. "The baby. Of course! How far along are you?"

"About seven months," Annet answered, remembering Alex had told her all Elise's pregnancies had ended in a miscarriage. She gave the elegant young woman a warm, compassionate hug.

"Oh, watch out for my crinolines," Elise shrieked, but then gave her a sympathetic smile.

Alex's father hammered with his knife on the table. "I have waited long enough," he said. "Tell them we're ready to be served."

Under her father-in-law's scrutinizing glare Annet slumped down next to Alex, picked up her napkin and placed it in her lap, hoping she wouldn't screw up any unknown etiquette while they ate.

"A woman who isn't eager to acquire new garments," Leo remarked patronizingly, helping Elise with her layers of petticoats and whatever else as she worked herself into a chair. "I didn't know those existed, did you father?"

A side door opened and two other servants entered. One of them carried an embossed soup tureen, the other a large spoon. They curtsied and, starting with Alex's father, dished up a clear broth, throwing curious glances in her direction. She nodded in return and they blushed, quickly lowering their eyes.

The conversation started with the weather and their sudden marriage, but soon the men entered in more serious dialogue. At first, Annet paid little attention. She was intrigued by the sumptuous foods she'd never had, served on exquisite silver and porcelain. Meticulously, she followed Elise's example, making sure she used the correct silverware for each dish.

Her ears perked with interest when the men talked about upcoming business opportunities since the colonization of New Zealand and Australia.

"The finest quality wool comes from Australia," she remarked, thinking about the well-known warm and comfortable Ugg footwear that came from there. She had a well-worn pair in her own closet and loved them.

"Well, well," Leo smirked. "What else does the new Mrs. Keizer know about New South Wales?"

"Not that much," she admitted, ignoring his sneer. "But I know the British claim Australia didn't belong to anyone before they took possession, completely disregarding the native Aboriginal people, and they shipped convicts down there to help build the infrastructure." She took another bite of her pudding and said, "This vanilla custard is delicious."

"Annet reads a lot," Alex said, giving her a warning frown.

A weighty silence fell around the table, the only sound the clinging of their silver spoons against the porcelain bowls as they finished desert.

"Alex," his father said, wiping his mouth with a white cloth napkin, a sharp frostiness in his eyes. "You better convey to your wife that her sole responsibilities are to run a respectable household, to ensure that her home is a place of comfort, and that her children are taught moral values." He dropped his napkin on the table and stood, looking down at her with disapproval. "A gentlewoman doesn't mingle in her husband's affair, and her illiterate opinion is not appreciated."

The frown on her father-in-law's face was so ominous that Annet felt the hair at the back of her neck prickle, but she wasn't backing down. "You would be surprised to find out how much I could tell you," she retaliated hotly, rising up from her chair, but a strong hand forced her back down.

"Not now, Amazon," Alex cautioned. His eyes flashed an urgent warning that couldn't be ignored. All she could do was bite her bottom lip to hold back the flood of words she wanted to spew forth.

Alex's father straightened his shoulders, tugging at the lapels of his long tail coat. "Although it was honorable to marry your pregnant concubine," he said before walking out, "you better keep her locked in her room until she knows how to behave."

Chapter 37

CLEANED UP AND DRESSED FOR THE OFFICE, in newer and nicer pants and shirt, Forrest took his new post behind the counter at the Keizer Manor. The museum would open its doors in ten minutes. Before the first visitors arrived he dialed detective Jaeger's phone number. He hadn't heard from him in far too long.

"We just finished watching the security tapes," the detective told him after he got him on the line. "Including the ones from the parking lot."

Although he knew he was innocent, his heart pounded in his chest. Suppose they had found something to incriminate him. After all, he had chased her down the parking lot, and who knows what they concluded.

"The tapes prove the only interaction you had with Miss Beverly Tjaverski during the course of the day was when you fixed a light bulb, and the few minutes you were together in Annet's office."

"I already told you that," Forrest replied, trying to sound nonchalant although his nerves were wired. "What else did you find out?"

"Not much. The exterior cameras showed us Annet running down the parking lot and disappearing into the dunes, to be followed by you one minute later."

Forrest heard the sound of rustling paperwork, Jaeger sighing audibly before he continued, "None of this will hold up as evidence against you. So far, you're still in the clear."

Forrest sagged down against the back of his chair, a sigh of relief escaping his lips.

"We did find her other shoe," the detective said.

Forrest shot back up. "You did? Where?"

"On the beach. About four miles from where we found the first one."

A group of people stared at him from the other side of the counter. It was past ten, the museum had opened its doors. Forrest ignored them. "Four miles? How is that even possible?"

"You tell me," the detective replied.

"How much is the entrance fee for a senior citizen?" a red-haired woman asked, irritation on her face.

"Adults are ten, seniors are six," he answered automatically, disconnecting the phone line.

The woman pulled out a large wallet from the colorful tote she carried around her shoulder and counted out the money.

"Thank you, Madam. Enjoy your visit." He handed her the tickets, with a brochure.

The hallway filled up, and although he felt awful, he plastered a smile on his face, welcoming the next guests to the Keizer Manor.

A steady stream of visitors made its way through the museum, keeping him busy the entire morning, but his anxiety shot back into overdrive when someone knocked rapidly on the counter. It was Annet's mom. A few feet behind her stood Chuck, glancing around him with interest.

"Barbara? What are you doing here?" he asked.

She impatiently banged her shiny fake diamond rings on the marble surface, the piercing clatter grating his nerves. He wanted to pull her over the counter and smack her.

"We decided to see where Annet worked and disappeared from," she informed him.

He looked at her, trying to remain professional. "Okay, that will be one adult and one senior." He entered the admission into the computer. "Sixteen dollars, please."

"Are you out of your mind? I'm not paying to see those stupid paintings," she hissed at him, a challenging, cold smile around her dark-red lipsticked mouth. "Screw that!"

Forrest bit his lip, straightening his spine. "I can't let you enter the museum without paying admission. Sorry."

"Like hell you can't!" she retorted, raising her voice and looking over her shoulder at Chuck for support. "I'll be damned if we are required to pay while my daughter has gone missing from this very fucking place. I'm a victim in this too, you know. They wanted my fingerprints, my DNA, my exact whereabouts. It's humiliating."

The people waiting in line behind her shuffled with their feet, looking away, uncomfortable with the situation.

Forrest inhaled a deep breath, his gut tightening in dread of the scandal that could ensue if she created a scene. "It's okay, Barbara, I'll take care of it," he said, zeroing out the transaction. "I'm sorry for not being more considerate."

"I thought so, you freakin' pathetic wimp," she snubbed, motioning with her head for Chuck to follow her to the first exhibit hall.

At the first chance Forrest got, he informed Dan about Annet's mother, warning him to tread carefully around the vindictive woman, but Dan shrugged off his concern.

"Don't worry. Annet is her daughter. She has every right to be distraught," he said.

Maybe so, Forrest thought, but while Annet had been around she had called once, maybe twice per year, hardly ever coming over to visit. In his opinion her whole grief-stricken mother attitude was a deception, used to her advantage, so she would get the attention she so desperately needed.

"Tell me what she looks like, and I'll take care of it," Dan continued.

"Long dark hair with fake blonde streaks, about forty-five to fifty, ripped blue jeans, high heeled black boots up to her knees, white tank top, and a leather jacket over her arm," he said, thinking that getting treated with courtesy by the boss was exactly the reason why she was here. "The guy she's with is in his sixties, bulging stomach, tattoos, and thin long grey hair. Should be easy to notice."

Fortunately, Forrest had been able to avoid Barbara during the rest of her visit, but as soon as he opened the door of his apartment, she was right there, in his face.

"I saw you hiding in that office when we were on our way out. Why was that?" she demanded to know. "Are you ashamed of me, or something?"

"You're darn right," Forrest told her, closing the door with all the calm he could muster. "I didn't want you there, and I don't want you here either."

At first, she was too stunned to speak, then when she did, her voice shook with indignation. "At least Annet's boss understands what I'm going through, you insensitive prick! I'm her mother. Don't you get that?"

Wishing the earth would open up and swallow her, he walked toward the bathroom where he downed two ibuprofens to stave off another headache. When he came outside, she waited for him, standing in a combative pose, her hands on her hips. "Where were you last night and the night before?" she spat at him.

"None of your business," he replied, Barbara blocking his path when he tried to go around her. "Please, get out my way," he said, trying to push her aside.

She stiffened and then slapped him across the cheek. "Don't you dare touch me!"

"What did you do that for?" he cried out in shock, his hand against his burning face. "You're not the only one who's suffering here, you bitch! I miss her a lot more than you." Swearing to himself, he turned away. *This was it!* He'd had enough and couldn't take anymore. He pulled a garbage bag from under the sink, opened it on his way to the bedroom, and stuffed it with socks, underwear, jeans, and T-shirts. Next, he went to the bathroom to collect a few other personal items, Barbara's cold stares poking holes in his back, her mouth set hard like a trap.

"What are you doing?" she asked. "Running away like a dog with its tail between its legs? You're pathetic."

He gave her one baleful glance before he marched to the door and yanked it open, the garbage bag hanging over his shoulder.

"Yes, run away," she yelled after him, her voice tainted by bitterness. "Like everyone else around me always does!"

Her voice sounded strangely muffled, and he turned around to look at her. Their gazes met across the room. To his surprise, there was nothing left of the furious hell woman he had seen earlier. All he saw was a pitiful, decrepit woman, weighed down with all the disappointments and mistakes she had made in her life. A woman who had fought hard, but had fallen harder. His anger disappeared, changing into empathy. "Tonight, I'll crash with my parents, and tomorrow, I hope to move in with a friend, so you and Chuck can have the apartment to yourself," he said. "If you need me, you can reach me on my cellphone." With a decisive click, he shut the door behind him.

Chapter 38

In high school, they had taught her that women in the nineteenth century had no legal, social, or political rights. They couldn't vote, and were barred from following a higher education. Annet got that, and tried her hardest to act accordingly, but she was raised in a tough environment, where women had to stand up for themselves to keep from being walked over by their men, pushed around by their peers, overlooked, dismissed, or mistreated. In her world, you had to fight for your place and defend your turf, or you would end up with nothing. The result was a potty mouth, a thick skin and a defensive attitude. Even in her work at the Keizer Manor, she had been outspoken and opinionated, quick to draw the gun. But now, for the first time in her life, she had to watch every single word that came out of her mouth. Not being able to speak freely was a challenge unlike one she'd ever had to conquer.

So, after six weeks of pacing their quarters, taking long warm baths, and learning to knit, she was bored to death. The bullshit about obedience and keeping her mouth shut drove her up the wall. This wasn't her era, and it never would be.

Her perfect sister-in-law Elise turned out to be not so bad. She was kind, supportive and good-natured. They had toured the grounds of the estate together, and she had been useful in the search for her personal maid, but an intelligent conversation, with contents and meaning, proved impossible. Her only interests, besides her appearance, were making flower arrangements, and playing the harp. She prided herself in speaking a little French and reciting poems, spending her mornings with walks through the greenhouse, to talk to her flowers. Each afternoon, she took a long nap, picked up her needlepoint, or read a little. On warm and sunny days, she strolled outside through the gardens, or she visited with a kindred lady friend. Annet couldn't comprehend a tedious existence like hers, where nothing else was expected other than to remain subservient to your husband.

When the three men left to do important things she wasn't supposed to be interested in, she got into the habit of spending time in the library. Alex had told her the library was his father's refuge, where he relaxed after work, read the newspaper, and drank rum or ale. Comfortable chairs surrounded the fireplace, and she enjoyed sitting in one of them, with her feet on an ottoman, the newspaper resting on her growing stomach. Her baby moved inside, making her, with growing fondness, wonder if it was a boy or a girl.

The newspapers were thin, with a minimal amount of advertisements, but it was an enjoyment to read lurid stories about crimes and murder cases, and the trial of an accused arsonist. Not to forget important historical events, like the election of William Harrison as the 9th President of the United States, and the American naval expedition under Charles Wilkes that identified Antarctica as a new continent.

After she finished reading the morning's paper, she searched the library for a specific book, called *The Time Machine*, written by H.G. Wells. She had seen a science fiction film adapted from this story. If it was already published, she hoped to find out where the author lived, and if she could pick his brain about her possible return to the 21st century. Each day, the urgency to return home built up inside her. Although Alex was great, and their quarters comfortable, she hated her degrading subservient status and the confinements of the mansion. Even though she could be here for a specific reason, or had to wait until another powerful May storm rolled in, her return might be more complicated, maybe even impossible, after her child was born. She was running out of time.

She stretched her back and waddled around, pausing in front of the section devoted to everything Greek. Her index finger skimmed over the extensive selection. Names like Odysseus, Zeus, Poseidon and Athena jumped at her. The largest book had "Χάρτες της συλλογής" written on the spine. She pulled it out and placed it on the table, where she found a chair without arms comfortable for her expanded body.

"My wife's mother was Greek, hence the collection," a voice said behind her.

"Jeez, all mighty," she yelped, her heart racing. Alex's father had entered through a side door and watched her from the threshold, top-hat in hand.

"Sorry I scared you," he said. He placed his hat on the table, took off his long overcoat, and draped it over the back of a chair. "Her name was Lucinda. It means light of the day.

Alex had told her his mother was Greek, hence his strong features and distinctive nose.

"I would always find her here, absorbed in a book," he continued, pulling out a chair before sitting down at the table. "She loved to read. Seeing you in here this morning brings back a lot of memories."

She detected a hint of honest grief in his eyes and her heart softened. *Maybe he wasn't such a coldhearted despot after all.* "Why don't you tell me more about her," she said, but he had fallen into deep thought. The tall mahogany grandfather clock ticked the minutes away as she grew uncomfortable under his unwavering gaze.

"She died too young," he declared and cleared his throat, his expression turning hard and distant. "Now, explain to me what you're doing here. I don't like surprises."

She noted he was his old self again. "Oh nothing special," she replied, not interested in prolonging the conversation. "I was bored and just wandered in for some distraction."

"How can you be bored in a mansion like this?" he said, his voice aloof and condescending. "Besides, I heard you've been busy redecorating your wing."

With Jason's help, she had brought down Alex's old rocking cradle crib and a six drawer cupboard from the attic, both matching pieces hand carved with curved fronts and sides. She had also found a picture-frame maker in town, a genuine artist, who had framed several paintings. They hung in their drawing room and bedroom. "Preparing the nursery and hanging a few painting are not enough to keep me occupied, Sir," she told him, trying to match the tone of his voice.

His fingers drummed the table in an impatient tempo, "I understand from Alex you have an inquisitive mind. He also claims you're intelligent for a woman. Is that true?"

Intelligent for a woman? Did she hear that right? "No, he's wrong. I'm not smarter than most women," she corrected him haughtily. "I just gathered a lot of knowledge over the years, but there's still a lot to learn. Like importing goods, clothing manufacturing, steam engines, crinolines, and having babies."

"If you care to be accepted in Alex's world, solely stick to the latter two," he told her.

Every muscle in Annet's back stiffened at his misogynistic words. "Sorry, Sir, but that's not enough for me." With utmost effort, she kept her tone reasonable. "I need to stay busy, reading a book, doodling around, and watching the grass grow is not cutting it!"

He raised his eyebrows. "You can read? I didn't expect that."

His arrogance was beyond belief. "Of course I can read," she fumed, holding onto her last shred of patience.

Indifferent about her agitated response, he regarded her thoughtfully, "So you attended school?"

She scoffed. "Believe it or not, but I actually made it to graduation. The only reason I didn't go to college was that I needed to work and make money."

"Working? That's right. How could I forget?" he interjected.

For a moment taken aback, she regarded him until aversion took over. "Dammit!" she cursed, throwing her hands up in exasperation. *How could she have thought, if only for a second, there was a softer side to him?* "I'm not a hooker. Don't you realize that by now?"

Unwavering, they stared at each other across the table, his face wiped of all expression.

Deliberately slow, she pushed her chair back and got up, but before she walked out, she stopped next to his chair to give him one last message before leaving. "Screw you, you pompous ass!"

Chapter 39

Over dinner that evening, she didn't have to wait long before her father-in-law addressed their encounter in the library.

"I didn't know you spend time in the library, Amazon," Alex answered.

You would have, if you had shown a bit of interest in my daily activities, she thought, but hid her disgruntled frame of mind behind a sugary smile. "But dear, you know I'm not used to sitting around. If it wasn't for my huge belly and the need to take a nap in the afternoon, I would have gone nuts by now. I hope you're not upset with me?"

"But why in the library?" Elise asked in disbelief. "I'm more than happy to teach you to play the harp or walk with you through the gardens."

"That's very nice of you," Annet replied, smiling sociably, "But I'm used to a different pace and need to be … a … busy." Her job at the Keizer Manor had been hectic, especially after the economy had slipped into a recession and several jobs were eliminated, creating more work for the remaining employees. On the average, she had put in fifty hours per week or more, loving every bit of it.

"You'll be busy enough when the baby is here," Elise said, patting her hand.

"I can't wait," Annet replied with a grimace. "This baby is giving me heartburn."

Alex looked at her questioningly over a spoon of mashed potatoes and gravy.

"You know," she explained, "like when the baby takes up so much room, your stomach gets pushed up."

"We're having dinner," Leo interrupted.

Elise nodded in agreement. "Yes, Annet," she warned in a whisper. "You shouldn't talk about these private matters at the dinner table."

"Where I come from, that's exactly the time to share important information with your family," Annet challenged them, looking around the table until her eyes fell on her father-in-law. *What?* she thought surprised. *Did she see that right? Was he trying to hide a smile behind his napkin? Did he think this was funny?*

After the tense meal ended, Alex accompanied her back up to their rooms, his hand at her elbow. She had only eaten her vegetables, the rest of the food too heavy for her stomach to handle. "Are you nervous about the upcoming birth of the baby?" he asked.

She pulled a face. "I would feel much better if I knew I had the possibility of a spinal anesthesia. I'm not a hero and don't like pain." Placing her hands on the bed behind her, she slowly lowered her expansive body. "I'm feeling like an invalid elephant. Look at me, I'm humongous."

"Do you think it's time to alert Doctor Snow and Mrs. Fritz, the midwife?" Alex asked, helping her lift her legs.

Annet couldn't help but think about Forrest. How unfair it was that another man was by her side instead of him, watching the baby grow inside her, feeling it move.

Alex sat down at the edge of the mattress, taking her hand. "I know you don't care if the baby is a girl or a boy, but have you thought about names yet?"

She had thought about it many times, but had hoped to never have this conversation with him, and that instead of being here, she would have been back in her apartment, with Forrest, where she belonged. "If it's a boy, I want to name him Forrest."

"Obviously," he replied, a flash of pain shooting through his eyes.

"You're far too nice for your own good, Mr. Keizer," she said, reaching out to him to soften her words.

He scooted over and took her in his arms.

"You know, I really miss you," she confessed, making herself comfortable against his strong body. "You're gone all day, come home late. We don't have any privacy or time to talk."

"I know," he admitted. "I miss that too, but I had been at the cabin for far too long this summer and have to make up for lost time."

She raised her head to look at him. "Lost time? Is that how you look at it?"

"No, that's not what I meant." With tender fingers, he stroked a loose strand of blonde hair in place. "All I dream about is going back to the cabin with you, to make love under the stars, and paint during the day, but I can't abandon my responsibilities."

She knew all about responsibilities, and understood where he was coming from, but if he didn't take time off, how could he ever become the famous master painter?

"What if we turn one of the empty rooms into a studio?" she suggested, certain he would agree. "So you can paint, right here? Isn't that a good idea?"

But instead he shook his head. "That would be a complete waste of money, time, and effort."

"A waste?" she cried out in disbelief. "Why?"

He shrugged. "There's something blocked in my mind when I'm in this house. It makes me a different person."

"That's not healthy!" she protested. "You have to paint!"

"Hey, it's okay," he tried to calm her. "It's been like this my entire life, and it's the reason I escape to the cabin whenever I can. So I can break that barrier and get in touch with my other self."

"Oh, Alex. You're suppressing the most important part of you. I can't allow that to continue!"

He placed his hand against her cheek. "Let's stop talking about it, because there are more important things to discuss, like our baby, and its future."

Side by side, with Alex's comforting arm draped across her belly, they lay quiet for a few minutes, Annet's mind spinning in turmoil. Poor Alex, how horrible it had to be for him, not being able to be himself in his own home. They had to get away from this place.

"What if the baby is a girl?" he asked, returning to their earlier conversation. He rolled over on his side and propped himself up on one elbow. "I have a suggestion. What do you think of the name Fleur? The French word for flower."

"Fleur." She tasted the name on her lips. "I think I really love that."

Alex slid from the bed, unbuttoned his shirt and took off his breeches. It was a fascinating scene to watch as more and more of his long, lean body came exposed. She was spellbound by the play of his muscles, the breadth of his chest, and his brawny shoulders.

"Were you looking for something particular in the library?" Alex asked, with care hanging his clothes over a chair.

"Oh, no, just looking for a book I wanted to read," she said evasively.

He sat back down on the mattress, peeling off his knitted tube stockings. "A particular book?"

She felt the warmth of his body, exuding a sexual energy, and her heartrate spiked. Now if he would only stop pestering her about that stupid library, maybe they could snuggle up, and make love.

"It's called 'The Time Machine'," she replied, just to get it over with and move on to something much more interesting.

His jaw twitched and a flash of pain flickered in his green eyes. "I may not *want* to hear it," he said. "But you're my wife and I like to know what's on your mind."

She looked away. "It's about a scientist who states time is something like a fourth dimension. He builds a machine capable of carrying a person and travelling through it." Out of the corner of her eyes, she saw him pull himself up straighter, crossing his arms over his chest in a gesture, of what? Annoyance? Anger?

"I just want to see if there's any truth to his story. That's all."

"I know you still want to return to your time," he replied, his eyes reflecting understanding. "And although I can't bear the thought of losing you, I'll do what I can to help. That's how much I love you."

Her heart wrung with pain and she wanted to hug him for his innate kindness, patience, and tolerance. "Well, if it makes you feel any better," she blurted out. "I love you too."

He stiffened visibly. "You don't have to lie. I'm a grown man and not a child." He picked his clothes back up and headed toward the door.

Taken by surprise, she cried out, "Where are you going?"

"I need some air," he replied, "Don't wait up for me."

"No, no, no," she flinched and slid off the bed. Gripped by an inexplicable panic, she waddled after him. "You can't leave me!"

He turned around on the threshold with his hand on the door handle. "I'll be back," he assured her. "Don't worry." With a decisive click the door closed behind him, leaving her standing in the middle of the room by herself.

"Come on," she yelled, stamping with her right foot on the carpet. "I've loved you from the first moment I laid my eyes on you in the convent four months ago!" Frustrated with the whole screwed up situation, she hissed several more swear words, the idea he might leave her almost paralyzing her with fear. But she hadn't forgotten Forrest, and she never would.

Chapter 40

SINCE ANNET HAD GONE MISSING, Forrest's life had fallen apart. He felt her loss in every cell of his body, his mood changing by the minute. One moment, he was confident and optimistic about her return. The next he was depressed, thinking she could be dead and lost to him forever.

After the atrocious confrontation with his mother-in-law, he had spent the night on the couch in his parents' house. The next day he had gone to Caroline Rothschild in Heemstead and moved into the four poster bedroom. He needed solitude and a place to hide. Having to deal with the loss of his best friend, the police, and the public's criticism and hostility had taken its toll, giving him nightmares and making him feel unsafe. His life was in a pandemonium and the last confrontation with Annet's mother had brought him to his knees, making him beg to the heavens above to be released from the agony that had become his life. The not knowing killed him, his loneliness impossible to bear. All that kept him going was his work at the Keizer Manor, and the unwavering support from his parents, Dan Mockenburg and Caroline. They never left him alone, constantly pestering him, forcing him to face another hour, another day, convincing him to keep on believing in a happy ending.

Although deep down inside he felt she was still alive, that she was out there somewhere, believing these unfounded emotions only made him feel worse. Annet would never voluntarily stay away, the only possible conclusion that she was held against her will. Whenever he let his thoughts wander in that direction he broke down, not able to face the images of concrete cells with thick metal bars, nude bodies covered in blood, and other terrible horrors assaulting his mind.

So once in a while, he joined Rix, the rock musician, and shared a beer or two, or three with him. Or he popped in while his band practiced and smoked an occasional joint with the guys to help him relax. Other days, he spent the evening at his parents' house and watched a movie on TV, until he crashed on their couch for another lonely night without his best friend.

At the Keizer Manor, Dan had hired a new receptionist, allowing Forrest to move into Annet's office where he tried to fulfill her duties. It was nice to get a paycheck, so he could pay rent to Caroline, the insurance on the car and the gas to drive it, but he felt it wasn't his money. It was Annet's, and he had to come to terms with that too.

Slowly but surely, the long, long weeks turned into long, long months. Months in which the search slowed down to a crawl, and the police moved on to cases they deemed more important. Annet's file sank to the bottom of the stack, leaving Forest with nothing but despair and his own miserable thoughts.

First thing in the morning, he called Detective Jaeger, as he did every day, to keep Annet's unexplained disappearance on his radar. As far as Forrest was concerned, the case wasn't over until her body was found or there was other evidence that indicated she would never come back. Until that day, he would never give up. He would keep on searching and hoping. But the answer remained the same. No news, no tips, nothing to tell.

Deciding he needed a long break, he strolled into the dunes toward the beach. He wanted to be by himself, to think and recoup. It was exactly three months to the day of Annet's disappearance and although his life had taken on a new semblance of normal, he was still grieving for everything he had lost.

Once again, the dunes didn't offer any solace, his pain only intensified by the vivid memories of the storm when he reached the barbed wire fence at the Government Research Center. With a heavy heart, he returned to the Manor. When he caught a faint female voice calling out his name, he squinted against the sun, noticing Caroline waving at him from the top of the steps. A slender young woman stood next to her, the wind playing with her long blonde hair.

Afraid to believe what his eyes were telling him, he shook his head and looked again, but she was still there, wearing her classic blue jeans topped off by a white short-sleeve blouse. Anticipation surged through his veins. Annet! She had returned! He increased his step, sand kicking up beneath his sneakers.

The young woman watched him approach, crossing her arms in front of her chest.

"There's someone here I would like you to meet," Caroline said when he reached the bottom of the steps.

Disappointment moved across his face. *This young woman wasn't Annet. How could he have believed such an idiot thing?*

266

Deflated, he sank down on the concrete steps, expelling a sigh of disillusionment.

"Are you all right?" Caroline asked him with concern.

He raked his hand through his hair and stared at the ground. "I'm fine. I just need a minute."

Caroline placed her hand on his shoulder. "Come, get up, Forrest. I want you to meet my granddaughter."

Caroline had talked about it for days, but somehow it had slipped his mind. He forced himself back up, forcing a feeble grin when he shook her hand.

"Kara McNary, nice to meet you," the young woman introduced herself.

He looked down into her smiling light-brown eyes, thinking she had to be close to Annet's age, maybe a bit younger.

"Kara is in town for a job interview and is staying with me for several days. Come you two, let's go out for dinner. We have a reason to celebrate. My treat."

Forrest met them at Joe's Grill Bar and joined them in ordering a medium steak with fries and a microbrew. The two women talked animatedly over dinner, and sipped their beer while he tried to work up enough enthusiasm to take a bite of his own food. His emotions were already stretched thin, and although up close Kara didn't really look like Annet, her presence threw him off more than he cared to admit.

"Did you hear that, Forrest?" Caroline tried to pull him into the conversation. "Kara is telling me her father almost finished the entire Keizer family tree, dating back to the early nineteenth century."

"Has he now," he answered, his obvious apathy resulting in a disapproving frown from Caroline. Sheepishly he straightened his shoulders and plastered a smile on his face. "So what kind of job are you here for, Kara?" he asked and stuffed two now cold French fries in his mouth.

"Last week I had a very promising phone interview with Orange Fine Arts. They invited me to their gallery for a second meeting," she explained with a shy grin, her face tilted down a bit. "They are located here, in downtown Heemstead, and have been in that same location over two decades."

"Kara mastered in Art Conservation earlier this year. After traveling around for several months, she's ready to settle down, aren't you dear?" Caroline explained.

"Doesn't a gallery only sell new stuff?" Forrest asked.

Kara took a sip from her light pilsner and wiped the foam from her lips with a napkin before answering. "They sell paintings, sculptures, wood work, pottery, and jewelry from a large variety of artists, but I will be assisting in the processes involved in the conservation and restoration of oil paintings, watercolors, pastels, engravings, and those sorts of things." The smile she'd been unable to contain while discussing the job became more demure, "That is, if they hire me."

Caroline placed her bejeweled hand on her granddaughter's arm. "Of course they will! Especially if you tell them you're one of Alex Keizer's direct descendants."

"I don't want them to hire me because of that, Grandma," Kara refuted. "I want them to hire me for my own capabilities."

"Silly girl," Caroline pooh-poohed her with a kind smile. "I would definitely use that fact to my advantage, and I wouldn't hesitate to tell them it would be more than likely they can land the contract to restore all Alex's paintings if they bring you on board."

Kara almost choked on her beer and coughed.

"Are you okay?" Forrest asked, handing her a clean handkerchief, but she waved him off. "I'm fine," she replied, still coughing.

He turned toward Caroline. "Is Dan really considering restoring all the paintings?" He had heard rumors, but hadn't taken it seriously. All the paintings in the museum were extremely valuable and hadn't been moved since they'd been hung in place by the master painter himself. Besides that, it would be an expensive and perilous undertaking.

"After I've been pestering him about this for months, I believe he is," Caroline said, leaning back in her chair to give the waitress a little more room to clear their plates. "Although he claims there's not enough money due to the expenses of the two-hundredth anniversary celebration."

"But that makes sense, Grandma," Kara chimed in. Her face was still a little red, but her breathing was back to normal.

"Nonsense," Caroline countered. "The anniversary has renewed and augmented interest in Alex Keizer's work, and visitor attendance has almost tripled compared to last year."

The waitress stopped at their table. "Any room for dessert?"

They declined, and after Caroline took care of the check, they left the restaurant. "It can't hurt to use your connections," Caroline continued their earlier conversation when they were outside, but Kara stiffened. "Thanks for the advice, Grandma, but I'll do this my way." Turning around on her heels, she left. No doubt she wouldn't utter a single word about her famous ancestor.

Forrest applauded her well-founded stance. That girl had spirit!

Chapter 41

A lex walked for at least an hour under a black sky, thinking about his wife and their irrational situation. When it started to snow he went back inside to warm up in front of the flickering fire in the library. He didn't feel like going to bed yet. He was restless; his reasoning powers overcome by envy of a ghost of the future, of a man he could never fight.

Although he had assured Annet he would do anything to help her go back to the man she loved, he wondered if he could be so selfless and let her go when the opportunity arose. Just the thought of losing her already hurt more than he could bear, so how would he ever be able to get on with his life without her?

The tall grandfather clock chimed another hour gone by, the fire by now barely smoldering, and the temperature in the library gradually decreasing. He didn't notice. Struggling with his bitter emotions, he kept pacing back and forth.

He was a romantic man, who believed in love at first sight, until death do us part. When he had met her in the convent, he had known right away she was the one he had been waiting for. For him, there would never be another woman. She held his heart firmly in her grip and would take it with her, wherever she went. There was no use fighting it. He wanted her, needed her, and he would take whatever he could get, even if it was just a crumb.

A soft knock on the door woke Annet the next morning. It was still dark outside, but when she opened her eyes she noticed Alex's side of the bed was already empty. He had joined her in the dead of the night. Looking for reassurance everything was still good between them, she had reached out to him. All he had done was mumble a "goodnight" before he turned his back to her, and fell asleep, leaving her awake for hours, worrying, until she had fallen into a deep sleep by morning.

Gloria, her maid, stepped in and curtsied. She couldn't be older than fourteen or fifteen, the skin around her nose broken out with acne, her chest still flat. "Do you want me to make your bath, My Lady?"

"What time is it?"

"It's still early, but since it's Christmas Day, the family prefers to have breakfast together before going to church."

"What? It's Christmas? Are you kidding me?" Her spirit lifted immediately. She pushed the heavy blankets away and stepped out of bed. "No, thanks, Gloria. I think I'll just clean myself at the washstand this morning."

When she returned to the bedroom, she found the bed perfectly made, her clothes laid out, and Gloria waiting to assist her.

"Are you sure it's Christmas today?" she asked.

She was used to seeing decorations on the houses, months of commercials on television, with sales to lure shoppers to all the stores and shopping malls, and people picking out their Christmas tree weeks in advance. There was no way around this holiday back home, but here, no one paid attention and not a single word had been uttered. "I haven't seen a tree or a single decoration!"

Gloria helped her into her dress, and tied her bodice. "A tree, My Lady?"

"Yes, a Christmas tree with lights and ornaments."

Gloria's face lit up. "Oh, I've heard about rich people decorating a tree in their homes, but I don't believe that custom has entered the Keizer household."

Annet couldn't hide her disappointment. "But how about gifts and a festive dinner?"

"I know nothing about that either, M' Lady," the young girl replied, bashful, and confused. "But like you, I've just entered this household."

"I understand," she appeased the anxious maid before leaving the room and descending the stairs, wishing she had kept better track of time so she could at least have bought everybody a gift.

Entering the dining room, she found the rest of the family already seated at the table. Besides the lighted candles in the candelabrum sending a warm, flickering glow over the table, she found everything exactly like any other morning.

"Merry Christmas everyone." She rested her hand on Alex's shoulder, kissing him on the cheek.

"Merry Christmas to you," he returned her greeting. "Are you feeling well this morning?" He got up and helped her into her chair.

"I'm fine," she replied. "Just a little disappointed to find out you don't celebrate Christmas with a tree and gifts. Why is that?"

"I've heard about nobility decorating a tree with apples, nuts, or other edibles inside their homes, but we don't do that here," Alex's father commented, buttering a white fluffy biscuit. "Are you Protestant, Annet?"

Annet frowned. "No, I'm not. Why?"

He thought for a moment, the butter knife hanging in the air. "From what I understand, it's a Protestant custom that originates either from Norse mythology or from the German culture. Since you are so adamant about it, I thought you …."

"I have no clue where it comes from," Annet interrupted him, "but we always celebrate Christmas with a tree, good food, and lots of gifts."

"You don't celebrate by going to church?" Leo inquired, the tone of his voice accusatory.

Annet shook her head. "No, I consider myself an agnostic and never go to church."

"Have you ever heard such words coming from a woman?" Leo grunted. "Absolutely ludicrous and unacceptable."

Since she had moved into the house, Leo had treated her with indifference, ignoring her presence, which suited her just fine. He was an egotistic, pompous dickhead, and she wondered how the soft and kind Elise could tolerate her husband's constant superior arrogance.

"I don't mind joining you today," she offered quickly, trying to patch things up. After all, it was Christmas, and anything would be better than another boring day at the house.

"Since you married into a Catholic family, to a Catholic man, you're required to adopt his faith," Alex's father said.

"Please, Father," Alex interrupted. "We'll handle this issue together."

"That's fine," his father stated. "As long as you remember Paul saying in the Bible that Christians shouldn't be yoked together with nonbelievers." With that, he dropped the issue.

After breakfast, the coachman drove them to church in the family's shiny black carriage. Dressed in warm winter coats, the five of them huddled together on the red plush seats inside, but the atmosphere was frigid and strained. Annet looked outside at the empty streets. It was a gray day, the roads covered with a dusting of snow. "A white Christmas. At least I got that," she muttered to herself.

When they arrived at the church, she clutched Alex's arm, trying to walk with dignity, her head raised. She didn't want the churchgoers to think she didn't belong here. Since the entire family was already upset with her, she couldn't afford to stir up more trouble.

"You'll do great as long as you stick to normal pleasantries, and don't say anything peculiar," Alex encouraged her. He lowered his voice to avoid being overheard by the parishioners flocking around them on the concrete steps, but the moment they stepped inside the church, she knew that wouldn't be easy. They were the center of attention as they walked through the center aisle to the front of the church. As they seated themselves in the third row, she could feel curious eyes pricking her back. *Damn, why hadn't she just stayed home?*

"You're doing fine," Alex assured her, catching her negative vibes. He helped smooth out her irritating bulky skirts and smiled.

"It looks like I'm on display like a freak in a circus," she replied behind her hand, trying to ignore the whispers around them.

"People talk, Amazon," he said, trying to ease her mind. "But once they have seen you a few times, their curiosity will wane, and shift to something else."

With a straight back, she sat on the hard, wooden bench, fumbling with the book full of songs and hymns she had found on a little shelf in front of her. She leafed through it, noticing most of them were in Latin. "Salve Regina." *Wow, that's funny,* she thought, *one of my classmates in high school was called Regina.* Another song was called Panis Angelicus. She tried to read the text, but couldn't make heads or tails out of it.

Everybody rose and she followed their example. A priest, wearing a liturgical vestment in ornate green with a gold embroidered stole, entered the church from the vestry and walked up to the altar. He was followed by four young acolytes. After he reached the altar, the four acolytes set up in a straight line behind him. The priest raised his arms to acknowledge the congregation and solemnly crossed himself. "In nòmine Patris, et Fìlii, et Spìritus Sancti."

"Amen," the parishioners answered.

Next, the organ struck up the prelude for a song. The choir sang, the congregation joining lustily, and Annet glanced around. The interior of the church was spectacular with statues, paintings, and colorful stained glass windows. The ceiling was astronomical, the tall pillars and enormous oil lamps hanging down from long golden chains dazzling her.

As mass continued, her mind wandered back to previous Christmases at Forrest's parent's house, where they laughed over useless gifts and ate until they were sick to their stomachs from all the fat and sweets. Her heart ached when she thought about how much she was missing.

"Can't you sit still for one minute?" Alex muttered next to her.

What? How dare he criticize her? Didn't he realize the hoops of her petticoats were jabbing her? Or how uncomfortable these pews were? Her legs were falling asleep, her back hurt, her ass was numb. And it was as boring as hell.

Finally people moved around, getting up. "Is it over?" she whispered.

"It's communion, but you can't partake," he whispered back. "Just stay in your seat."

She watched as the worshippers lined up in the center aisle. After taking communion, they walked back to their seats, their heads bowed, their hands folded in front of them. She felt ignorant and stupid, left by herself on the bench. *Yes, take a good look*, she thought after she caught a woman casting a curious glance.

Alex came back and knelt down next to her, covering his face with his hands.

She shook his arm and he looked up. "What now?" he barked. "Can't you see I'm praying?"

That did it! Why had she even come?

After mass, Annet hurried out of the church without waiting for Alex. She was tired, cantankerous and fed up. People grouped around her. She worked her way through them until she reached the top of the steps in front of the church. Fresh air, finally. She tried to pass a group of women, chattering as they strolled down onto the parking lot. "Excuse me," she mumbled. She shrieked when she missed the bottom step, falling forward.

Her knees hit the gravel, her hands grabbing onto skirts and reaching arms.

"Oh, my goodness," the surrounding women exclaimed all at once, trying to catch her.

Annet struggled to get back up from the snow covered ground, two of the women assisting her. "Are you all right?" one of them asked.

She rubbed her painful hands against each other to wipe off the dirt. Then she bent down to pick up her skirts, lifting them up high to inspect her sore knees. "This is the first time I'm happy with all these layers of fabric," she told the concerned ladies. "They're great protection when you fall. See, I don't have a single scratch!"

A group of men ogled her shapely legs as Alex came rushing down the steps.

"Annet!" he hissed in warning. "Drop your skirts!"

This was the first time he had called her by her real name. This shocked her more than anything he could have thrown at her. "Considering my very pregnant situation, a word of concern would have been very much appreciated," she retaliated against his pissy attitude. With a snotty move, she stuck her nose up in the air and turned away.

One of the older women, who had been watching the entertaining incident from the sideline, walked up to her and took her arm in an unexpected friendly gesture. "I could tell you are literally and figuratively ready to explode," she said.

"Isn't that the truth," Annet agreed.

"My name is Agnes Bornholm," the woman introduced herself, her ill-fitting purple dress with a flounced skirt and brown bonnet an odd mismatch of clothes.

"Thanks for getting me out of there," Annet said, throwing Alex a dirty look over her shoulder. "I'm new to all this, and feel completely out of place."

"I know how you feel," Agnes smiled. "Although I try very hard, I'm never able to quite fit in myself."

Alex's arm slid around her waist. "Thank you, Mrs. Bornholm," he said, dismissing the woman. "I'll take it from here."

"You can't treat her like that, Alex," Annet protested as he pulled her toward the carriage, the rest of the family already waiting inside. *Dammit, he was behaving like his asshole brother.*

"Who was that peculiar woman?" her father-in-law asked after they got seated and the door closed.

"That's Leonora LaRouge's sister," Leo said at his usual imperious tone, "her husband passed away recently and if they hadn't allowed her to move into their guesthouse, she would have ended up on the street."

"Shame on the husband, leaving his wife not provided for," her father-in-law stated.

"I've met her once while I was having tea at their house," Elise joined into the conversation. "They say she can tell your fortune with cards." When Leo snorted his disapproval, she placed her gloved hand on his arm and added quickly, "Of course I don't believe in that."

Annet stared out the window, wishing this day to be over. When they got home she refused to join the family with the excuse she wasn't feeling well and needed a rest. Alex grunted with displeasure as she left him standing in the hallway. In her room, she lay down on top of the velvet comforter, the baby busier than ever, as if it was ready to fight its way out. Unable to fall asleep, she eventually left her room, thinking a book might help to distract her mind. Hoping nobody would notice her, she sneaked down the stairs and in the direction of the library. A door opened and Leo stepped into the hall.

"What are you doing meandering the house?" he growled, his features cold and assessing.

He was the last person she wanted to see. "I'm not trying to steal the table silver if that's what you're implying," she snapped.

Leo laughed without mirth in his dark eyes. "I can understand you've been able to wrap Alex around your finger. He's naive, inexperienced, and soft, but don't think for one minute you can fool me."

"That's too bad," she said, having no idea what he was talking about. When she tried to walk away, he caught her by the wrist.

"That baby isn't from Alex. He hadn't even set eyes on you when you got pregnant."

They were the same height, but he was a lot stronger, his shoulders massive underneath his coat. "How do you know that?" she retorted, trying to wrench her arm free from his viselike grip.

"Simple. People talk and not a single soul had ever laid eyes on you before you showed up at that convent four months ago in August."

She looked him straight in the eyes, noticing his hard features change into something calculating. Before she could pull back, his lips were on hers, hard and demanding, her arms caught between them, leaving no room for protest. With all the strength she could muster, she struggled to free herself, kicking and biting, until he let go.

"You bastard!" she spat out, pulling back a hand and slapping him across the face. "How dare you lay your filthy hands on me?"

"Ah, come on," Leo griped, rubbing his cheek, "don't pretend you don't like it."

"You're a pig, a pervert," she roared, fleeing down the hallway, his loud mocking laughter following her into the library. She slammed the door closed behind her and leaned with her back against it.

"That asshole," she muttered, her breathing ragged. It wasn't until then that she noticed her father-in-law standing in front of the fireplace, leafing through a book.

"I thought you were feeling poorly," he remarked.

Annet inhaled a deep breath, wondering what his reaction would be if she told him his oldest son just pawed her in the hallway, but she decided against it. It would only create more problems, and she already had enough of those.

"I was restless. Thinking a book might help to calm my nerves."

His sharp eyes rested on her for a moment. "You have lived under my roof for two months now. I believe it's time for a private tête-à-tête." He sat down in front of the cozy flickering fireplace, motioning her into the other chair.

"If this is about my behavior this morning, I apologize," she said quickly, uneasy under his scrutinizing glare. "With the upcoming birth of the baby, and the discomforts that come with it, I was a little testy."

"I hadn't noticed," he replied.

To her surprise, she noticed the same twinkle in his eyes she had seen the other day. Feeling slightly more at ease, she sat down in the chair, reorganizing her skirts.

"So tell me how you became acquainted with my son?"

Oh no, here we go, another inquisition. She squeezed her lips together, her defenses back on high alert. "How I met your son? Yeah, let me see," she mumbled, trying to formulate an acceptable answer. *What was it again they always said? Oh, yes, try to stick to the truth as best as you can, to avoid getting caught in a lie.* "I found out about your son during an art class in high school. I must have been sixteen or seventeen."

A flicker of surprise glided across his face. "An art class? What nonsense is that?"

"The teacher was an admirer of Alex's paintings. He even took us on a field-trip to the ....uh...dunes, because he knew that's where Alex prefers to work."

"Right, his paintings," her father-in-law replied, his tone degrading, giving no doubt how he felt about his son's passion for art.

"Alex is very talented, Mr. Keizer," Annet continued, not allowing herself to be intimidated. This could be her chance to talk some sense into the old man.

"Hogwash," was the brusque reply. "He can't afford to waste his time on frivolous pursuits. He's a grown man and is expected to take part in the family business."

"Yes, making money is important," she agreed, deciding to pursue this precarious subject another time. It was obvious he wasn't in the right mood, and she didn't want to stir up any trouble. Instead, she steered his thoughts in another direction. "So I understand you own a shipping company?"

"Indeed. Over the past fifty years, The Keizer Shipping Line has transported merchandise to and from many ports," he answered with pride in his voice. "Goods, ranging from letters to spices, leather, and lumber, come from far corners of the earth. But I'm sure that sounds very tiresome to you."

"Not at all! I'm *very* interested," she assured him. "If I remember correctly from my history classes, we currently live in the middle of the Industrial Revolution." She enthusiastically shifted to the front of her seat. "The construction of major railways will soon connect cities and towns, and if you take advantage of that, your business could increase considerably."

Her father-in-law stared at her for a lengthy time. "I don't believe they raise subjects like this in a girl's grammar school. You must have had a private tutor."

She dropped back into her chair. Damn, why was she always such a babble mouth? "Well, uh,... my tutor was an advocate for equality in education," she improvised, struggling to keep her wit. "To diminish illiteracy among women and to secure their independence. He was far ahead of his time."

He got up and straightened out his coat, his face solid, giving nothing away. "We will continue our conversation another time."

"Of course," she mumbled, feeling rejected and dismissed by the third member of the Keizer Family that day. She raised herself with difficulty. Her back hurt and it felt as if something in her belly had shifted. There was a peculiar pressure deep in her pelvis that hadn't been there before.

Chapter 42

A lex showed immediate concern about the change in her condition, but was distant and stayed out of her way. There was pent-up hurt in his eyes. Hating to see him like that, she cursed the tricks life pulled on her. She loved him, she really did. But what could she do?

For a second night, she lay awake, wrestling her way through her jumbled thoughts and conflicting emotions.

Her instinct told her to nest, put the finishing touches to the nursery, reorganize the baby's clothes, and stay home. She had some swelling in her feet and ankles, and she enjoyed reading a book in front of the fire, with her feet up, or taking a revitalizing nap.

Her heart told her to give her life in the nineteenth century a chance. Alex was handsome and had a great body. He was caring and honest, and in him, she had met her match. He was intelligent, hardworking, and not afraid of a decent and invigorating verbal altercation.

But her mind was crying out for her former life, and not only for her job, her friends, her mother, or Forrest, but also for all the modern conveniences, like electricity, computers, cellphones, grocery stores, drive-thru coffee stands, Chinese food, and pizza. She also missed their tiny one bedroom apartment, their comfortable kitchen and bathroom, and even their clunker of a car. But what she missed most of all, was her independence. Of that, she had none, and every effort she made to gain a little back, was frowned upon.

The days dragged on as she tried to come up with a solution, cramp-like pains in her abdomen bothering her. They were irregular, making her believe they could be the Braxton Hicks contractions she remembered her doctor talking about. Whatever they were, it meant her baby's birth was imminent.

Mrs. Fritz, the midwife, had moved into the servant quarters, watching her every move with exaggerated concern. The days were short, the nights long, the weather depressingly nasty. New Year's Eve came and went without fireworks, music, television or any kind of celebration, and she was ready to book a flight to Hawaii or the Caribbean. Then, on January third, just before midnight, her water broke and labor started.

Alex stayed with her for the first few hours, and although she begged him to stay with her through the end, he slipped away the moment they told her to push. In agony, she cried out in pain, cussing and screaming all the way until her child was born.

It cried, red-faced, its tiny hands grasping in the air. Mrs. Fritz wrapped it in towels, cleaned it, and put it on a scale.

284

"It's a girl," the midwife informed Alex after he rushed in, handing him the baby. Instead of looking at the small bundle in his arms, his eyes searched for Annet, the strain on his face disappearing when she reached out to both of them, her hands shaking. Her labor had lasted over twenty-four hours, and she was exhausted. He placed the baby in her waiting arms, her face haggard but exultant.

"Fleur is born," he smiled, gently touching the blonde fuzzy hair with his fingertips.

"A healthy nine pounds, and all ten toes and fingers accounted for," Mrs. Fritz informed them.

"Really, she weighs that much? How is it possible?" Alex replied, sinking down on the bed next to his wife. "She seems so small."

Tears welled up in Annet's eyes, her fingertips stroking the baby's cheek, nose, and lips. "She's so beautiful."

"She's gorgeous, just like you," he whispered, wiping her tears away with his thumbs. "I love you, Amazon. More than anything."

"And I love you too," she whispered back.

Fleur was a content and easy baby, the first week flying by. Annet's days and nights were filled with feedings, diaper changes and learning everything there was to know about infants. Each day, a doting Elise came to see her, cooing over the baby's crib and helping her change her cloth diaper. Even Leo and her father-in-law came regularly into her room for a brief visit.

After ten days, Annet made her way downstairs into the kitchen for the first time since Fleur was born. The cook was busy behind the stove, an apron over a loose fitting green and white dress gathered at her gargantuan waist.

A kitchen maid was mopping the floor. "Careful, Mrs. Keizer," she warned. "The floor is wet. We don't want you to slip."

"Dumb girl!" Mrs. Browning yelled. "Take her arm and help her into a chair. Don't you know she's still recovering from childbirth?"

"It's all right," Annet told the trembling maid, steering away from the wet linoleum. "Mrs. Browning, I have a request. Can you make a chocolate and hazelnut cream pie?"

"Chocolate pie is not a problem, Madam," the cook told her, taking three loaves of bread from the brick oven and placing them on a walnut butcher block. "But hazelnut?" She furrowed her eyebrows. "I'll do my best."

"And do you have birthday candles?"

The cook's hands fell silent in midair. "What was that?"

"I'm turning twenty-six today and where I'm from, we celebrate a birthday with cake, candles and a Happy Birthday song," Annet explained. "But don't worry. One candle will be fine, maybe two. Just see what you can do. Okay?"

"Of course. Will that be all, Madam?"

"A heel of that delicious smelling bread would be great," Annet said, looking around for a bread-knife.

Mrs. Browning eyes flashed a warning. "Let me do that for you, Mrs. Keizer."

Before the cook could place the slice on a plate, Annet pulled it out of her hand. "Thank you," she smiled. "You're the best!"

Nibbling on her bread, she read the newspaper in the library. Martin Van Buren was still president, the inauguration of William Henry Harrison not until March 4, 1841.

The names of all the presidents were drilled into her at school and she remembered Harrison had been the shortest serving US President, dying of pneumonia one month after he gave his inaugural speech. *Poor President Elect*, she thought. *Maybe she should try to warn him? But how? It wasn't like she could give him a call.*

Another interesting article was about the continuing Opium War between Britain and China, and the occupation of Hong Kong Island. The United Kingdom wanted to secure economic benefits and fought China over their conflicting viewpoints on diplomatic relations and trade. The second headline was about the Spanish slave ship, the Amistad. It had transported captives who had freed themselves, gaining control of the ship after killing the crew.

"Good for them," she mumbled when a knock on the door made her look up.

The butler walked in. "Good morning, Jackson. What's up?"

"Sorry to disturb you, but you have a visitor, Madam Keizer," he informed her, bowing with his hand in front of his stomach. "Do you want me to escort her into the drawing room?"

"Of course," she replied, thinking it had to be Amelia or Trudy Jonkers, "And could you send Gloria for refreshments?"

"Certainly, Madam," Jackson said, turning on his heel.

A minute later he ushered her visitor in, dressed in a maroon brownish dress, her sandy red hair uncovered and pulled up in messy bun on the top of her head. Annet recognized the eccentric fortune teller she had met at church on Christmas morning.

"Agnes, how nice of you to come," Annet said, inviting her to take a seat.

The women exchanged a few pleasantries about the library and the dreadful weather while Gloria brought in a tray and served them tea.

"I hope you don't think it's inappropriate for me to call this afternoon," Agnes said, the fine wrinkles at the corners of her grey eyes deepening with unease, "but I've been thinking about you every day since we met."

"Oh, you have? Why is that?"

"Now please, I don't want to offend you in any way," Agnes replied, shifting in her seat. "But the moment our hands touched, I felt a surge of energy shooting up my arm and into my head."

Annet couldn't help but laugh. "Well, that's cool."

"Yes. I had hoped to meet you again in church, but you haven't been back."

Annet stood and poured them a second cup of tea. "No, I'm not religious. Besides that I've been too busy with Fleur, our new baby."

A faint blush of pink rose to Agnes's cheeks. "Oh, how unthoughtful of me. I didn't even realize. Congratulations."

"No problem," Annet grinned. "Would you like to see her?"

After they finished their tea, Annet preceded Agnes up the stairs and into their bedroom. Mrs. Fritz sat in the rocking chair with Fleur in her lap, her needlepoint discarded next to her on the floor. Fleur was fussing and Annet picked her up.

"Does she sleep in your bedroom?" Agnes asked, looking at the crib placed in a corner. "That's unusual."

"Tell me about it!" Annet replied, slowly rocking in the chair. "It looks like I have to fight over everything in this household. Even over where my baby sleeps, when to feed her and what she's wearing."

Agnes laughed, shaking her head. "I can't believe I have met a woman who is more unconventional than me."

"Trust me, you have no idea," Annet replied gloomily. Although Alex tried very hard to be supportive of her peculiar ideas and unusual behavior, it was a constant struggle to fit into the wealthy, influential, and conservative Keizer family, each day bringing new challenges.

"You are a fortunate woman, Annet," Agnes commented. "You live in a beautiful house, with a husband who loves you very much, and with a gorgeous baby girl. I hope you cherish all this, because before you know it, it can be taken away."

Chapter 43

Agnes' words kept creeping through Annet's mind the rest of the afternoon, the idea that the fortune teller had seen something in the stars very disturbing. Even feeding her daughter didn't have its usual calming effect.

"You showed that crazy woman around the house?" Leo growled while they sat down for another late dinner that night.

For weeks, the men had been working every single day from before dawn until after dark. She was worried about Alex, who was often too tired to eat. Her hand searched for his beneath the table, and she squeezed it. "Just the library and our bedroom," she said, "I hope that's all right with you."

"I don't care," he shrugged, his indifference adding to her growing concern.

She looked around the table. "I thought the manufacturing of machine tools and the increasing use of steam-powered machinery in the factory would make life easier, but it seems it only takes up more of your time. What's up with that?"

"We're in an important, but difficult transition phase, Amazon," Alex explained, listlessly playing with his food.

With a loud thud, she placed her glass back on the table, water spilling over the rim. "I'm bored, while you're working your ass off, heading toward a mental and physical breakdown," she cried out. "That's not right. I want to help."

Leo laughed out loud. "A woman who wants to interfere with her husband's work. Preposterous!"

"You're lucky I'm not a fanatical feminist," Annet flared up.

Alex placed his hand on her arm, calming her, and she relaxed.

"Maybe it's time to invite Annet to the factory, so she gets a better understanding of the importance of your work, Leo," her father-in-law announced.

"Absolutely not," Leo objected indignantly while Annet's eyes lit up. "That would be wonderful."

"Then that's settled," her father-in-law decided, Leo's protest falling on deaf ears. "Now where is dessert? Jackson, why don't you find out what's taking so long?"

A few minutes later, Gloria, Mrs. Fritz, and Justine entered the dining room followed by Mrs. Browning, carefully carrying a decorated cake with ten small burning candles. The four of them sang, 'Happy Birthday, Happy Birthday' totally off-key.

"Now blow out the candles and make your wish," Mrs. Browning told her after she placed the cake on the table.

Annet clapped her hands with glee. "Oh, thank you!" she smiled.

Leo tapped with his fork against his plate. "Now what's all this nonsense?" he grunted, a frown of disapproval furrowing his forehead.

"It's Annet's birthday," Elise told him.

Leo glared impatiently at the ceiling. "Like I didn't understand!"

"It's me you're angry with, and you shouldn't take it out on your wife," Annet told him, coming to the defense of her sister-in-law. Elise personified gentleness and didn't deserve his wrath. "But don't believe for one second I'll back out of this trip. I'll go with you, no matter what you say or do!"

"Several days later, Annet dressed with excitement, ready the moment the men left for work. Finally, she would see the inside of the clothing factory.

Leo hadn't said a word since they left, continuing his brooding silence as they drove along the busy waterfront. Glued to the window, Annet looked at the hustle and bustle of people and carriages, and the kaleidoscope of moving, and moored sailing vessels, some with one mast, others with three or more. In the middle of the river, a wooden paddle-wheeled steamship with a big black funnel made its way out. Other vessels were moored onto the dock, unloading cargo and passengers from all around the globe, loading domestic cargo for export.

Before the carriage came to a stop at the rear of an uninviting brick building, Leo hurried out and slammed the door in her face, leaving her to fend for herself. Jason jumped down from the driver's box, reopening the door while she scrambled with her skirts.

With her head held high, her posture straight, she opened the heavy metal door of the building and entered the lobby. A young man, his blond hair cut into a stubble, rose up from a chair behind the counter. "Good morning, Mrs. Keizer," he said. "We were expecting you." He lifted the hatch and walked through. "Mr. Keizer told me to guide you around the factory, and answer all your questions. I'm Deagan. At your service, ma'am." He looked down at her from at least six feet, his black trousers too short, his leather shoes and brownish coat well-worn. "Right this way, Ma'am."

She followed him through a door into a hallway, the faint sound of running machinery in the distance.

"I started working here as a scavenger when I was twelve," Deagan continued.

"A scavenger?" Annet frowned, images of animals feeding on decaying carcasses coming to her mind.

"A scavenger works under the spinning mule, to sweep, and gather fallen material and dust," Deagan laughed, lifting his hand. "It's a dangerous job, but it wasn't until I progressed to piecer, I got hurt."

Annet counted three fingers. "Luckily for you that you work in the office now," she answered, wondering if worker health and safety regulations already existed.

"I don't work in the office, ma'am," Deagan corrected her. He opened the door at the end of the hallway, the clicking and clonking of the machinery much louder. "I can't read or write, and was merely waiting for you there."

They entered the factory floor where rows and rows of machines were operated by countless factory workers. "I operate the newly installed self-acting spinning mule and spin at least one hundred pounds of cotton in a mere week," Deagan yelled over the now deafening noise. "Our earlier mules were partially powered, handling a maximum of four hundred spindles, while our new self-acting mules have thirteen hundred spindles."

Annet covered her ears with her hands, staring bewildered at the smooth running gears and long strands of yarn.

"As the carriage travels on the track, it draws out and spins yarn," Deagan shouted, using his arms and hands to point out what he was talking about. "On the return trip, as the carriage moves back to its original position, the newly spun yarn is wound onto these spindles right here."

Yeah, yeah, yeah, she thought, not understanding a word of it. They walked further down the aisle and she waved at the workers as they passed, the air stifling, dust irritating her nose. *How could anyone work under these conditions?*

When they reached the other end of the floor, Deagan opened a narrow wooden door and Annet hurried outside onto a courtyard. A cold wind pulled on her clothes and it drizzled, but she was glad to be out of the noise. To her left, two large doors stood wide open, workers loading spindles of yarn onto various drays.

"Those are ready for transport to the weaving mill or to the harbor for export," Deagan explained.

"Are all these buildings still part of the Keizer textile manufacturing?" she asked, dodging rain puddles as they crossed the courtyard.

"Yes," Deagan replied. "The spinning mill, weaving mill, and warehouses are all owned and operated by the Keizers."

Holy moly! That's a lot of terrain to cover, Annet thought.

Deagan preceded her into an office, introducing her to Mr. Owlings, the supervisor.

"Welcome, Mrs. Keizer," Owlings said, his rheumy eyes regarding her with interest. "I was instructed to take you to the mill's steam engine, to explain the workings. Would you be so kind as to follow me?"

Before following him out of the office, Annet looked around. No phones, typewriters, printer, computer, ballpoints or markers. Only wooden desks, stacks of papers with ribbons tied around them, dip pens, and bottles with black ink. Their work had to be so meticulous.

"This steam engine powers the approximate eleven-hundred looms in the weaving mill," Owlings said. He continued his explanation, but all she heard were unfamiliar words like warp, heddles, shuttles, and shedding, his voice drowned out by the noise of hundreds of leather belts activating driving shafts, flywheels and crank mechanisms.

"I've seen and learned a lot," Annet said when they returned to the office. "But what I'm really interested in is where the clothes are made."

"Madam Keizer," Owlings replied, his face slightly baffled. "Virtually all clothing is handmade, either as home production or on order from dressmakers and tailors, the textile mill only concerned with the production of yarn and cloth."

"That's disappointing," Annet commented, her engorged breasts painful, a sign Fleur's feeding was overdue. "I'm in need of a new dress and had hoped to talk to someone here."

"The company employs several tailors, Madam," he responded, wringing his hands uneasily. "They make the bib aprons for the factory workers. I could accompany you to the workshop."

"I'd rather have Jason drive me home right now," Annet said, "but I appreciate the tour and will be back tomorrow. Thank you, Mr. Owlings."

After she fed Fleur, gave her a bath, and put her down for her nap, Annet wandered over to the west wing where Leo and Elise resided.

"I hope I'm not disturbing," she said after she entered their suite.

Elise plucked away on her harp, her light pink dress made of delicate muslin, her petticoats elaborately embellished, and her dark hair curved in intricate layers to her shoulders. She was the perfect picture of the wealthy sophisticated Victorian woman.

Annet plopped down in one of the elegant upholstered spoon-back armchairs, repressing the urge to put her tired feet on the matching rosewood table. "I heard you played with Fleur for about an hour while I was at the factory. Thank you."

"That was my pleasure," Elise frowned. "She's such a doll. I can't believe you would leave her alone for an entire morning!"

"It's not like I left her unattended," Annet defended herself, realizing Elise would never understand how cooped up she felt. "Have you ever been to the mill?"

Elise's lips curved down at the corners. "Of course not. Why would I?"

Annet scoffed. "Because it's your husband's workplace. Isn't that reason enough?" She took off her low-heeled ankle boots and wiggled her toes.

Elise kept on tinkering on the harp, an uninterested stare in her eyes.

"Leo has a lot of responsibilities on his shoulders. I could tell he's well respected by the employees," Annet continued, trying to stir up her sister-in-law's interest. "You should ask him to give you a tour."

Elise's hands fell still in mid-air, her eyes roaming over Annet's clothes. "I hope you wore a different outfit than this timeworn and tedious garment," she commented. On the

296

average, Elise went through three wardrobe changes a day, her immaculate looks more important than anything else.

"Oh, you're a terrible snob, Elise," Annet replied. "Of course I was wearing this. I went to see a mill, not the opera."

Elise pushed a fictitious stray hair in place and checked her fingernails. "To show off our family wealth and our prominent standing as noble ladies, we are obliged to dress elegantly, elaborately, and fashionably on every occasion, Annet."

Screw that, Annet thought. There were a lot of women outside these sophisticated walls who weren't dressed like a Victorian damsel or a haughty noblewoman. They were hardworking women, wearing warm comfortable dresses, without all the silly tassels, ribbons, petticoats, and other hoopla she detested.

"Well, it might please you to know I'll talk to a tailor at the factory tomorrow," she countered. "I want them to create something special for me. If you don't like my clothes right now, wait a few weeks until its ready and you might be in for a *real* surprise." She got up and paraded with her boots in hand from the room.

After cuddling Fleur and putting her down for a nap, Annet left Gloria to watch over the baby and headed toward the library. At the bottom of the stairs she ran into Mrs. Browning, who brought up a cast-iron bucket full of potatoes from the cellar.

"You didn't eat since breakfast, Mrs. Keizer," she said. "Can I fix you anything?"

Annet stopped in her tracks. "Actually, that sounds wonderful. I'm starving."

"What would you like?"

Annet thought for a minute, then gave her a warm smile. "I have to tell you, my dear Mrs. Browning. One of the biggest advantages of living here is having *you* around."

The heavyset woman wrinkled her brow in puzzlement.

"I was never good at taking care of myself, skipping meals all the time," Annet continued. "But just like Forrest used to do, you take such good care of me. I wanted to tell you how much I appreciate that."

Mrs. Browning blushed like a little girl, her fingers twiddling her silver-brown hair under the unexpected compliment. "You're a pleasure to work for, ma'am," she said and rushed off to the kitchen. Thirty minutes later she entered the library with a tray filled with scones, omelets, bacon, pudding, and cake.

"Holy smokes," Annet cried out, pushing a stack of books to the side to create room for all the food. "Since I'm breastfeeding, I know I have to eat for two, but this is enough for the entire family."

Mrs. Browning smiled modestly, pouring her a cup of tea. "What are you reading, ma'am?" she inquired.

For several ponderous moments, Annet gazed in front of her, wondering how she could explain why she had pulled out books about "Merchant Ships," "Building Materials," "Industrial Design," "Sail Makers," and "French Textiles."

"Although I appreciate the luxury and comfort around me, I'm dying of boredom," she began. "I need to break away from this contrived routine. I need excitement, and the feeling I'm contributing. Can you understand that?"

Mrs. Browning snorted. "You want to find meaning in these books?"

"Yes! These books will give me knowledge about import and export, the operation of steam engines, various fabrics. I want to help in the family business, and to make myself useful, instead of being a burden to the entire family."

The astounded cook stared at her in mute stupefaction.

"It's all right. Thanks for the refreshments, Mrs. Browning," Annet sighed with placid resignation, realizing the amiable woman had no clue what she had been talking about. Having worked in the kitchen since she was eleven years old, she could barely read or write. So how could she ever wrap her mind around the fact that someone from the upper-class, who lived under such privileged conditions, needed even more than what she already had?

Over dinner Annet couldn't stop talking about everything she had seen and learned that day. Her natural dynamism was rekindled, her gloomy state of mind out the window, her lethargy vanished. She felt renewed, almost her old self again.

"That poor young Deagan who's missing two fingers," she said. "Are there a lot of work accidents at the mill?"

"We've had numerous calamities in the mill with workers hair or clothing getting caught between the mule's roller beam and carriage, or between a belt and a shaft," her father-in-law explained. "To prevent these devastating injuries from happening, we require all workers to cut their hair short, and to wear tight clothing. Hence Alex's design of the stiff and tightfitting bib-aprons the workers are required to wear."

She turned to Alex, her face flushed with excitement. "I would love to see the tailor's shop, Alex. Can you show it to me tomorrow?"

"For heaven's sake," Leo sneered. "Why are you so interested in a simple outfitters workplace?"

Annet turned around in her chair to face him and declared hotly, "That's none of your business!"

Elise gasped and Leo's face darkened.

"Oh, come on, Leo," she said with a stern voice, "I gained admiration for you and your work at the mill today, so don't ruin it by degrading your own tailoring business."

Leo shot her a seething stare, but looked away after a few tense moments.

Annet gloated, thinking to herself, *I'll fight for my place in this family, and in the business. Nobody is bullying me away!*

A junior servant in livery entered the dining room, rounding the table to clear the dishes.

"Listen," she continued after he left, "I've been reading up on this in the library. Since clothes are either made at home or custom tailored, the manufacturing of clothing is still in its early stages. But it won't be long before the sewing machine is invented."

"A sewing machine? That sounds intriguing," Alex said, shaking "no" with his head.

She could tell he wanted her to stop talking, but this was too important, and not even her beloved husband was going to stop her. "The invention of the sewing machine will be the start of the ready-to-wear clothing industry. If the Keizer Mill is prepared for the arrival of this ingenious apparatus, and for the subsequent groundbreaking change, you can start producing these clothes before all the other clothing manufacturers get wind of it."

They gaped at her, her father-in-law rubbing his forehead in deep thought. "Ready-to-wear clothing? Like the aprons we hand out to each new worker the moment he starts?"

"Exactly," Annet replied, appreciating his swift understanding. "Sewing machines will reduce the time to make a dress shirt or a pair of pants. Therefore a manufacturer can decrease the number of workers needed to produce the same amount of clothing. This will reduce production costs and drop prices significantly, so more people can afford multiple outfits."

"Which in turn will not only increase the production of clothing, but also the production of fabrics, weaves, and cloths," Leo finished her dialogue. For the first time since she'd met him, he regarded her without his usual scowl.

"I don't understand," Elise complained. "Why would anyone want to wear or buy something customary, undistinguished, and ill-fitting?"

"Don't worry. This doesn't concern you, my dove," Leo said, patting her hand before he turned to Annet, hostility back on his face. "Since we've never even heard of such a device, please indulge to explain where you've gained this knowledge?"

Alex rose up from his chair. "Come, Amazon, let's go. I believe Fleur is crying."

The door opened and the servant came in with dessert. Leaving the dinner table before the meal was finished was against the family's etiquette. Reluctantly, Alex sat back down.

"I just know stuff," Annet replied vaguely, thanking the young liveried boy for her bowl with banana pudding and cream in an effort to direct the conversation away from her.

"I just know stuff," Leo mimicked. "Please, share more of your knowledge, if you would.

His patronizing superiority pissed her off, her words regretted the moment they flew from her mouth. "I know your new president will die about a month after his inauguration."

Her brazen statement shook even Alex. "What are you saying?" he cried out.

Annet lifted her shoulders in a shrug. "It's true. You'll find out soon enough."

Chapter 44

With admiration, Annet stared down at her sleeping daughter. "Isn't she beautiful?"

Alex wrapped his arm around her shoulders, pulling her into an embrace. "Yes, she is," he agreed.

She slipped her arms around his waist. "Sorry I'm such a pain in the butt," she said. "I realize it must be hard, having to live with me, but I feel so locked up in this house. It's like I'm suffocating."

Alex rested his chin on the top of her head, a look of distress on his face. "I know exactly what you mean," he sighed.

Something in the tone of his voice made her look up, his expression solemn as he continued, "Did I ever voice that the tailor's workshop is my preferred part of the mill?"

She shifted in his arms to look him straight in the eyes. "It is? Why?"

His forehead furrowed into a frown of deep thought. "Sometimes I find it difficult to comply with the world around me. If I can't escape to the cabin on moments like these, I find a semblance of solace there."

Annet nodded, encouraging him to continue in the hope he was finally opening up, sharing what had been bothering him for weeks now.

"At times, it feels I'm ready to burst, my inner soul pressing hard to emerge from the depths beneath my duties." His green eyes brimmed with yearning and unfulfilled desire. "The only means to release the pressure is to let my artistic passion leak up through the maze of responsibilities, dogma, and devoir. Something only possible in the confinement and seclusion of the cabin."

Oh, Alex, her heart cried out in pain as she recognized the locked up desires from the soulful artist buried inside him. I'm so sorry! I've only been thinking about my own needs. While I wallowed in self-pity, I never thought about how you were feeling. What a horrible, selfish wife I am!

"Every day, you're forced to bury yourself under paperwork behind a desk, while you should be out there, embracing your talent," she declared forcefully. "We have to get your ass out of here and go back to the cabin asap."

"I appreciate your support, my love, but painting is just an inane pastime," he half-grinned, releasing her from his embrace. "My sole responsibilities are right here in Heemstead, with my family, and at the office." He walked toward his dressing room, loosening his white linen cravat.

"I know you're just trying to convince yourself of that," she said, following him. "You know what your problem is? You're afraid of rejection. But let me assure you the world will embrace each painting, because they are unbelievable creations of beauty. You should never doubt your talent. Do you hear me?"

He continued undressing himself. "You're the most infuriating and outspoken woman I've ever met," he stated, tossing his dress shirt on a chair, "Why in the world I love you so much is beyond my comprehension."

His grin broadened, making her instantly aware of everything about him. The sparkle in his eye. The width of his bare shoulders.

"That's because I'm so freaking gorgeous, sexy, and irresistible," she said, her fingers seductively sliding through the sprinkle of hair on his chest.

He reacted immediately, pulling her up against him. "Yes, you are."

At his touch, a burn of desire overwhelmed her. She slipped her arms around his neck, her mouth seductively searching his lips.

With eyes radiating his adoration, he lifted her in his arms, and carried her to the bed.

The next morning Alex accompanied her to the tailor's workshop, introducing her to Gregory Skaar, a middle-aged man with thick eyebrows, an approachable smile around his mouth. He stood hunched over a long wooden workbench, pressing out the wrinkles of a piece of fabric with a burnished steel box iron.

"Greg and I worked together on the design of the aprons," Alex continued. "He's a former tailoring guild member, a consummate tradesman, and a great asset to the company."

The well-organized textile sweatshop was dusty, workbenches covered with durable-looking brown material, thread, and a variety of shears, hooks, and hole punchers. Tall windows brought in an abundance of light, giving the spacious workshop a bright ambience.

"Although this shop might be big enough for the current workload, it will be far too small for the assembly line I have in mind," she commented. "Is there a possibility for expansion?"

The next hour they walked through the building concocting plans, the tailor following them around, listening with keen interest. "We've already seen textile become cheaper since the installation of the steam power loom and spinning mule," he acknowledged Annet's theory. "Because unskilled workers are now able to perform tedious, time consuming tasks in a fraction of the time."

They concluded their conversation, but before they left, Annet pulled out a handful of crumpled black lace from the embroidered purse she'd carried along.

"I realize this is completely different from your current work, Mr. Skaar," she said. "But since you're an excellent needle worker and clothier, I was hoping you might create a few of these."

"What in the world is this?" he asked, holding the small wad of fabric up in the air.

A faint blush of pink rose to Annet's cheeks. "We call it a bra, short for brassiere. It's a woman's undergarment that supports her breasts," she explained. Although she wasn't a prude, he didn't have to display her underwear for everyone to see! "This will be very fashionable in the future."

"I can't make anything like this," he concluded. "Such fine work should be done by a seamstress."

"Then you better hire yourself a female apprentice, because this project is very important to my wife," Alex told him.

"A woman in our sweatshop? I don't know," Greg Skaar objected.

"She needs to be talented, innovative, and experienced," Alex continued. "But most importantly, she needs to be able to keep a secret, since this project will be confidential."

"Yep, and we will call it "Amazon's Secret," Annet laughed.

Chapter 45

A lex annexed the 8,000 square foot warehouse next to the mill. They emptied it out and prepared a full line-up, in the hope it could house about thirty sewing machines as soon as they became available. While Annet worked alongside her husband, Leo kept his distance, her father-in-law becoming increasingly skeptical.

"After convincing us about the imminent invention of the sewing machine, I agreed you could help Alex with the groundwork and preparation of the new sweatshop, but I don't want you to keep on interfering with his *real* work," he told her after she began spending more and more time in Alex's office.

His real work? she thought angrily. They had no idea what his real work should be!

All she could do was back down a little, to give him more time to adjust to the idea of a working daughter-in-law. Nothing could be accomplished without the approval of the patriarch of the family and, after all, Rome wasn't built in one day either.

Winter was losing its grip, the first daffodils, and snowdrops popping up their heads in the flowerbeds in the yard. The time to revisit the cabin had arrived. Annet couldn't wait to find out how it had survived the brutal winter storms, and bitter cold temperatures they had endured in January and February.

She gathered clothes to bring for the entire family, a crib, and blankets for Fleur. A knock on the door of their chambers interrupted her packing. To her surprise her father-in-law walked in. He seemed distraught, his demeanor strained. Frowning with concern, she looked at the clock. It was two o'clock. Far too early for him to be home already.

"Has there been an accident?" she asked, picking up her daughter. Fleur was three months old, and more aware every day. She slept for a nice stretch of six hours at night, held up her head, and smiled at the sound of a familiar voice. Changing her diaper had become a challenge, her chubby little hands trying to grab at everything.

"President Harrison died of pneumonia today," her father-in-law announced.

"Jesus!" she yelled, scaring Fleur. "Oh, baby, don't cry," she shushed her, holding her little head and pressing it against her shoulder. When Fleur stopped crying, she looked at her father-in-law. "You scared the hell out of me with your solemn demeanor, and now you tell me it's only because of that!"

He lifted his chin in a way that demanded an answer. "How did you know?"

She didn't answer.

"We need to talk," he ordered. "In the library."

Annet handed Fleur over to Gloria, obediently following him downstairs.

"Can't we talk about this when Alex is home?" she tried to wriggle herself out of the upcoming interrogation.

He gave her an unemotional, lengthy stare, one that convinced her there was no escape.

She sank down in a chair at the table. "I can't explain why I know things," she started out, her hands fretfully moving several books around. "Although I find the president's passing unfortunate, at least it proves I was telling the truth."

"Indeed," her father-in-law declared, his eyes narrowing distrustfully. "What *else* of significance can you share?"

In the movie Back to the Future, Dr. Emmett Brown had talked about a time paradox. That time travel was dangerous, coming face to face with yourself in another time period destroying an entire galaxy. So what could the consequences be if she told him about automobiles and planes, the telephone, the California gold-rush? Or about Abraham Lincoln, the civil war, and the end of slavery?

"I don't know where my knowledge comes from," she improvised. "Maybe it comes from a place somewhere deep within me, or from a dark hole somewhere far away in the universe. Sometimes, a peculiar awareness floods over me, making me blurt out what comes to my mind. I know, sorry, it's an annoying habit. I sincerely apologize."

"Why don't you share another example?" he said, regarding her with skepticism.

She avoided his gaze, looking at the sugar coated cookies Mrs. Browning had brought in. "You should look into importing wool from Australia."

He shrugged, taking a chair at the other side of the table. "So you said."

Okay, he was too smart to fall for the same information she had already spilled. What else could she tell him? Then she knew.

"I know what causes the horrible diarrhea and vomiting that makes hundreds of townspeople die."

He almost choked on a gulp of hot tea and coughed.

"They have contracted cholera, a disease caused by drinking water or eating food contaminated by the feces of an infected person."

"By what?" he said, wiping his face and cravat dry.

"You know, like when someone is sick and his or her shit, uhhh, body waste ends up in the water system. Then another person consumes this contaminated water and gets sick too."

Her father-in-law scoffed. "To my knowledge, this dreadful disease is only common among the unfortunate that live in the slums, but now you claim by merely drinking water, we could get sick too?"

"Of course," she cried out. "Because it's not a matter of being underprivileged. It has to do with poor sanitation, and the only way to protect our family and employees is by using boiled water."

Not able to resist the delicious smelling cookies any longer, she took one, enjoying every morsel in the quiet that followed.

"If what you're saying is true," he spoke more to himself than to her, "we can't keep this knowledge to ourselves. This is revolutionary. Lives could be saved." He got up from his chair and headed to the door. "I will conduct a visit with Doctor Snow right away."

Annet immediately got on her feet too. "Before you go, there's one more thing I need talk to you about, and you better listen to this one."

"From now on, you *have* to support Alex's painting. He's extremely talented, and one day, he will be famous worldwide."

Disbelief and anger spread across his face. "You almost had me believing you," he said, his voice quaking with wrath before he opened the door and slammed it in her face.

On Easter Sunday, she joined the family for church. It was an important holiday, the celebration of Jesus's resurrection, and her father-in-law had made it clear he expected her to be there.

After Fleur was born, Elise had insisted on taking Annet to her personal tailor, ordering her several elaborate gowns. When they were done, the new seamstress at the mill had finished her first soft-cup triangle bra from black lace, with mesh-lined cups, and hook-and-eye fasteners at the back. Today, Annet wore it under her new purple satin dress, the warm weather allowing her to drop several layers of petticoats, her new underwear comfortable against her skin.

She entered the church on Alex's arm, nodding to the left and the right as he guided her to their pew. With a straight back, she sat quietly through the entire mass, not giving a flinch when she was left by herself while the rest of the family took communion. Although still solemn and magnificent, the church didn't seem as impressive and overwhelming as before, the parishioners less hostile and condemning.

After the service, Agnes Bornholm approached her in the pebble-stone parking lot. Her smile did not hide her displeasure.

Seeing her reminded Annet of the ominous words she had spoken, and she felt guilty for not visiting the woman as she had promised. She left Alex's side and took Agnes by the arm. Together they strolled away from the crowd.

"I thought you were interested in having your fortune read," Agnes came straight to the point.

"I know, I'm so sorry," Annet apologized. "I thought about it more than once, but every time I wanted to go and see you, something held me back."

"Why? Were you afraid of what I might tell you?"

Annet frowned. "It's weird, but I'm not sure if I want to know my future anymore."

Disappointment was evident on Agnes' face. "Did something happen to change your mind?"

"That's a good question," Annet said, gazing off into the distance. "You know, to be honest, I have no clue!" She laughed uncomfortably. "But trust me, I will figure it out."

Agnes face softened. "You have changed since I first met you." With interest, she glanced at the young woman in front of her who seemed deep in thought. "You don't seem cross or ill at ease any longer. Are you more at peace?"

Annet blinked several times, her frown fading into a contented smile. "You are right. I was pissed off most of the time, believing the whole world was against me," she ruminated. "Since Fleur was born and I am able to prove myself, my outlook transformed."

A young woman marched in their direction, her golden gown with black crochet borders adorable and exquisite, her hair a true work of art. "Are you coming, Aunt Agnes? We're ready to leave!"

"My niece, Juliette LaRouge," Agnes said, rolling her eyes.

"Hi girl," Annet said cheerfully. "Long time no see!"

The young woman cast her a disdainful glance. "Do I know you?"

"Yes, we met at the pump in Dunedam, last summer. Do you remember?"

Uncomprehending, the young snooty woman raised her fine eyebrows.

"I know, I wasn't at my best that day," Annet laughed, extending her hand. "Annet Keizer, nice to meet you again."

Three young women chatting in the vicinity turned their heads, gaping at her before they started whispering behind gloved hands.

"Word is spreading you're working at the mill," Agnes clarified the women's condescending glances. "The only explanation for a lady assisting her husband at his work is financial trouble. Is it true the Keizer Mill is on the verge of bankruptcy?"

"Hell, no!" Annet protested. "The mill is on the brink of a major transformation in the clothing industry. I'm helping with the preparations."

A strong arm wrapped around her shoulders. "Are you ready to go, Amazon?" Alex asked.

Annet smiled sweetly at the group of prosperous and influential ladies that had gathered around her. "Some women like to get more out of life than being a housewife or a frivolous butterfly," she declared in a loud voice, for everyone to hear. "See you later."

Composed, she took Alex's arm and promenaded away.

Chapter 46

"THAT SMELLS WONDERFUL, CAROLINE," Forrest said when he entered the kitchen. "What are you making?"

"Oh, nothing special," she replied, her two cats circling her legs. "Just some ground beef with onions, tomatoes, and gravy that I want to serve over mashed potatoes."

He looked at the table, raising his eyebrows in questioning. "Just two plates tonight?"

Since Kara had joined the team at the "Orange Fine Art Studio and Gallery", and had moved into the right wing upstairs, they had picked up the habit of having dinner together every evening, taking turns on who would cook.

"Yes, she's meeting Rix for dinner somewhere in town. Afterwards, they're going to the Legion Hall, where they play for free drinks. Don't you remember?"

Shortly after Kara had moved in, Rix had charmed her into joining his band "The Dirty Dandies" as a backup vocalist. She also played a little tambourine. Forrest often joined them when they practiced in the old coach house. He had to admit Kara had a nice singing voice and the band sounded great, if they would just play a little less loud.

"You don't mind she spends so much time with him?" he asked.

"Why would I?" Caroline asked, keeping her eyes on the food. "She's a smart young woman and is just having fun."

Forrest shrugged, turning his head to stare outside. It had been eight months since Annet's disappearance and nothing had changed since then. Barbara and Chuck still lived in his apartment. Neither of them worked, but Chuck received Social Security and a small pension from the trucking company he had worked for before they went bankrupt, allowing them to take care of the rent and utilities. He had few dealings with them, but had come to appreciate them. Chuck had a great sense of humor and was the most patient man he had ever met. Even Barbara had mellowed out, paying him an occasional visit at work, bringing him cookies, and asking for an update that wasn't there. The police had basically given up on ever finding her.

Since there had been no tips that had pointed them in any direction or had shed light on her disappearance, they had gradually lost interest. Even the public was forgetting about her. It was old news, most people preferring to push her disquieting disappearance to the back of their minds rather than be reminded a woman had vanished without a trace, making their tight-knit community unsafe.

He was still working at the Keizer Manor, plucking away behind the computer. Although his work was a far cry from his anticipated high paying career as a civil engineer, the job he had studied many grueling years for, he was content with his current position. There were no high demands and no deadlines to meet, and although Annet had taken on far more responsibilities, he didn't feel compelled to do the same. He wasn't like her, not even close. All he wanted was to drift from one day to the next, feeling close to her behind her desk, and daydream about the day she would come back, just as miraculously as she had disappeared.

On the surface, it seemed his life was in order. He ate and drank, he slept, watched television and worked, but there still bubbled a volcano of grief and pain under his composed and somber appearance. His concerned parents had suggested counseling more than once. They recognized his pain and were anxious about his wellbeing, but he had declined. Although he was aware he was angry at life, and lived each day on autopilot, he believed all he needed was space and time to learn how to cope with the loss of his dearest Annet and their unborn child. Therefore, he kept to himself and dismissed all help, afraid if someone were to come too close or dig too deep, the volcano inside him would erupt into a spewing fire, all the bottled up grief and anger spilling out.

Caroline placed the steaming bowl of potatoes on the table and regarded him with concern. "Are you going to watch them play tonight?"

He woke up from his gloomy reverie and sat down in one of the hard backed kitchen chairs. "No, I don't think so."

She sat down on the other side of the table and spooned up her plate. "I think you should. You haven't been out since Annet disappeared. It might do you good."

He sighed. "Do you realize my child would be about three months old by now, and that instead of sitting here with you, I should be busy changing diapers and warming up bottles?"

"I know, my dear," Caroline replied and squeezed his fidgeting hand briefly to show her support. "But you can't keep on locking yourself away in your room. Annet would not have wanted that. You know how full of life she was, and she would kick your ass if she ever found out how you've spent the last eight months."

Despite himself, a smile escaped his lips. "You're right," he admitted. "Maybe it's time to stop feeling sorry for myself and get out."

Caroline sent him an encouraging smile. "Absolutely, and tonight is a great opportunity to start."

Chapter 47

On a clear and warm April day, Alex and Annet headed to the cabin in Alex's wagon. The tranquil, pleasant weather mirrored Alex's mood.

"Just before we left, my father came to see me in the stable," he said, grinning from ear to ear. "He asked for permission to roam through our wing and look at my paintings. I don't know if he was seriously interested, but nonetheless, I appreciate the gesture."

"That's wonderful," Annet replied, squeezing his arm. She held Fleur in her lap, wrapped in a warm blanket, so the baby could look around. "Now let's hope he develops some appreciation for your work, and becomes more supportive." Inside she was gloating and feeling proud of the role she had played in her father-in-law's change of attitude.

An hour later they stopped at the Jonkers' farm for fresh eggs, milk, and sausage. They were welcomed as long lost friends. After visiting awhile, they continued their trip into the dunes, finding the cabin exactly the way they had left it. The only difference was the heaps of sand banked up against the buildings.

"Luckily nobody stole the shovel and the broom," she joked after they entered the cabin, overjoyed to find everything untouched.

Alex unloaded and she put everything in place. By the time it got dark, it was almost as if they had never left. They fixed an easy dinner together and after Fleur had fallen asleep in her new bassinet, they snuggled up in their own bed.

"It's so wonderful to be here," Annet sighed, stroking her husband's arm.

"Yes, it's the best place on earth," Alex agreed, yawning. It had been a long and busy day. "Do you want me to blow out the candles?"

In reply, she brushed her fingers seductively over his chest and down to his navel, nuzzling the skin of his neck. "Are you tired?" She took his lips in a long deep kiss as he wrapped his arms around her, pulling her close.

"Not really," he lied.

Their tongues touched tenderly, savoring each other's company and the quietness of their surroundings until their blood heated up and kissing wasn't enough.

A deep rumble in the distance interrupted their lovemaking. Annet stiffened underneath his touch. *Was that thunder?*

Grudgingly, Alex stopped licking and kissing her abdomen and pulled himself up until he lay next to her on the pillow.

"Did you hear that?" she asked, her blue eyes large and troubled.

A faint flash of lightning lit up the room before another rumble rolled in from the ocean.

Alex raised himself up on one elbow, trying to catch her gaze, "What do you want to do, Amazon?"

Avoiding his intent stare, she sat up on the side of the bed and wriggled herself out of her nightgown.

"You're getting dressed," he concluded miserably. "You want to get out there in the storm, don't you?" He sighed and got up himself. "But don't think for one second I'm letting you go by yourself. No matter where you go, what you do, or how dangerous it is, Fleur and I will join you."

But instead of leaving, she sank back down on the mattress, stark naked, and pulled him down with her. Then she rolled on top of him and took his face between her hands.

"I'm not going anywhere. I'm staying here, with you."

Her mouth found his in a hard, ardent kiss, and she whispered with shaky urgency, "I need you! Fill me! I need you! Now!"

He took hold of her bare behind and rolled her over before entering her with one swift movement.

"Oh, yes," she groaned in pure pleasure as his hardness filled her, her eyes wide and brilliant with suppressed tears. She loved this man so much. He was her life, her everything. This was where she belonged, and nowhere else. She was home, right here.

His hands moved impatiently over her flesh as he slammed into her with brutal force. "Like this?" He breathed hard, catching his own gasp in fierce longing.

As his warmth wrapped itself all around her, enfolded her, her entire body throbbed, the feel of him inside her making her cry out for more. "Yes, my love, exactly like that."

Outside, the storm intensified and rain pelted noisily on the roof, while inside the dark protection of the cabin, their lovemaking was just as violent and tempestuous, the intensity of their emotions making them soar.

His breathing was still shallow and quick when he sagged down next to her, but she clung to his shoulders and kept on kissing him everywhere, not able to get enough of him.

Grateful to have her still with him, he cupped her face, her skin hot under his touch, her hairline damp with perspiration.

"You know you may have missed your only opportunity to return home," he said searching her face. "Aren't you afraid you made a huge mistake by letting this storm pass?"

At first, she tried to evade his intense gaze, her emotions still in turmoil from their lovemaking and the sudden revelation that had come to her, but then she beamed up at him.

"Everything is completely clear to me now, and I've never been so sure in my life. I love you, Alex Keizer. More than anything in the whole wide world, and I will never leave you or Fleur. Ever!"

His green eyes grew large and then misted over. "Do you know how I've longed to hear you say this?" His words shuddered as he spoke. "I love you so much. I couldn't bare life without you."

She stroked his back as he tried to regain his composure.

"I've loved you from the first moment I saw you in the convent," she confessed, "I truly did. But it wasn't right to betray Forrest. I had known and loved him for so long. I was expecting his child." Her voice was choked with emotion. "Over the last few weeks, I've done a lot of soul searching and came to understand that what had started as the infatuation of a teenager, had over time changed into a deep friendship. We got along so well. He was gentle, caring, and fun, but what I felt for him is nothing compared to what I feel for you. Really, Alex, I'm crazy about you. I love you with my whole heart, and am proud to be your wife."

At her passionate statement, Alex relaxed, but there was still concern in his eyes. "Amazon, although I'm overjoyed with your words, there's more to this situation than just Forrest. How about the rest of your former life? Your family, your friends, your colleagues? You've been telling me how much you miss all that too."

His stare seemed to pass through her soul, but she didn't avert her eyes. All she wanted was complete honesty between them.

"That's true, I miss all that terribly," she whispered, not hiding her pain, "but not enough to give you up. I want to stay at your side until I die. You're the love of my life, and I need you more than anything."

They spent two glorious, peaceful and relaxing weeks at the cabin, with just the three of them, completely happy, not needing anyone else. After their return to Heemstead, she continued working with Alex every morning, her father-in-law and the rest of the family gradually accepting her "inappropriate" behavior.

During a warm spell in June, they spent another week at the cabin, and in August they returned again. It had been a year since she had arrived in the nineteenth century, her former life and Forrest becoming strangely unreal, almost imaginary.

When September came along, she realized she was pregnant. Alex was elated and so was the rest of the family. In April 1842, she gave birth to a baby boy. They named him Frank Leonardus after respectively, his grandfather and Leo, who insisted he wanted to be the baby's godfather.

That summer, they spent ten days at the cabin and Alex was disappointed. He'd looked forward to their vacation, but Fleur was walking and they had their hands full with their two children, giving him no chance to paint. By the time they came back to the city, he was disgruntled and edgy, and Annet understood. His artistic blood needed to flow, but there was nothing she could do about it. Children took up a lot of time and energy, and if she hadn't been able to leave them in Gloria's care, she would have gone nuts herself. Being a full-time mother had never been in the stars for her.

Unfortunately, Alex didn't seem to get over his blues. Weeks later, he was still restless and quickly agitated. Something had to be done.

"Why don't you take off for a week," she told him, "just by yourself. So you can paint your heart out without being interrupted by crying children and a nagging housewife."

It wasn't hard to convince him and although he left, hesitant and halfheartedly, he came back revitalized and enthusiastic. She had made the right decision. She had her husband back.

The next summer, their short trips to the cabin were spent in a similar fashion, except now they had two toddlers running around, knocking over paint and touching everything. Alex picked up the habit of extending his stay with an extra week, to work in peace, but this time, when he hadn't returned home after ten days, Annet became worried.

She left the children with Gloria and had the coachman drive her to the cabin. When they arrived, she noticed Alex's horse tied to the shed. He had fresh water and was nibbling on a handful of hay. Her anxious heartbeat slowed down, and she was finally able to breathe. He was okay.

"Alex?" she yelled, running toward the cabin. "Where are you?"

She pulled the door open and marched inside, her eyes widening in disbelief.

Leaning against the wall stood a life-sized painting of a slender, very familiar, woman in a long white nightgown. She had a toddler by the hand. Their clothes were soaked and they seemed lost, the dark clouds behind them lightened up by thunder-flashes.

"Lost in the Storm," she cried out. "This can't be."

With both her hands in front of her mouth, she took a few steps closer. *Oh my God. I admired this painting for years. How could I not have seen it was me?* Tears started streaming down her face, her shoulders shaking with uncontrollable sobs.

When she felt a warm hand touch her arm, she turned around and cried against his chest, soaking his shirt. "It's *me*, Alex," she managed to say. "It's *me* and Fleur in the painting."

"Sorry you were worried, and had to come and look for me," he apologized, massaging her tense shoulders and neck with his thumbs. "I was so wrapped up in my work and couldn't let go,"

"Oh Alex, don't apologize," she interrupted him. "I understand."

With their arms wrapped around each other's waist, they stared at the freshly painted canvas.

"I still need to put the finishing touches to the background, but do you like it so far?"

"I don't *like* it," she half cried, half laughed. "I think it's incredible! How were you able to paint us so lifelike? So perfect?"

"I don't need to have you in front of me to see you, Amazon. You are engraved in my soul, and all I have to do is close my eyes and you are with me. Don't you know that?"

"No, I didn't," she whispered, still shaking inside. "But I do now."

After standing together for several more minutes she was still in disbelief. "Do you think I didn't recognize myself because I'm wearing an unfamiliar nightgown, or because my hair is so dark from the rain?" she asked. "Do you think I didn't see it because I'm holding Fleur by the hand? Or because I look so desperate and lonely?"

Alex only smiled. He had no answer. "When I first met you in the convent, you were wearing your nightgown. That's how I wanted to paint you."

Mesmerized, she reached out to the canvas, her fingertips touching her face, the dark clouds, her young daughter.

"This is your master piece, drawing people from all over the world to the museum," she told him. "You must have worked day and night on it. Aren't you exhausted?"

He planted a kiss on her hair. "When I paint, I drift into another dimension, and if you ask me to explain how that feels, I can only compare it to a bright, safe, and warm burrow. A place where I'm in touch with my inner self, where I'm free, and at peace. A place where I never get tired, and hardly sleep." His voice was hoarse and he cleared his throat. "I can even work in the dark, by the light of an oil lamp and candles, and sometimes don't see my bed until my work is done and I'm satisfied."

"Well sorry, buddy, but that's not happening tonight," she told him, snuggling closer up against him. "Right now I'm taking you to bed and won't let you finish until I'm done with you."

The next morning, she woke up with a start, their arms and legs still tangled, her face pressed against his ribcage. She shifted in his arms and found him still in a deep sleep, his breathing even, his features relaxed. Impatiently, she shook him until he woke up.

He gave her a lazy smile, turned around, and tried to fall back asleep, but she shook him harder.

"What is it?" he protested. "It's still dark."

"I have to tell you something. I finally figured out why I'm here."

He was immediately wide awake. "You did?"

"Yes, I'm here to build the Keizer Manor."

He raised his eyebrows and then burst out laughing. "You want to build a manor? How? Why?"

She frowned. "I'm not joking. I'm serious."

"Sorry, Amazon," he hiccupped. "But in my mind I saw you juggling with wheelbarrows, dirt, lumber, and bricks."

"I've done my share of dirty work back in the day," she snubbed, remembering how she had gone through the numerous garbage cans in the trailer park in Heemstead. The people that lived there had been selfish slobs, without a second thought discarding soda cans, beer bottles, and other recyclables into the trash. From a young age, she'd daily plowed through the trashcans, to collect the refundable deposits from the automated machines at the grocery store.

"Calm down, I believe you," he replied. Still grinning, he shifted in search of a comfortable position and pulled her into his arms until her head rested on his chest. "Now, tell me all about it."

She lay quiet for a moment, thinking about how to explain it. "Do you remember I told you I transitioned in time on the day of the two-hundredth anniversary of the Keizer Manor? Now, I was thinking, how could we even have had that celebration if the Manor was never built?"

"It's simple. Until today, I'm the only person in the whole wide world who appreciates your work and believes in your talent, so who else would ever be interested in seeing it built. Do you get it?"

"Hey, I'm interested in my paintings," he objected.

She scoffed. "But did you ever think of a real house, right here, instead of the cabin? Where your paintings will be safe from the elements? Where they can be displayed for the world to see?"

"No, of course not," he rebuffed. "This cabin has always been sufficient for my needs, and you know I've never been interested in sharing my work. So why would I have *ever* considered such a frivolous and pointless notion?"

She raised herself up on her elbow to look at him. "You see? That's exactly what I mean. Without me, that Manor would have never been built."

"Okay, I see your point," he admitted, "But my father will never agree, so let's get back to sleep and forget about it." He yawned and pulled the blanket back over his shoulders. "I haven't slept in days."

Indignantly, she picked up her pillow with two strong hands and slammed it on top of his head, before jumping out of bed. *How could he say he understood, then turn his back against her and tell her to take a hike?*

She slipped into her bra and panties, her fingers struggling with the tiny pearl buttons of her blouse, when she felt two strong hands on her shoulders.

"Let me assist you with that," Alex said.

She stepped away from him, her eyes still heated. "Only if you've changed your mind."

"I still think it's a ridiculous idea," he said, reaching out to touch her again. "But you're my wife, and I want to stand by your side."

"Come on, Alex. What's the big deal?" she argued. "You own the land free and clear, and don't forget I have complete insight into your financial status. There's a large chunk of change in your bank account, and you don't even need the support from your precious family."

His loving demeanor changed and with eyes blazing he snapped, "Unlike you, I care about my family, their opinion and their feelings."

Her fists planted solidly on her hips "You wouldn't if you were raised like me, between baboons, serpents, and pigs!"

"I'm sorry. That was unjust," he apologized without remorse, "but you have to understand my family's opinion *is* important. They have my best interest at heart, and always want what's best for all of us. Although their ideas don't always coincide with mine, I value their views, their insight, input, and observations."

She stared at him for a long moment, tamping down her anger when she realized she loved him so much because he wasn't afraid to stand up to her. He confronted her on her outbursts, corrected her mistakes, and expressed his own opinion. He took charge when needed, and was the rock she could build on.

Almost a full minute of thoughtful silence elapsed when he reached for her hands. "Did I mention how seductive you look in your brassiere this morning?" She hadn't closed a single button and her blouse hung wide open, exposing her bra and abdomen.

"Sorry my emotions occasionally fly off the chart," she said, the air cleared after their heated argument. She squeezed his hands before letting them go. "Why don't you finish the painting, and then let's clean up the cabin and go home. I can't wait to get in touch with a respectable and trustworthy architect who can draw up the plans, and get this ball rolling. I'm so excited!"

She picked up her skirt from the floor and finished dressing. "Uh, by the way, how about the logistics? Did you come here with the wagon or just on your horse?"

He chuckled. "Sorry, you're out of luck. No wagon."

"Darn! I would give anything for a phone call, to tell them to send the coach," she muttered. The fourteen miles from the cabin to Heemstead meant nothing by car, but having to sit behind Alex on horseback, getting bumped up and down with each gallop, would be torture all the way.

"I don't mind," Alex told her. "I'll enjoy feeling you behind me."

"Ugh, I bet you do," she commented.

Chapter 48

As Annet had predicted, the ride home had been challenging and taken forever. By the time they got there, her butt hurt, and so did all the muscles in her back and legs. Alex's horse had protested the entire way under the additional weight, while a strong sea wind had picked up, playing continuous havoc with her long skirt.

Alex had found it hilarious, so had passersby, but she had been cold, and fighting to stay on the rebellious stallion. *Darn. How could she have ever believed riding on horseback was romantic?*

"You're becoming an old lady," Alex teased her when she groaned going up the stairs to their quarters. She was ready to slap him.

After she cuddled with Fleur and Frank, she changed into another blouse and skirt, the children clinging to her legs. She had never left them for so long and they didn't want to let go.

With a child on each hip, she walked down the stairs to meet with her father-in-law. Alex had told her he'd come home and was waiting for them in the library with Leo. Her aching body protested under her children's weight, but the moment she tried to put them down, they screamed in protest.

What would her old friends and colleagues say if they could see her, she wondered. They had all known she'd never had the desire to marry or have children, and here she was, deeply in love with her husband, and expertly juggling two toddlers. Life was full of surprises.

The two original upholstered chairs in the library were replaced with four leather ones. The men were talking together, occupying three of them. When she entered, Alex stood and took Fleur from her, but the moment he sat back down in his chair, she squirmed out of his hands and climbed onto her grandfather's lap.

"Hi, Grampa," she said, making herself comfortable in his arms. Fleur had a way of being able to wind anyone around her little finger. Grandfather Keizer wasn't an exception.

Frank tried to slide down from her lap too, but he was after the delicious smelling butter cookies on the coffee table. She let him go, relieved to see both kids had forgotten about her unusual absence, feeling confident enough she wouldn't disappear again the moment they looked away.

"I want to build a new house in the dunes," she came straight to the point. "A vacation home for the entire family... a place to escape to ... so if someone is tired or needs a change of scenery, there is a place to go."

"Ridiculous," Leo blew her off. "I have no desire to get away, and Elise prefers to spend her time in her room."

Over time, Leo had softened toward her, but still often treated her with impudence.

"That's not true, Leo," she protested, grabbing Frank to keep him from taking all the cookies, and crumbling them in his hands. "It's the unfamiliar that scares her off, but what if she had the exact same quarters in a different location? With a closet full of her clothes, a harp, books?"

Leo leaned back in his chair and placed his foot on his knee, a disapproving frown on his face. "Then she might as well stay home," he declared.

"Just hear her out, Leo," Alex commented. "I think it's a brilliant idea, and all we're asking is to give it a serious thought."

Annet had grown used to Leo's arrogance and negative outlook and didn't let his words bother her. She had also come to know a softer side of him, watching him dote on Elise, and talking to her children when he thought no one else was around. Besides that, she admired his intelligence and business sense. She even appreciated his brutal honesty.

For a moment, she gathered her thoughts. "But what if she could open the window and smell the ocean? If she could hear the distant sound of the rolling waves? The squeaks of the seagulls? And all she had to do was open the front door to stroll through the dunes, toward the beach?"

She painted a beautiful and rosy picture of the surroundings of the cabin, the words coming straight from her heart.

Her father-in-law listened with Fleur still in his lap. She was playing with his golden pocket watch, but the shiny object also caught Frank's attention. On wobbly legs, he sauntered toward his sister and grabbed his grandfather's knee for support, his chubby baby hands covered with cookie crumbs and drool.

"What exactly are you suggesting?" he asked, searching his pocket for a handkerchief. He took a hold of the little boy's hands and wiped them clean.

"You know how much we enjoy going to the cabin," Alex continued. "But with the two children it's too small and uncomfortable, so Annet and I have been talking about building an actual house on the property." He got up from his chair to give his words more power, using his arms to express its proposed grandeur. "Instead of building this home solely for our own use, we want the entire family to enjoy it. Make it a refuge for all of us. A sanctuary, a safe haven, a home away from home."

Little Frank grabbed onto the golden chain that hung from the watch and pulled it toward his mouth. Fleur cried out in protest and fought him off, not willing to give up her toy. The next moment both kids were screaming.

Alex scooped up his son and planted him on top of his shoulders, the watch immediately forgotten. Fleur crawled from her grandfather's lap and dove underneath the coffee table, out of sight.

"I believe it's time to feed our children and take them to bed," Annet smiled in apology. "That will give you time to think about our plans, but before I leave I want you to keep one thing in mind. Most influential families in Heemstead have second homes in the country. Take for example the Parsons Family, and the LaRouges. Don't you think it's time we have our own Keizer Manor?"

Two weeks later, Annet and Alex sat down in the head office of the Keizer Shipping Line with the owner of the most prestigious architecture firm in Heemstead. After introductions were made, and coffee served, Alex explained the purpose of their meeting before Annet took over and continued the conversation. She had drawn up a floor plan and a sketch of the Keizer Manor, and handed them to him.

The architect skimmed over the wrinkled papers and the smudged pencil stripes. A frown of disapproval appeared on his forehead. "I can't work with that," he replied condescendingly, pushing the papers back toward her. "I'm a professional!"

"Sorry I'm not a better draftswoman," Annet spat out. "But come on, man. My children got a hold of them, and that shouldn't be a problem for an expert like you."

"Apologies," the man said, pushing his chair back. "This is a waste of my time. You better find somebody else." He grabbed his hat and overcoat and walked out of the office, the coffee untouched.

"Asshole!" Annet yelled after him.

Alex roared with laughter. "Oh my, oh my, Amazon. That temper of yours."

Annet burst out laughing too. "Did you see his face? What a jerk!" She leaned against the back of her chair with a grin. "You know what, I'm glad that arrogant prick walked out of the office. I wouldn't even *want* to have him around."

Alex pulled a crumbled piece of paper from his pocket. "Maybe we should start at the bottom of my father's list instead of the top? Benjie Flax," he read. "I like that name. Don't you?"

They set up an appointment and met with him a week later, Alex waving him into a chair after he was escorted in.

The young architect bowed politely. "It would be an honor to work for you, Mr. and Mrs. Keizer."

The door opened and one of the clerk's aides walked into the office with a tray. Benjie jumped to his feet, making room for her so she could easily access the table.

Annet appreciated the uncommon courtesy he showed the aide, most visitors and business associates would not even notice her, but Mr. Flax exhibited a different stance. Liking him already, she handed him the simple unsophisticated drawings, observing his reaction.

"Based on these sketches, do you think you can draw up the plans for Keizer Manor?" Alex asked.

The architect's Adam's apple bobbed in his thin neck, but that seemed the only sign of distress. "I'll do my utmost best," he replied.

"Then it looks like you're hired, Mr. Flax," Alex said, extending his hand over the table.

Two weeks later, they sat back around the table, going over the preliminary pen and ink drawings Benjie Flax had drawn up.

Annet wasn't pleased with what she saw. "This looks nothing like the Keizer Manor," she told the disappointed architect. "Didn't I explain it has three stories? And you completely missed the terrace and the double entrance doors."

"I apologize for my oversight," Mr. Flax said. "Is it all right if we meet again in seven days so I can make the necessary corrections?"

Annet searched for a piece of paper and began to draw with a wooden graphite pencil. "It has to be like this! With windows here and here, and stained glass everywhere. A side entrance on the left of the building. And the roof is four-sided with a double slope. Like this." She tried to draw it but failed miserably. "Damn, this is difficult." She was close to tears.

"You can't expect him to read your mind, Amazon," Alex said, rubbing the smooth skin at her wrist before he turned toward the flustered architect. "Your drawings are a testimony of your capabilities, Mr. Flax. Please, excuse our impatience."

The young architect nodded graciously. "I recognize this project is very important to you, and I am not a person to walk away at the first hurdle." He gathered his plans, including the

335

horrible picture Annet had made, and hurried out of the door followed by Alex.

When it was time for Annet to go home, Alex hadn't reappeared, but when he didn't show up for dinner that evening she became worried. Finally, after she had gone to bed, he slid in next to her.

"Sorry I'm late," he mumbled and fell asleep.

The next morning, he left before dawn, was gone all day, and by the time he came back in the wee hours of the night, she was freaking out. "Where have you been!" she spat at him. "You're worrying me!"

"There's something I have to take care of," he answered, pulling her stiff body close in an embrace to ease her concern. "That's all."

"But what is it?" she demanded to know. They had grown so close over the years. Keeping secrets from each other was disquieting.

"I can't tell you. It's a surprise."

No matter how hard she tried to press him he kept his mouth shut, and she became more apprehensive and distressed with each day that passed in the same manner.

When she came into the office a week later there was a letter waiting for her. "I canceled the meeting with Mr. Flax today. Don't be mad. I love you, my dearest Amazon," she read, causing all her anxiety and uncertainty to explode in anger. *What was he thinking? Disappearing for days, keeping secrets, and now cancelling her meeting. No way!* She walked out of the office and summoned the coachman to take her to the architect's domicile. This was her project, and she was not going to let Alex blow it off.

After a fifteen minute drive, the carriage drove through a neighborhood with modest houses, and came to a stop in front of a two-story plantation style home. The exterior was painted bright white, and a covered porch ran the width of it. Toward the back were a horse stable and an outbuilding.

Ignoring the coachman's extended hand, she jumped out and rushed across the finely cut lawn onto the porch. Next to the front door was a gold name sign mounted to the clapboard that read B.J. Flax. Architect. She banged the brass ring doorknocker. It didn't take long before she heard footsteps and the door opened. A young dark-haired woman wearing a red and white apron rubbed her hands dry on a kitchen towel. She was heavy with child and looked at her timidly.

Annet tried to look over the woman's shoulder down the entrance hall, into the house. "I'm Mrs. Keizer and came to talk to Mr. Flax. Is he home?"

"No, he just stepped out to buy more paint, but your husband is here," the woman replied with a gentle smile. "He's in the workshop behind the house. You're more than welcome to walk over there to see him."

Annet struggled to keep her professional composure while inside her thoughts were rioting. "You're very kind," she uttered. With long determined strides she rounded the house and approached the stable. A horse nickered, and sure enough, she recognized her husband's stallion in a stall.

She proceeded to the other outbuilding, and reached for the door handle, the hinges protesting as she pulled it open. The large room she entered was bright, with an aged wooden floor and a high ceiling. Two rickety wooden chairs and a table stood in a corner, a woodstove with a black single wall pipe disappearing into the wall behind it. Sun poured in through four ceiling high windows, the smell of fresh paint hanging in the air. She had an instant sense of déjà vu.

"That's fast, Benjie," Alex said without looking in her direction. He stood in front of an easel, working in full concentration on a painting, a brush in his hand, and jars of paint scattered on the floor.

"Instead of putting me through hell, why didn't you just tell me you wanted to surprise me with another painting," she cried out. "You're such a jerk! You know that?"

He stiffened and turned around. "Amazon? How did you find me?"

When she looked into the depths of his anxious green eyes, she recognized his insecurity. *He was such a fool, always wanting to hide when he was painting.* Her resolve melted. "I can't believe that after I told you so many times about the museum and your popularity, you still doubt yourself as an artist."

He drew in a deep breath and exhaled heavily. "Last Monday you were so distraught with Benjie's drawing. I wanted to help him by trying to paint the Keizer Manor."

She turned toward the painting, tears welling up in her eyes as she took in every single detail. "It's perfect. Everything is there. The steps, the decorative hoods on the dormers, the elaborate columned windows in the front, the roof line, the steeples, and pillars. How did you know?"

He smiled with relief. "From the moment I met you, you have been telling me about this beloved Manor of yours, so how could I not?" He put his brush down. "I followed Benjie to his house after the meeting. He's truly an honest and hardworking man. I trust he's the right man for the job."

Their shared smile lasted for several seconds, but then her expression turned serious. "Why don't you explain to me, my love, why you so easily trust *his* work, and not your own?"

He wrapped his arms around her slender body and caught her lips in a warm kiss. "I do believe in myself. After all, I am *The Alex Keizer*. Right?"

"Yes you are, and you better never forget that!"

Chapter 49

FORREST DROVE TO THE KEIZER MANOR, thinking about the fun and relaxing weekend he'd spent with Rix, the band, and last but not least, with Kara. Catherine had been right, forcing him out of the door every time the band played. It turned out Kara was incredible on stage. He loved to watch her sing and dance, her voice developing with each gig, her stage presence improving. Last night, the moment she took the microphone in her hand, and started to sing, her eyes had lit up when they met his over the heads of the crowd. She had blown him a kiss and winked. Something inside of him had lifted, and he had returned her kiss. He got warm, just thinking about that moment.

After parking his car, he crossed the parking lot, noticing a moving truck had backed up to the bottom of the concrete steps in front of the Manor, the two doors wide open, an automatic back lift lowered halfway down.

"We're having a delivery?" he asked Maria who worked behind the reception desk. She was professional, hardworking, and could type as fast as he could talk. He appreciated her a lot. Not only for her competence, but also because she had never met Annet. Therefore Maria didn't pay attention to the gossip about her disappearance a year and a half ago, or the speculation about his possible involvement.

Then he remembered. "Of course, they're picking up *Lost in the Storm* for restoration. Is Kara here, too?"

"Yes, she is. She's with the guys from the moving company who'll transport it to Orange Fine Art."

"How about the security firm?"

"They're not here yet," Maria replied. "Do you want me to call them?"

"If they're not here yet within the next ten minutes, I believe you should," Forrest replied and headed toward Storm Hall, his heart skipping a beat at the prospect of seeing Kara.

When he entered, four men, all dressed in blue coveralls, were setting up scaffolding. Kara stood watching them, wringing her hands, her expression strained. Forrest understood why she was so apprehensive. It would be quite the undertaking to take down and transport the valuable six by nine foot oil painting.

"Anything I can do?" he asked.

She turned around and smiled. "No, not really, but thanks."

He noticed a hint of insecurity in her brown eyes and his arm slipped around her shoulders. "Don't worry, Kara. These guys know what they're doing."

For a second, she rested her head on his shoulder, but then pulled away, letting out a deep sigh. "I sure hope you're right. This is his masterpiece. We can't afford to have anything happen to it."

The four men had set up two fourteen foot high towers of scaffolding on either side of the painting and were now busy connecting them.

"You see what I mean?" he continued. "They're experts in this kind of work."

Voices behind them made them turn around, and when they noticed a group of visitors entering the hall, Kara hissed. "Can you believe these people, ignoring all the signs not to enter?"

Forrest quickly walked up to the unwelcome spectators. "We're sorry," he said politely, "Storm Hall is closed for cleaning and restoration."

The visitors protested disgruntled. "*Lost in the Storm* is the main reason for our visit," one of them said.

"I understand," Forrest replied, his tone apologetic, "but it's clearly posted at the entrance, the reception desk, and the website that *Lost in the Storm* would be taken down in November."

The discontented visitors left and he turned toward Kara. "I'll make sure the entrance to the hall will be completely blocked off, so you won't have other curious visitors marching in."

There was gratitude, mixed in with uncertainty, and something else he couldn't define, in the darting look she sent his way. Thrown off by the intensity, he tried to make light of the situation. "You shouldn't curse like you just did, young lady. It doesn't suit you."

She pulled a funny face at him before she shifted her attention back to the work at hand.

Laughing out loud he walked to his office.

The next morning, Forrest shrugged out of his rain slicker and shook the water off it before he walked into the hall with the mail.

"Look at me," he told Maria who was already at her post behind the reception. "I got soaked in the hundred feet from my car to the front door. What a downpour!"

She smiled at him. "It's winter. What do you expect?"

Water dripped of off him onto the marble floor, and when he noticed, he cursed, "Darn, I better get to my office. Sorry about that, Maria." But before he took off, she stopped him in his tracks. "Dan wants to talk to you. He's in his office, waiting for you."

"Something wrong?"

Maria shrugged. "I don't know. All I know is that Kara called, asking for you first, and then for Dan."

Forrest's heart dropped. "I sure hope nothing is wrong with Caroline." At eighty-two she wasn't a spring chicken anymore, and anything could have happened. Completely forgetting about his dripping rain coat, soaked hair, and wet shoes, he rushed toward Dan's office, finding him behind his desk with his coat on, a colored cashmere scarf around his neck. That couldn't be good.

"Did something happen to Caroline?" he asked, his eyes revealing his concern.

Dan shook his head. "No, this is not about her. Kara called from the Orange Fine Art Studio telling me they found something disturbing within the wooden stretcher of *Lost in the Storm* this morning."

Forrest let out a sigh of relief. "Phew. I'm glad it's not something serious. So, why the coat and the scarf? Are you on your way out?"

Dan stood and joined him at the door. "Yes, I'm going to the art studio and you're coming with me."

"I can't. I have too many things to do."

Dan took the mail from his hands and dropped it onto the reception desk as he pushed him toward the exit.

"Hey, I'm sure my presence isn't needed," Forrest protested further, donning his slicker when they stepped outside in the pouring rain. A strong west wind howled around the Manor, whipping up sand from the dunes that piled up against the steps. It was the first serious storm of the winter, and he hated it, his nerves jolting with every gust, his heart racing after each clap of thunder.

"Somehow this involves you more than me," Dan explained as they crossed the parking lot. He started the station-wagon and unlocked the doors with his remote.

Forrest stepped in on the passenger side. "Great car with lots of room," he commented, stretching his long legs, sinking down into the comfortable leather seat. "So what's going on at Orange?"

"They just started the preliminary evaluation of the painting," Dan answered. Traffic got busier on the road as they approached the city and he slowed down, before continuing, "You know that as time passes, oil paintings darken due to the accumulation of dust, and yellowing of the protective varnish layer. The restoration work we're having done deals not only with the removal of this surface dirt and the discolored varnish, but also to the treatment of the support of the canvas called the stretcher."

"I know a frame protects a painting from the front, and the stretcher protects it from the back," Forrest commented. He had picked up some knowledge about oils and watercolors since he worked at the museum, and Kara had explained to him extensively what they would do after the paintings were brought into the studio one by one.

"That's right," Dan acknowledged, stopping for a red light. "A stretcher is found on the backside of a painting, the canvas tautly wrapped around it and nailed onto the wooden bars on all four sides."

The rain diminished, and he adjusted the speed of the windshield wipers before he continued, "Alex Keizer had his paintings framed by a professional craftsman, the frames works of art in themselves, whereas he made the stretchers that are an actual part of the painting himself."

Why did he keep going on and on about those stretchers? Forrest wondered, getting bored. His mind drifted off to this unexpected trip, and on to seeing Kara.

A few minutes later they pulled into the parking lot. Forrest followed Dan through the main entrance. A young woman, dressed immaculately in a bowknot blouse, straight black skirt, tights, and high heels welcomed them with a polite smile. "What can I do you for you gentlemen?" she asked. "Are you looking for something in particular?"

The atmosphere in the gallery was tranquil, warm, and luxurious, some of the art on display worth thousands of dollars.

"I'm Dan Mockenburg from the Keizer Manor. This young man is Forrest Overton. I believe we are expected?"

The young woman's eyes widened and she took a step back, staring at Forrest until he became uncomfortable.

Dan cleared his throat to get her attention and she blushed with embarrassment. "Mr. Greenwood, the art conservator, and his team are waiting for you. I will take you straight to them. Follow me."

Kent Greenwood was specialized in the restoration and conservation of old and contemporary paintings, not only restoring age-related damage to the valuable artwork, but also salvaging paintings affected by fire, water, and vandalism. He was also the owner of the Orange Studio, and Kara's boss.

The woman preceded them through the gallery until they reached a hallway lined with several offices. "You'll find them in the studio at the end of the hall."

"Thank you," Dan said, nodding his head politely in her direction.

Forrest opened the door and they walked into the studio, the spacious workplace airy and light. A group of people stood gathered in front of a six by nine painting elevated onto a sturdy wooden frame. It was turned around, with the backside toward them, but he knew right away it was *Lost in the Storm* due to its sheer size. Kara stood among them. To his surprise, Caroline Rothschild was there also. She sat on a chair next to the painting fanning her frail hands in front of her face, her eyes bright. Kara had her hand on the back of Caroline's chair, as if she was in need of support. When their eyes met, Kara let go of the chair and approached him, her long blonde hair a chaotic mess, her cheeks flushed with excitement.

"Glad you're here, Forrest," she said, pulling him toward the painting.

Forrest nodded. "Hello everyone, what's going on?" He recognized one of them as Kent Greenwood.

When no one answered, he looked back to Kara and then to Dan, wondering why he was summoned here. The atmosphere felt laden with tension, all the attention focused on him, and he had no clue why.

Kent Greenwood broke the silence. "Unlike Mr. Alexander Keizer's other paintings, the backside of *Lost in the Storm* was protected by unbleached linen, the kind that's usually used as a backing in vintage rugs. It's very strong, durable material, and still in excellent condition considering its age."

"Well, it was his masterpiece," Forrest shrugged, by now feeling a little annoyed with the situation. "So I don't find an extra layer of protection unnecessary, right?"

No one said a word for what seemed like a long time. Forrest took a deep sigh, lowering his eyes to escape the scrutinizing stares. Even the air he breathed seemed filled with a sense of urgency, and expectation. Or was it an accusation, and hostility? Completely at a loss, he broke out in a cold sweat, regretting he had come.

"That's what we concluded," Mr. Greenwood agreed. "Unlike the other paintings, this one has an elaborate stretcher due to its size. We can tell extra care was put into the framework as well. But after we removed the frame and the linen backing, we made another peculiar discovery."

The art conservator narrowed his eyes, sizing Forrest up, making him feel even more uncomfortable.

"What do you want from me?" he protested, turning around toward Dan. "This is ridiculous. Can we get out of here?"

Kara took a step in his direction. "Not yet. There's something you have to see." She pointed toward the back the painting. "Do you see that?"

He took a few steps closer. In between the dark wooden boards, he noticed four numbered yellowish colored envelopes.

"Take a good look at them," she urged him on.

He took another step forward. When he was close enough, he read out loud, "Forrest Overton, White Castle Apartments, # 14, Sixth Street in Dunedam." He turned around in disbelief. "What is this? Some kind of stupid joke or something?"

"We wanted to ask you the exact same question," Mr. Greenwood said, his gaze stony and unrevealing.

In the silence that ensued, all eyes were on him, waiting for him to say something.

A rush of annoyed emotion appeared on Kara's face. "I don't want to be disrespectful," she protested, her irritation directed at her boss, "but earlier you said the paper of the envelopes looked old. After I asked you how old, you estimated from the texture and the discoloration that it could be around one hundred and fifty years, maybe more."

The art conservator raised his hands up in the air. "I'm only trying to stay rational here."

"Why don't we let him open those envelopes, Kent," Caroline suggested, finding immediate support with all the others.

With trembling hands, Forrest carefully removed the first envelope, the tension in the studio increasing even more. "It feels heavy," he commented, turning it around in his hands, his palms slick and sweaty. "I've no idea how to open it. It doesn't have a flap."

"Let's go to my office where you can use a letter opener," Kent Greenwood suggested, walking toward the door. Kara helped Caroline up from her chair and they all followed him out of the studio down the hallway into a large office. Kent sank down behind a huge desk, the others gathered around the conference table.

After Caroline was seated, Forrest lowered himself into a chair next to her and placed the envelope on the shiny black surface of the table. With great care, he pried the tip of the opener in a corner and cut it open while everyone breathed down his neck. His heart raced when he pulled out a stack of folded papers.

"I think these are all letters." He glanced over the first page, blood draining from his face. "What the hell! It can't be! That's Annet's handwriting."

Kara leaned over his shoulder and read out loud, "January five, 1851." She turned toward her boss, her eyes dancing with excitement. "They're really old." When she looked back at Forrest, she found him leaning forward over the table, covering the letters, hiding his face in his hands. With immediate concern she placed her hand on his shoulder, finding it shuddering beneath her touch. "Are you all right?" she asked, shaking him gently.

When he looked up, his face was ashen. "Letters for me? From Annet? It's impossible."

Dan took a step forward. "Come, let's clear the room everyone," he ordered, coaching everybody out. "This man needs some time alone."

"Thanks, Dan," Forrest sighed, "but could you, Caroline and Kara stay please? I don't think I should read these by myself."

"Of course," Dan replied, sitting down across the table.

Bracing himself for what was to come, Forrest cleared his throat.

My dearest Forrest,

How hard it must be to believe what happened to me, I can imagine. It took years to come to terms with it myself, and all I can hope for is that my letter will somehow reach you soon after my disappearance, so you will get some closure, making it possible for you to move on with your life, like I did.

I promise you, this will be the first of many other letters, explaining what happened to me during that terrible storm and how my life unfolded afterwards.

I didn't die, wasn't kidnapped, or run away. I wandered through the dunes for several days after that fateful afternoon, and woke up in the monastery of the poor ladies from the Second Order of St. Francis, the Sisters of St. Clare, outside Dunedam.

It turned out I had landed in the year 1840, where I raised hell in the convent, believing I was being played. Now I can laugh about it, but at the time it wasn't funny.

Forrest raised his head, shock darkening his eyes. "What is this bullshit?" he cried out, "1840? Do they expect me to believe this?"

Dan picked up one of the letters and scanned it over. "It's definitely her handwriting. Why don't you continue? I can't wait to find out more."

"I don't think so," Forrest refused. "This is sick."

Caroline placed a calming hand on his arm. "I'm sure it will make sense if you continue reading, Forrest."

Forrest handed her the first letter. "Why don't you read it," he sighed, slouching down in his chair.

Caroline took the pages, adjusted her glasses, and continued reading where he had left off.

Today is Fleur's tenth birthday. She's my daughter, and I realize this must come as another shock to you, she is your daughter too. Unfortunately, photography is still in its early stages, but a few days ago I recruited a photographer, who was able to make a beautiful black and white photo of her. I will include it with this letter.

Kara picked up the yellow envelope and held it upside down. Four photographs fell down onto the table, all of them of a young girl with ribbons in her long blonde curls, dressed in Victorian clothing, smiling into the camera. Each photo had a date on the back. She put the first one on the table right in front of Forrest. "Look, here she's ten," she said, placing the other pictures next to it. "Eleven, twelve, and thirteen."

But Forrest pushed them away. *This was completely ridiculous. Did they really believe they could fool him like this?* "I don't want to listen to this any longer," he cried, rising up from his chair. "I've had enough."

For the second time, Caroline placed her hand on his arm. "Hold on one moment, my dear," she urged him to stay put. "This is very exciting. It may be about my heritage. My family. Please, let us read further."

Not wanting to upset the sweet old lady who had been there for him in his darkest days, he sat back down in his chair, bracing for what more nonsense was to come.

"My sweet Forrest," Caroline continued. *"I know how hard this must be to believe, but all you have to do is look at "Lost in the Storm." That woman wandering through the dunes isn't just a random woman. It is me, Annet Sherman, currently known as Amazon Keizer. I married Alex Keizer in October 1840 and a few years later he brought me and Fleur to life in what will be known as his masterpiece. Please, go and take a look before you continue reading.*

Forrest jumped up so fast that his chair tipped over, falling to the ground with a loud bang. He ignored it and rushed out of the office, into the studio. Dan and Kara followed on his heels, leaving Caroline absorbed in the letters.

"Turn the painting around," he yelled at Kent Greenwood. "Turn it around!"

Muttering his confusion, Kent and the crew complied.

When it was securely back in place, Forrest pushed a hardback chair in front of the life-sized oil and climbed on top of it. "This is outrageous," he yelled. "How is this possible? What did you do to the painting? Did you change her face?" He trembled with contradicting emotions. The rickety chair shook precariously under his weight. Before he could fall he jumped off and began pacing in front of the painting, grumbling loudly. "It can't be her! What the hell is happening?"

Dan climbed on top of the chair to take a look for himself, scratching his head.

Kara watched both men in silence, her hands clenched into tense fists by her sides. "Come, Forrest, let's get out of here," she said after a few minutes. She reached for his hand and pulled him out of the studio, past the office, through the gallery, and onto the street.

"We can't leave Caroline sitting there by herself?" he protested, freeing his hand from her firm grip.

"My grandmother can very well take care of herself for half an hour," Kara grinned. Resolutely she grabbed his arm and guided him toward a nearby coffee shop, the smell of espresso and glazed donuts in the air. It was still early in the morning, but almost all the tables were occupied.

"There's an empty booth by the window," she pointed, giving him a gentle push. At the counter, she ordered two sixteen ounce coffees.

Not minding Kara was taking charge, Forrest sunk down on the red vinyl bench, placing his elbows on the table. With his head in his hands, he waited for her to join him, his mind wandering. "All of this is so ludicrous," he said when she sat down across from him. "I can't believe this is really happening."

"I have a hard time understanding it too," she replied, placing one of the steaming cups in front of him. "But somehow we will sort it out."

He sighed, squeezing his eyes shut in an effort to think. "How can she be in that painting?" He sighed even deeper. "What about those letters and photos? Do you think they are real?"

Kara stirred sugar into her coffee, listening while he vented his thoughts, giving him time to ponder over the uncanny revelation.

"All these long months, I was convinced she was still alive," he mumbled, more to himself than to her. "So how can she be dead? How can my unborn child ... my daughter be dead?"

They sat in silence, trying to wrestle their way through their jumbled thoughts, their coffees forgotten, until she reached out to him with a comforting hand, her eyes brimming with compassionate tears. "This affects me too, Forrest, making my heritage the most unusual one you can imagine."

Her astounding statement shook him out of his tangled reverie. Slowly he raised his head, the noise of the espresso machine, the chatter from neighboring tables, and her concerned face coming back into focus.

"My grandmother Caroline is Alexander Keizer's great-great-granddaughter. If Alex was married to Annet, Annet must have been her great-great-grandmother."

He had a hard time following her and didn't know how to react or what to say.

"If this is true," Kara continued, "than Annet was my great-great-great-grandmother. But since one of her children was your daughter Fleur, we could be related." She let go of his hand and leaned back in her chair. "My father has documented the entire family tree from the Keizer family, dating back to the late seventeen hundreds. Let me give him a call."

For several moments, he gazed at her while she fumbled with her cellphone. She seemed agitated, dropping it on the table and having trouble to find the right buttons. He caught a whispered swearword as she kept on pressing the screen, her eyes avoiding his stare.

"You and me related? That wouldn't be so bad," he teased in the hope she would turn back into her normally calm, happy, and confident self. He had gotten to know her as an honest, caring, and lovely young woman with a great sense of humor. Seeing her upset bothered him. Not understanding why she was upset bothered him even more.

Instead of seeing her relax because of his remark, she only tensed up more, her fingers holding the phone so tight that her knuckles turned white.

"Hi, Dad," he heard her say. "Are you home?" With one hand holding the phone against one ear, and the other covering her other ear against the noise in the coffee shop, she nodded. "That's great. I want you to check something for me. Can you find out from what family line within the family tree I come?"

He watched her chewing on a fingernail, phone still pressed against her ear. Seeing her so distraught and anxious worried him. She had been his rock all those difficult months, and he had heavily depended on her energy, optimism, and support. This wasn't like her. Wondering what he could do to ease her mind, and make her feel better, he played with his napkin until she released her breath in a deep sigh. Closing her cellphone, she rolled her shoulders in an effort to relax. Next, she gave him a dazzling smile.

"Alex and Annet had two children, Fleur and Frank. Frank was my great-great-grandfather, so we are not related."

"I'm glad that news makes you happy," he commented, raising his eyebrows in questioning. "But can you explain the importance of that fact?"

"Darn you," Kara replied. "She opened her wallet, threw several dollars tip on the table, and got up from her chair.

He tried to grab her hand before she walked off, but missed. Within seconds he bolted after her, out the door. "Don't run away," he told her, after he caught up with her on the sidewalk. "Talk to me."

Her face was flustered, tears welling up in her eyes. She didn't speak.

Slipping his arm around her shoulders he pulled her off the sidewalk into the entrance of a nearby movie theatre. There was nobody there this early in the day, so they could talk in private. "I can't stand seeing you upset, Kara. Please, explain it to me."

She sighed deeply. "Do I really have to spell it out for you?" A tear trickled down her cheek, and then a second one.

He reached out with one hand and took her chin in a soft grasp, raising her face. When their gaze met, he noticed the warmth and love for him radiating from her eyes. His insides melted. With a knuckle, he brushed the tears away, then buried the fingers of one hand in her hair.

"I like you... a lot," she confessed, her eyes trying to avoid his penetrating stare. "Because of that, the idea of us possibly being related didn't sit well with me." She blushed deeply.

Seeing her shy away from him pulled on his heartstrings. The urge to take her into his arms increased. He lowered his face to within inches of hers, close enough to feel her warm breath. When she didn't shy away even further, he tentatively let his lips roam her face. They had grown so close to each other the last several months. How could he have missed noticing that his feelings for her had changed from friendship into much more than that? She was gorgeous, passionate, caring, and her slender body fit perfectly next to his.

"You're amazing, and I'm so grateful you're here with me," he whispered. He inhaled deeply, loving the smell of her. Gently, he brushed his lips against hers, before taking them in a deep, seductive kiss. Her arms folded around his neck and he pulled her closer against his chest. He had never thought it possible that he could fall in love with another woman, but as she melted in his warm embrace, he felt a flicker of hope for his future.

A hope he had lost in a thunderstorm.

Two lives
Two names
Two loves
Too beautiful to die
Too special to lose
Disappearing as the dunes
Making place for others

The Old Pump in Hillegom, The Netherlands.
The inspiration for my story, and therefore so important.

Three decades ago, Ramcy Diek fell in love with the United
States, and moved from the Netherlands to the
Pacific Northwest where she now lives with her husband.
They are both self-employed and work in the tourism industry,
giving Ramcy ample opportunity in the winter to indulge in her
favorite pastime: reading and writing.
Read more at my site: https://www.ramcydiek.com

Acorn Publishing, LLC.

Made in the USA
San Bernardino, CA
18 March 2018